FOREST OF RUIN

KELLEY ARMSTRONG

HARPER

An Imprint of HarperCollins*Publishers*

Library of Congress Control Number: 2015943565

ISBN 978-0-06-207131-6

Typography by Anna Christian

17 18 19 20 21   PC/LSCH   10 9 8 7 6 5 4 3 2 1

❖

First paperback edition, 2017

To Julia

FOREST OF RUIN

ONE

"You'll be coming back with me, Keeper."

Moria stared at the young warrior. Gavril Kitsune had escorted her across the Wastes after her village was destroyed, her people massacred. A massacre orchestrated, as she'd later discovered, by his father, the former marshal—a man long thought dead. Orchestrated and carried out with Gavril's full knowledge. If that betrayal had not been enough, she'd been taken in battle nearly a fortnight ago and held captive at Alvar Kitsune's compound, under Gavril's care. Locked in a dungeon at Gavril's command. And now, a mere day after her escape, he stood before her, with the emperor at his side, telling her she was going *back*?

Moria took a slow step backward, bumping into her wildcat, Daigo, and the emperor's son, Tyrus. Daigo pressed against her legs, growling, his fur on end. Tyrus stepped in front of her.

"Is this sorcery?" Tyrus said. "And do not tell me you aren't a sorcerer. When we were children, you swore you were not. Lied to me, as I now realize. I told Moria once that I knew you as well as anyone could, but you have proven that I did not know you at all."

Gavril flinched at that. After everything, he actually flinched, as if wounded by his old friend's words.

Tyrus went on. "This is sorcery. It must be, to convince my father to let you take Moria."

"It is not sorcery," Emperor Tatsu said, his voice soft but firm. "It is war. I need a spy in Alvar's camp, and Gavril has convinced me he is not our enemy."

"Then make *him* the spy," Moria said. "If he is telling you he is innocent, let him prove it."

"It is not that simple," the emperor said. "Gavril's position is precarious enough. He must maintain the fiction of allegiance to his father."

"Fiction?" She looked at Gavril. "Is that what it is? But of course. It's all a terrible misunderstanding. How wronged you have been, Lord Gavril. How poorly I have treated you, when you have been nothing but kind to me."

He wouldn't meet her gaze as she spoke.

"There is no fiction here," Moria said. "Only another kind of sorcery. The one Kitsunes are best at: lies."

She turned on her heel to see Dalain, son of Warlord Okami, whose lands they were on. Her hand moved to her dagger, ready for him to block her path, but he dipped his chin and stepped aside, allowing her and Daigo to walk into the forest.

Behind her, she heard the clatter of swords—Tyrus starting to come after her. She knew that without looking. But his father said, "Let her go," and to Moria's relief—and yes, a little to her dismay—Tyrus obeyed.

Moria walked until she was out of sight, and then she broke into a run, a headlong dash through the trees, her chest feeling like it was going to explode, her eyes threatening to fill with tears.

What sin had she committed against the goddess to deserve this? She might not be as pious as a Keeper ought to be, but did her petty rebellions truly warrant such punishment? Her twin sister missing, the children of her village missing, her emperor handing her over to a traitor, and Tyrus . . .

No, Tyrus had done the right thing, staying by his father's side. Filial piety above all, including any attachment to young women. Tyrus was honorable. Always honorable. And she loved him for it, even if she might desperately wish to hear his footfalls—

Boots pounded behind her. Daigo growled and she knew it was not Tyrus. She pulled her blade as she turned. When she saw who it was, her fingers gripped the dagger, and the urge to whip it with all her might was almost too much. Instead she shoved the dagger into her belt and kept running.

"Moria!"

She kept going, veering past a gnarled oak, over a stream, one boot sliding in mud, Daigo pushing against her to keep her upright.

"Keeper!"

She stopped then. Stopped and turned and saw him. A tall,

dark-skinned warrior, his figure as identifiable as his braids and his green sorcerer eyes.

"Wait, Keeper. We must speak."

"Do not call me that," she said through her teeth.

"I have always called you that."

"And so you will no more," she said. "The one who called me that was a boy I knew in Edgewood. A scowling, surly, exceedingly difficult boy . . . one who traveled with me and argued with me and fought with me. Fought at my side and told me his secrets. That boy is gone. It seems he never existed."

Gavril sighed and pushed back his braids with an impatient hand. When Daigo growled he said, "I'm no danger to her, Daigo. I never was. I think you know that as well as she does, but you're both too stubborn to admit it."

"Stubborn?" Moria stepped toward him, her dagger drawn. "You dare call me *stubborn*? As if I'm a child who has made a silly error?"

"Of course not. I—"

"You will tell me you had nothing to do with the massacre? I have heard that already, *Lord* Gavril—"

"Don't call me that."

"Why not? That is your title now, as one of your father's warlords. Yes, you've told me you knew nothing of his plans in Edgewood. But only after repeatedly insisting that you were indeed responsible. But let's not discuss your role in Edgewood or Fairview or Northpond or the massacres there or my father's death. Let's talk about what you cannot deny. You said you are no threat to me. Yet within your compound, you left me in a dungeon—"

"I—"

"A dungeon. A cold and dark dungeon, without a word about my sister or Daigo or Tyrus, no idea whether they lived. In a dungeon with a guard who pissed on my blankets and spoiled my food and tried to *defile* me."

"What did you say?" said a voice behind her.

Moria turned as Tyrus walked from the forest, breathing hard, as if he'd run ahead to cut her off. He had indeed defied his father and come for her. She felt only the first spark of mingled dismay and pleasure before she caught sight of his face—the awful expression as he bore down on Gavril, his sword out.

"Moria told me you had taken care of her," Tyrus said.

"I did not wish you—" Moria began.

He glanced back, his eyes softening. "I know why." He turned to Gavril again. "She told me you'd treated her well, because when she was captured, duty compelled me to make for the city, to warn my father of Jorojumo's betrayal rather than hunt for her, and the only thing that allowed me to do so was the conviction that you *did* care for her and *would* care for her. That whatever you had done, there was still honor and decency in you. If she'd admitted otherwise? I would have blamed myself. Now I discover not only was she mistreated but . . ." Tyrus seemed to choke on the words, gripping his blade tighter. "Unsheath your sword and defend yourself."

TWO

Gavril shook his head as Tyrus challenged him. "I'll not."

"You will!" Tyrus roared, and both Gavril and Moria fell back in surprise. "If you have one shred of honor left, you will defend yourself."

"Then I have none, because I'll not fight you, Tyrus. I understand you are upset."

"*Upset?*" Tyrus's roar rang through the forest again. "You threw her into a dungeon and allowed her to be—"

"I allowed nothing. I can explain."

"Are you telling me you have an excuse? Does it involve sorcery or magics? Something that made Moria believe you abandoned her in a dungeon when you did not?"

"No, but—"

"Then there is no excuse."

Gavril paused. "All right. Yes. There's no excuse. I made a mistake."

"A mistake?" Tyrus's voice rose. "A mistake is drinking rice wine before your host. Putting a Keeper into a dungeon, when she has committed no crime, fought in no battle? That is an act of cowardice and cruelty that has no excuse. You are no longer the boy I called my friend. You are a treacherous son of a whore, and either you draw your sword and defend yourself or I will cut your head from your shoulders."

Gavril straightened. "Then do it."

Tyrus raised his sword tip to Gavril's throat. "You mock me?"

"Never. I'll not stop you. I'll not fight you either. If this is the penalty I've earned, then I accept it."

Moria rocked forward, dagger gripped. She ought not to interfere, but if she didn't, what stayed her hand? Was it truly respect for Tyrus? Or because she *wanted* Gavril's death? Wanted someone else to do it? Not Tyrus. Never Tyrus. He might be enraged now, but if she let him do this, he would suffer, more than Gavril.

"Defend yourself, Kitsune," she said. "Please."

Gavril's gaze flickered her way. His green eyes revealed nothing, but sweat trickled from his hairline and his braids seemed to quiver.

"Do you care at all?" she asked.

His mouth opened. Nothing came out for a moment. Then he collected himself and said, in his usual dispassionate way, "I was concerned for your well-being but I did what I thought necessary."

"I'm not asking if you care about me. Do you care about *him*?" She nodded to Tyrus. "Was there ever anything in your friendship? Or were you merely using him, as the emperor's son?"

"Of course not."

"Then prove it by showing him the respect of a fair fight."

Gavril's mouth worked, but nothing came. Sweat dripped from his chin now. He turned his gaze back to Tyrus.

"I am sorry. I deeply regret any pain I have caused you—"

"Caused *me*!" Tyrus's boot shot out and he kicked Gavril square in the stomach, knocking the young warrior onto his back. "You betrayed my trust, but you betrayed *her* in every possible way. And it's *me* you wish to apologize to?"

Tyrus brandished his sword. Even standing behind him, Moria realized he could not bring himself to swing it—as enraged as he was, that went too far. Yet having said he would, if he failed to follow through, the loss of face . . .

"Tyrus!"

Moria lunged, as if he'd been about to make the fatal blow. She put her hand against his back, feeling the bunched muscles, smelling the stink of sweat—of rage and grief and fear—as she whispered into his ear.

"Please, don't," she said, loud enough for Gavril to hear. "You'll suffer more than he will, and I'll not have that. Please."

When Tyrus hesitated, Daigo leaped onto Gavril.

"Daigo!" Moria said. She gripped her dagger, ready to whip it if Gavril made one move to hurt her wildcat, but before he could move, Daigo had him pinned, his powerful jaws around Gavril's throat. And that's when Moria saw true terror in Gavril's eyes. The honest realization that he might die.

"Call off your wildcat, Keeper," a voice said.

Moria looked up to see Lysias walking toward them, followed by the emperor.

Lysias said again, "Call him off. Please, my lady."

"She cannot," Gavril managed. "He is a Wildcat of the Immortals. Possessed by the spirit of a great warrior. Bond-beast to the Keeper. Not her pet. Not her hunting cat. She cannot command him."

"I would suggest she try," Lysias said.

"No," Emperor Tatsu said as he walked into the clearing. "Gavril is right. This choice is Daigo's. Please sheathe your sword, Lysias."

"Let me speak to Moria," Gavril said, looking the wildcat in the eyes. "Allow me to explain, Daigo, and she will under-stand."

"And therefore not deserve an apology?" Tyrus said, sword still in hand as he moved alongside Gavril and the wildcat.

"Tyrus . . ." Emperor Tatsu said.

"You think I misspeak?" Tyrus turned on his father. "Did he tell you how he cared for her? He put her in a *dungeon*, father. A squalid dungeon with a sadistic guard who tried to violate her."

Emperor Tatsu hesitated before looking over, and while his face gave away no more than Gavril's, Moria knew this came as a surprise. He said slowly, "Mistakes were made, but I'm sure Gavril will ensure Moria is not touched."

"*Touched?* Forgive me, Father. Let me be more blunt, if that helps. She was almost *raped* while under his care. Now you wish to send her back?"

"Moria can handle herself," Gavril said. "She fought off her attacker, and this time I will be sure she is secretly armed with her dagger. I would never allow—"

"You *did* allow!" Tyrus bellowed. He spun on Lysias, and before the guard could draw his sword, Tyrus's blade was at his throat.

"Run, Moria," Tyrus said. "Take Daigo and run."

She stepped backward, her gaze on Gavril. He shifted, but at a look from Emperor Tatsu, he did not move.

"Where will she go, Tyrus?" the emperor asked. "Lord Okami has some of the best hunters in the empire. They will find her."

"That depends," Tyrus said. "You said yourself that I was safe here because the Gray Wolf is no slave to the emperor. Perhaps we'll test that. I'll put the case to him, and while I'm certain he'll send men, I would not be quite so certain he'll tell them to look very hard if I beg otherwise."

Emperor Tatsu's lips curved.

"You laugh at me?" Tyrus said, prodding Lysias's neck hard enough to draw blood.

"No, my son. I'm pleased with you. While you may claim to have no head for politics—"

"Do not praise me!" Tyrus snarled. "You are trying to send a Keeper—our sacred Keeper, who has been nothing but loyal to the empire—back to a traitor. Do not cheapen my outrage by praising me."

Emperor Tatsu dipped his chin. "I apologize."

"Go, Moria," Tyrus said. "I will come to you when I can, but your priority right now is your sister. Find her."

Moria wavered there, torn between fear for his safety and fear for Ashyn's. As much as she cared for Tyrus, Ashyn was her sister.

"Go," Tyrus said, his voice low. "I expect no less of you."

She'd just started to run when something flew through the air. It struck Daigo and he let out a yelp. Moria saw a dart in his shoulder. She plucked it out, but he toppled, unconscious. She dropped beside him, her fingers going to his neck.

"It is but a sedative," Emperor Tatsu called.

Moria glared into the dark woods, looking for the attacker. "You said it was only us out here. You lied."

"I took precautions. Your wildcat is fine. Now come back, Moria."

She peered into the forest, and it felt as if a dozen eyes watched her.

Tyrus turned to his father. "Have I ever asked you for anything before?"

"Tyrus . . ."

"I have asked you for one favor. Only one. Do you remember what it was?"

Silence. Then the emperor said, quietly, "You asked me to allow Gavril to visit his father in prison before his exile."

Gavril's studied blank expression cracked. He looked at Tyrus, and even from where she stood, Moria could see the shock there. Shock and then pain.

"Yes," Tyrus said. "Almost eighteen summers of my life, and I have asked only for one thing. Now I ask for another. Let Moria go. Whatever you need to do, find another way."

"It's not that simple."

"Yes, it—"

Lysias grabbed for Tyrus's sword arm, apparently thinking him distracted. Tyrus's sword swung and it caught the captain of the guard in the arm, blade cutting through to bone. Lysias did not stagger back. Did not fall, howling, to the ground. He

11

pulled his blade with his other hand and faced off with Tyrus. Blood gushed from his wounded arm. Lifeblood. Moria knew that, and she started forward instinctively, then stopped herself as Lysias's blade swung up. Tyrus countered, steel clanging.

"Tell him to give way, Father," Tyrus said.

Another swing. Another clang.

"Father! Tell him now. He's badly injured, and he cannot fight me with his off-hand. I do not wish to hurt him."

The emperor did nothing. He would do nothing, Moria knew, and not out of a callous disregard for his captain, but because he did not need to intercede. Tyrus knew Lysias. Knew him and respected him and cared about him, and it didn't matter if he could end this standoff with a single blow—he would never deliver that blow.

Moria caught a glimmer of motion and saw two men step from the forest. They quietly advanced on Tyrus.

"I'll go with Gavril," she said.

"What? No!"

Tyrus started to spin toward her. Lysias lunged, but Tyrus countered with a clash of swords that sent Lysias stumbling back. One of the men from the forest pulled his blade and stepped up behind Tyrus. Moria did not warn him, but she readied her hand on her blade for the slightest sign that the man would do more than capture him.

At the last second, Tyrus saw the second man. He spun and Lysias tried again, but as Tyrus wheeled toward the other man, he kicked Lysias, and the weakened captain toppled. Tyrus's blade swung at the second man. It hit him in the shoulder, embedding itself in the lacquered armor, but slicing through flesh, too, the man letting out a gasp. The other warrior from the forest rushed Tyrus as Lysias staggered to his feet, his sword still in hand. Tyrus spun so fast that Moria saw only blades flash and blood arc and she charged, shouting "No!" Out of the corner of her eye, she saw Gavril dart forward. She wheeled on him, but he hadn't drawn his sword. He only moved into her path, stopping her before she leaped into the fray, and by the time he did, it was over.

Tyrus had two swords at his throat. One man lay on the ground, blood soaking his breastplate. Tyrus breathed hard, more rage than exertion, like a trapped beast, face hard, nostrils flaring, watching his captors for any twitch that would allow him to escape, knowing he'd find none.

Moria started past Gavril. He put his hand on her shoulder. She shook him off.

"Let me speak to him," she said. "I can—"

"Stay where you are, Moria," the emperor said.

She bent and laid down her dagger. "There. Now let me—"

Two more men stepped from the forest. Both had blades raised.

"I'm not going to try anything," Moria said. She put out her hands and turned to Gavril. "Here. Bind me."

"That isn't necess—" he started again, but before he could finish, one of the men had grabbed her and was taking a rope from his belt.

"No," Tyrus said. "Don't. Father—"

"I'm fine," Moria cut in. She smiled for him. "I can handle this. You know I can."

There was an eerie calmness to her voice, as if her sister

was there, infusing her with her quiet reason. A moon ago, Moria would have been snarling like Daigo and fighting like Tyrus, taken down only at the end of a blade. But she'd watched Tyrus—always so calm, so even-tempered—explode, and it was as if he vented her rage for her.

She let the warrior bind her, and she kept her gaze—and her smile—on Tyrus. Behind her, the emperor called for other men, presumably from the forest, telling them to transport the wounded men quickly to Warlord Okami's compound.

"Tend to Lysias's arm first," Moria said, in that same calm way. "He's lost a great deal of blood, so bind the arm before you go."

"Yes, my lady," one of the men said.

Emperor Tatsu ordered others to take Daigo back to the compound, and that's when Moria turned from Tyrus. "What? No. He must come with me."

Tyrus flexed, but one warrior had taken Lysias's place and another had stepped up behind him, so that now three blades at his neck held him as tightly as any bonds.

"Daigo must go with her," Tyrus said. "Gavril can tell his father he found them together."

"And the moment Moria misbehaves, Alvar will kill him as punishment."

"He's right," Gavril said. "As much as I would like Daigo at her side, the risk is too great."

"Then take me," Tyrus said. "Gavril found the two of us and took me prisoner, too."

"Then you would suffer the same fate as her wildcat," his father said. "If Alvar knows she is attached to you, he will kill you to punish her. If he does not, then he will kill you to punish me."

"Why? I'm only a bastard prince."

"Exactly. Killing you is not an act worthy of retaliation. In fact, given that the empire believes you betrayed it, Alvar would be lauded for executing you, and I would be unable to retaliate." The emperor walked to Tyrus, who was still locked between the sword blades. He lowered his voice. "Alvar knows me well. He knows how to hurt me the most."

Tyrus looked away. "All right. Then I will follow them. I will camp nearby and be there for Moria."

"No, Tyrus."

"Yes, I—"

"*No*, Tyrus. Another word, and I'll take you back to the imperial city and put you in my own dungeon. If that's what it takes to stop you."

"I'll go," Moria said. She moved in front of Tyrus and faced the emperor, no one stopping her now that her hands were bound, her dagger on the ground. "I've said I'll go, and I'll do it alone."

"No," Tyrus said. "You—"

She turned to him. "I cannot get out of this. You know I cannot. Find Ashyn for me. Please." She looked into his eyes. "That's what I need you to do. Make sure she's safe." She walked to him, passing between the men holding him still, and pressed her lips to his. "Please."

"No," the emperor said.

"What?" She spun on him. "My sister—"

"—will be found by Goro Okami's men."

Tyrus stiffened. "If you think I would pursue Moria—"

"He won't," Moria said. "If he gives me his word that he'll go straight after Ashyn, then there is no doubt he will."

"Just because he stays away from Alvar Kitsune does not mean he'll be safe. He's been branded a traitor."

It was *Tyrus* who had been betrayed, by an imperial war-lord. But the only witness to return to the imperial city claimed the prince had been seduced by Moria, and that he'd fled the battlefield after leading his men to certain death.

The emperor continued. "With a bounty on his head, I'll not have him roaming the lands."

"I am a man, not a child," Tyrus said, his voice chilling. "Perhaps you forget that. I can do as I wish."

"Not if your emperor commands otherwise."

"And if my emperor acts as a father and not a ruler?"

"He acts as both."

Tyrus leaped back. The move was perfectly timed—the warriors had been intently following the conversation. They were caught off guard. Tyrus's sword swung up, hitting one blade and then a second, and both were knocked free of the men's grasps. Then he swung on the third, but the warrior was already in motion, the one quickest to recover, his sword firmly in his hand. Tyrus's blade caught him in the side, not quite piercing the armor, but Tyrus yanked it free and danced back, ready for another—

Moria heard the *thwack* of the dart before she saw it coming.

Tyrus pitched forward. "No." He staggered, turning on his father. "No. You would not . . ."

"I would," Emperor Tatsu said softly. "To keep you safe."

Tyrus fell, and Moria knelt beside him. Tyrus's eyelids fluttered as he struggled to stay conscious. She gripped his hand, and he squeezed hers back.

"Take . . ." he whispered. "Take . . ."

His eyes closed. She leaned down and kissed him.

"I'll take care," she whispered. "You know I will."

She started to rise. Something hit her shoulder. A dart. She pushed up, turned on the emperor, and thrust her bound hands at him. "Was this not enough?"

She bore down on him, her feet tangling under her as the sedative took hold. One of the men moved as if to stop her, but Emperor Tatsu waved him back. He stepped toward Moria and caught her as she fell. As he lowered her to the ground, she said, her words slurring, "I am no spy."

"I know," he whispered.

"You do not wish me to spy on Alvar Kitsune, do you?"

"No," he said, his lips to her ears as she drifted from consciousness. "I wish you to kill him."

THREE

Ashyn stared at the man. Pale-skinned and white-haired, he had tribal tattoos of dragons on his cheeks. Not imperial tattoos like Tyrus's, but rather the intricate art of the North. His eyes were golden with slitted pupils. Dragon eyes. Then he blinked, hard, and the illusion vanished—his eyes were as blue and clear as hers.

"Ashyn," he said gently, when she didn't respond.

"You're my . . . grandfather?" she said.

He nodded. "Did your father not mention me?"

"He did not speak of my mother's family. Or his own. Once, when Moria asked, he said . . ." She swallowed. "He said it was another life. Best forgotten."

"Yes, I can see that he would. Safer for all, given the circumstances."

The circumstances. Their mother's suicide. Taking her

own life to protect their father's. To ensure her daughters would not grow up orphans.

Except now they were. Not merely orphaned but without any family at all. Ashyn had spent the past moon trying to forget that. There were other things to worry about.

Yet now . . .

"My grandfather," she said slowly.

"Edwyn, if that is easier."

"Do I have . . . ?" She was about to ask if she had other family. A grandmother. Aunts. Uncles. Cousins. But that only made her think of the family she did have—namely the sister who was not here. Her gaze went to Tova, the giant yellow hound sitting at her side. Her thoughts moved slowly, still lost in the fog of the sedative.

Sedative. A noxious-smelling cloth shoved over her mouth and nose. Frantically fighting to be free, seeing a boy, slumped on the ground, arrow lodged—

"Ronan." Ashyn looked up sharply. "There was a boy—a young man—with me, felled by an arrow. Did you see him? Did you—?" She stopped short and her hand went for Tova, who rose, growling so softly only Ashyn could hear him. "The arrow. That was you. You shot him and—"

"No, child. We were following you, but Lord Okami's men felled your escort, and we took you before you were hurt."

"Escort? No. I mean, yes. Ronan *was* escorting me. But he's a friend. A good one." Her heart thumped so hard she could barely get out the words. All she could think about was Ronan, on the ground, that arrow—

"Did Dalain Okami take Ronan or . . ." She swallowed

again and forced out the words. "Did you see if he lived?"

Edwyn did not answer. He simply looked at her, studying her expression.

Ashyn turned to go. Then she froze and gaped at her surroundings, her mind still fogged, having forgotten exactly where they were. In a cave. A cave that contained the skull of a dragon.

The skull of a dragon? There *were* no dragons. Creatures of myth, lost in the distant past, or perhaps never having existed at all beyond collective imagination.

Like thunder hawks and death worms. Creatures of myth, now made real by Alvar Kitsune. And dragons . . . ?

Questions for later. Actions for now. That's what Moria would say.

"I must go," she said. "I need to find out what happened to Ronan."

"He lives," Edwyn said. "We have him."

"What? Why didn't you say so?"

"He is not well, child. The outcome is uncertain."

Ashyn struggled for breath. "He might not survive?"

"The wound should have been mortal. Only swift intervention ensured it was not immediately so. But he has lost a great deal of blood and his heart is weakened. I hesitated to tell you we had him, because I am not certain we will have him for much longer."

"I—I need to see him. Now. Please."

"You say he is a friend." Edwyn studied her again. "Is he more?"

Ashyn felt her cheeks heat, but she could say with honesty,

"No, he is simply a very good friend. He came with us from Edgewood." *From the Forest of the Dead, actually. Where he'd been exiled as a criminal.* But she was not explaining that. "He escorted me across the Wastes. He was with me here as we sought to reunite with my sister and Prince Tyrus."

"That seems very attentive for a friend."

"Prince Tyrus hired him to accompany us."

Edwyn frowned. "A friend who takes money to escort you?"

Frustration lashed through Ashyn. It was too much to explain, and she should not have to explain at this moment, perhaps not at any moment. As naive as she might have been leaving Edgewood, she was no longer that girl, and yet she had absolutely no doubt of Ronan's loyalty.

She channeled her sister, straightening and saying, "Ronan is my friend and I wish to see him," though Moria would have said something more akin to *Take me to him now*, with one hand resting on her dagger hilt.

The sterner tone seemed to startle Edwyn. Then he laughed. "You are indeed your mother's daughter. I will send word to the healer, and after we've dined—"

"I will not be able to eat while a friend lies near death."

He nodded. "I understand. Come, and then we will return here to speak. You must have many questions."

Outside the cave, Ashyn found herself on a path, looking *down* at the forest. She gazed up at the sparsely wooded rocks rising toward the sun.

"These are the Katakana Mountains," she said.

"Yes."

"That's . . ."

"Home of the Kitsune clan. I know." Edwyn motioned for her to go ahead of him on the path. As they stepped out, two hooded figures joined them. Edwyn paid the men no mind, and they fell into the rear, as guards.

"This is not the place I'd wish to be," Edwyn said. "Not now particularly, but not at any time. I know what Alvar Kitsune has done, and I count myself in the small portion of the empire that is not the least bit surprised by any of it. Not that he survived his exile in the Forest of the Dead. And not by the rumors I've heard, of what happened to your village and your father."

Ashyn glanced back quickly.

"Yes, child, most of the empire may know nothing of what transpired in Edgewood, but my sources are excellent. Alvar Kitsune raised shadow stalkers to massacre your village. Is that correct?"

She nodded, her chest seizing with grief as she thought of it. Tova pushed at her hand, and she patted his head.

"I heard the story, and I did not doubt it for a heartbeat. I know exactly what sort of man Alvar Kitsune is. I've known for thirty summers—since he put my village to the torch."

"What?"

Edwyn motioned for her to turn on the path ahead. When she did, he continued. "Our family originally came from a town not much bigger than your Edgewood. It was called Silvershore."

"I've not heard of it."

"You won't. It has been erased from time and memory. An inconsequential town that fell in the conquest of the North." Edwyn waved for her to head upward with the path. "Jiro Tatsu and Alvar Kitsune were still young warriors, looking to make names for themselves. Fearsome warriors and closest companions, but very different men. They split their forces that day, on the former emperor's orders. Have you heard of Icewynne?"

"My father mentioned it. A pretty town on the side of a snow-covered mountain. He took my mother there when they first married."

Edwyn smiled. "Yes, I recall that. Icewynne is indeed beautiful. That is the town Jiro Tatsu conquered. He rode in, demanded their surrender, put a few objectors to the sword, and captured the town. It pledged fealty to the empire, and he left it exactly as he'd found it. Over in Silvershore, Alvar Kitsune also rode in and demanded surrender. Then he put *every* objector to the sword, along with a few dozen innocents as a lesson in resistance. The town begged for mercy. He accepted it and made as if to leave. I was hiding with your mother and my wife, and as he rode past, I saw him throw sorcerer's fire into the livestock enclosure. The straw and the wooden buildings caught flame, and the town burned. Then Alvar told the emperor we must have burned our own town in spite, so the emperor ordered Silvershore razed and stricken from all history books."

They climbed a particularly steep section of the path in silence, and Ashyn looked back to see if Edwyn was having difficulty, given his age, but he didn't appear to be winded or struggling. When they reached a flatter section, he continued speaking.

"When Alvar Kitsune was exiled, I was more pleased than I ought to admit. I would certainly prefer *not* to be on his ancestral lands. However, as you may have noted, that dragon skull is embedded in the cave wall. Unmovable. This, then, has become one of our sacred places, despite the proximity to an old enemy."

"Sacred places?"

He smiled. "More on that soon, child. For now, there is a cave opening hidden just ahead. Inside, you will find your friend."

If Edwyn had not told her that Ronan lived, Ashyn would have believed she was viewing his corpse, laid out for her to send his spirit to the second world. He lay absolutely still on the straw-filled pallet. His brown skin looked as pale as hers. His eyes were closed and dark-lidded as if bruised. She had to take his hand to feel his pulse, and even then, the chill of his touch sent one through her. As she lowered his limp hand back to the pallet, Tova whimpered.

A woman crouched beside Ronan's supine form. She wore a thin cloak of hemp weave. Her hood was pushed down, revealing a woman perhaps in her fourth decade, with graying yellow hair. The healer, Ashyn presumed, along with another older woman who seemed to be her assistant. Ashyn did not want to bother the healer, who was busy, but when she asked the assistant about Ronan's condition, the woman didn't lift her gaze.

"She does not speak the common language," Edwyn said. "The North may have been conquered three decades past, but for many of the small settlements, that is their protest."

"Not learning the empire's language?" Ashyn said, looking over. "One would think that would be more hindrance than help."

He shrugged. "People do what they can to retain some power when most of it has been stripped from them. I am not particularly opposed to life under the emperor. We feel he often forgets us, likely because we have little to offer but snow and ice, but he does send warriors to protect against the tribes, and wagon trains of rice to sustain us during the long winters, so I offer him my fealty and learn his language. Others do not."

Ashyn went to examine the bandages around Ronan's neck. The assistant jumped then, as if to stop her, but halted at a word from Edwyn.

"Is the wound closed?" Ashyn asked.

"Yes, it has been sewn. The problem is the loss of blood."

"Then he needs fluids. Water may not replace blood, but it does aid in its replenishment."

"You know healing, child?"

"Mostly from books. Battle healing is one of a Seeker's responsibilities."

"Ah, I will admit that I know little of your position. There has never been a Seeker in the North. It is an imperial custom."

She turned, frowning. "But it's not a *custom*. Moria and I hear the second world, at least when the spirits choose to communicate. I can soothe spirits and Moria can banish them. That is not merely training."

"Perhaps, but it is not the gift of *every* twin girl either, is it? Only those the empire allows to survive."

Ashyn nodded and turned back to Ronan. The empire was a place of both kindness and cruelty. Right now, she needed to focus less on that and more on her immediate corner of it.

"Has he woken to receive liquids?" she asked.

"No, he has yet to regain consciousness. Which is the problem with replacing his fluids."

She leaned over and laid her hand on his forehead, clammy and cold beneath her fingers.

"Ronan?" she said. "It's Ashyn. Can you hear me?"

No response.

"If you are conscious but too weak to open your eyes, can you let me see you move?"

Still nothing.

"He is deeply unconscious," Edwyn said. "We have not witnessed so much as a flutter of movement since he first passed out." He said a few words in another language to the woman, and she nodded, confirming that.

"He is as well as he can be, child," Edwyn said. "Now, if you'll return with me to the other cave, I will answer your questions and tell you what we have planned. Then you may come back here and sit with him."

"It's real then," Ashyn said, running her fingers over the eye socket of the dragon skull. It protruded from the wall, as if mounted there, but upon closer inspection, it was indeed embedded in the stone itself.

"It would be difficult to manufacture such a thing,"

Edwyn said with a dry laugh. "Although, to be honest, people have tried. We've been summoned to verify remains of dragons, only to discover they're bones from an ancient cave bear or even parts carved from soapstone. But something of that scale, I assure you, is impossible to fake."

He was right. The eye socket alone was as big as her head, and she had to reach up to touch it. The teeth were each larger than her handspan. Some were missing, and she could feel wear on the intact ones, less sharp after a lifetime of ripping apart prey. She shuddered at the thought. Moria had told her about their horrific fight with the thunder hawk, and this creature would be larger still. One chomp of its great jaws . . . Ashyn might not have her sister's imagination, but she could still picture a man sliding down that massive gullet in a single swallow.

"How old is it?" she asked.

"Ages."

Ashyn smiled. "Moria will be disappointed. They were selling dragon eggs in the city, and I could tell she was tempted. She might know they're simply pretty rocks, but still . . . the possibility . . ."

"Yes," he said, returning her smile. "That possibility keeps many a shady merchant in business. They are very pretty rocks, though. Nothing like real dragon eggs."

"There are real—?" She stopped and nodded. "Fossilized."

"You've heard of such a thing?"

"The process, yes. I grew up in the Wastes. After the volcanos erupted, the cooling lava left many petrified remains. Traders used to come and collect stone-hardened beasts to sell as monsters. Never dragon eggs, though. The stones were too dull for that. I suppose real fossilized eggs *would* look dull."

"They do, though if broken open, they are a thing of beauty. Every color, like diamonds refracting the light. Not that we would ever break an egg, but sometimes they are discovered already shattered."

"Who discovers them?"

He didn't answer, instead walking to the skull. "Your sister is called the Keeper. Ironic, because that is her true heritage—yours and hers both. Our family's heritage. The keepers of dragons." He walked to the skull and touched the snout. "Keepers of memories now and keepers of bones. Or so most believe. But the truth, child? The truth is that we keep so much more."

He ran his finger over one front fang. "You spoke earlier of your powers. Yes, you have powers over spirits, and in the empire, where spirits are the subject of religion, that is what they focus on. It is the manifestation of your connection to the imperial goddess. But there are other faces to the goddess. Sometimes she is not even a goddess but a god. A supreme power that men and women recognize as their faith tells them to." He looked over at her. "Do you understand what I'm say-ing?"

"I . . . I think so. Many people worship a deity, and you believe it is the same one, with different names and faces."

A broad smile. "You are indeed clever, child. That is a con-cept rarely understood by people twice your age."

"Perhaps it's not so much a matter of understanding as of accepting."

"Clever and wise. So the empire has its goddess, who rules the second world. She is also associated with dragons, particularly under the rule of the Tatsu clan."

"Because the dragon is their totem, so it benefits the emperor to strengthen that connection."

"Do you know where that connection comes from?" He did not wait for her to answer. "From the North. Our goddess is the queen of dragons. And in our world, twin girls born blessed of the goddess have a special gift, beyond the ability to hear the dead."

He took her hand then, his fingers warm and surprisingly strong as he moved her to stand with him in front of the gaping jaws, both gazing up in awe at the beast before them. Then, still holding her hand, Edwyn leaned down and whispered in her ear, "They have the power to wake dragons."

FOUR

Moria woke with her hands bound and her head pounding. Her first thought was of the dungeon, of the cold and the dark and the terror, and she was certain she was back there, and she tried to jump upright and—

A whinny. She barely had time to realize she'd been lying over a horse like a sack of rice before she was flying clear, hearing a shout of "Moria!" as she struck the ground hard enough to jolt her out of consciousness. She came to lying against someone's chest, an arm holding her up, a voice saying, "Moria? Are you all right?" Green eyes over hers. Dark braids brushing her face. And again, another flash of treacherous memory, and she was back in the Wastes, and Gavril was there, and they had just fought the thunder hawk and . . .

Then the rest tumbled back like rocks down a cliffside, bashing her, each blow bringing fresh pain, and she slammed her fists into Gavril's stomach and scrambled off his lap.

"You cannot run, Keeper," he said.

"No, truly?" She lifted her bound hands. "That much is obvious. I'm no fool, whatever you may think of my intelligence."

"For my father's sake, I pretended to dismiss your intellect."

"You've *always* made your opinion of it perfectly clear."

He sighed. "I've needled you, but I do not think you a fool. Your intelligence is above average. Not as high as your sister's . . ."

"You do not even know how to pay a compliment without lacing it in insult."

"Your sister is simply more book-learned than you. Perhaps that does not imply a difference in innate intelligence. You were wombmates, after all. One might presume your fundamental capacities are as identical as your appearance, and the difference lies in what you do with those then."

"Enough. Stick to insults, Kitsune. They're shorter." She lifted her hands. "Now untie me so I may ride." When he hesitated, she said, "I gave my word that I'd go with you. You will untie me, and you will return my dagger."

"I cannot—"

She smashed her fists into his gut again, and when he stumbled, she leaped on him, toppling him to the ground. Before he could strike, she was crouched on his chest, her bound hands at his neck, the rope cutting into his throat.

"You will untie me, and you will return my dagger. I do not need either to kill you." She pressed down harder, making him gasp. "Nod when you agree."

He shook his head and managed to say, "You will not find him."

"As hard as it is for me to be separated from Daigo, I will not attempt."

"You'll return and try to free Daigo and Tyrus. Then you'll go after your sister."

"Truly? You do think me a fool. A mad child who believes she can outwit the emperor and free an imperial prince from captivity. Then they'll run off together through the empire, hoping to trip over her missing sister by sheer luck, apparently."

"I know you, Moria. You are impetuous and obstinate, and your actions often ill-conceived."

"Enough with the flattery, Kitsune. I am no longer the child who flits after butterflies. I have endured enough in the past moon to ensure I'll never be that girl again."

A look passed over his face. Something almost like grief, gone too fast for her to see more than a flicker.

"I would have it any other way, Keeper," he said, his voice low. "I know you have suffered greatly."

"Spare me false sympathy. You do it as poorly as flattery, and I require neither. I am not the girl I was, and I will not dash off into the forest at the first opportunity. Nor will I ram my dagger into your back the moment you turn it. I could kill you now if I wished. I do not, for the same reason I stopped Tyrus from ending your life. Because we would suffer for it much longer than you would. It's no small thing to take a life. I understand that now."

Another flicker of emotion. "You've taken—"

"It is a war, Gavril. That's what happens when you launch

one. Now, do I get my dagger?"

Silence. Then, "If I return it, will you let me speak as we ride?"

"I cannot stop you from speaking. However, if you insist on defending your actions, you may not want to return my dagger, or my impetuous nature might win out."

More silence.

"I wish my hands freed," she continued. "I wish my dagger returned. And I do not wish to hear your voice. If you can grant these, you will find you have a riding companion as quiet and courteous as Ashyn. If you cannot, you will be reminded that I am not my sister."

Gavril agreed.

They stopped for the night. They had no tent to sleep in. No blankets either. When Moria went to lie on the cold ground, Gavril said, "I have something for you."

She turned away, ignoring him. He rustled in his horse pack, and when he came and crouched in front of her, she kept her eyes shut. But then she caught a whiff of tanned leather and ermine fur and campfire smoke.

Her eyes flew open to see him holding her cloak. The one she thought had been left on a bloodied battlefield when she'd been thrown into the dungeon.

The last gift from her father. She'd been wearing her old cloak when she'd fought the thing that had possessed her father's corpse. The shadow stalker had grabbed her right before she banished it, and the last she'd seen of her cloak, it was clutched in the gnarled, misshapen claw of the monster

33

her father had become. Covered in his blood. She'd refused to return for it, and Gavril had insisted they take a new one from her father's shop. He'd found this on the shelf. A wrapped gift from her father. Her Fire Festival present, complete with the last words she'd ever have from him.

Losing that cloak had physically hurt, like having the last piece of her father wrenched from her grasp.

"They found it near the battlefield," Gavril said. "One of the men who brought you to my father had taken it for his wife. I recognized it and bribed him for its return. I know how much it means to you."

"Yes, it means a great deal. Which makes it valuable, does it not?" She lifted her gaze to his. "A tool to control me?"

Gavril rocked back on his haunches. "Blast it, Moria. I cannot do one kind thing, can I?"

"Because you do not do kind things, Gavril. Even at your best, you do not, and so I will suspect everyone."

He lowered himself, cross-legged, to the ground beside her. "We are embarking on a very dangerous mission, Moria. Together. It will be as it was in the Wastes, where you must watch my back and I must watch yours. Where we must trust each other."

"*Trust* you—?"

"Within those walls, there will be only two people you can count on. Myself and Rametta. And while Rametta is loyal to me and fond of you, we cannot involve her in the heart of this deception."

"Thank you for the cloak. It is appreciated."

She took it and stretched it out on the ground. Then she

lay down with her back to Gavril.

"We need to speak of this eventually, Keeper," he said.

"No, you need merely to provide me with the script for my performance. My life depends on carrying it out. That is all the motivation I require."

FIVE

Gavril had stalked off into the night. Perhaps he was scouting. Perhaps he was performing his nightly ablutions. Perhaps he was sulking. Moria did not care. She was drifting toward sleep when she heard a footfall. It was not the crunch of a rock or the crack of a stick under a misplaced step. Not even the whisper of dry grass. Simply the faint movement of soil beneath a foot. Which meant it was not Gavril, who would make no pains to cover his approach.

Moria pulled her dagger and opened her eyes just enough to peer out. It was a dark night, unlit by stars or moon. They'd camped well off the road, on a barren patch, with the forest at least twenty paces away, making it impossible for anyone to sneak up. Yet someone was, even if the horses didn't stir.

Moria kept her eyes open just enough to watch, and finally she made out a dark shape against the dark night. She shot up, her dagger ready.

"You are far too good at this game, little Keeper," sighed a softly lilting voice.

"Or you need more practice playing it, Sabre."

"True."

The figure moved closer, still bent, until she reached Moria and lowered herself to the ground. A girl of about eighteen summers, with gray-blue eyes; wild, dark curls; and skin somewhere between copper and bronze. They'd met only briefly, earlier that day, under remarkably similar circumstances, as Moria and Tyrus had been making their way to the Okami compound.

"At least I didn't end up flat on my back under your wildcat this time," Sabre said.

When Moria tensed, Sabre's smile vanished, her look uncharacteristically somber. "My apologies, Keeper. That was ill-considered. Perhaps I can acquit myself of the offense with the reassurance that your beast is well. As is Tyrus. They'll wear ruts in the confinement house from their pacing, but they are fine, and they are together. They are safe, as well. I may not be as fond of the emperor as a citizen ought to be, but he would never harm his son nor anyone his son cared for, including a wildcat." Sabre rose to a crouch. "If you wish to flee, your captor is well enough away that we may do it if we act quickly."

When Moria didn't respond, Sabre settled in again. "The fact that you were already remaining here, when he is not, suggests you have no intention of escaping."

"If Tyrus expects—"

"He does not. He hopes you will escape, for your own safety, but he would not in your place and so he does not expect you to. I simply offered to help if you wished to go." Her gray eyes met Moria's. "You make a hard choice, little Keeper."

"I make the only choice."

"There are always others."

"Then I make the only one I can."

"That is a very different thing. You are a fine match for the prince." She smiled. "Or for the prince he has become. You'd not have been a fine match for the silly boy I remember. He has matured, thank the ancestors."

Sabre tilted her head, lips pursing. "I ought to qualify that by pointing out that any admiration I have for the prince is like the admiration I might have for a brother, not for a handsome young man. You've nothing to fear from me there." She leaned down. "And you would do well to play to my ego by expressing relief at that, as if you were genuinely concerned."

Moria gave a small laugh. "I might have been . . . if I did not suspect your eye looked closer to the Okami compound."

"Dalain?" Sabre snorted and rolled her eyes. "Let's simply say that while I'm pleased to see how much the little prince has matured, I regret that I cannot say the same for his former blade instructor. And from what I heard of that fight before you left, the student has surpassed the teacher in that, too."

"Tyrus is a very fine swordsman."

"Is he?" Sabre's eyes sparkled wickedly.

Moria laughed. "I do not know about *that*, though I have high hopes of surviving this ordeal long enough to find out."

Sabre grinned. "Oh, I do like you. The court girls I've met would faint if I asked such a thing. Now I truly do regret that you won't come with me. We would have a fine time—"

They caught the sound of footfalls at the same moment,

and both stood as a tall figure ran toward them, his blade in hand.

"Stop there, traitor," Sabre said, raising her sling. "Or I'll fell you before you take another step."

"The advantage of a missile weapon," Moria said.

"Exactly. And it appears he has enough experience with yours to respect mine."

"No, he'll only pretend he's listening, as he talks and distracts, and then creeps close enough to use his sword."

"I can hear you," Gavril called.

"Good," Moria said. "Then you can hear that I'm not under any duress, and you can presume that if our visitor was helping me escape, we'd be gone by now, not chatting like girls at a tea ceremony. Since I know you'll not stay where you are, you may approach half the distance, then lay down your sword and come closer."

"May I?"

"Only if you behave. And keep quiet. Otherwise, stay where you are."

"I think you forget who is—"

"—in charge here? No, Kitsune, I do not. I am in charge, because if you do not return with me, you will pay the price. That is why you've accommodated me so far and it's why you'll continue to do so now."

Sabre chuckled. Gavril stalked closer.

"I'll not lay down my sword, Keeper," he said as he sheathed it. "I will concede to your demands by keeping my hand from the hilt."

He didn't wait for a reply, only walked to them, his arms

crossed, presumably to keep his hands from his hilt, though the stance complemented his scowl quite well.

"Gavril Kitsune," Sabre said as he approached. "I almost feel I know you. When Tyrus was apprenticed to the Okamis, he spoke so highly of you. Such a good friend." She glanced at Moria. "Did I mention Tyrus was quite a silly boy? Very gullible."

"Whoever you are, I presume you have come for some purpose other than needling me?"

Sabre lowered herself to the ground. Gavril remained standing.

"This is Sabre," Moria said. "She is—"

"The bandit king's daughter," Gavril cut in.

"My father is no bandit," Sabre said hotly. "He is a nomadic tribal chieftain." She paused. "Though if he were a bandit, I do rather like the title of *king*. Would that make me a bandit princess?"

"Tyrus said you like to talk," Gavril said.

"I take that as a compliment. As for why I am here, as I told the young Keeper, I was sent by her prince to set her free and accompany her on the search for her sister. However, being not nearly as silly a boy as he once was, Tyrus realized there was little chance Moria would abandon this duty. He merely wished to ensure she had the opportunity. More important, he wished her to know that Lord Okami is taking the hunt for her sister very seriously. So is the emperor, but right now, Tyrus has more faith in the family that hosted his apprenticeship. Lord Okami sent his best hunters and tracking hounds. The mission is being led by Dalain, since he was the one who *lost* the Keeper's sister. I will be joining him as soon as I can. Whether he wants it or not." She grinned. "Almost assuredly not."

Gavril opened his mouth, but Sabre continued. "I am asking my father to send men as well. The Okamis are fine hunters . . . when the prey is a giant pig. My father's men have more flexible talents."

"More experience tracking humans?" Moria said with a smile.

"I admit nothing, little Keeper. I only say that my tribe are excellent trackers and that with my assistance, even Dalain cannot botch this too badly."

"You have a high opinion of yourself," Gavril said.

"I do. Thank you. Now, if you are reassured that we're not preparing to flee into the night . . ." She flicked her fingers. "Away with you. We are talking."

"I wished to ask about Tyrus." Gavril cleared his throat. "The fight . . . It was . . ." He straightened, that cool look returning. "He is as impetuous as the Keeper, and his actions often as ill-advised. Taking on three warriors was madness, and while he did not seem injured . . ."

"Tyrus is an excellent swordsman," Sabre said, straight-faced. "Or so I've heard."

"Yes, I know he is," Gavril said impatiently.

"Do you?" Sabre's brows shot up, that wicked look returning.

Gavril scowled. "Of course. We were sparring partners for many summers."

Sabre choked on her laugh as Moria tried to keep a straight

41

face, failing miserably, and joining Sabre as Gavril's scowl deepened.

"I don't know what you both find so amusing," he said. "If you're suggesting I was a poor match, while I am clearly no longer on his level, Moria knows my prowess is—"

"Stop," Moria said, holding up her hands. "Please. Stop that sentence there. Now, you were asking whether Tyrus is well. Sabre has assured me he is, and I will refrain from adding that you've forfeited the right to show concern about his well-being."

"You did add it."

Moria turned to Sabre. "I appreciate all the news you have brought."

"You are most welcome, my lady."

"Moria, please."

"I have one more task to carry out before I go, Moria." She turned to Gavril. "You may leave us."

"I may . . . but I will not."

"Ignore him," Moria said. "I do. As much as possible."

"I do not blame you. He seems very ill-tempered. Traitors ought to be more charming or they'll never woo anyone to their side." She turned to Gavril. "Is your father more charming?"

"I do not wish to speak of my father."

"I don't blame you. I ought to thank you, Gavril Kitsune, for teaching me a valuable lesson. I may bristle at hearing my father called a bandit, but at least he has never betrayed the empire. Nor massacred innocents. Nor—"

"Enough," Gavril said, between his teeth. "I have no illusions about my father, and you waste valuable resting time cataloging his crimes to me. Tell Moria what you need to tell her and be gone."

"He is a very poor host," Sabre said.

"You have no idea how poor," Moria said, looking at Gavril.

"Finish your business," Gavril said. "Quickly."

Sabre reached under her cloak and took out something. In the darkness, Moria could only make out that it seemed to be a strip of cloth. Then Sabre opened her hand, and Moria saw a red silk band with tasseled ends. Tyrus's name was embroidered across it.

"That's . . ." she began, and her breath caught. "Tyrus's amulet band." His mother had given it to him. It was an old custom—long out of fashion—but he wore it faithfully, tied around his upper arm.

"He wanted to give it to you before you left," Sabre said. "But he lost consciousness. He asked me to bring it to you."

"No." Moria reached out quickly and closed Sabre's hand around the band. "Return it to him. Please. He ought to be the one wearing it. Especially now. It will protect him."

Gavril snorted. "Superstitious nonsense. You are as bad as he is, Keeper, with your stories and your—"

She turned sharply on him. "I am well aware that the band is likely little more than superstition. The point is that Tyrus believes it works, and if he believes it helps the ancestors protect him—"

"Then he is all the more likely to engage in foolhardy recklessness."

"No, then he is more confident in his abilities."

"Which makes him more reckless."

"You both make very interesting points," Sabre said. "But I will make another. If Tyrus is sick with worry about you, Moria, and he believes this will help keep you safe, is it not better if he knows you wear it?"

"She cannot," Gavril said. "My father might discover it. Tell Tyrus you delivered it, and keep it safe for him."

"You wish me to lie to an imperial prince?"

"I suspect that offends your sensibilities less than it ought," Gavril said dryly.

"True," she said. "I do not in *principle* have a problem with lying to an imperial prince. But I will not lie to a friend."

"Nor will I lie to Tyrus and pretend I took it," Moria said.

"It is settled then," Sabre said. "Push up your sleeve."

Moria did and Sabre tried to tie the band, Moria instructing her and Sabre fumbling and cursing, until Gavril said, "We'll be up all night at this pace. I'll do it. I've tied it for Tyrus before."

He crouched beside Moria and tied it. Then he tugged her sleeve over it. When the ends showed, he shoved the sleeve up and wound the tassels through the band.

"With that, I will take my leave," Sabre said. "I'll report to the prince that you wear his band, and he will rest easier." She squeezed Moria's hand. "Take care, little Keeper." And then to Gavril, she said, "As for you, I would say to take care of her, but I'm not sure that is wise."

"I am perfectly capable of looking out for her."

"Not what I mean." Her gaze lifted to Gavril's. "I've said I count the prince as a friend. And anyone with eyes can see the depth of his regard for the Keeper. Watch yourself."

"I've said I'll not harm her nor allow harm to come to her, and I do not require the threat of Tyrus's vengeance—"

"I cannot tell if you are as obtuse as you seem or only play the part."

Gavril's eyes flashed. "I understand you perfectly, and I will take care of the Keeper."

Sabre sighed. "You understand me not at all. Foolish child."

She stood, and they watched her lope off into the darkness. Then Gavril opened his pack and took out dried fruit, fish, and rice balls. Moria did not consider refusing. It would do no good, and regardless of Gavril's promises, she was not convinced she'd get proper meals once inside Alvar Kitsune's camp.

They were finishing the meal when Moria reached for the last rice ball and her cloak fell open, and she realized the ends of the prayer band again dangled past her short sleeve. She gave them an impatient tuck up again.

"This is what I mean, Keeper," Gavril said. "It is not as easily hidden as you seem to think. If my father finds it . . ."

"He'll not."

"I'd rather avoid taking the chance and—"

"Shhh."

Gavril glowered at her. "Don't shush me."

Moria slapped a hand over Gavril's mouth. Before he could wrench it off, she pointed to the east, where she'd seen movement in the long grass. He caught it, too, and then he did push her away, yanking his blade as both of them rose, weapons ready.

Four figures stood in the distance. Four armed men, with

swords and cudgels. Not warriors, then, despite the blades.

"Sabre's father's men?" Moria whispered.

Gavril shook his head, and Moria lifted her dagger to hurl at the first man who moved. None did. Then two more appeared beside the others. Gavril swung toward them, his sword raised, and Moria spun just as yet another two men stepped into the clearing. Big men. Rough men. Armed men.

"The traitor and his whore," one said, stepping forward. "The goddess has smiled upon us tonight."

SIX

"Stay your dagger, Keeper," Gavril murmured as Moria flexed her throwing hand.

"I can fell—"

"Only one, which will then leave you unarmed."

"You can give me *your* dagger, Kitsune," Moria said. "And I'll take down two."

"I gladly would, but the odds are still against us. Heavily against us."

Moria surveyed the bandits encircling them. She now counted eleven, possibly more behind them, lost in the night.

"Listen to your lover," the lead man called. "You cannot escape this alive. Letting us return you to the emperor is your only choice. He has not yet reinstituted executions. He may only exile you. Torture you, yes. Perhaps enough that you'll wish you were dead. Yet there is a chance of survival. Strike against us, and there is none."

He was right. Moreover, while Moria still worried what punishment the emperor might need to inflict on them for appearances' sake, that would not include execution. Not when Emperor Tatsu was the one who'd sent them here in the first place.

"Lower that dagger, whore," the bandit leader said. "We'll take your weapons."

"I would ask you not to call her that," Gavril said, his voice low.

"Oh, that's very sweet. The traitor loves his Keeper whore, and he does not appreciate hearing her maligned."

Gavril opened his mouth, but Moria whispered, "Do not argue. Just lay down your weapons. You'll not be able to keep them. Nor to fight."

They both set their blades at their feet. The bandit leader approached. He looked to be from the steppes—almost as light-skinned as Moria, with shaggy, brown hair. Not nearly as intimidating as Alvar's man—Barthol—but Moria knew better than to put much credence in appearances. She'd learned much since Edgewood.

"Bind them," he called to the others, then scooped up their weapons and examined them like a merchant eyeing new goods. Which was apt, given that Moria doubted she'd see her dagger again.

Two other men approached with ropes. Gavril and Moria held out their hands as the leader walked through the camp.

"Good horses," he said. "Take them. Oh, and what do we have here?" He lifted Moria's cloak. "This is particularly fine. I believe I'll keep this for myself."

Gavril's mouth opened in protest, but Moria stomped on his foot to silence him.

"You're in no position to demand anything, Kitsune. He'd likely cut it to shreds if you tried." She gave him a look. "And you call me the impetuous one."

"You've changed."

"I've had to," she said, and let one of the men lead her away.

The smell of sweat did not particularly bother Moria. If one engaged in physical activity, it was rarely convenient to draw a bath immediately after. So long as bathing—even with a bowl and cloth—was a regular part of one's routine, the smell rarely escalated to a stink.

In the Wastes, with no access to spare water, both she and Gavril had reeked. She'd grown accustomed to it quickly enough, and would only notice when she woke in the night, confused and unsettled, and then the smell was actually comforting. Gavril was there, and whether they were tolerating each other or barely speaking, if danger came, he'd be at her side and she'd be at his.

Gavril was there; she and Daigo were not alone; all was well.

Had someone asked exactly what she'd smelled, waking up those nights, she'd have said it was simply the stink of an unwashed body. Now, having been put in a wagon by the bandits and left to sleep, side by side again, Moria realized she recognized Gavril's scent as well as Daigo might.

And now she smelled it again, tossing in her sleep, and it tormented her with memories. Gavril in the palace court when she confronted him about his father. Gavril admitting he knew who had massacred her village. Gavril holding her at sword point before he escaped. Gavril in the dungeon. Gavril turning his back on her, telling his father he did not care what happened to her. Telling his father she was a foolish, stupid child, and leaving her in that dungeon, to the guard's torments.

She dreamed she was back in that cell, fighting off the guard—Halmond—pulling back the knife to stab him. Only in the dream, he wrested it from her fingers and slammed it into her gut, and she gasped, her eyes closing and then opening to see, not Halmond holding the blade, but Gavril.

Moria shot upright, screaming, still feeling the agony of the blade buried in her gut, and then she saw Gavril, right there, his hands on her shoulders, saying her name. She fought wildly, half asleep, seeing Gavril's face in both dream and reality, his cold and empty expression as he plunged the blade in deeper, and then the other Gavril, his eyes wide with alarm, her name on his lips, his hand over her mouth to stifle her cries.

"It's all right," he said. "It's me. I'm here."

She kicked and clawed, biting his hand and struggling with everything she had while he fought to restrain her, muttering, "Not the right thing to say, apparently."

Moria scuttled backward as Gavril crouched there, his hands raised, talking to her in what he must have thought was a soothing tone, but sounding more like he was trying to calm a spooked horse.

The floor rattled. She could feel the vibrations, and they scattered most of the dream, leaving her staring about in confusion. Vibrating wood floor. Low wooden ceiling. Dark, cave-like space lit only by the moon shimmering through a hole in the roof.

They were in a wagon. They'd been tossed in here, their bindings removed, apparently deemed unnecessary given that they were surrounded by mounted and armed men.

"We're in a wagon," Gavril said.

"I see that," she snapped. She continued looking about, orienting herself. There were blankets on the floor. She tugged on one and backed farther from Gavril. Then she lay down and pulled it over herself. When silence fell, she could hear her teeth chattering as she shook convulsively, as much from the dream as from the chilly night.

Gavril took the second blanket and passed it to her. When she ignored it, he started to stretch it over her.

"Don't," she said.

"Until the dream passes," he said, and pulled it onto her. "Was it about your father?"

"It was about many things."

"We ought to talk—"

"No."

A hiss of air expelled through teeth. "I know you think I cannot explain, and you are correct," he said. "There is no excuse. I do not expect you to understand, but it would help me to say my piece."

"Yes, it would help you." Moria rose, sitting, pulling the blanket up to her chin. "You think I'm punishing you, don't you? Not allowing you to explain."

"I understand that I deserve your anger."

"Do you? After you left the city, I wouldn't speak to anyone

51

of what you did. I could say I had made up my mind about you and would not waste time discussing the matter, but Tyrus determined the truth. He wanted what I wanted: an explanation, an excuse. To have you return and say, 'This is not as it appears.' Because no matter what you'd done, we both remembered another Gavril. He remembered his childhood friend. I remembered a boy who fought at my side through the Wastes." She lifted her gaze to his. "But you are not that boy."

"I—"

"If you explain yourself to me, I'll see that boy again, and I'll realize it's not as simple as I thought. That you are not one thing or the other. That you can be both. That I can trust you with my life, and that I can trust you not at all. And how would that help me? Am I safer to be on my guard at all times? Or to rest certain that you will always have my back?"

"I have your back, Keeper. Always. Yet you are safest to pretend otherwise, to watch it yourself, and work with me, as best you can, to escape this situation. Then you may decide what you wish to hear. I will wait for you to do so. I will not ask you again."

"Thank you."

She tried to hand him back his blanket, but he said, "Keep it. I'm sitting watch anyway."

"Wake me at dawn so you can sleep."

SEVEN

Gavril did not wake her, but the morning sun did, and she insisted he sleep. They needed to keep their wits about them, which meant they both needed to be rested. He slept fitfully. When he stopped tossing, she shifted closer and saw that his eyes were open.

He pushed up, gazing around.

"We're in a wagon," she said.

He gave her a look, and she countered it with a faint smile. He did not return it, but his face relaxed, and he nodded, acknowledging the jest.

"Have we stopped at all?" he asked.

"No. It's midmorning if the sun is any indication." She turned to him. "We need to talk."

The look on his face made her stomach clench—seeing his hope and relief and knowing she was about to crush it, hating herself for that and then hating herself for feeling guilty.

It was so blasted complicated. So fraught with emotion and all of those emotions painful, and she was struck by the overwhelming urge to leap out the back of the wagon, fight their captors. Because whatever happened, it would be action and a pain she could deal with so much more easily than this.

"About our plans," she hurried on. "You know the emperor better than I do. What will he do when we are delivered to his doorstep?"

Gavril took a deep breath. "That is . . . difficult to say. I knew him well enough when I was younger, but my opinions on the man have changed. Justifiably in some ways and yet in others . . . I'm realizing now . . ." He shook his head. "You didn't ask for my opinions on the emperor himself."

"No, go on. I'd like to hear them."

Gavril hesitated. "It is impossible to explain without touching closer to breaking my promise than you might like. Everything is colored by the past, and in explaining that, you may think I'm trying . . ."

"Anything you say about your experiences with the emperor helps me understand what we might be about to face."

"All right, but I warn you, this may be more about my father than the emperor. It's . . . difficult to separate the two."

"I can imagine."

He seemed to relax at that and sat cross-legged before he began. "You know that they were best of friends. Boon companions. They grew up together. They fought in the imperial wars together. When Jiro Tatsu was made emperor, I'm certain my father felt slighted. It happened before I was born, so I know little of it, though I do recall once hearing them talking, alone together, and the emperor saying it was only luck of birth that gave him the throne over my father, because my father was not empire-born."

"That is true," she said.

"In public, they remained as close as ever, but even as a child, I felt the tension between them. At the time, I only worried it would affect my friendship with Tyrus. My father . . ." Gavril shifted. "My father did not encourage me to form relationships."

"What do you mean?"

"He . . ." Gavril shook his head. "It adds nothing to the tale, because my father *did* encourage my friendship with Tyrus. Or, I should say, he encouraged . . . No matter. The point is that we remained friends, and so the emperor was like an uncle to me. He was very kind to me, and always had time for me, and I greatly admired him and often wished . . ."

"Often wished what?" she prompted when he trailed off.

"My relationship with my father was not easy. I envied Tyrus's with the emperor. It was the difference between being a bastard to a man with four legitimate heirs and being the only child. My father said that someday I would be glad of his harshness, because Tyrus could never be more than he was, and I could. I did not care. I would have gladly shared my father's attentions with a dozen brothers, if I could be as free as Tyrus."

"Tyrus is not free."

"I know. His burden is different but no less. A child doesn't see that. Later, my view of the emperor changed. I was confused for a long time. No one truly explained what my father had done, and people thought him either a martyr or a monster. I was still friends with the son of the man who had sentenced my father to exile, and the emperor himself was as kind to me as ever, as if nothing had changed. But then I grew up, and I heard how my father had been betrayed by his best friend, how the emperor exiled him on false charges because he feared my father's power. I heard that from my uncles and in the streets. Then Tyrus went away to the Okamis and I was moved into the barrack for training. That separation also meant a separation from the emperor himself, and my opinions on the man changed. My view of his actions changed."

"He became the enemy," she said softly.

Gavril nodded. "Time tempered my memories of my father, too, and all around me I heard what a great man he was, and how any rumor of his ruthlessness or cruelty or, yes, madness was from his enemies, who spread lies for the emperor. Even my opinion of Tyrus altered. I was . . . more influenced by others than I like to admit. I felt alone and . . ."

He cleared his throat. "That is no excuse. The fact is that it was simple for me to believe we had grown apart and the fault was more Tyrus's than mine, and that if he continued trying to renew our friendship, he had an ulterior motive."

"Tyrus never has ulterior motives."

"I know, and I know it does not speak well of me to admit I thought him guilty of that. It was easier to believe I had avoided a trap than that I'd lost a friend, which I now know I had. I now know many things. About Tyrus, about myself, about my father, and about the emperor. But it is the last that concerns you. What do I think of the emperor?"

He took a deep breath. "I am almost certain we face no hero's welcome. Jiro Tatsu is not the kindly uncle I once believed him to be. Nor is he the monster I later thought. He is the emperor, and all that entails. He must put us into the dungeons, exactly as these men expect. If he makes any other move, his enemies will pounce, and the empire will be further split. It will not be comfortable nor pleasant, but it will be safe. We will be there for appearances only, and only until he can find some reason to free us."

"But then we cannot go to your father's camp."

"No."

"Which is a problem."

Gavril exhaled and stretched his legs. "It is."

"Because not only does it mean I can't spy on him, but when he discovers we've been taken, it gives him more fodder for his cause—his only son and an imperial Keeper thrown into the dungeons."

"Yes."

"How will this affect his next move?"

Gavril looked over and frowned.

"You said he is planning a major move. I'm presuming now you can tell me what it is."

"I would, if I knew. My father realized . . . he did not have my full devotion. I was simply too poor an actor, as I'm certain you saw. I could not feign the degree of filial loyalty he expected. I led him to believe it was simply because we'd been too long apart—he was a stranger to me—but he took care not to tell me anything of a sensitive nature. I know only that he was mobilizing troops and that he had some grand move in mind."

"Martial or sorcery?"

"I . . . I would like to say that, given the mobilization of troops, it was the former." He looked at her. "But I fear it was not."

EIGHT

At midday, the wagon stopped, and they were escorted out to a spot where Moria was expected to relieve herself.

"It's been nearly a day since I drank water," she said. "I have none to spare."

The bandit leader grunted and handed Moria a small bag, which she opened to find dried meat and fruit. She gave it back.

"I'm not hungry."

"Your rumbling stomach says otherwise." The leader took out a piece of meat and bit off a chunk. "There? It's not poisoned."

"I would prefer water."

He motioned to Moria's guard, who took out his own waterskin and passed it over.

She took a gulp of the water. The leader passed her the bag

of food again. She accepted a piece of meat and chewed on it.

"Have you ever heard the story of King Hokkai?" the leader asked. Moria stopped chewing, and he laughed. "Ah, you *have*. Good King Hokkai, who invited all his enemies to a banquet. Then, in a show of good faith, he sampled from every plate before they dined. His enemies dug in, and one by one, fell foaming and convulsing to their deaths, the king having built up an immunity to the poison over the moons proceeding the meal."

His gaze moved to Gavril, judging his reaction. When Gavril gave none, the leader laughed and said, "Eat, girl. I jest."

Moria still hesitated, much to the leader's amusement.

"It's one set of rations between you," the bandit said. "Give the boy some."

"Do I have to?" she asked.

The man smiled. "No, you do not. It's entirely your choice."

Moria took another long draught of the water. "Then no. He gave me nothing after he captured me. He needs nothing now."

"Perhaps a sip of water?" the leader said. "The day grows hot, and if he's to survive the journey . . ."

"Is that necessary?"

The bandit chuckled and elbowed Gavril. "Did you hear her?"

"I'm well aware of the Keeper's opinion on my continued existence, and her hope of seeing it end soon, preferably at the point of her dagger."

"Seems you survived the night together just fine."

Gavril gave him a baleful look. "Does it appear as if I slept?

I would ask that when we resume our journey, she walks behind the wagon so I may get some sleep."

"You'll sleep well soon. I hear the emperor's dungeons are very quiet . . . in between the screams of the tortured."

Another called the leader, hailing him as "Toman." The leader walked off. Moria glanced about. They were still surrounded by a half-dozen bandits, eating and drinking and resting yet keeping an eye on them.

"I could not—" she began, whispering without looking Gavril's way.

"I know. Well played."

"You do need to drink. Perhaps if I soak dried fruit and conceal it—"

"No."

"But you must—"

"They'll not let me die. Spare no thought for me. Nor will I for you. That is safest."

Moria moved a few steps away and crouched to finish her meal. Out of the corner of her eye, she saw Gavril glance over, and a couple of the bandits laughed.

"You might beg her for a scrap," Toman said as he returned.

"I need none," Gavril said stiffly.

"Good. Because you'll get none except from her. Now let's talk about your father."

"I'd rather not."

"Oh, but you should be so proud of him. It takes a strong man to survive the Forest of the Dead. And then to come back and wreak vengeance by murdering hundreds of innocents? The actions of an honorable warrior."

"Whatever the warrior code might say, my father realizes it is impossible to fight treachery with honorable deeds. He was betrayed by the empire itself. If citizens must fall in his war, then they ought to consider the choices they made, supporting a monster on the imperial throne and allowing a hero to be exiled."

"Pretty speech, boy."

"I do not make pretty speeches. Only plain ones, ringing with truth."

The advantage to an impassive demeanor, Moria reflected, was that one was not expected to infuse any speech with passion or even emotion. Gavril spoke the words with monotone conviction, and the bandit leader studied him for any sign of dissembling, but Moria knew he'd find none.

"Your father is no hero," Toman said finally.

"That is your opinion. I trust you will see the error of it before he takes the imperial throne. Otherwise . . ." Gavril met the leader's gaze with a cold stare. "You will regret it, as will every citizen who stands between us and—"

The bandit's slap rang through the quiet, the blow hard enough to make Gavril stumble back.

"Apologies, my lord," Toman said. "I had to make you stop. You were talking madness."

"You asked me to speak of my father."

"Let's change the subject. Your mother."

Now there was a slight stiffening in Gavril's back before he composed himself and said, "What about my mother?"

"Where is she?"

Silence.

Toman continued. "I had much time to think, riding through the night, and I realized my gift to the emperor is incomplete. He will reward me handsomely for you two but . . ." He shrugged. "There is a limit to what gold can buy, and there are things I want that I cannot purchase. I have wives. Three. Not that they *know* there are three of them, of course," he said with a smile. "More important are my eight children. What they need most is a better life than a bandit can provide. I want a pardon for my crimes and land for my families."

Gavril lowered his voice. "Which I can guarantee you will receive if you return me to my father."

"Your father has neither land nor pardon to offer."

"He will."

"No, he will not, and I would sooner see my children put to the blade than take a copper from that traitor." Toman stepped closer to Gavril. "And if I may offer a word of advice, boy? You would do well to look deep into your heart and reconsider your loyalty to him before we reach the city gates."

"My loyalty to my father is absolute."

"For now. Wait until they're slicing into you—a thousand times. Do you know what that's like?"

"I'm certain I'll find out if I'm captured."

"Brave words for a child. Perhaps I ought to do you a favor and torture you myself. Give you time to change your story before the experts take over."

"I have no story to change."

"But you could. Show the emperor that you have seen the error of your ways, recant, and throw yourself on his mercy."

Gavril's eyes narrowed. "And how would that help you?"

"As I said, I have children. I am a father and you are a boy. Perhaps I fear you've been led astray."

"I may be young, but I am not a child, foolish enough to be led astray by my father, nor to be tricked by you."

"It's no trick, boy. I know the torture methods the emperor employs—intimately—and I am suggesting you may wish to avoid learning of them yourself. There is a way you can do so that will benefit us both. Tell me where to find your mother."

The bandit leader got his reaction then. An honest one, too great for Gavril to conceal.

"You plan . . ." Gavril could not finish.

"Some argue today that our laws are too lenient. They long for the old days, when crime was almost unheard of, those past ages where to commit one meant the lives of your entire family were forfeit. Personally, I'm quite glad that is no longer a possibility, but still, in matters where the crime is treason? The emperor was too lenient when he exiled Alvar Kitsune. Not only did he leave you and your mother alive, but he allowed your family to retain their caste, their wealth, their social standing . . . look where it got him."

"My mother played no role in my father's escape."

"But *you* did. Your uncles did. Your family turned the emperor's mercy against him and used the wealth they retained to raise an army. The only way to punish that? Retract his mercy. All *traces* of his mercy. Annihilate you and your mother and your uncles and their wives and their children and wipe the Kitsunes from the empire. That is what the emperor wishes now. I will help him achieve his revenge."

Gavril's jaw worked, but he said only, "My mother did not

even know my father was alive."

"She does now."

"I presume so, but he has not seen her. He had her taken from the imperial city and put into safekeeping before this began. I do not know where she is."

Toman peered at him. "Are you saying your father does not trust you? That he has reason to doubt your filial loyalty?"

"No, it is my maternal loyalty that concerns him. He knows I worry about my mother, and he knows that it would be unsafe for me to contact her. So he has given me no way of doing so. For both our sakes."

"Hmm, well, I was going to suggest that it would help your cause if you willingly turned her over, but I can see that's not likely to happen. Perhaps, then, I can appeal to your maternal concern myself. There are others searching for your mother, hoping to win a reward from the emperor. He would not require her to be returned alive. If you are certain she played no role in your treason, perhaps it is best if you allow her to be returned—with you—to the imperial city, where she can plead her innocence to the emperor."

Gavril's cold gaze met Toman's. "Even if I agreed, as I said, I do not know where to find her."

Toman nodded slowly and paced in front of the two of them, as if thinking of a new tactic. Then the bandit grabbed Moria, wrenching her around so fast that she didn't have time to react before his dagger was pressed against her throat.

"Are you certain, boy?" The bandit leader pushed the blade edge into Moria's neck and pain sliced through her, hot blood dripping. "Perhaps you wish to rethink that. And rethink your affection for the Keeper."

"I do not need to rethink either," Gavril said, his words chill and brittle. "I cannot tell you what I do not know. I could tell you a lie, to save the Keeper's life, but her death means only that I do not have to share the wagon or the rations. Or worry about falling asleep and waking with her hands around my throat. If the emperor would be satisfied with her corpse, then that is your choice."

Toman shifted his weight, the blade digging in, and Moria gasped. Gavril tensed, as if ready to react, the movement so slight the bandit seemed not to notice.

"You're quite certain you don't know?" the man said.

"I am entirely certain."

"Then you have a point, even if you may regret inadvertently making it." The bandit leader threw Moria aside. "The people will not be satisfied with your whore's corpse. You are stuck with her for the duration of the journey." He motioned for the others to take them to the wagon. "And there's no need to tell me where your mother is." Toman grinned over his shoulder. "I already know."

NINE

*H*e's mad. That was Ashyn's first thought when Edwyn told her she had the power to wake dragons. There was no such thing as dragons . . .

Nor shadow stalkers. Nor death worms. Nor thunder hawks. Truly, Ashyn, you are correct, as you have always been. Such things exist only in your imagination. Like that dragon skull you see before you.

She imagined her sister's voice. Not mocking—simply light and teasing as she rolled her eyes and sauntered away. And for one moment, picturing Moria, Ashyn wanted to lunge after her, to grab her cloak and pull her back.

I'm as mad as he is.

No, simply lonely. So very lonely and unsettled and incomplete without her sister.

Are you well, Moria? Are you safe? Did Gavril look after you?

Has Tyrus found you? Are you reunited with him and with Daigo?

"Ashyn?" Edwyn said.

She looked at him, and she didn't see madness in his eyes. She saw calm resolve and strength of purpose. She glanced at the dragon skull. Proof that he was not mad, at least not in believing there had been dragons once.

She looked up at the skull. "How would I wake . . . ?"

His laugh startled her. He reached to squeeze her shoulder. "Sorry, child. I'm not laughing at you, but at myself. I truly ought to have explained more before I blurted that, but this is such a moment for me, the culmination of both a life's work and sixteen summers of grief and longing. It is fate, of course. A gift from the goddess, whatever she might be. I spent my life with these empty relics." He waved at the skull. "Preserving them and the memory of them for our people. And then my own daughter bears children who could waken the dragons? If that is not the work of a beneficent goddess, I do not know what is. Reunited with my granddaughter, who is also the young woman who can make my greatest dream a reality, at a time when the empire needs it most?"

He shook his head. "But that is not straightening out this matter at all, is it? You'll have to excuse me. I'm overexcited and overwhelmed, and my thoughts can be a jumble even at the best of times."

She knew what that was like. Moria's thoughts seemed to run in a linear path, clear and decisive and leading straight to action. Ashyn's were more like a spiderweb, with infinite possibilities, and she could get lost in them.

"Let me start with the simplest answer to your question,"

he said. "When we reach our destination, you will not be asked to transform bones to flesh. We have a sleeping dragon. A mother and two young offspring."

"Sleeping dragons?"

"Asleep for almost an age now. That was the custom. A dragon is not an easy creature to control. When our people had no further use for them, those with your power would put them to sleep, and then wake them when needed. But there had not been Northern twins with your ability born in so many generations that people forgot it was even possible, forgot the dragons altogether. Fortunately, some of us did not, and we cared for them. Then you were born and we knew they could be wakened, but they ought not to be. Not yet. Just as I knew I could have my daughter's children back, but I ought not to interfere. Not until the dragons needed to rise. Until the empire needed them."

"Which is now. Because of Alvar."

He smiled. "Because of Alvar. So, Ashyn, are you ready to wake dragons?"

To Edwyn's confusion and dismay, Ashyn did not rush to say *yes, of course, and when can we leave?* It was thrilling, to be sure. To wake dragons? To see a living one? Beyond her dreams. But at the moment Ashyn had more prosaic concerns.

"I need my sister," she said. "I don't know what you've heard of her plight . . ."

"I have caught rumors," he said carefully.

"They are lies. All of them. Moria is not Gavril Kitsune's lover. There was never anything of the sort between them. She despises Gavril as a traitor. As for Tyrus, she cares deeply for him as a friend, and he for her. We were all in battle together when Tyrus was betrayed by a warlord and Moria was taken. We presume she is being held captive by Alvar Kitsune. She would sooner kill Gavril than willingly share the same room with him."

That, Ashyn would admit, overstated the matter. Her sister's feelings for Gavril were complex. Rage and hate and hurt and betrayal. She did care for him, though it was not in the same way she cared for Tyrus. But to present such a convoluted picture to Edwyn wouldn't help her sister's case.

"I understand you are close—" he began.

"No," Ashyn said, with some snap in her voice. "If you need to comment on that then you don't understand at all. Until a moon ago, I'd never spent more than a day away from her."

"I do not mean to be indelicate, Ashyn, but you are both in the time of life when the body and mind can be at odds with each other. If she was alone with Gavril Kitsune in the Wastes, as I understand, for many days—and nights—it is possible that something occurred between them and she is too ashamed to tell you."

Ashyn's laugh rang through the cave. "Another girl, perhaps. But not my sister. If anything happened between them, I'd have had a full and enthusiastic accounting of it. For Moria, there is no war between mind and body. They both want . . ." She felt her cheeks heat then, realizing what she was saying in her haste to defend her sister. "The same thing."

"Ah."

"My sister is not shy about such matters. She made it clear

to me that nothing occurred." She paced across the cave, Tova at her side, her hand on his head. "I'm sorry if this agitates me, but I'll speak on it no more. My sister is innocent. My sister is in trouble. Whatever else you need me to do, first I must find her, and hopefully Tyrus and Daigo as well. They search for her, too."

"That is a lot to do, Ashyn."

She straightened and turned to him. "It is. If you can help me, I would appreciate it. If not, then I'll take my leave, and you can tell me how to contact you once I've found them."

"I would not let you undertake anything so dangerous without help, child. Let me bring dinner and then we will discuss how to best handle the search."

To help Ashyn understand what they faced beyond the safety of this mountainside, Edwyn explained what had been happening in the empire. It was, unfortunately, what Ashyn feared. Alvar might be banging the drums of war, but he seemed to have no immediate plan to actually appear on a battlefield. While he continued to muster and train troops and to sway warlords to his side, his primary tactics seemed to be lies and treachery and fear-mongering, which suited the clan of the Kitsune, the nine-tailed trickster fox.

Ashyn and Ronan had witnessed this in a tiny, nameless outpost—an inn on the road with a small community grown up around it. Alvar's men had tempted the locals into joining them. Then they'd pretended instead to be imperial guards and beheaded every "traitor" in front of their friends and family, before mounting the heads on pikes. In an empire that had outlawed capital punishment, that had been an unimaginable insult and cruelty to hitherto loyal citizens, and it was not the only such "punishment" visited on similar communities that night. By morning, word was out that the emperor had apparently become the tyrant that Alvar Kitsune's men claimed he was.

"So that is how he's winning troops among the commoners," Ashyn said when Edwyn told her more of Alvar's treacherous deeds.

"No, that is how he's inciting sedition. Alvar Kitsune might have been the empire's marshal, but he was never its greatest warrior. That distinction goes to Jiro Tatsu, and Alvar knows it. Do not expect to see war anytime soon. If at all."

"What?"

"There are ways to break an emperor without engaging him on a battlefield. Ways to divide an empire without ripping it asunder in war."

"Does Emperor Tatsu know this? He's preparing for war, and if that's not . . ." She remembered what the emperor had said, when he first discovered Alvar Kitsune lived.

Prepare for a war unlike any the empire has known.

To Ashyn, that had meant war on a grand and unimaginable scale. But that was not what the emperor had meant at all. He knew what kind of war this enemy would fight.

"The emperor must rally his troops and prepare for battle," Edwyn said. "If he does not, then *that* is the moment Alvar would indeed strike. Emperor Tatsu must be ready for war, and yet prepare himself to fight a very different battle on much less familiar terrain. I do not envy him the task. I only trust he is up to it."

As do I.

After that, Edwyn explained his plan for them. Moria would have fought it tooth and nail, because it involved sitting and doing little while others took action. But in the end, Ashyn recognized her limits. She was no warrior. Tova would protect her with his life, but he was not a battle dog or a tracking hound. She had no idea where to begin hunting for Moria. Ashyn herself was both easily recognizable and easily mistaken for her supposed-traitor sister. And Ronan was here, deathly ill, and she did not know these people well enough to leave him in their care.

Edwyn said he would send scouts to make contact with those he knew in the imperial city and elsewhere. They would seek news on Moria and Tyrus, and in the meantime, Ashyn would stay where she was, while Edwyn prepared her for the dragons. That was the important thing. Alvar Kitsune might be lying low for now, but he would make a move soon. Edwyn was sure of it.

"Traitorous sorcerer that he is," Edwyn said after he took a drink from the waterskin. "He'll keep to the shadows for as long as he can. Alvar Kitsune plans to lead the emperor on a terrible chase, horror and destruction in his wake. But this dragon knows this fox, and Tatsu's trying to run him to ground rather than launching his army to an empty battlefield. When we bring Jiro Tatsu an actual dragon . . ." Edwyn smiled. "That is when things will change."

"Will one dragon truly make a difference?"

"In battle? It would help, but it would not guarantee easy victory. What matters here, child, is not the beast itself but the symbolism."

Ashyn nodded. "The dragon has woken dragons. The goddess has chosen her champion."

A smile crinkled his face. "Your mother would be so proud of you."

"Can you tell me about her?"

That smile broadened, lighting his blue eyes. "With pleasure, child." He passed a plate of dried persimmons. "When she was a child, she used to . . ."

TEN

Ashyn blamed the dream on the talk of young men and women and the yearnings of the body. While her sister was much more aware—and interested— in those yearnings, Ashyn was not unfamiliar with them. Nor, if she admitted it, did she find them unwelcome. Yet it was certainly uncomfortable and confusing when she'd find her gaze lingering on a young man she would never consider romantically interesting, because unlike Moria, Ashyn could not fully untangle the two. She wanted someone she could kiss and, yes, more, when the time was right, but she also wanted someone she could talk to, laugh with, and love, and the thought of one without the other confounded her.

That night, she dreamed of being curled up on a sleeping pallet, another body beside hers, lean-muscled and hard, her fingers running over his nakedness, exploring as she kissed him and as he whispered in her ear, telling her how much she meant to him, how much he cared for her, how he'd always cared for her, and she was whispering back, telling him not to talk so much, not now, that she wanted him to kiss her and to touch her and—

She woke then, at some noise or disturbance, hearing herself make a sound not unlike Tova's growl as she pulled the blankets back up and tried to snuggle back into the dream, that delicious dream. It was the first time she'd ever experienced such a thing, though she remembered Moria talking about similar dreams, and she remembered how she herself had felt stabs of confusion and relief and envy, all rolling together— confusion because she didn't quite understand, relief because she suspected she would not enjoy such dreams as much as her sister, and envy because, well, because she might not enjoy them as much as her sister. But now, having had her first, all she wanted to do was return to that dream, and it made her ache and sigh and struggle to reclaim it, to find him again. For there was no question who *he* was—it was not some mysterious figure haunting her dreams. Her heart and her desire never changed, no matter how often she might fervently wish they would.

Ronan.

Always Ronan, much to her dismay when she woke and recalled the dream. But for now, lost in that warm fog of half sleep, she had no problem admitting to herself who it was, and envisioning him there, in her blankets, enjoying the dream, feeling the heat and the—

"My lady?"

Now Ashyn did bolt upright, as Tova growled and rose

from her side. A figure appeared in the entrance to the small cave where Edwyn had put her for the night. It was a young man, and all she could see was his outline. A little under average height, but well-formed, with tousled curls, and her first thought was *Ronan*. She blamed the dream, because Ronan would never call her "my lady." She was Ash, unless he was annoyed, and then she was Ashyn.

The young man standing in the entrance was Ronan's stature, but Northern in his coloring, with light hair, blue eyes, and skin as pale as her own. She knew him, too. Tarquin, the guard Edwyn had assigned to watch over her cave as she slept.

"Hmm?" she said.

"You called out, my lady."

Her cheeks flamed red-hot, and she was glad for the darkness. "Did I?" she managed to say in as calm a voice as possible. "I must have been dreaming. It has been a very difficult fortnight. My dreams are often unsettled."

"Yes, it did sound unsettled." He lit his torch and ducked to step into the low cave. "I could summon the healer with a sleeping draught."

"No, I am quite fine. But thank you for asking."

He lifted the torch, and she realized she was still sitting up and her bedclothes were . . . less than adequate, having been borrowed from a woman significantly larger than Ashyn. She tugged the blanket up, but not before Tarquin had gotten a good look, and he stopped short, staring even after she covered herself, and continued to stare, as if he'd never seen a girl on a sleeping pallet. She dropped her gaze, trying to be demure, only to discover that she'd dropped it to his breeches, where she could see the proof of his thoughts.

She tore her gaze away as her cheeks flamed.

"I—I'm sorry, my lady," he stammered. "I did not mean to intrude. I only wished to be sure you were well and did not need my assist—"

He stopped there, and when she looked over, his face was as red as hers must surely be.

"I do not," she said evenly. "But again, I thank you for offering."

"Then I'll leave you to your sleep. If you need me—I mean, if you require assist—that is, a sleeping draught . . ."

She tried not to smile as she lifted her gaze to his. "Thank you."

She did smile then, offered it to him along with the thanks, and when she did, he stared again and said, "You are beautiful, my lady." Then his eyes widened, as if in horror, and he said, "I did not mean—that is to say—"

"There is no harm in a compliment. Thank you, Tarquin."

And there was no harm in it. If anything, it was welcome. Ashyn had grown up knowing her looks would not appeal to many young men in the empire. Either she was too pale and odd in her appearance, or she was exotic and desirable because of that and no other trait.

Even when young men in Edgewood did find her looks to their taste, there was another who looked exactly like her, and whose brash and bold personality always outshone Ashyn's quiet timidity. The only young man who'd sought to court her was the scholar Simeon . . . who'd then named her sister and the prince as traitors. Not quite a pleasant memory. So to have a Northern boy tell her she was beautiful? It was a small thing, but it felt warm and comforting, even if her return smile held no hint of invitation.

"I—I'll leave you, my lady," he said, backing up . . . and hitting the cave wall.

She tried not to laugh. "Thank you again, Tarquin. I will see you in the morning and—"

A cry sounded beyond the cave. Tarquin raced out. Tova lunged in front of Ashyn as she pulled her dagger from under her sleeping pallet, grabbed her cloak, and started for the cave entrance. Tarquin stood a few paces outside it, his sword drawn.

Edwyn said they had only a few warriors in their group, and most had gone seeking news of her sister, but he'd kept two behind, leaving one to guard Ashyn. From the way Tarquin held his sword, though, he might be a trained warrior, yet he was not an experienced one. When Tarquin saw Ashyn, standing in the entrance, dagger raised, his eyes widened.

"My lady," he said. "Go back inside. I will handle this."

"I am trained with my dagger." Not untrue, though she'd come to realize she needed much *more* training.

"Perhaps, but my orders—"

Another cry, and they both went still.

"Is that an animal?" Ashyn whispered. "Or a bird? I'm unfamiliar with this area."

"It does indeed sound like a beast, my lady, and these forests are filled with them. I would ask that you retreat into the cave while I investigate."

"And if it circles past you and comes into the cave?"

He hesitated.

"I will accompany you," she said. "Let me pull on my boots and cloak."

"I truly ought to—"

"Abandon me?"

He paused again, and she said, "Give me but a moment."

ELEVEN

The other caves were silent. There were perhaps four of them, in addition to the one with the dragon skull. The settlement was hardly a village—simply caves in the mountainside big enough for temporary lodgings, which meant they were spaced far enough apart that Ashyn could not even see the other entrances. A cry would bring Edwyn and the others, she'd presumed, but the cry they'd heard had not. Did that mean they could not hear well enough, sleeping in their caves? Or that they'd heard and recognized the sound as a harmless animal? The high probability of the latter is what kept her from suggesting they call for aid. They would investigate first.

The night had gone quiet. Unnaturally quiet, she realized when both she and Tarquin stopped simultaneously, and without their footfalls she could not hear anything. Goose bumps prickled along her arms, and when Tarquin resumed walking, she stayed where she was, surveying the silent forest.

It ought not to be silent.

She'd encountered such a quiet wilderness once before. The Forest of the Dead.

Tarquin turned. "My lady?"

"It's too quiet," she said.

He looked about and frowned. "It is night, my lady."

"And it is always this silent at night? It was this silent earlier?"

He tilted his head as if listening. "I can hear water, my lady. And the creak of trees in the wind."

"But beasts? Birds?"

"I saw an owl at dusk. Perhaps that is what made the cry. I heard one a few nights ago, and it was a terrible shrieking sound. The owls in the North are very different. As is the silence. You've not heard quiet until you've been out on the ice, my lady."

It *was* too silent. But Tarquin didn't realize that, just as none of the villagers of Edgewood had thought the Forest of the Dead unnaturally silent. It was Ashyn. She sensed . . .

What do I sense? Spirits?

She continued after Tarquin as she sent up a silent and polite query to the spirits, in case that was what she sensed. They did not answer. Beside her, Tova was looking about and walking so close his fur brushed her cloak. He sensed it as well.

She recalled the trip from the imperial city, when they'd discovered mummified monks possessed by spirits. She'd detected something then, too. Was it the same? In a way, yes. A disturbance in the second world. She'd felt it even before the possessed monks, when she'd first encountered the shadow stalkers. This was the same . . . and yet not the same. Interesting.

Another manifestation of Alvar's magics? Or was she overly quick to jump to that conclusion?

"May I take the torch, Tarquin?" she asked. "So you may be ready with your sword?"

He handed the torch over wordlessly, and Ashyn lifted it high as she walked, peering into the dark forest for signs of shadow stalkers or anything else. When a bat flitted overhead, she ducked with a yelp and Tarquin spun so fast she was nearly impaled on the tip of his sword. They both stumbled to apologize, and then laughed, softly.

"Continue," she said. "I will be more careful."

"As will I, my lady."

Tova harrumphed and glanced back toward the caves, as if wishing they'd brought someone more experienced on this excursion. Ashyn made a face at him. She'd relaxed now, seeing the bat, proof that the forest was simply quiet, perhaps from the lateness of the day. She knew from her reading that many supposedly nocturnal creatures were actually crepuscular, most active at twilight and dawn, so the deep night would be quieter.

Yes, she was overreacting. It was not only Moria who let her imagination run away with her these days. She truly ought to—

A scream rang out and Ashyn fell back, Tarquin leaping in front of her, his sword at the ready, the blade quivering slightly. The sound stopped. They both turned in its direction.

"Someone is hurt," Ashyn said. "Just over there."

Tarquin looked toward where they'd heard the sound, then back at the caves.

"It is farther to return," she said. "It sounded as if a woman was being attacked. If whatever did so—human or beast—sees us fleeing . . ."

"It will give chase," he said grimly. "And yes, if we can help her . . ."

He started forward, motioning for Ashyn to stay at his back. When another scream came, he broke into a jog with Ashyn at his heels. Tova ran into the lead. The hound leaped over a bush as another scream came, so close she swore she felt it. She raced forward, almost passing Tarquin before he picked up speed to stay ahead. Tova had disappeared. Ashyn strained for some sound of him, some—

The hound growled. And something growled back. Tova snapped and snarled and there was a clang like metal, and in Ashyn's mind, she saw a sword. She ran, passing Tarquin now and barreling through the thick brush until she could see Tova's pale fur ahead, and she pushed into the clearing where he stood and . . .

A fox. That was what had growled. A young fox stood a few paces from Tova, its tail puffed as it snarled. It lunged and seemed to stop short, and Ashyn heard the metallic clang again.

"It's hurt," Ashyn said, moving forward carefully as Tova growled.

The fox had something around its leg. Wood and metal and rope.

"A trap," Tarquin said. "It's not unlike the ones we use in

the North for our foxes. For their fur."

"And they simply capture the poor beast and leave it to die?"

He shook his head as he moved forward, his sword lowered. "It ought to have killed it mercifully, but the trap was damaged. See over here . . ." He pointed out the problem, though all Ashyn truly cared about was the poor beast, whining now, bloodied and in pain.

"Can you free it?" she asked.

"I can."

"Should you?" She lowered her voice. "Will it survive?"

"I'll see."

He put his sword back into his belt and approached the fox with care, his fingers extended. Ashyn tensed, ready for the fox to bite his hand, but Tarquin kept his gaze lowered, crooning under his breath, and the fox only sniffed at his fingers.

"You know animals," she said. "You're good with them."

"We have Northern dogs. That's what my family does—raises and trains them to pull sleds over the ice." He hunkered down beside the fox. "It's not going to like me taking off that trap, though. Perhaps if you speak to it, try to comfort it."

"I think you'll be better at that. Tell me what to do with the trap."

"It's bloody, my lady, and you ought not—"

"I can do it. Comfort the beast. And try not to let it bite me."

He smiled. "It won't. I'll make sure of that. Now, take your dagger . . ."

He talked her through removing the trap. As he'd said, the

fox did not like it, and he had to subdue it. Once it was free, though, the beast made no move to escape, but lay on its side as they both examined the wound.

"It's the foreleg, which is better than the rear," Tarquin said. "They can survive with only three if this one does not heal."

The fox whined, as if understanding, and Tarquin absently rubbed it behind the ears. At first, the fox tensed at the touch, but then it relaxed and closed its eyes, as if enjoying the scratch.

"You have a new friend," Ashyn said.

He laughed softly. "It's a wild beast, my lady. Best left wild. And it would not like my dogs at home."

"What are they like?" she asked as they continued examining the wound. "I've heard of Northern dogs, but never seen one."

"Your hound would make a good one," he said. Then he looked at Tova. "No offense. I know the legend, that he is a warrior in beast form. I meant only that his size and thick fur would serve him well. Our dogs do not grow quite so large."

The fox whimpered, and Tarquin resumed scratching it while he bent beside Ashyn.

"We should clean the wound," Ashyn said. "Would it let you carry it back up to the caves?"

"I can try, my lady. It's small. Likely a young one and a vixen. Here, move your hand under the leg while I lift."

When she didn't do it the way he meant, he took her hand, blushing madly and stammering as he showed her how to brace the injured leg.

Tova growled.

"Yes," Ashyn said. "We're taking the fox with us. I might even make you share your food."

Tova's growl sharpened, and she laughed.

"That growl might be for me," Tarquin said. "Warning me I ought not to touch his Seeker. He——"

Something leaped at Tarquin. A shadow come to life seemed to jump from the forest in a single bound. Tarquin spun and it pounced, and he fell back with a scream. He dropped the fox and Ashyn grabbed for him, but Tova lunged between them and she stumbled into the torch, planted in the ground, extinguishing it as Tarquin let out a scream more horrible than the fox's and then——

And then blood. Blood sprayed and Ashyn screamed and something hit her and she looked down to see Tarquin's hand lying at her foot. She could see other . . . other pieces of him, and she staggered back, still screaming, until Tova grabbed her cloak in his teeth, and she saw something else in the forest, running toward her, a black shadow with red eyes.

TWELVE

on't look!

DMoria's voice seemed to scream the words in her ear, and Ashyn couldn't process what she was seeing, only knew that she should not look, that she could not look. The fox was long gone. She glanced back at Tarquin. At what remained of Tarquin. The darkness covered some but not enough, certainly not enough to leave any doubt that he was dead. That the boy she'd just been speaking to, the sweet Northern boy who'd helped her free a fox, now lay in pieces—

Run, my lady.

The words whispered all around her, as if from every side. Tarquin's voice. His spirit's.

Run, my lady. Please run.

Ashyn saw the shadows forming again, taking the shapes of beasts with red eyes, and she did not spare a moment to consider what she was seeing. She heard Tarquin's voice, his urgent whispers, and she ran, and even as she did, she didn't think of what she'd seen, but sent up prayers for Tarquin's spirit, to ease his passing and guide him to the second world.

She continued to run, uphill now, toward the caves, Tova behind her.

What are you doing? Don't run!

That was Moria's voice again, from deep in her mind.

Don't look. Don't run. Black shadows. Red eyes.

Not shadow stalkers. That's what she'd thought at first, remembering another forest, another attack, another shower of blood, when the shadow stalkers had killed Ronan's uncle. These were not shadow stalkers.

Don't look. Don't run. Black shadows. Red eyes.

Fiend dogs.

Ashyn exhaled a ragged breath as panic filled her. Fiend dogs. Another spirit-driven creature of legend, like shadow stalkers. Yet not like them at all. Fiend dogs were the spirits of warriors who'd been damned for cowardice, forced to spend their afterlife in the form of shadowy hounds. To look at them meant death. To run from them meant death.

There was nothing to be done now, no way to avoid her fate, if Moria's old stories were true.

All of Moria's old stories were true. Why would this be any different?

She thought of Tarquin. Ripped apart by shadow dogs. There was no question. If they caught her, they would kill her.

Yet they had not caught her. While she was not a fast runner, they were still at her heels.

No, not at *her* heels. At Tova's. They were not passing Tova.

Hound of the Immortals, possessed by the spirit of a great warrior.

Fiend dogs were shadow hounds possessed by the spirits of cowardly warriors.

There was some answer there. Some reason they were not attacking him or passing him to get to her. The reason mattered not, only that she could keep running, escape to the . . .

Escape to the caves? To the others? To Edwyn? To Ronan? Lead the fiend dogs to them?

When she slowed, Tova nipped her hand. Telling her to keep going, keep running. She looked around for another option, but Tova growled, warning her not to look, and a fiend dog appeared, right at his side, its red eyes flashing. In the shadow she saw a hound begin to take form and she wrenched her gaze away. She veered to the side, leading them away from the camp, but ahead, she heard voices, someone shouting. Then, "Ashyn!"

It was Edwyn. A snarl sounded behind her. Not Tova. The fiend dogs. She caught a glimpse of shadows in the forest beside them. The fiend dogs circling around, realizing there were other targets ahead, easier targets.

"No!" Ashyn shouted. "Begone, spirits! I command you, begone!"

Even as the words left her mouth, she knew they were a waste of her breath. Banishment was Moria's power, not hers.

Moria, where are you? Why aren't you here? I can't do this without you. I can't do any of it without you.

"Ashyn?" Edwyn called again.

"Go back!" she shouted. "Into the caves. Fiend dogs. There are—"

"There are *what*?" yelled another voice, and she said it louder but she knew it would do no good. It was like saying a dragon was attacking. Worse, because her grandfather and the others believed in dragons.

Ashyn continued running in the direction she'd heard Edwyn's voice. There was no need to lead the fiend dogs away now. The damage had been done.

"Don't look at them!" she shouted. "Don't run from them. Just get back into the caves."

And do what? Cower with their eyes shut? Tarquin had barely glanced at it, before it ripped him apart. If that was all it took, how did anyone survive?

Someone screamed. A terrible scream that told her the fiend dogs were upon them.

"Into the dragon cave!" Edwyn shouted. "Retreat to the cave! Do not run. Do not look at the shadows. Do not look at the eyes. They are—" He said a word Moria didn't know, a word in some other tongue, and someone shrieked, not with pain but with terror.

"Do not panic!" Edwyn roared. "I can hold them off! Do as I say and you will live." Then, "Ashyn! Can you hear me, child?"

"I can."

"Follow my voice. I know how to deal with such beasts, but I need your help to escape them. Focus on me and follow my voice, and if you see the shadows, banish them."

"That is Moria's power. It is not—"

"Do it, child!"

Ashyn kept running. She glanced back, but there was no sign of the fiend dogs. They'd circled around to attack the others. She did not know the way to the dragon cave, certainly not in the dark, but she continued following Edwyn's voice as he spoke in another tongue. Using magics.

Her grandfather was a sorcerer?

Finally, she could see him ahead, standing in the mouth of a cave . . . surrounded by fiend dogs. She stopped short just as Tova was grabbing for her cloak.

"Ashyn?" Edwyn said. "Is that you?"

She swallowed. Would the fiend dogs come after her if she spoke? She was trying to decide what to do when Tova barked.

"Listen to me, child. I'm going to do something that will scatter them, but only for a moment. Do not look directly at them. When you see them disperse, come to me as quickly as you can without running."

Tova barked again.

Ashyn waited with her trembling hand on the hound's head. He nudged her reassuringly. Edwyn started to speak in that foreign tongue again, his words rising. When they hit a crescendo, the shadows seemed to break apart, as if blasted by a gust of wind.

Ashyn moved quickly toward the cave. She'd run before and if she was doomed, then she was doomed, but this wasn't the time to panic Edwyn by running. When she finally reached the cave entrance, the fiend dogs were re-forming. Edwyn pushed her into the cave, telling her he could handle this now. Tova stayed outside with him, growling at the fiend dogs as

Edwyn continued working his magics.

There were seven others inside the cave, the remaining members of their party and the other warrior. When Ashyn saw the healer among them, she looked about frantically.

"Where's Ronan?"

No one answered. There was not enough room in the cave to hide an unconscious young man.

"Where is Ronan?"

"He's safe, my lady," the healer said.

"Is someone with him?"

"There was," the warrior said, and the others gave him a hard look.

"He is fine, my lady," the healer said.

"The elderly woman. Your assistant. Where is she?"

Silence.

Ashyn remembered the scream. That terrible scream. And the warrior's words—that someone *had been* with Ronan.

The warrior grabbed Ashyn's arm as she made for the cave entrance. "You cannot leave, my lady. Your young man will be fine. He cannot see the creatures nor run from them. He is safe."

Do you know that for certain? For absolutely certain?

They didn't know and couldn't care. Ronan was not important to them. Only to her.

Moria would storm out against their wishes. Yet Ashyn was coming to accept that she could not be her sister, and it was not a failure of nerve. It was a difference of inner composition. They might look identical without; they were not identical within. Running to Ronan's side would do little except make her feel better. It would not save him. It might even kill him, if she brought the fiend dogs with her.

Instead of trying to flee, she stepped out behind Tova and attempted to calm the spirits, and while she was not convinced it did any good, Edwyn encouraged her efforts.

When the fiend dogs had finally dispersed, one of the women came up behind her and whispered, "You are covered in blood, my lady," and when Ashyn looked down, she saw she was speckled and splashed with Tarquin's blood. Her throat tightened and tears filled her eyes as she said, "Yes, I am."

"Tarquin . . ."

"I—I'm sorry. We—there was a fox. Injured. We heard screams and—"

The woman squeezed her hand. Edwyn reached out and drew her into an embrace, in spite of the blood.

"He died as a warrior," Edwyn said. "In our faith, as in the empire's, that means his spirit will be honored in the second world."

Ashyn nodded. "I heard his spirit depart. I said prayers for it, but I wish to say more. First, I must check on Ronan."

"I will send someone—"

"No," she said, walking from the cave. "I will do it."

"It is not safe yet, child."

"If it is safe for others, then it is for me." She could tell he was going to argue the matter, so she broke into a run. Edwyn tried to come after her. Then the warrior cried out and Ashyn looked to see a shadow lunging at Edwyn. A fiend dog. But hadn't they been dispersed?

"Back in the cave!" Edwyn shouted. "Everyone get inside! Ashyn!"

She turned away and pretended not to hear him. That would have been difficult a moon or two ago. One did not disobey one's elders, particularly family. Yet now she assessed the situation. The fiend dog was intent on Edwyn and the others, and the beasts had already proven that Tova made them uneasy. So the chances of the fiend dog abandoning the others to come after her were minimal. Edwyn could handle it.

As terrifying as fiend dogs were, they'd been easier to handle than she expected, perhaps because of Edwyn's magics. She slowed to a fast walk, to avoid running, but she continued on up the path that led to Ronan's cave.

The old woman lay right outside of the cave mouth. Ashyn did not look closely. She saw blood and she saw a limb, and that was enough. She kept her gaze averted and told herself that she was stepping over stones and branches. Finally, she burst into the cave and . . .

Ronan was gone.

She heard a low moan, and Tova dashed ahead and ran to a dark shape in the rear shadows.

"T-Tova?"

Ronan's voice came thick and fractured, and Ashyn raced over to find him on the cave floor, the blanket wrapped and twisted around him. She dropped beside him and he turned to her and he smiled. No, more than a smile. He grinned for her.

"Ash."

She kissed him. On the forehead, but a kiss nonetheless, and as much of an embrace as she dared give in his condition. That's when he noticed the blood.

"You're hurt," he said, scrambling up.

Ashyn held him down. "It's not mine. You're the one who's

been injured. Badly. The blood is not yours either, though. We . . ." She took a deep breath and felt grief surge as she thought of Tarquin. She pushed that back. "Later. We're safe for now." A glance at the cave entrance, where she could see parts of the old woman beyond. *Reasonably safe.*

His hands rose to his bandaged throat. "The arrow."

She nodded. "You've been unconscious since then."

"Okami . . . There was a young warrior. Dalain Okami. Is that who . . . ?" He squinted about the cave. "Where are we?"

"The Okamis didn't take us. They shot you, but someone else . . . It's a long story. We're safe, and you're awake and alive, and that's what counts."

"Hopefully if I'm awake I'm also alive. But I suppose these days that's not a given, is it?"

She struggled for a smile. "Sadly, no. Now, lie back down. Help will come soon. I'll get you water. You must be thirsty."

When he didn't answer, she stopped looking for a waterskin and turned to him. "Ronan?"

"Sorry, just . . . Something about being thirsty. I was dreaming . . ."

"That you were dying in a desert? I don't doubt it. You must be parched. Probably famished, too, but we'll start with water." She found the skin near his sleeping pallet. "Here, I'll help you."

She opened it and held it out. He motioned that he could handle it and took the skin. After one gulp, he spat it out and made a face.

"The water's fouled."

She sniffed at it. "There is a smell, but I think it's from the skin. Perhaps it wasn't cured properly." She capped it and set it aside. "I'll get you more once I'm certain the fiend dogs are gone."

"Fiend . . . ? Did you say . . . ?"

"She did," said a voice from the entrance. Edwyn walked in. "I see you're awake. That is a relief. To us, but especially to my granddaughter. She was greatly worried."

"Your grand . . ."

"There are dragons, too," Ashyn said. "Well, only bones here, but we're going to see a sleeping dragon. Then I'll wake it to fight at the emperor's side."

She had to smile as Ronan rubbed his hands over his face.

"I'm still asleep, aren't I?" he said.

She took his hands, just to pull them down, but he gripped her hands and squeezed and quirked a smile for her.

"So . . . dragons now?" he said.

"And fiend dogs."

"I think I'll prefer dragons." He tugged her to sit beside him. "All right. Tell me the whole story."

THIRTEEN

While Ashyn talked, the healer came in and tried to insist that Ashyn leave while she examined Ronan, but he refused to let her go.

"If she leaves now, something else will happen and the story will only take longer."

"It will be but a few moments, my lord."

"I'm not—" he began, and then looked at Ashyn.

"Ronan is from a warrior family," she said, which was technically true. "His does not rank high enough to be accorded the title of lord, though."

"Ronan will do," he said. "But Ashyn's not leaving until she's done with her tale. Given that it is my neck that's injured, there's hardly any impropriety in you examining me with her watching. She's trained in battle healing. She can assist—while she talks."

Ashyn did that, filling Ronan in on everything that had

happened since his injury, even as she assisted the healer with his care.

The fact that the arrow had penetrated to the side, hitting neither his windpipe nor his spine, meant there was no damage beyond the wound and the loss of blood. In other words, he was weak and ought not to exert himself, but the danger had passed and he'd suffer no long-term effects beyond a scar.

"I'll follow Tyrus's lead in this," Ronan said with a faint smile, "and tell myself a scar will make me more dashing. Even if it doesn't require an eye patch." He winked at her then, and she laughed, remembering their reunion in the Wastes, when she'd teased him about rogues requiring eye patches.

"If that is all," Edwyn said, "the young man needs to rest, child, and you and I need to discuss our new plans, in light of what has transpired."

"I need to see to Tarquin . . ." She swallowed. "To his remains first. They must be buried, and before that, I wish to say words to put his spirit at peace. I know that is not your way, but it is important to me."

Edwyn nodded. "It is also our way, and his family will be honored. We will do that then, as soon as we have spoken outside."

"Speak here," Ronan said. "As Ash's guard, I ought to be privy to any plans."

"You are hardly in any shape to function as her guard, my son. Rest, and when you've recovered, you can—"

"I've recovered enough to stay by her side," Ronan said. "Which I will, particularly now, after what happened to the guard you assigned."

"It was not Tarquin's fault," Ashyn said.

"I do not mean to minimize the tragedy of his death," Ronan said. "But he wasn't up to his task. You require better. You require me."

"You have a high opinion of yourself," Edwyn said dryly.

"No, I have a high opinion of the danger Ash faces, and I don't trust anyone else to understand it. Clearly your guard did not expect fiend dogs."

"No one expects fiend dogs," Ashyn said.

"True, but at least you and I expect the unexpected."

Edwyn cleared his throat. "Perhaps so, but I still ask—"

"No," Ronan said. "If you wish to have Ashyn, you must take me as well. As her guard. At her side. Always."

Edwyn's brows rose. "Are you her guard? Or her *guardian*? To suggest that you would prevent her from helping me, when she clearly wishes to . . ."

"Ronan speaks brashly," Ashyn said. "He is a warrior. It is their way. He knows he cannot determine my path for me. Yet I will insist he stay at my side, as my personal guard. I presume we'll be moving on as soon as your scouts . . ." She looked between the two of them. "And that doesn't matter now, does it? We cannot wait for the scouts to return with news of Moria. Fiend dogs mean Alvar Kitsune is near, which means we must flee, quickly, before he sends something else after us."

"Or comes himself," Edwyn said. "Yes, we must presume that the creatures are his work and that they were sent to attack us and allow his men to capture you, which would explain why you were not attacked. We must leave. Quickly."

"We will," Ronan said. "But as we go, I want to know more about these dragons. How far is the journey? How long will this require? Because I know Ash's main concern is her sister, and while duty to the empire will take her along with you, she will not wish to be gone far or long."

Ashyn glanced over with a faint smile, thanking him for saying what she dared not.

"Come then," Edwyn said. "I'll explain as we pack."

FOURTEEN

The bandits had lied. Shocking, truly. They apparently hadn't "stumbled upon" Moria and Gavril the night before. They'd already been on the trail of Gavril's mother when the source they'd paid handsomely for that tip had brought them another—the traitor and his supposed lover had been spotted together nearby.

When the bandits left them in the wagon again, Gavril sank into the corner, his expression one she'd seen before. At Edgewood. When he'd discovered that she had not lied about the massacre.

Moria had spent the last fortnight telling herself she'd imagined that haunted horror in his eyes. But now, seeing it again, she knew it was not a reaction he was capable of manufacturing.

He hadn't truly believed her when she'd first said Edgewood had been destroyed. She'd thought then that he believed her a foolish child with an active imagination. But while he'd suspected his father had raised the shadow stalkers they'd fought in the forest, he still had not believed him capable of massacring a village. Then he'd seen it for himself.

She remembered him staring at the corpse of the baker's wife.

"It's all . . . I don't understand. This isn't . . . Something's gone wrong."

He'd known his father had planned some sorcery. Likely the raising of the shadow stalkers in the forest. But letting them massacre a village? Never.

Moria crouched in front of him now. "These men will not harm your mother."

"He said her corpse was sufficient—"

"He lies. You know the emperor has no bounty on your mother. Toman only *hopes* one will be paid. He said he wouldn't take a chance delivering my corpse. He will not with hers either."

Gavril looked up. "I wouldn't have let him—"

"—kill me? You wouldn't have had a choice, Gavril. I did not suspect you were serious when you said you'd be happy to see me dead. Not yet anyway. Perhaps after another day in this wagon together."

She smiled, but he didn't seem to notice, too lost in his thoughts.

"Tell me about your mother," she said.

He shook his head. "It is not important."

"When we stop at her hiding place, there may be a chance

of escape. For all three of us. So allow me to distract you and clear your head. Tell me about her."

He was quiet for a moment. Then he said, "Have you met Maiko? Tyrus's mother?"

"No. She was out of the city when I arrived and had not returned before we left."

"Ah, then that's why the emperor was also away." He caught her look. "Yes, I'm well aware of Maiko's fondness for pilgrimages and the emperor's habit of vanishing when she's gone. I remember, growing up, I used to listen to bards' tales . . ." He paused at her raised brows. "Yes, I listened. Wild stories are not to my taste, but if others were singing them at parties and such, I had little choice."

"Of course."

"As I was saying . . . I recall those tales often ending with the warrior marrying the lady, which I always found a very unsatisfying resolution. If they were truly in love, they would not marry. One married for duty. Love was something altogether different."

"Your parents were not in love."

"My father married to produce heirs, as is common for a man of his stature. Unfortunately, as you well know, it did not work well. After three successive wives, he has only me. As you've rightly pointed out before, the problem almost certainly does not reside in the women. I'm quite certain he has not produced any children even through . . . ah . . ."

"Mistresses?"

Moria had chosen the most delicate way of putting it, but from Gavril's expression, she might as well have said something far more vulgar.

"Yes," he said. "There were no children despite . . . outside dalliances. Which clearly would have affected his relationship with Emperor Tatsu, given *his* seemingly endless offspring."

"The ability to father children is a mark of virility."

As Gavril squirmed, Moria resisted the urge to sigh with impatience. Truly, sexual relations were a fact of life, and this conversation only skirted the edges of the subject.

She continued. "It added salt to the wound of his friend becoming emperor. But this does not concern your mother."

"It does. In many ways. He married her because she was very beautiful. And very young. She was your age when they wed."

"What? That hasn't been legal for—"

"It has always been legal if the girl's parents consent. My mother was very young and . . ." Gavril pushed back his braids. "You may have heard my father say my mother lacks intelligence."

"He made an unkind jab. I put no stock in it."

"My mother is not a stupid woman. But she is very sheltered and she is not . . . I asked if you'd met Maiko. I think you would get on well. She does not have your sharp tongue or your impetuousness, but she is a strong woman, an independent thinker who does not bow to convention. My mother is not Maiko. She is not you or Ashyn. She grew up in a world where she was expected to be a powerful man's wife. No other options were presented to her before or after she married my father."

"That can be the way of things," Moria said slowly. "At least she had you."

"No, she did not. That, too, can be the way of things in

the warrior world, and my father adhered to the old customs. I was raised by a succession of caretakers, none permitted to stay long enough for me to form any maternal attachments, which are not fitting for a young warrior."

"Not even if they are to your actual *mother*?"

"Particularly then. When Tyrus would chatter about life with his mother, my father would mock him behind his back, saying that letting Tyrus stay with his mother meant the emperor must want more daughters, not sons, and that Tyrus would never become a proper warrior. I wish he'd been there yesterday, to see Tyrus fight, and—" Gavril sucked a breath. "No, I ought not to say it."

"Your father *was* wrong."

A weak smile. "On many counts. I mean only that I ought not to say that because it makes me . . . It makes me things I do not wish to be."

"Angry?"

He seemed ready to answer, then shook his head. "As I said, when I was a child, I had little contact with my mother. That changed when my father was exiled. Ours was still . . . not the usual relationship between parent and child. My mother did not know how to be a mother, but she was sorely in need of a friend."

"I can imagine she was."

"She is a good woman. She's kind and she's caring, but she . . . She needs to be cared for more than she is capable of caring for others. My father has hidden her someplace and I've tried to find out where, because I'm concerned for her well-being."

"And what Toman said only ignited those fears."

"Yes."

The bandit train wasn't moving fast—it could not, given that it took roads that were little more than paths. But it moved steadily, all through that day and into the night, making only brief stops to rest the horses. Too brief, in Moria's opinion, but she suspected if the poor beasts wore out, the men would simply liberate more from the nearest homestead.

Each time they stopped, the captives were allowed out of the wagon. Moria got food and water, precious little of both but still more than Gavril. At the end of the first day, they'd given him water, yet only a few mouthfuls, enough to ensure he didn't die on them. Toman delighted in mocking Gavril and reminding him that he could have more, if only Moria deigned to share. The truth, Moria realized, was that Toman hoped she wouldn't share, and the lack of rations would keep Gavril weak. In other words, the bandit leader had no desire to tangle with a true warrior, even if he was young and unarmed. A coward, then. Unsurprisingly.

The next morning, they'd barely woken when Moria heard a commotion outside. The scout had returned, riding hard, and was warning Toman that a troop of soldiers was coming their way.

"On *this* road?" Toman's voice carried in the quiet morning. "Blast it. They must be Alvar's men, sniveling cowards who don't dare take the main route. Get the horses and wagons to that forest there. Quickly!"

That took some effort. The road was rough enough—

leaving it meant the wagon tipped and veered wildly until Toman finally stopped it and ordered Moria and Gavril out.

"You're weighing it down," he grumbled, though Moria was sure he just wanted to get his prizes to safety before the soldiers appeared.

He bustled them off, making them run on foot ahead of his horse. That was not easy, given how little she'd eaten. For Gavril, it must have required every bit of strength he had left, but he pushed himself to keep up, needing not a single prod from Toman. When they reached the woods, though, he looked ready to collapse, and she caught his arm, only to have him shake her off with a whispered, "Mind yourself, Keeper." She nodded and motioned for him to lean against a tree instead. When he hesitated, she said, "Accept the support of that oak or collapse at Toman's feet. Your choice, Kitsune."

He leaned against the tree. Toman finished dismounting and tying his horse, and came over to where they watched the soldiers, who'd just rounded a bend.

The men were not warriors. Not even militia, but farmers pressed into service—ordinary men who'd grabbed whatever weapons they could find, and walked in something akin to military formation behind a man who, on closer inspection, did bear the dual swords of a warrior.

"Recruits," Gavril whispered.

"But not your father's," Moria said. "Look at the warrior's helmet. It is imperial. These are the emperor's men."

"You are correct," Gavril said. "Your man misjudged, Toman. There's no need to hide. Perhaps you ought to speak to the warrior there, see if he bears any news."

"You think you're clever, don't you, boy?"

"Not particularly. I'm merely suggesting—"

"They're recruits for Alvar," Toman said to Moria. "See the band around the warrior's arm? In order to pass through the empire unharmed, they dress as imperials, but wear some sign to show they are not, so they are not cut down by other recruits spoiling for their first skirmish. The sign changes as quickly as the emperor can get out word to his men. Or, I should say, *almost* as quickly."

Moria watched the men. There were twenty-two of them, all but the leader armed with only cudgels and scythes.

"Your men could defeat them," she said. "That's what the emperor would want."

"I'll leave that to the emperor's troops."

"But those men have supplies. You could defeat them and take what they have."

He snorted. "Dry rice balls and rotting cabbage? We do not need supplies that badly."

And so they let Alvar's recruits pass unharmed, and all Moria could do was fervently wish the emperor's side attracted a better class of bandits.

FIFTEEN

The wagon stopped again at dusk. There was no announcement. No escort either. Moria and Gavril waited for someone to open the wagon flaps. Then the bandits' voices faded, replaced by an odd keening sound that made the hairs on Moria's neck rise.

"Do you hear that?" she whispered.

He nodded, which meant it was not spirits. Moria opened the flap, and a blast of whistling wind nearly knocked her back. She looked out across a windswept plain. It was not a term she'd ever used before, having only read it in books, but seeing the landscape before her, it was the first one that came to mind. A windswept plain.

Brown. That's what she saw. A sea of yellow-brown grass, bent even when the wind died down. There were scrubby trees, also bent, as if from a constant northern wind.

"What is this place?" she whispered as Gavril moved up beside her.

"I don't know."

"Is it the steppes?"

"I don't know."

His tone suggested annoyance, but when she glanced over, his gaze scanned the vista, assessing and wondering as much as she was.

"Perhaps the steppes," he said. "I've never seen them."

"I don't like it."

He looked over, frowning, and Moria rubbed a hand over her face. "Ignore me, Kitsune. I'm tired."

He studied her then. "It's difficult for you. Without Daigo."

She started, surprised that he'd struck so close to the truth. Then she nodded. "I feel . . . unbalanced."

"You seem it. Off-kilter. Not yourself. More . . . vulnerable."

She straightened quickly, injecting some bite into her tone. "Having my dagger would help as well."

"I know. Your wildcat, your dagger, and a change in companions would settle the ground under your feet."

"None of which I'm likely to get soon, so I should shake this off, and get on with it. Your point is taken, Kitsune."

"It was not a point, Keeper. Merely an observation, one meant to say that you do not need to explain yourself to me. But is it the lack of balance that disturbs you now? Or . . ." His green eyes turned to look over the plain. "This?"

This.

The thought came unbidden as she looked out at the emptiness. She shivered.

"Spirits?" he asked.

She shook her head. "I'm simply unsettled, as may be

evidenced by the fact that I'm chatting when we appear to have been left alone, without guards, able to escape."

He motioned to two bandits on a ridge. The mounted men watched them.

"Oh," she said.

"Hmm."

She stepped out. The bandits didn't move, and she flashed back to entering Fairview with Tyrus, the dead bodies in the guardhouse. She faltered, but only for a moment before calling, "May we come out?"

One bandit waved his hand in an indeterminable gesture. Moria walked a few steps and looked around. The wind whipped up again, shrieking past and blowing a fine layer of soil into her face, making her sputter. The bandits laughed, but Moria had experience with sandstorms in the Wastes, so she only pulled up her tunic over her nose and mouth and put her back to the wind.

When she turned, she saw the house. It was mud-daubed, the same color as the soil, with a flat roof and no distinguishing features. One could ride right past and never realize it was there.

Despite the falling sun, she saw no sign of light from within. After a few more steps, she realized there weren't any windows, but simply a door, shut tight. The bandits clustered at the front, as if waiting. The wind whistled again, and this time, in it, Moria thought she detected . . .

"Keeper?" Gavril's fingers closed on her elbow, as if to steady her. "Do you hear spirits?"

No, I hear memories. My memories. With the wind and the

emptiness and the desolation, all I can think of is Edgewood, after the massacre, when I found my—

"Do not heed me," she said.

"I'm only—"

"And I'm only reminding you that we are being watched. Do not heed me, Kitsune."

He nodded. "Do you want to go back inside the wagon?"

Yes, I wish very much to go back inside the wagon.

"No, I believe they are waiting," she said, jerking her chin toward the bandits.

She strode forward, struggling to throw off her unease. It was merely the isolation of this place, preying on her imagination and—

She stopped short.

"Why does no one come out?" she asked.

"Hmm?"

"If we are here because your mother is within, should she not be guarded?"

"Well guarded, yes, if only to save my father from the humiliation of having his wife taken by his enemy."

"Then why have they allowed us to get so close? There's nothing out here. *Nothing.* There ought to be a scout perched on that ridge. Does your father have no decent archers?"

"He does." Gavril turned in a full circle, shading his eyes.

"Come along, boy!" Toman shouted. "I wish to leave before sundown."

"It's a trap," Moria murmured.

"By the bandits?" Gavril said. "Or someone waiting within?"

113

"Does it matter? Either way is equally dangerous to us."

"Come on, boy!" Toman said. "Bring out your mother!"

Gavril looked at Moria. Then he called back, "You do it."

"If you insist . . . and you don't mind me bringing out her head."

Gavril shot forward. He stopped himself but rocked there, glancing between Moria and the house.

"Why do you look to the girl, boy?" Toman called. "Does your enemy give you counsel now?"

"No," Moria called back. "He fears turning his back on me, lest I have only been cordial to him in preparation for attack. Come on then, Kitsune. Let's get this over with." They started for the house. When they drew up alongside it, she turned to Toman. "You stand out here because you fear walking into a trap. Do you trust that Lady Kitsune's guards will not mistakenly cut down Gavril and spoil your chance for his bounty?"

"True. You'd best go with him, then, to be sure they do not."

Moria snorted. "I hardly care—"

"Start caring." Toman strode forward and slapped her dagger into her hand. "He is the one Emperor Tatsu truly wants. If he dies in an ambush, I'll not take you back to the city alive, for fear you'll tell the emperor what happened and he'll have my head for it."

"Arm him as well," Moria said.

"Listen to you, little girl. Talking as if you're a warlord—"

"I am the Keeper. I outrank every warlord in this land. If you wish the traitor to survive this trap, provide him with a weapon."

114

Toman motioned for someone to bring Gavril a sword.

"I'll take a sword, too," Moria said. "I have been training and—"

"Do not push your luck."

"Luck is meant to be pushed."

"And *you* are lucky that I admire your mettle, little girl, or I'd not appreciate your tongue." His grin turned wolfish as he stepped toward her. "Perhaps I can come to appreciate it more on the remainder of this journey."

"I'm sure you will, though not in the way you hope."

He only laughed. "We'll see." He winked. "There's a reason I have three very happy wives. Now take your dagger and bring me a true traitor's whore."

SIXTEEN

"I think I prefer you unsettled," Gavril muttered as they moved toward the door. "You are less a danger to yourself and others. Don't provoke the man, Keeper."

"I was getting you a blade, Kitsune."

"And I'm asking you to be careful. Now, if we may . . ."

He motioned at the closed door. His face was calmer, the strain and worry temporarily vanished. For Gavril, that brief argument had been steady ground, settling him as much as the dagger in her hand settled Moria.

She eyed the door. "Perhaps we ought to look for a secondary entrance, to avoid ambush."

He nodded, and they both stepped back.

"What are you doing?" Toman called, his voice echoing across the plain.

"So much for the element of surprise," Moria muttered.

"I believe we lost that when they decided to stand in the yard and wait for us."

"True." She turned to Toman and motioned that they were looking for another way in.

"Why?" he called. "That door is as good as any."

Moria muttered, "He truly wants us going in this way."

"Hmmm."

"When Tyrus and I walked through a door into a potential trap, I kept to the rear to cover him."

"When did you and Tyrus do such a thing?"

"In Fairview."

"You returned to—? Yes, of course you would." He glanced at her. "So you saw . . ."

"Yes, I saw what the shadow stalkers had done."

He swallowed. "You ought not to—"

"—have returned to try to free the town and save Edgewood's children?"

"Ought not to have needed to witness that. I had no idea my father intended—"

"Kitsune? I know. We will speak later. For now . . ."

"Yes. Your plan is sound. I will go first."

Moria stood at his back, dagger raised. Gavril pushed the door. It did not budge. He eyed it and seemed ready to bash his shoulder into it when she whispered, "You cannot fight with a dislocated sword arm, Kitsune. Kick it."

He hesitated.

"If you fall on your arse, I'll not laugh." She paused. "Or not loudly."

He gave her a look and then positioned himself and kicked.

The door flew open. Gavril lunged through with his sword at the ready and Moria at his shoulder, and they swept into a darkened room. When nothing inside moved, Moria pushed the door open farther, allowing the rays of the falling sun to light the interior.

"Kiri?" Gavril called, and when Moria frowned in confusion, he said, "My mother."

To call one's mother by her given name was not something she'd ever heard. A mother who would not own the title and a father who did not deserve it. What kind of childhood could one have under such circumstances?

"Kiri?" he called again. "It's Gavril."

Silence answered, a quiet stillness that crept into her bones. She shook it off and walked about the small room. It was sumptuously decorated, as comfortable as any court lodgings. There was a lantern beside a pile of pillows. When she turned the light on, she saw a book tucked into pillows. A romantic novel, the simple sort, well illustrated for those without enough education to read a lengthy tome. She looked down at the pillows and imagined the woman who'd been here. Held a virtual prisoner in luxury, left alone with pretty stories of other lives, better lives, happier lives.

She set the book down. "Kiri?" she called, in case a feminine voice might help. "I am Moria, Keeper of Edgewood. I'm here with Gavril to help you."

Not even a distant rustle answered. She motioned to Gavril that they ought to check the other rooms. He approached the first door. He opened it and went through while she guarded and then followed.

This room looked like servant or guard quarters. Empty. They backed out and tried the next. The kitchen. There was only one room left and it had to be Kiri's bedroom. But when Moria stepped in, all she could think was *There's a child living here, too?*

It was as perfect a bedchamber as any girl of nine or ten summers could wish, filled with dolls from every part of the empire, every shade of skin and style of clothing. There were books, too, some of them simple romances but others more suited for children. An easel sat in one corner, with an inexpert watercolor of flowers on it. Gaily colored cushions covered the sleeping pallet. On a low table there was a collection of bright hair ribbons and jeweled clips and stones that seemed to serve no purpose but to be pretty stones.

When Gavril saw her staring at the room, he looked abashed. "My mother . . ."

"She is your mother. Nothing more needs to be said. She has not had an easy life."

"No, she has not."

"The house is empty then," she said. "That is why no archer attacked. They knew we were coming and left."

"Yes . . ." He looked about, his green eyes dark with worry.

"She's not here, Gavril," Moria said, her voice lowering. "If you are concerned that she is, and that harm has come to her, look about. There is no place for her to be."

"Yes . . ." His gaze still surveyed the room.

"Fine, we shall search. To ease your mind. Perhaps she hides—alive and safe—under a trapdoor or such, and if so, we will leave her there, but you will know she is well."

"Thank you."

"I'll start in here. You take the kitchen."

He nodded and left. Moria began her search, and as she hunted and moved aside Kiri's belongings, a clearer picture of the woman formed. Alvar had said she was as "empty-headed as one of her dolls." Moria now understood what he meant, at least about the dolls. As for the rest, she did not think Kiri Kitsune was a woman of low intelligence. Gavril was proof of that.

Instead, she seemed a girl who had never quite become a woman, never been allowed to grow up, taken from her family and thrust into a loveless marriage where her only duty was to provide children, which she had not been terribly successful at. When she did give Alvar a son, any chance for her to mature with motherhood had also been wrenched away as her son was raised by others, returned to her when he was ten summers old.

From what Moria knew of Gavril, he would have been ten summers going on twenty.

"Where are you now, Kiri?" Moria whispered as she checked under the rugs and moved pillows, looking for a trapdoor. "You left quickly, taking none of your treasures. Did you leave willingly?"

Moria suspected that, whatever the circumstances, Kiri *had* left willingly, regardless of whether those coming for her were friends or foes. Her life was one of being guided, day by day, step by step, and perhaps even kidnapping might have seemed only like the possibility for a change of scenery.

At that thought, Moria looked about the dark and dreary room. Kiri's paintings did little to lift the gloom. Moria could not imagine Kiri stuck in this place, a woman who obviously loved color and beauty and worlds beyond her life's walls.

That's when Moria saw the peephole. She'd been thinking that Kiri might insist on more, and as Moria scoured the wall, she'd noticed one painting, hung oddly low and quivering slightly, as if from a breeze.

Behind that painting she found a hole, painstakingly dug into the mud wall. It was right beside Kiri's sleeping pallet, as if she'd lain here at night, staring out. Kept a prisoner in her own home, she'd had this one small act of rebellion, a peephole to freedom, perhaps even seeing haunting beauty in that desolate world. A lost girl who loved beauty and longed for freedom, had likely longed for it all her life.

Moria bent to get a glimpse at Kiri's secret world and saw—

A man's face. Moria fell back, her dagger raised. Then her mind replayed the image and . . .

By the ancestors, that expression. The horror.

It was not the face of a living man. His expression had told her that, as had the placement of his head, set below her direct line of vision.

A head. Lying on the ground. She swallowed and glanced over her shoulder for Gavril. He was still busy in the next room. Good. He did not need to see this. Nor did she. However . . .

She looked through the peephole again to assure herself she was correct. Yet she was not. She had imagined the poor man had been decapitated, but that wasn't the case. The case . . . She swallowed again and squeezed her eyes shut, but the image of the man's face was branded in her mind.

Whatever she had seen in the villages—the horror on the faces of those cut down by their own families turned into monsters—it was not like this. Their deaths were not like this.

The man had been buried alive to his neck. Then he'd been left there. Left to slowly die of dehydration in this desert-like wasteland. No one to hear his screams. No one to come to his aid. Trapped for days . . .

Moria pulled back from the hole, her breath coming hard. Then she spotted something behind the man. Another head and shoulders. Another man buried and dead. And beside him, an old woman, her face twisted in a final scream.

Moria raced from the room, stumbling over everything in her path. Gavril came running from the servants' quarters and she plowed into him, then pushed past.

"S-stay here," she said, forcing the words out, her chest so tight she could barely breathe. "I'm going out, but you need to stay right here."

"I don't—"

She ran to him and grabbed his hands, startling him, and he stumbled back, but she kept hold of him. "Gavril, please? Just do as I ask. For once, do as I ask."

"I don't understand."

"Do you trust me?"

"Of course."

"Then stay here." She dropped his hands and ran for the door. She threw it open. Two bandits stood there as if listening in. She didn't look at them. Just said, "Keep him inside. Please," then ran behind the house, ignoring shouts to stay where she was.

She rounded the rear of the house and stopped short. Five figures were buried there. Three guards. One old woman.

122

Moria ran to the fifth figure. She dropped in front of her and pressed her hands against the woman's neck, knowing even as she did that the skin would be cold. Ice-cold.

The woman had to be thirty-five summers, but she seemed so much younger. And she looked . . . Moria let out a heaved breath, tears prickling her eyes.

She looked like Gavril. Like an older sister. A beautiful woman with skin as dark as her hair, short curls wrapped in bright ribbons, like a child's. And her expression . . . That was a child's, too, and it was Gavril's as well, that look on his face when he'd witnessed the massacre and again today, when he'd realized the bandits were going after his mother. Shock and confusion. The other victims looked terrified. Kiri Kitsune looked bewildered and lost, a little girl who did not understand what had happened and, moreover, why it had happened to her. And that was the worst of it, the look on her face.

Moria looked over at the bandits, who had now come to the side of the house, watching her, and she swore a couple of them were smirking. As if they'd already seen this, circling the house earlier. Seen it and yet played out the sadistic game, letting Gavril look inside for his mother, perhaps being relieved she'd escaped and then coming out to find . . .

Her hand tightened on her dagger, red-hot rage filling her. Then she heard a shout followed by running footsteps, and she forgot about the bandits. She raced back around the house just as Gavril appeared. She charged toward him and stopped so suddenly that he smacked into her.

"No," she said.

He reached as if to shove her aside.

"No, Gavril." She put her hands against his chest, pushing him back, and she knew the bandits would realize there was more between them than hate, but she didn't care. Nothing mattered now except stopping him from seeing what lay behind the house.

"Keeper . . ." he said, his voice low.

"She's gone," Moria said quickly.

His breath caught. "My mother—"

"—is dead. She's been murdered, and I'll not have you see her. Not like that."

"I must—"

"*No.*" She looked up into his face. "Do you remember my father? The last time I saw him? I would give anything to pluck that image from my mind, and if I can block this from yours, then I will."

"How was she—?"

"No."

"I—"

"No!"

He stepped sideways then, too fast for her to stop, and she lunged into his path, but he'd frozen there, staring. When she glanced over her shoulder, she could see one of the buried guards.

The look on his face was the exact image of his mother's final one. Loss and confusion and disbelief. Moria struggled to keep her voice steady as she said, "Please, Gavril. Don't take another step."

"I need . . . I need . . ." He swallowed hard and looked away from the dead guard. "She must be buried."

"Looks like she already is," one of the bandits said, but Moria spun on him, and he had the decency to close his mouth.

"I must dig her out and bury her properly," Gavril said.

"I will."

"You cannot, Keeper. Digging is a difficult chore."

"I will. If these men wish to be gone before dawn, they will help me."

Gavril started forward. "No, as her son, I must—"

Her dagger tip flew to his throat. "I'm asking you to do one thing for me, Gavril. You will allow me to free your mother, and then you will see her to say good-bye. You will help me bury her properly, and I will say the rites over her. But you will not take one more step in that direction until I summon you."

"It is my duty. You ought not to have to."

"I'm asking to do this." She wiggled the dagger against his throat. "Or insisting on it. Interpret as you wish."

A slow nod. Then, gaze lowered, voice barely audible, he said, "Thank you, Keeper," and returned to the house without another look into the yard.

SEVENTEEN

Moria found shovels behind the house, abandoned after their gruesome task. The bandits didn't move, and her rage flared inside her thinking of the terrible trick they'd played on Gavril, ready to challenge them on it. Then Toman ordered one of his men to assist her, and she channeled Ashyn and tamped down that fury, knowing it would do no good and this was not the time. For Gavril's sake and for Kiri's, it was not the time.

How much the bandit actually helped dig that hole was debatable. It was long and exhausting work, and by the end of it, Moria was ready to collapse, every muscle quivering.

At one point Toman had offered the opinion that it was unnecessary, that he could simply take Kiri's head for her bounty, since that was exposed. But he seemed to be more taunting her than seriously suggesting it, and at a snarl from Moria, he'd chuckled and wisely wandered off without pressing the matter.

Finally, she had Kiri out. The bandit did not help with that, leaving her struggling to pull the corpse from the loosened earth. She managed it and then insisted on help to carry Kiri to the side of the house, so Gavril would not see that telltale hole or the horrible faces of the other victims.

Kiri had been bound hand and foot. Marks on her cheeks suggested she'd been gagged. Had they sedated their victims to keep them from struggling as the holes were filled? Moria did not know which was worse—to be conscious in that hole as the dirt fell around you or to wake trapped in your grave. She knew only that, once again, she wished she had not been blessed with such a vivid imagination.

The whole time she'd been digging Kiri out, her mind had plagued her with scenarios, not only of the victims but of those who'd carried out the horrible task. How could they fill in those holes? How could they rip off the gags and walk away, casually dropping their shovels behind the house, listening to the cries and the pleas of five innocent victims, knowing the unimaginable torment they faced in the days before death would come? How does one do such a thing and remain human?

Moria removed Kiri's bonds and placed her on her back, hands folded on her stomach. She shut her eyelids. She massaged her face and managed to wipe away that look of loss and disbelief and find a quiet expression of peace. She cleaned dirt from Kiri's face and brushed it from her gown, and she fixed hair ribbons that had come loose. She was fussing with one of the last when she heard a noise and looked up to see Gavril a few paces away, watching her.

"Didn't I tell you to wait for my summons?" she said.

"I brought him," Toman said, walking up behind Gavril.

"The night is half passed, and we don't have time for you to make a corpse look pretty."

She quickly finished tying one of the ribbons. Then she pushed to her feet and bowed her head to Gavril. "We will give you a few moments."

"We don't have time—" Toman began.

"We will give you a few moments."

She started to leave, but Gavril touched her arm as she passed and said, "Stay."

Moria still remained standing, with her back to Kiri as Gavril crouched beside his mother. When he said, "I'll bury her now," Moria walked over, bent, and clipped a beribboned curl with her dagger, then handed it to Gavril. He pulled away, that grim mask falling as he said, "I do not require—"

"Then I will." She tucked the lock into her pocket. "Now, we must bury—"

"How will I collect my bounty without a body?" Toman said.

"You can tell the emperor where to find her."

It was a poor solution, and Moria expected him to refuse, but he only grumbled and said, "Do it quickly."

Moria and Gavril dug the hole while Toman watched.

"You do know this is the emperor's work," Toman said when the hole was almost deep enough.

Neither replied, simply dug in their shovels again.

"You're educated children," Toman continued. "Surely you recognize this for what it is?"

"Yes," Gavril said.

"Tell me."

When Gavril didn't respond, Moria looked at him and he nodded.

"It's the traditional execution method for the Tatsu clan," Moria said. "From ages past. I have heard of it . . ."

But never imagined it. Words she found herself saying and thinking so often lately. All the things she'd read in books or heard in bards' tales and never given a second thought because they'd been merely words. However vividly described, words of a thousand deaths did not begin to convey the horror of a single one witnessed.

The stories said that the Tatsu clan used to bury their enemies to the neck and leave them to perish. It was not a violent death, so it seemed merciful compared to the infamous death of a thousand cuts. Now, Moria could not say for certain that she would choose this over *any* other method.

Toman said, "You know then that this is incontrovertible proof that the emperor has taken his revenge."

"Is it?" Moria said. "Everyone who has read a history book knows this is the Tatsu's traditional method of execution. Anyone could emulate—"

"Do not defend him," Gavril said, his voice low, gaze fixed on the hole.

"I'm simply saying—"

"And I know well your feelings about the emperor, Keeper. As you know mine. He has allowed you to be cast as traitor, and yet you continue to defend him. My father is not the monster here. The man who did that?" He pointed to his mother's corpse. "He is the true monster."

"No," Toman said. "He is a true *dragon*. At rest, he slumbers peacefully. But one does not provoke a dragon. Not if one has a grain of sense. Our emperor has acted with the brutality and the cunning I expect of a Tatsu. I was glad to call him my emperor this morning. I am proud to call him that tonight."

Gavril threw down his shovel. "He murdered an innocent woman."

"Your mother lost her innocence the day she wed that treacherous fox. Do you wish to blame someone for this, boy? Blame your father. He abandoned her out here with an inadequate guard. That tells the empire how much he cared for the mother of his only child."

"My father cares—"

"Not a whit for anyone but himself, and the sooner you acknowledge that, the easier your life will be."

"Do not taunt him," Moria said to Toman, her voice as soft as she could make it. "Not in his time of grief."

Gavril turned on her. "Don't defend me, Keeper."

"I'm not. I'm showing you a moment of kindness as one who has suffered such a loss herself."

"Your emperor—"

"I do not believe *my* emperor did this."

"Then you are a fool."

"No, you are the fool, if you continue to believe your father . . ." Moria sighed and stuck her shovel in the ground. "Let's not argue, Kitsune. We'll bury your mother, and I'll say the words to ease her passing."

Moria said the rituals for the dead. Gavril did not mention the fact that they weren't hers to say. The Seeker calmed spirits while the Keeper fought those who would not be calmed. Yet Moria knew the words, and so she said them and prayed the ancestors would understand.

They returned to the wagon and set off. Moria turned from Gavril, leaving him to his grief, sitting in the corner, his knees drawn up, arms around them, gaze lowered. They hadn't gone far before he said, "Thank you."

She nodded, still not looking over, in case that was all, but his boots scraped the wooden floor of the wagon as he moved closer. He lowered himself to sit cross-legged near her. She held out the lock of Kiri's hair and when he hesitated, she tucked it into his pocket. He did not stop her.

"Everything you did back there was both appreciated and undeserved," he said. "In equal measure."

"I did what was right."

"I know. Thank you."

"You performed very well at the gravesite." She turned toward him. "I presume it *was* a performance?"

"Of course. My opinions may change, Moria, but not so tempestuously. We must maintain our roles."

"I will be more careful in our interactions as well."

He shrugged. "We are not what the rumors accuse us of being, so perhaps it is simpler to allow them to see that the truth is . . . complicated."

That was the word, wasn't it? Complicated.

"I am deeply sorry about your mother's passing," Moria said after a few moments. "I ought to have said that earlier."

"You showed it. That's enough." A few more moments passed before he said, "Did I ever say the same to you? About your father? I was. I am. Deeply sorry."

Moria nodded and listened to the creaking of the wagon wheels. Wind blasted through the cracks, and she reached as if to pull her cloak tighter. Gavril handed her a blanket. She wrapped it around her shoulders.

"We'll get your cloak back," he said. "I know it means a great deal to you."

"Whether I get it back or not, I'm glad you found it in his shop."

"I wish I never had to find it. I wish he could have given it—" He shook his head and lapsed back into silence, his knees pulled up again, chin resting on them.

"Can you tell me what happened in Edgewood?" she asked.

"Madness."

She glanced over. The moon had passed behind clouds, and only darkness came through the hole in the top of the wagon. All she could see of Gavril were the whites of his eyes and the green irises, glowing as if by sorcery.

He continued. "I've told you I played no role in your father's death or your town's massacre, but that is disingenuous. Of course I played a role. The mere fact that I knew my father lived and that he planned to launch his bid for the imperial throne from there—the very place he'd been exiled—means I must share blame."

"It was the massacre you knew nothing about."

"I . . . I expected a military attack. Against the guards. I knew the military was still favorable to my father, so I thought he would strike but tell them the truth, how he'd been wronged, and with his eloquence, the guards would understand and capitulate and join us and . . . And I was a fool."

"What did you think was happening when the shadow stalkers attacked?"

"Truly?" He lifted his head to look at her. "I thought it was a mistake. My father knows powerful magics, and I feared he had accidentally unleashed them against innocents. Or that sorcerers working with him had done it. When you told me the town was gone, well, you *do* have an imagination, and you are fond of bloody and terrible stories. I thought a few people had died and you . . ."

"Saw a lizard and thought it a dragon?"

"Yes. Even when I witnessed it myself, I thought it was a tragic accident. The fact that the children were safe seemed proof of that. The magics had gone terribly awry, and my father mitigated it as best he could by rescuing the children."

"Which was not the case."

Gavril went silent so long that Moria thought he was finished speaking, and she began to move away. Then, he said, "I was wrong about many, *many* things, Keeper. In Edgewood, I called you a child flitting after butterflies, but that was me. Chasing a dream of a parent who never existed. My memory turned him into a father who was harsh but fair. A man struggling against fate and a traitorous friend, a man who became embittered because of it, but still good and honorable."

"And he is not."

Gavril's harsh laugh startled her. "I'm not even certain he's human."

She remembered the bodies behind the house, thinking that whoever had done such a thing could not be human. She shook off the chill. No, Alvar was capable of many things, but not that. Kiri Kitsune had been his wife. Mother to his child.

"In the compound, you called him mad," she said. "He slapped you for it. Do you believe he is?"

"Perhaps I'm still clinging to excuses. But if it is madness, it is not the sort that pardons his actions. He knows full well what he does." Gavril shook his head. "That's enough. You ought to get some sleep, Keeper."

"I don't think I could."

"Would you like me to tell you a story?"

She laughed softly, but he looked over and said, "The offer is a true one. You did much for me tonight. More than . . ." He shifted. "You did much, and it is appreciated. To save me from that horror, you had to face it yourself and . . . And I . . . cannot imagine what it was like, but I am grateful. So I offer you a story, though perhaps not one well told."

"Do you even *know* any stories?"

"One or two, but I'll not admit it past tonight."

She smiled. "All right then, Kitsune." She stretched onto the floor. "Tell me a tale."

EIGHTEEN

"Keeper."

Moria woke to Gavril shaking her shoulder, his voice taut with urgency.

"Moria."

When she moved, his hand shot to her mouth. That startled her enough to make her leap up, but as sleep scattered, she remembered Kiri's death and went still.

"Stay quiet," he said, and waited for her nod before lowering his hand.

Quiet. That's what it was outside the wagon. Completely silent. Gavril's whisper had echoed through the dark wagon. They had stopped, and Moria couldn't even pick up the sound of the horses sighing or stamping.

She felt something though. Her skin prickled, as if she'd caught a smell or a sound. But she hadn't. She rubbed her eyes and gave her head a sharp shake to clear the last fog of sleep.

"It's still night," she whispered, looking up at the stars through the hole.

Gavril nodded. She tried to calculate the time. The moon had been at its zenith when they'd left Kiri's compound. Then they'd talked and Gavril had told her a story. One about the Keeper of Edgewood, from ages past. An old and comforting tale. She'd fallen asleep as he reached the end.

"Were you awake?" she asked.

"I thought I was, but I must have drifted off. I woke to this."

He crawled to the door flap. Moria resisted the urge to pull him back. She held herself still, ready to leap at the first sign of trouble, but he undid the flap and opened it, and the silence continued.

Moria crept up beside him and looked out. There was nothing to see. Nothing at all. They were still in the steppes, the land an endless plain of grass, dotted with distant hills. But that was all they saw. There was no sign of the bandits.

"Are they waiting for us to follow on foot again?" Gavril murmured.

"It's not the same," Moria said, the words coming before she could consider them.

"Hmm?"

She shook her head, but he peered down at her. "What's wrong, Keeper?"

When she didn't answer, he said, "You're unsettled again, and it has nothing to do with the lack of your blade and your beast." He drew back onto his haunches. "Nor was that it entirely the last time. You sensed something. The passing of spirits. Death."

"I have no ability to—"

"You are attuned to the spirits. You could not hear them at my mother's house, but you sensed their anguished departure." He considered. "A learned ability, having been in such spirit-disturbed places repeatedly. Now you sense that here."

"Yes, and yet . . . no. It's . . ." She rubbed her arms briskly. "I'm no good at analyzing such things, Kitsune. I am unsettled, and it is not the same as earlier. That's all I can tell you."

He nodded and carefully stepped from the wagon. Again, she had to fight not to yank him back in. She shook that off. Cowering in a wagon was not her way or his, and she was hardly going to make it so now.

She lowered herself to the ground and peered into the night.

"Do you see anyone?" she whispered.

"No."

"Is it a trap?" She answered her own question with, "Best to presume so."

He made a noise of agreement.

Moria walked around the wagon. Then she stopped. The harnesses were empty, the horses gone. She walked over and picked up one of the straps. It was wet and slick and she dropped it, lifting her fingers into the moonlight, knowing what she'd see there.

"Blood," Gavril whispered, and she glanced to see him at her shoulder.

He moved to the second harness while Moria lifted the bloody strap again and examined the end. Cut, as if with a blade.

"The horses were freed, and the blade must have cut the horse as well." She looked at the wagon. "How would we not hear that? The strap is soaked in blood, meaning it was not a shallow cut. The horse would have shrieked and bucked, and yet we felt and heard nothing. That makes no sense."

"No," he said grimly. "It does not."

As they continued looking about, clouds covered the moon. At a sound in the darkness, Moria tensed, her back going to Gavril's, his to hers, both of them reaching for weapons they did not have.

He said something, and Moria looked over her shoulder to say that she could not hear him, when his fingers lit in an unearthly glow.

"This may be a trap," he said. "But if it is, they're looking for more than proof of this." He waved his glowing fingers. "Given all my father has done, there's little point in continuing to protest that we are not sorcerers."

"I don't suppose you can conjure me a dagger?"

A strained smile. "Sorry, Keeper. When I said in the Wastes that I know no sorcery to protect us, I was telling the truth. I have only the simplest of magics."

They fell quiet, backs together.

"You did hear something, did you not?" Moria said.

"Yes, but it's gone now, and I could not determine the direction."

Moria headed back to the wagon.

"Keeper?"

She motioned for him to follow.

"But we ought to investigate—" he began.

"We will. Now come. I need your light."

When she'd been on the road with Tyrus and Ashyn, their wagons had resembled these. Common imperial wagons, the lower half being a storage compartment, accessible from hatches in the sides. She unlatched one hatch door and crawled inside on her stomach while waving for Gavril to light her way.

When she tossed out a waterskin, he said, "This is hardly the time—"

"Drink while I look for weapons."

"Oh."

She glanced out at him. "Truly, Kitsune? You think I paused for a snack?"

"No, I—"

"Drink. But keep the light in here."

He grumbled that it would be nearly impossible to do both, given that the light came from his hands, also required for drinking. She ignored him and, after some digging, found not merely weapons, but *their* weapons. They were in a small stash with others, and she quickly selected a short sword to go with her daggers, and then pushed from the compartment. She handed Gavril his dual blades. He grunted his thanks. Then, before she could close the compartment, he reached in and pulled out something else.

Her cloak.

"I don't need—"

"Take it, Keeper. That hair of yours is as much a beacon as my hands."

She put on the dark cloak and raised the hood. When he

noticed she wore a sword, he opened his mouth to comment, but a sound cut him short.

It was the same noise they'd heard earlier. Clearer now. It sounded like the moan of the wind through eaves. Yet there was no wind here. Certainly no eaves. The sound came from somewhere ahead of the wagon.

She started forward. Gavril moved in front of her, but she tugged him back.

"At a doorway, yes," she whispered. "Out here, you block my vision." She motioned for him to walk behind her. He backed to her side instead. She sighed, and they continued on.

Her nerves had settled some since they'd come out of the wagon. Finding those cut harnesses had helped—it meant they were looking for something human. She could handle human.

As they neared the spot from which the noise had come, Moria saw a hand lying on the pathway. It appeared to be attached to a body, which was a relief. Again, these days, one could not guarantee such a thing.

The attached body lay in a heap, just beyond the grassy edge of the path. At another moan, they stopped short and Gavril extended his hands, lighting the scene. At first they could see only a collapsed figure, but then Moria could make out long braids with bright, colored beads, and knew it was the wagon driver.

"Extend your other hand," Gavril called to him. "And we will come to your aid."

The man only groaned.

"There is no one else here," Gavril continued. "No one to

140

fight you nor to bind your wounds. Place your right hand where we can see it."

The man went still and silent. Gavril extinguished his light. Then he called, "I will not hesitate to kill you. I trust you understand that."

He proceeded toward the man with his sword at the ready.

"Do not move or I will slice off your hand," he said. "I have retrieved my sword from the compartment under the wagon and the Keeper is poised with her daggers."

The man gave no sign he'd heard. Gavril took another step. Then he stopped. He quickly cast the spell to relight his fingers, which meant removing one hand from his sword, and Moria scanned the grass for any sign of an ambush. When Gavril let out a curse, she hurried forward.

As Moria approached, Gavril drew his hand into a fist, all but extinguishing the magical glow, yet not before she saw the wagon driver. Or at least, saw the bloody mess that she knew was the driver only by those beaded braids. His clothing was shredded and caked in dirt and blood. His nose seemed pushed into his face, as if it had collapsed on itself. One eye was . . . unmoored.

"He's been trampled," she whispered. "He freed the horses, and they trampled him."

The man's good eye stared as if dead, but he exhaled, the sound wheezing through collapsed lungs. Moria dropped beside him and put her hands to his chest. It was caved in, ribs broken, one pushing through skin, blood soaking his tunic. Still she pressed her hands against his heart.

"I can't tell . . ." she said. "Blast it, I'm no healer."

"I believe he is beyond that," Gavril said, his voice low, as if hoping the man could not hear. Moria suspected that even if he could, he didn't understand them. His head had been bashed in on the same side, blood and gray matter oozing out. Yet he lived. Clearly, he breathed, so he must—

"Moria!"

The man's right hand rose, his fingers curved and twisted, like claws. Moria saw that and flashed back to her father—

The whistle of a blade. The *thwack* of steel cutting through flesh and bone, and the man's hand sailed free of his body. She leaped up, staggering back as the wagon driver's body bucked and flailed, the stump of his arm thrashing, bloodless. His other arm pulsed, as if trying to change itself into the claw-like thing but finding itself unable to complete the transformation, crushed and nearly severed by the horse's hooves.

Gavril's sword sailed up, ready to strike the killing blow, but Moria said, "Wait!"

"It's—" he began.

"A shadow stalker. Which means you cannot kill it with that. We're safe at a distance—it can't fully manifest when the body is ruined, and it seems trapped inside. I can banish it but . . ." Her gaze crossed the open land. "Where there's one . . ."

"Yes, of course. Conserve your powers."

They stepped back onto the path. Gavril's gaze lingered on the wagon driver.

"His spirit has fled," Moria said. "He is at peace."

"I wasn't—"

"You're allowed to express concern for a fellow human

142

being, Gavril. No one will judge you for it." When he opened his mouth, she said, "No one *here* will judge you for it."

He nodded. "Thank you."

"Let's look around."

NINETEEN

They walked in ever-widening circles around the wagon. There were no other bodies. No other signs of death. Nor of shadow stalkers. What they feared most was discovering the other form, the shadows and fog that could possess a man—or rip him to pieces. Moria's powers allowed her to protect them against that, but she did not care to test how long it would last. Yet they saw no sign of fog or shadow.

"The horses are gone," she said. "The livestock in Edgewood had vanished, too. Is that part of the sorcery?"

Gavril shook his head. "Creatures will flee ahead of the shadow stalkers if they can. They sense them, much as you seem to."

"I'm not sure I—"

"You've come to recognize their presence. It's a matter of trusting and understanding that, which we will work on later."

He'd taken the lead while they crested a rise, being nearly a head taller and thus able to see over it sooner. She stared at his back as he said they'd work on it later, as if they were back in the Wastes and nothing in the interim had happened. And truly, at this moment, that was how it felt. As if all the lies and the betrayals and the pain belonged to some half-remembered nightmare.

Complicated.

Yes, it was indeed.

"So the horses fled in panic," she said.

He nodded.

"And we did not hear them? Did not hear the bandits trying to control them or free them before they injured themselves? Did not hear a man trampled to death?"

"I . . . I don't know how. Only we did not. The explanation isn't important."

"Is it not?" she said. "We just saw a shadow stalker, Kitsune. They do not randomly occur in nature."

He slowed, as if only just considering this, and she sighed. "If there are shadow stalkers, then there is a sorcerer who raised them to attack our wagon, and likely magics that kept us both sleeping and safe. It must be someone who is on your father's side, mustn't it? I presume this is not common sorcery."

"No, it is not." His voice was low, his words slow, as if working them through.

"Well, then, how many sorcerers would know it? Since there is no chance we've just happened to stumble on your father himself, out here in the middle of the steppes."

"I believe we are on the *edge* of the steppes."

Her sigh bordered on a growl now. "That is not my point, Kitsune."

"I know. Just . . . I did not consider . . . The problem is—"

He stopped suddenly and one hand shot up, warning her back. Then he gripped his sword with both hands, and she heard the sound of something being dragged over the hard earth.

"Help me."

The words came muffled and soft, and if it had not been completely silent on the plain they'd not have heard them. The voice came from the same direction as the dragging sound, and they both looked over but saw only the grass. Then the grass swayed as something moved through it.

"Who's there?" Gavril said.

"Help . . ." A garbled sound. "Help."

"Stay where you are," Gavril said.

"Help—"

"Stop moving. We will come to you."

The grass went still. Gavril waved for Moria to circle around while he approached straight on. He kept his gaze fixed on the spot where they'd last seen the grass move while Moria scanned the plain. Both drew steadily nearer until they could see it was Toman. Leader of the bandits.

Gavril took one look at him and said, "Moria! Back! He's—"

"No, he's not possessed," she said. "This is not the same."

Toman was indeed misshapen. Not twisted and wizened but inflated, his skin stretching like an overfilled waterskin. His clothing had split at the seams, flesh bulging through the gaps, some of it ripped and oozing. His face was nearly as unrecognizable as the wagon driver's had been, his eyes and mouth almost lost in bloated flesh.

Gavril stared in horror as Toman's distended arms reached toward Gavril's boots, his fingers digging into the ground as he pulled himself forward. Toman lifted his head, wobbling on his neck, as if he could no longer support it.

"Help me," he said.

Gavril started to look over at Moria, then stopped and squared his shoulders, as if deciding not to seek her opinion in this, not to ask for her complicity. He lifted his sword.

"Keeper?" he said. "Turn away." Then, "Please."

She did. She heard the sound of steel cutting flesh and bone and then a distant growl, and she spun to see Gavril with both hands gripping his bloodied blade, Toman's head at his feet, severed from his body. Gavril breathed hard, his eyes shut. And behind him—

"Gavril!"

A growling figure flew over the ridge. A shadow stalker. She launched her daggers, one after the other, and both hit their target and stopped the stalker just as it came within arm's length of Gavril.

Gavril's sword was already in flight. It hit the thing at the waist and cleaved clean through it. Both halves of the shadow stalker fell. Then the upper half began to twitch, and the thing launched itself at Gavril as Moria caught the back of his tunic and yanked him away.

The shadow stalker's torso continued toward them, dragging itself on twisted arms as it gnashed its teeth.

"Begone!" Moria said, focusing her energy on the creature. "In the name of the goddess and the ancestors, begone."

It continued coming as they backed away and as Moria commanded the spirit to leave, which only seemed to antagonize it. Finally, it dug its clawed hands into the earth and hurled itself again at them, and she shouted, "*Begone!*" and the thing dropped to the ground as a cloud of fog swirled up from it. Moria pulled Gavril to her, but the cloud made no move to come for him as it whirled up in the air and disappeared into the night.

"Anger," Gavril said. "That's what it needs. Anger and force."

She looked at him, not comprehending, but he was gazing out over the plain, surveying it for more trouble.

"Your banishing power," he said when he caught her look. "You need to infuse it with anger and force. Command them to leave with full authority and confidence. Clearly you have no shortage of either. Simply channel that better when you are banishing."

This was, she could point out, not the time for a post-battle analysis, and in the past she'd have bristled at it. But she knew by now there was no insult intended. He was unnerved, and this was how he calmed himself.

"And I must learn not to be so disturbed by . . ." He glanced down at Toman's decapitated corpse. "By what I must do."

"It was the most merciful way."

"Hmm."

He started to return his sword to its scabbard, his gaze still distant.

"Clean your blade, Kitsune," she said.

"Hmm?"

She pointed to Toman. "We have seen that condition before. The creature in the Forest of the Dead. The one you claimed was a natural evolution for the environment."

"The quilled rodent?"

"Yes. Tyrus and I saw rats at Fairview that were the same. Bloated and misshapen. I believe it is a byproduct of the magics. I killed one with my dagger and Tyrus insisted on cleaning it to be safe. You ought to do the same."

He nodded and began wiping it on the grass as she retrieved her daggers from the dead shadow stalker.

"This is not one of the bandits," she said.

Gavril looked closer at the shadow-stalker-abandoned corpse. "You are correct," he said, as if with some surprise.

She gave him a look. "Thank you. So it seems we are stuck in the middle—sorry, the *edge* of the steppes—with no horses and a useless wagon and a landscape populated by shadow stalkers. If they are indeed raised by some confederate of your father's, then we should be safe enough. We simply need to find this sorcerer and turn ourselves in to him to be returned to your father and resume our original mission. However, the fact that it"—Moria waved at the shadow stalker—"attempted to attack you suggests we are not safe at all. What is going on here, Kitsune?"

"I . . . I'm thinking."

"If you do it aloud, perhaps I can help. Unless you still think me a dull-witted Northerner."

"I only said that to needle you."

149

"You also did it in front of your father."

"As I said, it was to convince him you were not intellectually capable . . ." He stopped and scowled at her. "You're needling *me* now, Keeper. Playing on my guilt to make me share my thoughts."

"I do not believe I am intellectually capable of such cunning—"

"Enough. You asked who else could do this, and that is the problem I am working out. As far as I know, the magics are my father's alone. He spent three summers living well beyond the empire's borders to learn this particular sorcery, and he claims to have killed the man who taught him."

"Were there other students?"

"Others who would spend over thirty moons studying for one purpose? Who would have the power and the will to do such a thing? Very few, and no chance that another has coincidentally arrived in the empire and begun also raising shadow stalkers."

"So it must be your father."

"But how? Why?" He brushed back his braids impatiently. "This makes no sense, Moria." He waved at the dead shadow stalker. "*He* makes no sense. Where did he come from? My father carefully guards the warriors he has raised."

"Where are they?"

"I don't know. The point—"

She stepped in front of him. "No, the point is exactly what I'm asking, Kitsune. This man is not dressed as one would expect in this climate. Is it reasonable to think he might have come from Fairview?"

"Yes, but—"

"Then he did not simply wander off from the others and appear here. You say you do not know where your father keeps his army of the undead?" She waved across the land. "How about here?"

"I cannot imagine we have stumbled . . ."

He trailed off as she started back toward the wagon.

Gavril stalked after her. "What have I done now?"

"Nothing, which is the problem. It is night. There are shadow stalkers. Discussing the situation with you has proved tedious. I am taking action. Food, water, perhaps a lantern if I can find it. Then I am walking until I find a settlement. If you wish to be useful, help me find supplies. Including a sharpening stone or another sword for you. We will almost certainly encounter more shadow stalkers, and the only ways to stop them are banishment and hacking them to bits. We must be ready."

TWENTY

Gavril did as he was told. But the moment they set out, as dawn began coloring the horizon, he renewed their conversation as if they hadn't paused.

"My problem with your scenario is that it lacks plausibility and probability, Keeper," he said as they passed the wagon driver, the shadow stalker still seemingly caught within his battered corpse.

"Note that," she said, pointing as the thing reared up at them, hissing. "The shadow stalker is trapped. Why? They've seemed to be able to come and go at will before."

"Perhaps it is the condition of the corpse. The creature entered it and, unable to mobilize it, could not exit either."

"I think there is more to it than that. But for now, simply make note."

Gavril had fallen behind to examine the thing. Now he

caught up. "As I was saying, what are the chances that our wagon just happened to pass near where my father is keeping his army?"

"Is it not also near where he was keeping—?" She broke off.

"My mother."

"I did not mean to remind you."

Silence for the next fifty paces. Then he said, "I take your point. However—"

"Halt."

A growl of frustration. "I want to discuss this—"

"And I said *halt*. Not *stop talking*."

She stopped several paces behind and was looking about when a shadow stalker shot from behind a stand of bushes. It ran toward them. Or attempted to. Its gait was oddly uneven, and it moved in a staggering, stumbling run they could easily outpace.

"Save your sword, Kitsune," Moria said. "Let me practice on this one."

She worked on banishing it while staying out of its way. She tried various methods. Speaking the words aloud. Saying them in her head. Shouting. Whispering. Invoking the ancestors. Invoking the goddess. She saved one method for last, and when it worked, she turned to Gavril.

"You are correct. The wording and the invocation do not matter as much as the force of my delivery. And you can stop clutching your sword like that. You don't need to cleave anything in two. Not yet."

As she walked to the fallen body, she saw why the thing

had moved so awkwardly. It was barefoot, and its soles were worn to bone. She flipped the corpse onto its back. The dawn light hit it, and she reeled.

"Jonas?" she breathed.

"What?" Gavril sheathed his blade and stepped closer.

The creature's face had contorted beyond recognition, but scar tissue marred one forearm. He had dark skin, only a few shades lighter than Gavril's, and close-cropped curly hair. Her gaze slid back down to his feet and she imagined shabby boots, already on their way to the dust heap. She would not forget those boots. They were the last thing she'd seen of Jonas, as he'd been dragged into the undergrowth in the Forest of the Dead. She'd lunged, trying to catch them as he disappeared.

Now her gaze rose again to his arm and she touched the scars. "He told me he'd burned it saving a child from a fire."

Gavril snorted. "No, he . . ." He shifted his weight. "Yes, I'm certain that's how it happened."

"I'm certain it is not. He was a warrior trying to impress a girl, in a village with too many warriors and not enough girls. I heard many stories. Jonas was kind, though. Too old to be eyeing girls barely past their sixteenth summer, but he was kind." She laid his hands on his chest and then stood. "We have seen one man likely from Fairview and another we can both attest was from Edgewood. Do you still doubt your father's army is housed nearby?"

"While I do not like the sheer magnitude of the coincidence, I would accept it if it were not for a bigger question, Keeper. Why are *we* encountering them *here*?"

"Is it possible your father has indeed found us, and he

thinks you've betrayed him, and this is his punishment? Perhaps not to harm you but to frighten you with the possibility?"

Gavril said nothing, and when Moria glanced over, his gaze had gone blank. Deeply immersed in his thoughts. A look flickered over his face, but he blinked hard and it vanished. He motioned for them to resume walking, and they did.

"It is certainly not impossible that my father would attempt to frighten me," he said. "He did so many times in my youth. But he takes too great a risk here. I am his only heir. There is little point in winning an empire if one cannot launch a dynasty. With both his age and his past . . . performance, he is not foolish enough to believe he can father more sons. That is why I can get away with some degree of disrespect. Yet there is a limit, as I've learned. My sons could be his heirs as well as I could. He has threatened me with that when I am overtly impudent."

"Threatened you with what? Forcing you to father children? I'm hardly an expert in the matter, but my rudimentary knowledge of the process suggests that would be difficult."

She swore Gavril flushed. Impossible to tell with his skin tone, of course, but his expression said if he was a Northerner, he'd be as red as a summer plum.

"My father would not threaten it if there was not a way," he said. "A potion or a spell." When she stared at him, he said, "My father knows more magics than simply raising the dead."

"I do not doubt that. Even alcohol can influence behavior. My shock, Kitsune, comes from the fact that after receiving such a threat, you still believed he had no intention of actually forcing you to marry me."

"He did not. As he said, it was a matter of political posturing."

"And he would never insist on your marrying me to accomplish the other purpose?"

"What other purpose?"

She had to shake her head sharply before she could find the words. "To produce heirs."

His mouth opened. And stayed that way.

"I did not make the connection," he said finally.

"Between marriage and babies? By the ancestors, Gavril, I find it hard to believe you spent two summers in barracks and can still be so naive. Your father hoped to push you into taking me as a lover, and when that failed, he moved to marriage. He wants heirs."

"From a Keeper? To force one to bear his grandchildren is an insult to the goddess and to the ancestors and . . ." He seemed to run out of words, sputtering into silence.

"To your father, an arranged marriage is a fact of life. You would wed me, and I would do my duty as a wife."

Silence for at least ten paces.

"The shadow stalkers have escaped his camp," she said.

"What?"

"I am reverting to the original topic of discussion. Your reasoning is sound. Your father would not risk killing you before you produce an heir. Therefore, he did not set those shadow stalkers on our captors. The shadow stalkers escaped."

"My father would never be so careless."

"Then the magics have gone awry. I told you to make note of the wagon driver. Something is wrong there, some reason the stalker is trapped. Think of Toman. His condition—and the similarly affected rodents—are a sign that the magics have unwanted consequences. Ashyn, Tyrus, and I saw more of that on our journey to Fairview. We met monks conveying mummies to a shrine. Spirits had become trapped within the corpses."

"How is that connected to this?"

"The monks had passed close to Fairview, presumably as the shadow stalkers were loosed on the town. The magics are too strong even for your father. He has, presumably, left others in charge of his undead army?"

"Sorcerers, yes. They cannot raise the stalkers, but they can control them."

"Or *fail* to control them."

He nodded grimly. "Yes."

"The question now is, do we flee to the imperial city? Or return to your father as planned?"

He fell into silence as they tramped along, the morning light illuminating an empty plain and equally empty path, leading nowhere. She looked over at him and caught something like panic on his face. Both choices were equally dangerous, equally difficult.

She softened her voice. "Tell me what you'd *like* to do, Gavril. Even if we cannot do it. Let's begin there."

"What's the point?" he said, his voice hollow with bitterness.

"Just tell me."

"You already know." He looked straight ahead. "I told you in the courtyard, Keeper. I admitted to my cowardice, and I'll not do it again."

The imperial courtyard. The night she'd discovered his betrayal. She'd been taking the seal to the library to have it identified, and she'd found Gavril in the gardens. He'd been out of sorts, fevered even, telling her he was leaving and asking her to go with him, bring Ashyn, forget everything and leave the problem in the emperor's hands and flee with him.

She'd thought he was unwell and overworked from the journey. She'd shown him the seal and told him her intentions. He'd tried to stop her, but not hard, seeing she was resolved. He'd only asked her to spend a little time with him before she researched the seal. Before she discovered what it meant. That's what he'd wanted. Some last time together before she realized his betrayal.

"Oh," she said. And that was all she could manage.

"Yes," he said, that bitterness still ringing in his voice. "My nerve failed, Keeper. I wanted to run away like a child. I still do. Run and hide and live a normal life, as if I were a normal . . ." He sucked in his breath and squared his shoulders. "To run is worse than cowardice. It is complicity. If I run, I help my father because I cannot thwart his plans."

He looked over at her. "I know the emperor did not truly wish for you to simply spy on my father, Moria. He asked you to kill him."

"I—"

"But you are no assassin. To attempt that alone would gravely endanger you. I have said I will do everything in my power to see that no harm comes to you, Keeper. You have a duty, to your emperor and your empire, yes, but more important to your village and your father. To avenge them. And I will make sure you get that revenge." He looked at her again. "Do you understand?"

She did. And so they decided they would find Alvar Kitsune's shadow stalker camp and, in that way, be returned to him. It was, in the end, all they could do.

TWENTY-ONE

They'd been on the road since the fiend dog attack. They'd set out that night, ridden all day, and then taken turns sleeping in the wagon the following night. Now it was day again, and Ronan wasn't happy.

"He said it was a day's ride," Ronan grumbled. "We are on the second day."

"I know."

"He says we had to divert to avoid the towns, but he didn't add that to the estimate of time, did he?"

"I know."

He looked over. "And you'd like me to stop complaining about it."

"Not truly." Ronan was only saying what Ashyn was thinking. Her grandfather was eager to get her to the dragons—it was the culmination of a life's work and dreams. Was she surprised he'd misled them about the distance?

"I understand you wish to return to Jorn and Aidra as quickly as you can," she said. "If you want to do so, I understand, as I always have."

A flash of emotion. Then his face hardened. "My brother and sister will be fine for a little longer. You need me more than they do. But I'm hoping it'll be a brief delay." He peered out at the landscape. "Our destination had better not be in the North."

"It is a fortnight's ride to the North," Ashyn said. "Edwyn would not expect to get us that far before we revolted. We seem to be heading toward the steppes."

"Which border the North."

Ashyn shook her head. "The steppes begin a four-day ride from the imperial city. We were already to the northwest and . . . And you do not wish a lesson in imperial geography."

He shrugged. "I'm happy to listen if it will distract you from worrying about Moria."

"I'm not—"

His look cut her short.

"I'm trying not to," she said.

"I know. So if it helps to talk about anything else, I'm happy to listen, Ash."

When she said nothing for the next hundred paces, he drew his horse up closer to hers and said, "I ought not to have mentioned Moria."

"It doesn't matter. She's never far from my mind. Moria and Daigo and Tyrus and the children of Edgewood and

Fairview and . . ." She turned to look at him. "Am I doing the right thing, Ronan? They're back there. All of them. And I'm riding this way to do something I'm not even sure is possible, and I don't know if I'm doing it because I believe it's the best choice or because I feel useless otherwise. I want to find Moria, but Tyrus and Daigo are better equipped for that, and all I did was get Guin killed and nearly get you killed and—"

"You had *nothing* to do with Guin's death. If anyone could have handled that situation better, it was me. As for the arrow in my neck, I'm the one who told you to run, and if I had the chance to do it over, I'd still do the same, because clearly Dalain Okami was not the ally he claimed to be if he let his men try to kill me."

"But am I doing the right thing, Ronan? Are *we*? I know you want to get back to your siblings, and I've not brought that up, no more than you've brought up Moria, but we're both thinking it, aren't we? That there's someplace else we need to be, and this path is taking us further from it."

"I know." He cast a grim glance back at the others.

"Do you fear they wouldn't let us leave?" she whispered.

"I could leave. But you are not simply the person Edwyn believes can awaken his dragons, Ash. You're his granddaughter. He's not about to let you run off with a thief."

"He doesn't know—"

"I'm quite certain he realizes I'm no warrior. And a young man who can wield a blade but is not a warrior is a criminal. He knows what I am, and he's not pleased that I've planted myself at your side."

He went quiet then, as if falling into his thoughts, and

162

after a moment, she ventured, "If you think he realizes you are casteless, I cannot see how that would matter. He's not from the empire. The North historically does not have castes in the way we do."

Ronan said nothing.

"I'm sorry for bringing up that, too," she said. "I do not wish you to regret having told me your secret." One of them at least. She could tell when he'd confessed that there'd been more—some darker secret. But when she'd pressed, he'd been past talking.

"I don't," he said. "And it's not that. It's true I don't particularly want him to know I lack caste, or it will give him more cause to drive me from your side. But more than that, I'm simply frustrated with the entire situation. If we *were* to leave, we'd need to sneak away."

"Do you think we ought to?"

"I think we will not get the chance before nightfall, and we should be at our destination by then, so the point is moot. Let's see these dragons. Find out if this can be done quickly and, if not, we'll discuss our departure."

TWENTY-TWO

They did indeed arrive at their destination before sundown . . . the next day. The horses had tired, and Edwyn had apologized for the delay, but they'd needed to make camp for the sake of the beasts. Ashyn would never argue with that. If Ronan disagreed, he'd wisely kept it to himself.

Already today they'd stopped briefly for a midday meal, and when they had, Edwyn had sent two of the women on ahead to "tell the others and begin the preparations." When Ashyn had asked what that meant, he'd only smiled enigmatically and said, "Patience, child."

They had not gone overly far when they stopped again. Ronan grumbled under his breath as he and Ashyn both gazed out over the landscape, seeing nothing that would explain their halting. Simply another delay, they presumed.

"We have arrived," Edwyn said.

Ashyn looked out again, as if she might somehow have missed a dwelling. To the west was a distant hill. The rest was flat, grassy land. There seemed nothing for a quarter day's ride in any direction.

"Well?" Edwyn said. "Ronan? I may be old, but I've clearly heard your grumbling about the distance. Perhaps you'd like it to be farther?"

Ronan grunted and slid from his horse. When Ashyn tried to do the same, he stopped her with a raised hand, then said to Edwyn, "Show me where we're going first. I do not like the looks of this."

"There," Ashyn said, pointing at the hill.

Edwyn smiled, pleased. Ronan only looked confused.

"Does not the hill look odd?" she asked.

"If you're saying it isn't a hill at all, but concealing some building, then I'd say you share some of your sister's imagination. Look at the ground, the way it's split and scarred all along here. I'm no scholar, but clearly there was some sort of break or eruption ages ago. That strangely shaped hill is the result."

"Exactly," she said. "Which makes it unusual. Which means that is why we've stopped." She glanced at her grandfather. "Is it some sort of sacred place?"

He smiled. "You might say that. Shall we ride closer?"

"Could you not have mentioned that *before* I dismounted," Ronan muttered as he got on his horse again.

Edwyn ignored him, and the three of them rode off with Tova and two of the warriors, leaving the rest of the party behind. As they drew near the hill, Ashyn realized it was more of a small mountain, seeming to have erupted from the very earth. The rough, barren rock was made of layers, some of the top ones overhanging lower ones, which gave the formation its very odd appearance.

Edwyn dismounted and walked to an area where the layers overhung the most, leaving a cave-like dip in the side. It was not a cave, however—Ashyn could see the rear wall of it, which did not extend more than a dozen or so paces. Edwyn continued to a corner hidden by the shadow of the overhang. And then he disappeared.

Ashyn scrambled off her horse and jogged over with Tova at her heels. She expected to see there was indeed a cave entrance. Instead, she saw a solid rock wall.

"Around here," Edwyn called, seemingly from inside the mountain itself. Then his hand appeared, and she followed to see the solid wall was an illusion, created by shadow and the jutting rock. Squeeze past that jutting rock and there was indeed an opening, enough for a man to easily pass through.

She was about to step when Ronan caught her arm. He tugged her back.

"Move aside." Then he paused and squinted through at Edwyn. "I mean, would you please allow me to go first, my lady, to ensure your safety?"

As he passed her, she murmured, "I must admit, I do rather like the sound of that better."

He grunted and continued past her into the cave. She glanced at Tova, who made it through the gap with his fur just brushing the sides.

Ashyn continued behind Tova and Ronan as they followed Edwyn, who now carried a lit torch. The passage was narrow and winding, as if hacked from the rock itself, and soon they were in near darkness, the torch flickering, the air thin. Then Edwyn stopped, and they were in a small room with no doors. No exits.

Edwyn reached up and grabbed what looked like a chunk of rock. When he pulled, there was a click, and he pushed at the wall. A door-shaped piece opened.

Edwyn walked through. Ashyn started after him. Ronan rocked forward as if to stop her, but only motioned that she should take out her dagger. She did, as she stepped into . . .

"Oh!" she said, stumbling back as she came face-to-face with a skull peering from the dirt. A human skull. An entire skeleton, actually, embedded in the wall.

Edwyn let out a word in a foreign language. It sounded like a curse.

"My apologies, child. I'm so accustomed to it that I never thought to warn you."

"You're accustomed to corpses hanging from walls?" Ronan said as his gaze traveled across seven bodies, in various states of decay, all upright, as if they were part of the walls themselves.

"It's to discourage anyone who manages to get that hidden door open," Edwyn said carefully, as if trying not to snap at Ronan. "The locals are very superstitious. In their lore, there is a demonic spirit that lures people into caves and underground caverns, devours them, and hangs their bodies for decoration." He waved at the corpses. "Like so. Now I'm afraid this next part is a little unsettling. Ronan? Would you help me remove these three bodies? They're tied around the necks and limbs. Ashyn? You may wish to turn away for this."

Instead, Ashyn stepped to the nearest skeleton he'd indicated and began unfastening the ties. It was not, admittedly, the most pleasant task, but these three bodies were dry and mostly mummified.

Once all three were removed, Edwyn had Ronan set them aside. Then he opened the doorway they'd been covering. He walked through first with the torch. Then Ashyn and Tova. Ronan came through last and then Edwyn raised the torch and—

Ronan breathed a curse. It was one Ashyn had heard from him before, and would never repeat, given that it was a very impious reference to the goddess's anatomy. Under the circumstances, he could be forgiven for it. Even Ashyn whispered, "By the ancestors," under her breath as she stared at the cavern before them.

Ronan sheathed his sword and walked to a pile that glittered in the torchlight. He dug in, lifted his hands, and watched the gold and silver and red and blue sift through his fingers. Then he shook his head, dumped the remainder, and wiped his hands against his trousers as if they'd been contaminated.

"It's a trick," he said. "An illusion."

"Did it feel like an illusion?" Edwyn asked. "Look closer. I have a feeling you're quite adept at telling real from fake."

Ashyn stared at the pile. Golden coins and necklaces and armbands. And jewels. Every color of jewels. It wasn't simply one pile either. More stretched into the darkness.

"Go on," Edwyn said. "Taste it or scratch it or whatever your sort do to distinguish real from counterfeit."

Your sort. Ashyn tensed, ready to jump to Ronan's defense.

But Ronan stared at the pile, and in his face, Ashyn no longer saw the brash and audacious young warrior-thief. She saw a casteless boy risking his life for a few of these coins, dreaming of a pile a tenth this size, of what it could buy, the life it could buy, the freedom to tell his family he was done with thieving and conning.

The whole pile? That was not merely freedom for his family but from the stain of his ancestors. With one of these piles, he could buy caste. *Warrior* caste. Buy back his birthright. Bequeath a better life to his children and his siblings.

Ronan took a handful of gold and jewels, and he did not test it. He simply stared at it, his eyes dark with hunger and need and longing. He rose, still clutching that small cache of treasure, and he turned to her, with that same look on his face. Hunger and need and longing. He stood there, hand extended, offering it to her. Then he snapped as if from a trance and threw the gold and jewels aside so hard the echo pinged through the cavern.

"Let's go, Ash," he said, pulling out his sword with one hand while propelling her toward the exit with the other. "I'll not be tricked like this. I'll not."

"Ronan . . ." She caught his hand and he pulled away, as if burned. Then he shook his head sharply and took her by the arm. Beside her, Tova whined, unsettled.

"Come on, Ash. He's setting a trap with his magics, and I'll not see you hurt." A glower Edwyn's way. "I'll not."

"Not see *her* hurt?" Edwyn said, his voice soft, his gaze locked hard on Ronan's. "It's not her you're worried about, boy, is it?"

Ronan's grip tightened on his sword. "It's always her. She is the reason I'm here. To watch over her. To look out for her interests."

"Because she's a mere girl and cannot be expected to do so for herself?"

"Do not twist my words against me, sorcerer."

"I'm no sorcerer, boy. I am what they call in the North a cunning man, meaning I have devoted my life to the mysteries of our world, in particular dragons. That is all."

"Enough," Ashyn said. "Please." She took Ronan's hand again. This time he didn't flinch, but let her lead him to the side of the cavern, while turning so he kept his eye on Edwyn.

"I don't know if it's magical or real," she said, her voice lowered to a whisper. "But I'd not be swayed by gold and jewels. You know that. They mean nothing to me. If he truly sought to tempt me, he'd have a vast library down here, with every book I've dreamed of reading."

Ronan's gaze shifted to Edwyn. "It's not you he tempts, Ash. He knows what I am. He said as much. He mocks me with this, and he thinks to entice me into proving I cannot be trusted. He hopes I'll slide jewels into my pockets. That I'll be unable to resist. And then he can say I'm no warrior and place his own man at your side."

She lowered her voice further. "You think that's what he wants? That he has some motive and seeks to replace you?"

"He seeks to replace me because he finds me unworthy of his granddaughter. Unworthy as a guard. As a friend. Certainly unworthy as—" He swallowed and straightened. "I won't fail you, Ash. Even if this was real. Even if it could buy . . ." His gaze slid to the piles and he recoiled, as if the very sight of the riches was poison.

"Don't," she whispered. She clutched both his hands and leaned toward him. "I know what this would mean to you, and you do not need to pretend otherwise. I don't care if you sneak jewels into your pockets, Ronan. If they're real, I'll do it for you."

"No. Never—"

"But I *would*, and I would defend you if you did, and I could not see it as any betrayal of your loyalty. So stop thinking that."

"I want to leave," he blurted. "Now. I don't like this, Ash, and we've no time for it. Moria is out there. Tyrus is out there. My brother and sister—"

"Then we'll arrange for you to go."

"No." His eyes widened. "That's not what I mean. I won't leave you. I'd never—"

"Ronan? Shhh. It's all right." She leaned as close to him as she could, raised on tiptoe, and he went still, breath catching as if she was about to kiss him. But she only whispered, "If you wish to leave, we'll leave. When we can. I've said that and I mean it. For now . . ."

Ronan swallowed. "Hear him out."

"Please. If you'd rather go back outside and wait—"

"No." His chin lifted, the old Ronan sliding back. "Let's get this over with."

TWENTY-THREE

Ronan seemed to be correct about one thing—that Edwyn had apparently been hoping to tempt him into revealing his true self. He continued to insist Ronan test the veracity of the gold and jewels, and while Ronan claimed lack of skill and feigned lack of interest, it was obvious neither was true. When Edwyn held up pieces, Ronan's practiced eye reflexively assessed, and she could tell by his expression they were real.

"Do you know what this is, Ashyn?" Edwyn asked as he held out a handful.

"Gold coins from past ages, and a ruby, two emeralds, and a diamond."

He chuckled. "You are observant and quick, child. But I mean this." He waved at the cavern. "Do you know what this is?"

"It would appear . . ." She cleared her throat and chose her words with care. "In a bard's tale, piles of treasure in a cavern means dragons. A dragon hoard."

Edwyn took her hand and led her deeper into the cavern, past piles of gold and jewels, until they reached the farthest corner. Then he lifted the torch and murmured, "And among the treasures, the greatest of them all."

At first, all she saw was more gold and silver and rich jewels glistening and dancing in the torchlight. Then she realized she was *not* looking on golden coins or diamonds or rubies. She was looking at iridescent scales, like the ones in the mountain cave.

Ashyn touched one. Tova growled, but softly, uncertain. The scale was as cold as the rocks surrounding them. She looked up and saw scales reaching over her head. Then she began to walk around the thing. When she tripped, Ronan grabbed her arm, and she looked down to see what she'd stumbled over. It was a toe as big as her forearm, ending in a sharp claw.

She started moving again. Ronan kept hold of her arm, but she peeled off his fingers and continued around. When she craned her neck up, she could see wings folded on the creature's back, too high for her to reach. Then another fearsome clawed leg. Only when she reached the front quarters did she see the beast's head, tucked around its body, its chin resting on the dirt floor.

The head of a dragon. A head with eyes almost closed, the barest sliver of yellow irises peeking out. One lip was curled over a fang. A curved and pointed fang, not dulled by age as the skeleton's fangs had been. This was a young dragon. Perhaps two-thirds the size of the monstrous one in the cave. A female. Ashyn knew that when she saw why the dragon was curled the way she was—what she protected. The *dragon's* greatest treasure.

"Are those . . . ?" Ronan asked, squinting against the dim light.

She nodded and walked to crouch beside the two smaller dragons. They were the size of Daigo—whelps rather than hatchlings. She bent over the dragon on the left—ran her hand over its nubs of horns and down its snout. When she reached its nostrils, warm air tickled her hand, and she pulled back with a sharp "Oh!" that had Ronan brandishing his sword. She took his hand and put his fingers in front of the tiny dragon's nose.

"It's . . . breathing," Ronan said.

"I should hope so," Edwyn said as he finally came around to join them. "Or we've brought Ashyn here for nothing." He waved at the three dragons. "This is your task, child. This is what I've brought you here to do. To awaken our dragons."

Naturally, Ronan wanted to do it right away. Say the words, perform the ritual, whatever, and get back to finding Moria and Tyrus. That had offended Edwyn, and Ashyn couldn't blame him. He'd brought them here to awaken the most legendary of legendary creatures, and Ronan acted as if he'd asked Ashyn to remove a sliver from his foot. An inconvenient interruption at a very busy time.

Edwyn said that preparations had to be made. They would not even begin the ritual for another day at least. Ronan hadn't been thrilled with that, but he'd kept quiet—for now.

The festival began as soon as they emerged from the dragon's den. More people had arrived, strangers to her, and white tents were going up, and everyone was laughing and chattering. Ashyn was the center of attention, until finally Edwyn shooed them off and took her into one of the tents for a nap. Ashyn argued that she wasn't tired, but Edwyn insisted. It would be a long and glorious night, and she needed to rest for that. So she did.

It was indeed a festival, as elaborate as any Ashyn had enjoyed in Edgewood. A massive white tent was erected. Fresh goat was roasted, songs were sung. Music was played. Tales were told. Wine was drunk. Too much wine. By the time the moon passed its zenith, Ashyn was curled up at the fire with Tova at her side and Ronan at her back, his arm hooked around her waist, pulling her to lean back against him, as she ignored the whispered speculations and enjoyed the buzz of the wine and the warmth of the fire and the stories of the bard.

Stories of dragons. That's what they got that night. Especially tales of the one that slept beneath them. There were four types of dragons: sand, snow, timber, and rock, corresponding to the major areas of the empire. This one was, like the skeleton in the cave, a snow dragon. Her name was Isobo, and she was, like the other, a long way from her home. But after the Age of Ice, when the snow receded to the North, not all the snow dragons moved with it. Their iridescent scales meant they could reflect any terrain and blend with it. And there were few dragons in the steppes, with its lack of mountain caves. That must have been what appealed to Isobo, a young female seeking her place in the world. She'd found that odd hill and made it her home. Then she'd begun amassing her wealth, taking it from travelers, easily spotted on this open plain. The problem, however, was that the open plain also meant she was easily spotted. Soon tales from the survivors reached the dragon seekers of the North.

That was what Edwyn's people—Ashyn's people—had been. Seekers and keepers of another kind. Their lives had been spent hunting dragons and using magics and skills to tame them. Young dragons were required. No one dared attempt such a thing on the ancient bulls that darkened the skies and set entire villages aflame. While Isobo was an adult, her youth and isolation made her a possibility. Even better, as they'd been bringing food and treasure and wooing her, she'd left temporarily and returned to lay her eggs. Two eggs. Two successful births. Two baby dragons who *could* easily be tamed: a female they named Zuri and a male they called Ponto. Isobo seemed a gift from the goddess herself.

But they never got the chance to do more than accustom Isobo's young to the smell and sight of humans. The Age of Fire came and there was no time for war and no reason to train dragons. In fact, as the volcanos erupted across the land, dragons took advantage of the chaos and rained down terror, and the people—unable to control the volcanos—turned their rage on the threat they *could* tackle.

Edwyn's ancestors tried to stop the dragon slayers, but they would not listen. One by one, the dragons fell. Three great bulls. Seven younger bulls and females. Soon, the only known survivor was Isobo, safe in her isolation, busy caring for her young. The decision was made to protect her by putting the three into a magical sleep. The opening she'd used had been sealed, to be blasted open when the time was right for them to wake. When the empire needed them. As it did now.

TWENTY-FOUR

The festivities continued into the night. So did the wine. By the time Ronan tried to sneak Ashyn off behind the tent, she was intoxicated enough to think . . . well, to think that perhaps *he* was intoxicated enough to do more than hold her hand. There was part of her mind still sober enough to panic at the thought. She'd had enough of this dance with Ronan—friends and then perhaps more, and then . . . no, sorry, just friends.

As much as she might want more, she wouldn't be the foolish girl who tried to woo a boy who balked like a skittish colt. She had too much dignity and, yes, pride, for that.

Yet, that night, with the wine swirling through her head, she couldn't help but think *What could a few stolen kisses hurt?* She could take those kisses and enjoy them for what they were. Moria would. But Ashyn was not her sister, and she would be unable to avoid hoping for more; and even if she somehow did avoid it, come dawn she'd have to endure Ronan's apologies and the humiliating insistence that he'd meant nothing by it.

So when he tried to pull her behind the tent, she dug in her heels and said, "Where are we going?"

"Someplace where they won't find us." He tossed her a drunken grin. "Where we can be alone. I'm tired of being responsible, Ash. I want to have some fun."

She could imagine her expression at that, because he laughed and threw his arms around her neck.

"Not like that, my lady," he said, a teasing lilt on the title. "Your honor is perfectly safe with me tonight. I simply want to be with you."

"All right . . ." she said carefully.

"Don't give me that look, Ash." His hands entwined in her hair, pulling her face beneath his. "Ash, my Ash, my beautiful, brilliant Seeker." He kissed her forehead and pulled her into a tight embrace before moving back and taking her hand. "Come with me."

She followed him, half stumbling and blaming the darkness rather than the wine. Tova sighed but trudged along, resigned. As they passed a lantern, Ronan grabbed it. When he snuffed out the flame, she said, "Umm? Doesn't that defeat the purpose?" but he only grinned and said, "We don't want anyone tracking our escape, do we?"

When she saw where they were going, she slowed, but Ronan tugged her hand, and said, "Don't you want to see it again? Without him? Just us?" and she did.

There were no guards posted at the hillside. She supposed everyone in the group could be trusted not to pilfer from the piles within.

They went inside, and Ronan lit the lantern. When they

got to the den, he set the lantern down. Then he pounced, making Tova let out a startled bark as Ronan scooped Ashyn up and tossed her onto a pile of gold and jewels. Treasure tinkled all around her, spilling over her as she laughed.

"Exactly how much honey wine did you drink?" she said.

"Enough that I don't care," he said, plunking onto another pile and letting it rain onto the earthen floor. "I don't care about being responsible tonight. I don't care to be anything other than what I am, and I don't care what anyone thinks of that."

"I think that's perfectly fine," she said, sobering as she looked at him. "I would not want you to be anything else."

"I know, and that's why I—" He cut himself off with a rueful smile and a shake of his head. "None of that. Not tonight. Tonight . . ." He dug his hands into the pile. "Tonight I'm going to find you a gift."

"Not to deny your good intentions, but this isn't a marketplace."

"It is for me. I'm a thief, Ash. I take what's not mine. What can never be . . ." He looked at her and went quiet, then yanked his gaze away and scooped up handfuls of treasure. "My gift is not in the purchase. It is in finding exactly the right piece for you."

He dug through the piles, pulling up necklaces and armbands and other jewelry. He'd hold up a piece and say, "No, too gaudy," or "No, not your style," and keep sifting. She let him. He was happier than she'd seen him in many days, and she'd do nothing to spoil his game.

Even he had to know it was a game, that she would return

whatever he gave her. It didn't matter. What mattered was the moment, and it was wonderful, watching him in his element, his eye assessing every piece, telling her the stone and the origin and sometimes the value with no avarice in his assessments. None of that hunger and longing from earlier. This was pure fun. And, admittedly, some flattery, as he'd find a piece that "matched" her eyes or would "bring out" the red in her hair or one that wasn't good enough for her.

"The right piece must complement you," he said. "The perfect . . ." He stopped. Then he nearly dove into the next pile, making her laugh as he shoved aside jewels and coins, digging like a bird chasing a worm down a hole. He snagged his goal and pulled it out.

"Yes, this. *This*." It was a bracelet of gold, one that would weave up a woman's forearm. Delicate and intricately designed, with etched birds.

"Doves," he said.

"Oh! Yes, I've read about them."

"A man down the street from us raised them for sending messages. They were perfect, all white, as smart and as gentle as anything you could imagine. But I once saw a hawk twice their size try to steal a fledgling from a nest, and the dove drove it off." He held up the band. "That's you, Ash. Smart and beautiful and gentle, but ferocious, too, when you need to be."

Her cheeks burned as he put it onto her arm.

"It fits like it was made for you," he said with a grin. "Do you like it?"

She ran her fingers over the gold, only now seeing the

tiny onyx in the birds' eyes, and the incredible intricacy of the metalwork. "It's amazing."

"Like you."

Her cheeks blazed hotter. She opened her mouth.

"Uh-uh. Don't duck the compliment, Ash. I've had enough honey wine to say anything I like and not be held responsible for it in the morning. Just know that it's the truth. I might complain about being in the middle of the blasted steppes, on a mad quest to wake dragons. But there's no place I'd rather be than with you. Wherever that is."

His brown cheeks darkened, as if he'd gone too far. Then he took a wineskin from under his cloak and gulped it.

"No regrets," he said. "Not tonight."

He handed her the skin. She might have thought she'd had enough, but she suddenly felt the need to drain the entire thing. Get so drunk she would stop blushing and do something mad and rash and definitely unwise. *Be* unwise for once in her life. Of course she did nothing of the sort. She took a gulp, heat surging through her, and then she handed it back.

Ronan put the skin under his cloak and grabbed her hand. "Come on. Let's go visit your dragons."

They went over to the beasts.

"So we stay then?" she said, as she sat beside the whelps, petting one and feeling the slow beat of its heart. "Until the ritual."

"You're going to wake dragons, Ash. You can't walk away from that. You'd never forgive yourself."

"There's no guarantee—"

"But you're going to try, and it's only one more day. Moria

has Tyrus and Daigo. Aidra and Jorn have my aunt, and while that's not the best situation, a few more days in her care will not harm them."

"I know but . . . you worry."

He shrugged and said nothing.

"You could go on ahead," she said. "I'd understand—"

"Don't."

"But—"

"Tell me I can't leave," he said, the wine flush leaving his face as something like panic touched his eyes. "If you truly want to make this easier, tell me I can't leave. That you need me."

She hesitated. Then she said, "Because you feel guilty if you choose not to leave."

"I feel . . ." He shook it off and gulped more wine. "None of that. Not tonight. Just don't tell me to go, Ash. Don't make this my choice. Tell me you need my help and remind me that I'll be home soon, and that an extra day will make no difference, and my brother and sister will be fine."

"They will be," she said. "You know that. And, yes, I do need you. I'm loathe to say so, when you have other responsibilities—"

"But this is the important one. This is for my empire, because perhaps, if we succeed, if I watch out for the Seeker and she raises dragons, perhaps . . ." Another gulp of wine. "Perhaps something will come of it."

Ashyn rose to stand beside him as he leaned against the dragon. "Something *will* come of it. You'll get caste. There's no doubt of that. You brought me safely from Edgewood and stayed by my side through it all. The emperor cannot refuse you now, and the more you do for me, the higher your caste will be. I truly believe that."

"Then that is all the reason I need. I stay for my empire and for my family and for myself. For a better life. Not because . . ." He glanced over at her. "Not for any other reason, and no one can accuse me of it."

"They cannot. You have the best intentions, Ronan. You always do."

He let out a sharp laugh at that and leaned to give her cheek a smacking kiss. "No one else would ever accuse me of *that*, Ash. It's not true, but I love—I appreciate you saying it."

He handed her the wineskin. She took another drink and slid to sit beside the dragon whelps again. He lowered himself beside her and they sat in comfortable silence, Ashyn with her eyes closed, feeling the warm buzz of the wine and the warmer heat of Ronan, pressed up against her side, his hand clasping hers.

"Ah, blast it," he said suddenly, startling her. "Forget what I said. I'm going to do this. I'm drunk enough to say blast it all, I don't care if I regret it in the morning. I need to do this. I need to tell you."

A lick of panic ran through her. *Not this, Ronan. Not again. Don't tell me you care, only to tell me in the morning you do not. It isn't fair. I don't care how drunk you are or how good you feel, please do not—*

"I used to have another brother. I . . ." He swore, spitting the curse. Then he drained the wineskin. "Gonna do this. I am. You gotta know, Ash. All my crimes laid bare. Whatever that means."

"Ronan . . ."

"No, I've got this. Just give me a moment." He took a deep breath. "I had another brother. Eder. Three summers my junior. My father expected me to watch over him. Eder was . . . slow of thought. He fell as a baby. When our mother left he became my responsibility and I . . ." Ronan swallowed. "I was tired of it."

"I can understand—"

"There was a girl. A merchant's daughter. I would go to her shop, and she would encourage me to come, and I thought that meant . . . I was thirteen summers, and she was pretty, and she flirted with me, and I thought me being casteless didn't matter to her. It didn't. Not for that. To flirt. To steal a kiss. It's safer actually. A casteless boy isn't going to tell someone she allowed the kisses, and if he did, who would believe him? It—" He stopped with a sharp shake of his head. "And that isn't what I'm trying to tell you. *She* isn't what I'm telling you. She was incidental. I don't even recall her name."

Liar, she thought. The story might not be about the girl, but she was still essential to it. A girl—likely his first kiss. A girl who'd toyed with him. Who'd said his caste didn't matter, exactly as Ashyn herself had. The girl lied, and while Ashyn hoped Ronan wouldn't suspect her of the same, the lesson he'd learned was that the barrier could not be crossed as easily as he'd hoped.

"I was with her," he said. "I told Eder to sit on a crate outside. I did not plan to be long, but I was longer than I ought to have been. Something caught his eye. There was a wagon coming and . . . He ran right in front of it. The wagon was moving fast and . . ."

He didn't need to say more. When Ronan talked about his siblings, he spoke of two.

Ashyn squeezed his hand as hard as she could. "I'm so sorry."

A light kiss on her cheek. "I know you are. You're good to me, Ash. Even when I don't deserve it."

"You always deserve it. You were young. And there are many older than you who have lost children. It only takes a moment. Your father ought not to have expected—"

"He did. And I ought to have taken care of Eder. Properly." Another kiss. "I'm not looking for pardon. I just . . . I wanted you to know. What I'd done. And if it changes anything, if you no longer wish me to guard you or . . . or anything else, I'll understand. I was careless—"

"You made a mistake that anyone could have made. It changes nothing, Ronan. There is no one I'd rather have at my side."

He nodded and sipped the wine now, then passed the last to her. They sat there, holding hands and leaning against a dragon and staring at dirt walls, and thinking.

Ronan claimed he'd told her the tale in case it changed her mind about him, but there was more to it. She remembered what he'd said, only moments ago, begging her not to give him a choice in leaving. Making it clear that staying was for the good of his family. That he was staying for duty. Not for a girl. Not to be with a girl. Because that was what the story truly said. His brother had died because he'd been distracted by a girl . . . and he could not, *would* not do that again. He could not let himself feel that he was staying for Ashyn.

He stayed for the Seeker.

The best thing she could do for him, then? Close that door. Firmly. No more longing glances his way. No more wishing and hoping. Give him no cause to fear he was lingering for her sake, lingering to be with her. This was about duty. It had to be.

TWENTY-FIVE

Ashyn honored that pledge to keep her thoughts of Ronan pure and untainted by any romantic longing . . . by sharing a sleeping pallet with him. Moria would laugh at that, but for Ashyn it was, in her way, a statement, as much to him as to herself. That they could share a bed, like friends, and she would not lie awake hoping he would slide her way, that his hands would wrap around her, that his lips would find hers . . .

No. There would be none of that. And there wasn't.

They'd staggered back from the dragon's den, drunk and flushed, only to discover that the bitter wind on the steppes made Ronan's pallet outside her tent completely unsuitable. He'd come inside to see if there was a way of rearranging her pallet to make room for his, but the tent was not big enough, and in their intoxicated exhaustion, they'd just collapsed onto hers, Tova curled up at their feet.

Ashyn did wake once, hearing a noise, and Ronan was no longer on his side of the sleeping pallet, but curled up against her back, his hand on her hip, his face in her hair, his breath warm on the back of her neck. She accepted that. She even allowed herself to enjoy it. But she did not press against him, hoping to wake him and, well . . . just *hoping*. Instead, she lay there, fingering her bracelet and thinking about their night, about all of it, everything he'd done and said.

Would things change once they got back to the city? Once he'd returned to his family and fulfilled that obligation?

She'd like to say yes. That the way he'd looked at her and spoken of her meant that this was simply temporary. But after their first kiss, he had reunited with his family . . . and then told her he'd made a mistake.

Was she, to him, like the shopkeeper's daughter? A pointless fancy for a casteless boy? She'd told him none of that mattered, but it did, to him. If he got caste from the emperor, would *that* change?

If he returned home. *If* his brother and sister were safe. *If* he got caste. An endless string of *ifs*, like mountains to be climbed, and there was no way of seeing how many more waited, whether there was indeed an end.

Was that what her dreams of Ronan amounted to? Endless obstacles? And perhaps, if they did end, the biggest one of all: the realization that, as much as he enjoyed her company, he had other plans, other dreams, of a lover he could marry, children of his own.

Ashyn could not wed, and could only have a child with the dispensation of the emperor himself. She might dream of

189

a lifelong love, an informal partnership, but a man could want more. Even if she was happy to say, "Don't worry where this will lead—let's be happy together for as long as we can be," it might not be enough for him.

Was it worth risking her heart? Risking her dignity? Risking the pain of rejection?

Ronan shifted in his sleep, his hand gripping her hip, his face burrowing deeper into her hair, his sleepy voice whispering softly.

"Ash, my Ash . . ."

Ashyn smiled and let her hand rest on his with a soft squeeze. Yes, it was worth it. This was about her. Her choice. Her heart to let break. And if it did, she would still have the memory of a boy in a dragon's den, one perfect night when anything had seemed possible and nothing else had mattered but them.

It was enough. Her heart. Her choice. Her Ronan.

When Ashyn woke, she was alone on her sleeping pallet. Well, Tova was there, but Tova was always there. Ronan was gone, which did not come as any surprise. He'd have slipped out with the dawn, before anyone realized where he'd spent the night. She stretched and immediately regretted it. Her mouth felt like it was stuffed with sawdust. Her head pounded. Moving hurt. It just hurt.

She reached for her waterskin, opened it, and drank slowly but deeply. Alcohol dehydrated, as she knew from her healing studies. Preferably the water should be taken much sooner, but the problem with drinking to the point where she required water? She was past the point of being able to remember that she needed water.

"Mmmph," she said, lifting her head. "I hope today's preparations don't require movement. Or clear thought."

When Tova didn't make any answering noise, she lifted her head—gently—to see him still sprawled at her feet. His chest rose and fell in deep sleep.

"You didn't get into the wine, did you?" she said, laughing under her breath.

She shifted down her pallet to pat his neck. When he still didn't move, alarm darted through her and she sat up quickly—too quickly—nearly vomiting as her stomach rocked. Tova opened one eye and snarled a yawn.

"You're fine," she said. "Just as tired as I am. Do you think we ought to get up?"

He snorted and closed his eye.

"Good idea," she said, and stretched out with her head on his flank. "We'll sleep until we're woken."

She didn't even get her blanket pulled up before someone scratched at the door. It wasn't Ronan. He would walk in saying, "You dressed?" without actually giving her time to fix the situation if she wasn't.

"Who is it?" she called.

"Edwyn."

She groaned under her breath and murmured to Tova, "That didn't take nearly long enough." Then she called, "I'll be out shortly."

"May I come in? I must speak to you."

She looked down at herself. She still wore her clothing from yesterday.

"Yes," she said.

She sat up and tried to run her fingers through her hair, but as the sunlight hit her, she winced and shielded her face. Edwyn gave a soft laugh and closed the tent flap behind him.

"More wine than you are accustomed to, child?"

She flushed.

"You seemed to be having a good night," he said, "and I was very glad to see it. You deserved that after everything you've been through." He glanced down at his hand and Ashyn saw a scroll in it. "I . . . I have news that will make your day less pleasant, I fear."

She rose. "What is it?"

"Ronan has left, child. He placed this scroll outside, and I will admit that I read it before I realized it was for you."

"No, that's not—there's a mistake. He wouldn't . . ."

Wouldn't leave because he'd promised not to. Last night. When he'd been drunk. Then morning came and . . .

No, he still wouldn't sneak off.

Wouldn't he? She remembered when he'd left her behind in Edgewood. She'd found a small group of survivors, and he'd said he'd wait outside. When she'd come out, there'd been a note—and he'd been gone.

She unfastened the scroll. Inside was writing in a familiar hand. Ronan's.

I couldn't stay, Ashyn. I know I said I would, but I must get home to Aidra and Jorn. You know why. I explained it last night. I tried to justify . . . but in the end, I couldn't. Your grandfather will take care of you, and you'll awaken dragons,

Ashyn. I wish I could be there to see it. But my brother and sister need me. You do not. I will see you in the city.

She reread the note, looking for some sign that it was a trick, that someone had taken Ronan in the night and left this note. But it was his hand, and it said things no one else could know.

Ronan had said he'd stay, and he'd changed his mind. Was she truly surprised?

Ashyn rolled the scroll and tucked it into her pocket.

"I know I was not always kind to him," Edwyn said. "And I hope that played no role in his departure. If it did, then I sincerely apologize, child. I was harsh toward him yesterday, because I knew he was no warrior, and I feared you did not realize it, and he was misleading you."

"He was not."

"Either way, I feared he was using you for his own purposes. That he was feigning devotion to you. That is, I admit, why I showed him the treasure in the dragon's den. I almost hoped he would fill his pockets in the night and leave. He did leave, but my guard has told me no one went in there since the two of you during the festival."

"We were just—"

"—taking a closer look. Marveling at it all. And, perhaps, finding a private spot."

Ashyn shook her head. "It wasn't like that. We are only friends."

"You are still friends," he said gently. "That letter was not a good-bye, Ashyn. It was a temporary leave-taking for the sake of his family. One cannot argue with that."

"Family above all," she said.

"Yes." He reached out to squeeze her shoulder. "Which is why I apologize if I hurt you by being unkind to him. I truly was only trying to protect you."

"He didn't steal anything last night. He just . . ." She looked down to see the bracelet. "I'll put this back, of course. He was playing around and found it for me. As a joke."

"No, child. As a gift." His lips twitched. "Even if it was not his to give. Keep it, as a reminder that he is waiting for you in the city, once this is done. Now, while you probably do not feel much like eating, I'll have the cook make something bland. We have a full day of preparations ahead of us. Because tonight . . ." He looked at her, his eyes sparkling.

She managed a smile for him. "Tonight I wake dragons."

TWENTY-SIX

Moria lay in the long grass, watching two men at a night's campfire. They were dressed in drab clothing, blending with the endless brown of the steppes, but her eye caught almost-hidden ornamentation. Shimmering, jeweled rings. A bright-colored tunic under a cloak. Tasseled boots. Braids woven with golden thread. Not merchants themselves—their clothing was of inferior fabric and construction. These were the kind of men merchants loved, because they had money and no taste.

Both men bore swords, though—the dual swords of warriors.

"Mercenaries?" she whispered to Gavril, who was stretched out beside her.

"Imperial bounty hunters."

"What do they do?"

"Hunt bounties for the empire."

When she gave him a look, his lips twitched. Not mocking her outright. Nor calling her a fool. Gentle teasing instead. They'd been searching all day and into the night for the camp where Alvar might be keeping his shadow stalkers. While they'd passed settlements and hidden from two wagon trains, these were the first warriors they'd spotted.

Gavril's mood was not unlike what she remembered after a few days in the Wastes, when he'd begun to relax, to tease, and to talk. There were still snaps and snarls and glowers, yet that was Gavril, like the weather of the Wastes themselves—never what one would call easy, but the sunny patches almost made the storms worthwhile.

Gavril did occasionally sink into his grief, but it was quickly shaken off, which did not make it any less genuine. Sometimes, that was the only way to handle grief. One started falling into the pit, and then had to slingshot out of it and carry on. So it had been with Moria after her father's death, and so it was now with Gavril and his mother's.

"An imperial bounty is a price set on the head of a criminal," he continued. "These hunters try to collect it. Most are little different from mercenaries. If you see those forelocks, though? It marks them as an elite corps, permanently employed by the emperor."

"One would think an elite corps would dress better."

A soft chuckle. "True, but bounty hunters are a culture unto themselves, with their own rules and codes and, yes, manner of dress. They're hunters, so they need to blend in. Yet they're arrogant. The jewels and such advertise their success."

"Do you think they hunt for us? Toman sounded as if he expected a bounty, but it was not clear one existed. Would the emperor do that? Lay a bounty on our heads when we were declared traitors?"

"He'd likely have had no choice. Despite Toman's threats, though, I believe that Emperor Tatsu would have made it clear he wanted us alive—saying that we needed to answer for our crimes."

She nodded. "Thereby ensuring our safety as best he could."

Moria eyed the two. The one without rings looked only a few summers older than her. The other seemed a couple of decades older. A bounty hunter and his apprentice, she supposed.

She told Gavril her plan. He thought it mad. Naturally.

"Would you rather hunt for your father's camp while *we* are being hunted?" she asked.

He grumbled.

"All right," she said. "I'll take the older one, if he's too much—"

Gavril was off before she could finish.

Gavril crawled through the grass until he was about fifty paces from the campfire. Then, when neither man was looking directly his way, he rose and began walking toward them.

"Draw your blades and I'll draw mine." Gavril's voice echoed over the plain. "If you are imperial men of honor, you will rise and meet me as such, with your hands folded at your waist."

Neither moved. Gavril stopped. He wore his sleeveless

tunic, his cloak left with Moria, and his clan tattoos were on full display. Yet they were not as easily seen as others—black ink against dark skin, spots of green the only color.

Gavril raised his forearms and said, "I'd hope you would recognize the man you are hunting, even in the night, but shine your torches if that helps."

The two looked at each other, confused. Was it truly so difficult to identify Gavril? It was not as if the empire was filled with tall, green-eyed, dark-skinned, inked young warriors.

But they still apparently needed to shine their torches, and when they did, the young bounty hunter let out an oath.

"Gavril Kitsune?"

"You sound surprised."

"We—"

The older man shushed his apprentice with a look.

"Were you hoping to find my father out here?" Gavril said.

"Our target is our concern," the older man said. "But since you have foolishly presented yourself, we'll gladly accept you as an alternate. The bounty on you is as high as the one we sought." The man smiled, teeth flashing in the firelight. "And the public acclaim will be significantly higher."

They weren't hunting Alvar or Gavril then. Was it Moria herself? It didn't matter. They still needed to be dealt with.

"I wish to surrender," Gavril said.

The older man chuckled. "I don't blame you."

"I do not appreciate being mocked," Gavril said. "What-ever my father has done, it does not change the fact that I am a Kitsune and a warrior, and I expect to be treated as such. You will escort me back to the imperial city, where I will explain everything to the emperor. I will not be taken in chains or bound in any way. I am still—"

"Yes, yes, come along, boy. We'll treat you properly. Eat with us and then we'll head out. It's a four-day hard ride to the imperial city. I don't suppose you're hiding a horse out there."

"I am not, but I'm certain you'll lend me one until we can acquire another."

"Of course, my lord."

The moment Gavril got within striking distance, the older man drew. The younger hesitated, perhaps honestly thinking his master intended to accept Gavril's demands. By the time the older man had his sword out, Gavril's was slashing. The younger man drew his—but a dagger in his shoulder sent him staggering, his blade falling into the fire, sparks exploding.

Gavril and the older bounty hunter fought, their swords clanging. Moria had her other dagger raised, one eye on them and the other on the younger man, who was now trying to rescue his scorching-hot blade from the fire. When the young hunter drew his short sword instead, Moria launched her second dagger. The young man let out a cry, falling to his knees as he fumbled to pull the dagger from his back.

Gavril did not have Tyrus's skill, but he'd been the prince's sparring partner for a reason—he was a fine swordsman for his youth. The bounty hunter seemed a middling one for his age. So they were matched, which meant Moria had every intention of helping, should Gavril falter. This was not a bout for honor. But when the younger hunter fell, it startled his master enough for Gavril to get the upper hand. A perfect parry knocked the man's sword aside. A sword tip against the man's throat stopped him from going for it.

"Come out, Keeper," Gavril called. "You ought to watch the young one."

"Which is why I'm right here, Kitsune," she said, walking up behind him with her short sword drawn.

"It's true, then." The older man snorted. "I told you, boy. The Keeper is indeed this traitor's whore."

"Yes, yes," Moria said. "It's an old story and a dull one. Also untrue, but I'll save my breath and swallow the insult."

The younger man lifted his second blade, but unsteadily, one dagger still in his shoulder, the other on the ground, the end bloodied.

"If you ever intend to properly use your sword arm, you'll put that blade down and let me tend to your wounds," Moria said. "Although, I hear it doesn't take long to learn to fight as well with your left. Only a decade or so of practice."

The young man's gaze shot to his master.

"Don't you dare, boy," the older man growled. "There's a sword in your hand, and that is an imperial traitor. You have a duty here."

"But is it a duty worth losing your livelihood for?" Moria said. "Particularly if your injuries mean I'll be able to pluck that blade from your hand before you can swing it? Also, if I am not your prey, then you have no true duty to apprehend me."

"Don't listen to her, boy."

In the end, the young man did lunge, but it was half-hearted, and she dodged easily, grabbing her dagger from the ground and turning on him, the two facing off.

"We lay down our blades together," Moria said. "Then I will tend to your wounds."

"We have no intention of killing you," Gavril said. "We simply cannot afford to have two imperial bounty hunters out here with us. We will tend to your wounds, and then take your weapons and your supplies."

"Oh, in other words, let us die slowly instead of quick."

"We passed a settlement within a half-day's walk," Moria said. "Taking your supplies only gives you cause to head for them rather than pursue us. Now, boy, show us you're brighter than your master."

He pulled the second dagger out of his shoulder, wincing and tossing it aside. The man began cursing his apprentice with dire threats should he dare lay down his—

Moria and the young bounty hunter laid down their weapons. The older man dove for his sword, but Gavril saw that coming and kicked it aside.

"I do not wish to—" Gavril began.

The bounty hunter dove again—this time at the sword in the fire. He howled as his fingers touched the white-hot metal handle, but he kept his grip, leaping up and swinging the sword. Gavril countered it with his own blade.

"Do not make me—" Gavril began again.

"Die? Yes. I will make you die, boy. The emperor may want you alive, but I'm sure your head will suffice. Your head on a pole at the palace gates."

Moria eyed her daggers. Gavril was parrying the blows, but making no attempt to land one of his own.

"I think you are mistaken," Gavril said. "The people of

the empire would much prefer me alive. Executed as a traitor. A platform erected for me to commit ritual suicide before the crowd. *Then* my head put on a pole. I think that would quench the empire's thirst for vengeance far better."

The man laughed. "You'll say anything to avoid death, won't you? A coward, like your father. Do you honestly believe he was innocent of the charges against him? He was not. I was there. He withdrew from the field under cover of sorcery and left us to die. I saw it, boy, and you are as much a coward—"

The man charged then. Gavril went to parry, only to have nothing to parry, because the bounty hunter's sword swung the other way suddenly, heading for Gavril's neck. Moria lunged to knock Gavril aside, but he spun out of the way just in time. His own blade swung and the bounty hunter feinted . . . and a blow sliced clean through the man's forearm and into his chest. The man's arm fell. Then so did the man himself, gasping, wide-eyed, his severed arm pumping blood, more gushing from his side.

The younger bounty hunter bolted. Gavril followed. Moria grabbed both daggers and tore after them. Once Gavril saw she was coming, he circled back to deal with the other man.

Moria threw one dagger, aiming for the same shoulder she'd hit already. The dagger was still in flight when a dark shape shot from behind an outcropping of stunted trees. A black, four-legged shape running for the bounty hunter. Moria stumbled in her shock, Daigo's name on her lips. Her wildcat pounced at the same moment the dagger struck, and the young bounty hunter let out a scream of pain as he fell face-first to the ground. Daigo pinned him by the back of the neck.

"I'd say 'surprise,'" a voice called, "but someone ruined it for me."

Tyrus strolled out from behind the trees, walking toward her as casually as if they'd parted only moments ago.

TWENTY-SEVEN

Tyrus shot Moria a grin that made her heart somersault.

"Stealing my prey, are you?" he said. "I don't know who's worse. You or your wildcat."

Daigo growled. Tyrus walked over and stopped right in front of Moria, so close she could feel his breath on her upturned face.

"Hello," he said.

Then he bent and kissed her. A soft, sweet kiss that had her rising on her tiptoes to follow it as he straightened.

"I thought we should catch up," he said. "See how you were doing, if you needed our help. We'd have been faster, but, you know." He shrugged. "Dungeons. They're very inconvenient."

She laughed and kissed him again, her arms going around his neck in a brief, fierce hug.

"You can thank me for the rescue later," he said as she stepped back.

"Umm . . ."

"Not even going to pretend to cushion my ego, are you?"

"You came closer this time."

He sighed.

She smiled. "Given the number of times I seem to need rescue, think of them as practice drills. Eventually you'll succeed."

"You don't *need* rescue at all. That is the problem."

"Could someone please get this beast—" the fallen bounty hunter began.

"You did *find* me again," Moria said, ignoring the young man. "That's a feat."

"Y . . . yes. We did find you, didn't we, Daigo?"

The wildcat growled.

Tyrus continued. "We absolutely found you and did not accidentally stumble upon you while waiting for those bounty hunters to go to sleep so we could capture them. Absolutely not."

Moria laughed and kissed him again. "Do I presume you were their target then?"

"So it seems, though they're doing a very poor job of catching us considering we've been tracking them for half a day."

"Hello, Tyrus."

They looked to see Gavril there, his sword at his side, his face taut. Tyrus's gaze dropped to Gavril's blade.

"Do I need to draw mine as well?" he said, that jaunty tone evaporating from his voice.

"No, of course not." Gavril put his sword away. He looked at Moria. "The other one is dead. The blood loss was too much." When the younger bounty hunter groaned, he said, "We should tend to him."

He started toward the man. Then he stopped, turned slowly, and, his tone formal, said, "I am glad to see you are well, Tyrus."

Tyrus accepted the courtesy with a nod, and they walked to the bounty hunter. Moria hugged Daigo while Gavril stripped off their captive's cloak and tunic and Tyrus stood watch. Moria retrieved water from the campfire and set about cleaning and then cauterizing the man's wounds. The first step came with muffled grunts of pain. The second brought screams, and Gavril had to stuff a cloth in the man's mouth before everyone within a quarter-day's walk heard him.

When they finished, the bounty hunter passed out. They stood, staring down at him.

"Well, that's inconvenient," Tyrus said.

Daigo chuffed in agreement. Gavril opened his mouth, but Tyrus cut him off with, "We'll bind him while we talk. I'll use the other man's belt. Leave that gag in his mouth, too, so he doesn't wake screaming."

Tyrus walked back to the dead man. Gavril stared after him.

"He's changed," he murmured when Tyrus was out of ear-shot.

"He's had to."

Gavril nodded, his gaze lowering. "I am sorry he's become involved in this. We were friends. Yes, I've denied it. But we were."

"I know."

"I should have known he'd follow you into this. I could

206

tell . . . at the court . . . even on so short an acquaintance."

"He did not follow me, Gavril. He isn't a puppy."

A faint twist of a smile. "He used to be. That's what his father called him, when he trailed after me, letting me lead our adventures. He's not a puppy anymore. And you're right, Keeper—not a follower either. That is what I did not expect."

"He's an imperial prince. He knows how to lead. If you know him as well as you should, you know why he's never done so before."

Gavril nodded. "His brothers. Yes. I mean he's more adept than I would have expected. At leading. At fighting. At surviving. I can see why you care for him."

"I care for him because of who he is, Gavril. Not because he's a fine warrior."

"Who's a fine warrior?" Tyrus asked as he came back.

"Him." Moria pointed at the young bounty hunter.

Tyrus laughed. "I could tell. Good thing I didn't try to take him on myself. I might never have survived."

Belt in hand, he headed for the inept young bounty hunter. Daigo followed, growling.

"Yes, yes," Tyrus said, reaching to turn the young man over and bind him. "You're very brave around those who have lost consciousness and—"

The bounty hunter's hand shot out. He grabbed Tyrus by the tunic. Steel flashed. A thin dagger, from under the young man's clothes. Tyrus was already wrenching away, Daigo leaping on the bounty hunter to pin him. Gavril ran, sword out, Moria right behind him. She had her dagger poised, but Daigo was grappling with the bounty hunter, and she dared not throw it, for fear of hitting her wildcat.

The steel flashed again. That thin dagger headed straight for Daigo's throat. She launched hers. She had to. It was a moment too late, but Tyrus was not. His blade sliced into the young man's side an eyeblink before hers hit the bounty hunter's heart. As blood spurted from the boy's side, Tyrus wrenched out her dagger and slammed it in again, as deep as he could, giving the bounty hunter a quicker death.

Gavril and Moria stopped a couple of paces from the body. Tyrus pulled out the dagger, walked to the side, and cleaned it in the grass. When he handed it back to her, his hands shook. He noticed and gave Moria a rueful twist of a smile.

"It is not as easy as they make it seem in training," he said. "Taking a life."

"I don't think it ought to be."

He nodded, and she leaned against him, his hand going to her hip as he gave a shuddering breath. Then he pulled back, straightened, and looked about, still regaining his composure.

"I'll say a few words for both of their spirits," she said. "I'm not sure it works, coming from me . . ."

He squeezed her arm. "Thank you."

Gavril's swords clicked, and they turned to see him kneeling beside the young bounty hunter. He took the thin dagger from where it had fallen and examined the blade. It was needle-thin and seemed as if it would fold on impact, but when he tested the blade, it didn't bend.

"It's a stiletto," Tyrus said.

Gavril frowned at the unfamiliar word.

"I've read of them," Moria said. "They're foreign. From

beyond the empire. Very rare. They're also known as assassin's daggers."

Tyrus nodded. "An imperial bounty hunter ought not to be carrying one. Which is no excuse for me nearly losing Daigo's life to the trick. Particularly after he tried to warn me." He turned to the wildcat. "My apologies."

Daigo swished his thick tail against the prince, his way of saying the apology was accepted.

"While warriors cannot carry hidden weapons . . ." Tyrus held it out to Moria.

"Thank you," she said. As she accepted, she recalled taking another dagger from a dead warrior—Orbec, back in the Forest of the Dead. While her intention had been to return the ancestral blade to his family—which she had—she'd still felt guilty taking it from his body. Now, even with no such purpose, she did not. She regretted the young man's death. It was senseless. Foolish, too, given that they'd tended to his wounds and obviously did not wish him ill. But he'd made his choice, and if his weapon could aid her, she would take it.

"We ought to go now," Tyrus said. "Say your words for the dead, please, Moria, while Gavril and I take what we can from their supplies."

TWENTY-EIGHT

s they walked, they told their stories of what had transpired since they'd parted outside Lord Okami's compound. Moria asked Tyrus to speak first. Their tale would end with the death of Kiri Kitsune, and Gavril didn't need to revisit that any sooner than necessary.

Tyrus had been held under guard at Goro Okami's compound, while his father had returned to the imperial city. His captivity had lasted only until he'd heard that the emperor's spy had reported Moria and Gavril had never arrived at Alvar Kitsune's compound.

Escape hadn't been difficult. Tyrus may have joked about dungeons, but it was simply house arrest, Lord Okami having presumed that once Tyrus calmed down, he'd see the futility of following Moria. Tyrus and Daigo had escaped and found the place where Sabre had reported meeting up with Moria and Gavril.

"We discovered the remains of your camp, along with signs of a wagon train heading up to it and then retreating north. Presumably you'd been taken captive. We followed the wagon as best we could, but your wildcat needs tracking lessons, Moria."

Daigo fixed Tyrus with a baleful look.

"Yes, I know," Tyrus said. "You aren't a hound or a hunting cat, but you could try harder. It's never too late to learn new skills."

Daigo growled and laid his head against Moria's leg as they walked. That was usually something only Tova would do with Ashyn, Moria and Daigo being less overt in their affections. But tonight he stayed close, and she rubbed him and scratched his ears and felt one hollow part inside her fill again.

"We lost the trail completely this morning," Tyrus said. "Your wagon must have ridden over hard ground, and we could no longer track it. I knew exactly where I was, but your wildcat got hopelessly lost."

Daigo rolled his eyes and flicked his tail at Tyrus, who laughed. Moria saw Gavril watching them. In their days together on the Wastes and beyond, Daigo had gone from barely tolerating Gavril to grudgingly accepting his companionship, a far cry from the easy camaraderie Daigo had with Tyrus.

"That's when we found the bounty hunters," Tyrus continued. "We overheard enough to realize they were looking for me, so we planned to attack under cover of night. If we'd seen their poor fighting skills, we could have struck sooner. But then we'd never have found you, so . . ." He smiled at her. "It all worked out."

"It did."

"Now tell me your story."

Moria explained that their captors had said they'd only stumbled upon them, when they'd actually been in pursuit of Kiri Kitsune.

"Your mother's out here?" Tyrus said to Gavril. He caught the young warrior's expression. "Gavril?" He turned quickly to Moria. "What—?"

"My mother is no more," Gavril said. "I will . . . I'll let Moria explain. She's . . . better at such things. I should—I should check over that rise ahead." He strode onward before either could speak.

Moria told Tyrus what had happened. With each word, the horror on his face grew. When she finished, he jogged ahead to Gavril.

"I am deeply, deeply sorry," Moria heard him say.

"Thank you," Gavril replied. "And I know your father did not do this, though you're refraining from saying so."

"I do not wish to belittle your loss by defending him, but I'm glad you do not suspect him of it. My father is capable of many things, some of them cruel and even callous, but—"

"If he took my mother, he would do much as Lord Okami did with you. House arrest. Even if he felt he had to make a stronger statement, he would never have killed her and certainly not in such a fashion. Someone did this to frame him, in the expectation that others would not realize he isn't capable of such monstrosity."

"Thank you for understanding that."

"I understand much," Gavril said, his gaze dropping to his still-bloodied blade. "I always did. I simply did not wish to."

***

With that, silence descended, and as it grew, the strain between Gavril and Tyrus returned, like a metal bar that kept them together yet apart. They walked within a few paces of each other but said nothing. What had happened outside Lord Okami's compound was not easily overcome. Moria knew that, for Tyrus, learning Gavril had held her captive had been a greater betrayal than anything that had come before it.

Yet Tyrus didn't seem entirely comfortable with her either. He'd seemed to be, when they'd first met, with his smiles and kisses. But now he seemed anxious, walking close enough to brush her hand with his, but never taking it. He kept looking over at her, as if trying to work something out. When they finally stopped for the night, Tyrus asked Gavril if he'd make camp while Tyrus and Moria found water.

They walked until they reached a stream and filled their waterskins. As Moria rose, she nearly bashed into Tyrus, standing right beside her with an oddly guarded expression on his face.

"Something's wrong," she said.

He started to shake his head. Then he stopped and cleared his throat. "I need to know . . . That is, I ought to ask . . ." He looked back toward camp and went quiet.

"Tyrus . . . ?"

"Has it changed?" he blurted.

"Has what changed?"

She followed his gaze to see Gavril setting up the bounty hunters' tent. "Are you asking . . . ?"

"The first time you kissed me, I said I could not be with you, no matter how much I wanted to. Not until I was sure of how you felt about him."

"And I told you—"

"You told me there was nothing between you. Not that way. But I worried that if he somehow had an excuse for his betrayal, things would change." He looked at her. "I presume he's given an explanation."

"He has, insomuch as I wished to hear it. I am satisfied that the massacre of my village was as great a shock to him as it was to me. As for the rest, I will hear more when I'm ready, but I accept his explanation. I will not say that I have forgiven him. But I no longer plan to kill him as soon as I get the chance."

She said the last with a smile, but Tyrus stood there, holding himself tight, that wary look in his eyes only growing, as if braced for the worst.

"And so . . ." he said.

"If anything had changed, do you truly think I'd have greeted you with kisses?"

"It was spontaneous. Perhaps—"

She kissed him. Deep and long and passionate enough to leave him staggering back when she pulled away.

"That was also spontaneous," she said. "But if you think I would kiss you that way if my relationship with Gavril had changed—"

He cut her off with a kiss, even deeper than her own, his hands in her hair, his body against hers, heat licking through her until he left her gasping.

"That was my apology," he said.

"Then I certainly hope you make more mistakes that require them."

He laughed, pulling her into a fierce embrace. When they parted, she pushed her cloak over her shoulder and laid his hand on the amulet band.

"I make up my mind, Tyrus, and I do not change it, and if you are going to question my loyalty every time we are apart . . ."

"I'm truly, *deeply* sorry," he said. "If it had been anyone else, I would not have questioned."

"There has never been anything between Gavril and me."

"I know, but . . ."

"Not a look. Not a word. Not a touch. Nor ever a time when I longed for one."

"Yet there is a bond between you. I saw it from the moment we met, and even if you did not think of him in that way, I cannot help feeling that could have changed, that if the possibility had been there . . ."

"It was not."

"But if it had been—" He cut off his own words, kissing her. "No, that isn't a question. Or if it is, I'll not ask it, because it does not matter. The possibility is no longer there. That is what counts. He is your friend. I am your lover. That is enough. More than enough. It's all I want, Moria, and I apologize for the rest. It'll not happen again."

"Good." She looked him in the eye. "I'll never give you any reason to question my loyalty, Tyrus. I expect the same from you."

"You have it. Without question."

She nodded and began to take off his amulet band. He put his hand on hers. "Keep it."

"No, it's—"

"Yours. For as long as I am. When you tire of me, you can give it back."

"Then I don't imagine I ever would."

He pressed his lips to hers. "I'll not argue with that. Now, it looks like Gavril has that tent ready. It's yours for the night."

"I ought not to take—"

"I insist. And I am still a prince, so you must listen. Or at least pretend to." He took her hands and pulled her to him. "If I were to join you—"

"Yes."

He chuckled. "You didn't let me finish."

"It's still yes."

"I was going to qualify that by stating my intentions before I shocked you with the suggestion. But I forgot who I'm speaking to."

"You did. It's yes. And please."

His smile evaporated in a look that sent a shiver through her. Then he pulled her to him and gave her a kiss that made her think they weren't going to make it back to the tent at all.

"Don't tempt me, Moria. I'm going to be honorable."

"Blast it."

He laughed then, loud enough to ring out over the empty plain. "I was going to ask if I might share your tent without the expectation of anything that might normally come with sharing your tent." When she opened her mouth to protest, he put a finger to her lips. "I know you're curious, but I'll not take advantage of that, and I'll not rush." His mouth moved to her ear. "Or you might discover that my experience with girls is not quite as extensive as my reputation suggests. Though I'll trust you to keep that between us."

"Of course."

"Good. Then you will allow me to proceed slowly and explore . . ."

"Yes. Please."

He grinned. "All right. You get the idea then. I'll share your tent with no expectation of anything. And if you wish, more, though I'll do nothing that could leave you with child."

"I know how babies are made. And I know that precautions can be taken to prevent that, though I suspect we wouldn't have such devices on hand. Unless you carry them around with you."

"Did I mention there might be a discrepancy between my experience and my reputation? I most certainly do not carry any such thing with me. Which means we have the perfect excuse for limiting our nights to—"

"Yes. Now can we stop talking and get to the tent?"

He grinned and led her back.

TWENTY-NINE

Gavril was laying out his sleeping blanket at the campsite.

"Moria will take the tent," Tyrus said.

"As I presumed."

"And I will be bidding her good night. Go ahead and get some sleep." He looked at the proximity between the tent and Gavril's sleeping blanket. "Perhaps you should move to the other side of the fire. The wind seems to be shifting, and you don't want to sleep with a face full of smoke."

"I will," Gavril said. "But I'll not be sleeping yet. After you've spoken to Moria, I'd like to talk to you."

"I . . ." Tyrus glanced at Moria. "I'm rather tired."

"I will be brief. I will rest better if we speak."

Tyrus's shoulders slumped. Moria could see the struggle in his face, wanting to do the right thing . . . and yet truly not wanting to do it, not at this moment.

"Could it possibly wait?" Tyrus began.

"No," Moria said quickly. "Go and speak now. You can say good night to me later."

He took her aside and whispered, "Are you certain? I would truly rather . . ."

"I should certainly hope so," she said. "But *I* would truly rather have your full attention."

"You shall. I'll keep this as brief as possible." He kissed her cheek and headed off with Gavril.

When Moria first climbed into her sleeping blankets, she congratulated herself on being so selfless, insisting Tyrus speak to Gavril before she got her time with him. As she lay there, though, she began to worry about what Gavril would say. No, she knew what he'd say—an explanation. The question was how Tyrus would react. He'd want to forgive Gavril. It was in his nature, because deep down he still considered him a friend. What if Tyrus couldn't forgive him? What if he returned preoccupied by what Gavril had said?

Could she change his mood if that happened? Distract him from his thoughts with kisses and . . . other things? That would be much easier if she knew what "other things" were. There were kisses and there was sexual congress. That was the extent of her understanding, in spite of all her efforts to expand her knowledge. The furthest she'd ever gone past kissing was with Levi in Edgewood, and that was only rather awkward groping, and entirely one-sided, as he'd grab her breasts and arse through her clothing, rough squeezes that suggested he knew no more than she did.

It was very vexing, to be so ill-informed. There were books, Ashyn had said, blushing madly as she'd admitted to hearing of such things. But they were not to be found in Edgewood. Nor with any of the traders—Moria always checked. Was one expected to simply wait for a lover to demonstrate? And what if neither knew more, like her and Levi?

Moria had explored her own body, but that was no less frustrating. It felt good and yet, she had the feeling she was trying to get somewhere she could not quite reach. An itch she couldn't scratch, and those explorations left her overheated and feeling rather thwarted.

From Tyrus's hint, she suspected answers were coming. If he was not overly distracted. She could try to refocus his thoughts. Disrobing would help, although, personally, she'd rather disrobe him. But what if she disrobed, and he didn't refocus? That would be a humiliation beyond bearing.

No, the proper thing to do, if he came back distracted, was to remind herself that there would be other nights and to talk to him about Gavril instead. Moria sighed. Sometimes doing the right thing was not nearly as easy as one might think. Which was perhaps why people did the wrong things so often.

Finally, the flap on the tent opened.

"Out you go, Daigo," Tyrus said.

The wildcat growled.

"Someone needs to stand guard."

Daigo sniffed but slunk out of the tent. Tyrus fastened the flap. Then he opened the one on the roof, letting moonlight stream through. Moria studied his face, but the angle left it in shadow. He deposited his cloak by the door and lowered himself to the sleeping pallet, staying atop the blanket, which seemed a bad sign, but then he kissed her, and while he kept it light, it was as sweet and heartfelt as any kiss that came before it.

"Did he . . . explain?" she whispered.

"He did, and it is a lot to think about, but I'm not going to do so tonight."

When she hesitated, he stroked her cheek. "It's fine, Moria. I understand what he did, and while I do not think he always made the right choices, he made the choices that I would expect of him. He tried to keep his honor. He knows he did not, and that burns most of all, and that absolves him most of all, to me. The friend I knew has not changed, however much he may think he has. He is still as difficult and as exasperating and as wrongheaded as ever. But as idealistic and, yes, as honorable, too. That is all I needed to know. That he made mistakes, and he owns them. That many of those mistakes were a choice between two evils, and the other was no better."

He looked down at her. "Can I stop talking now?"

"Please."

"Do I need to ask if you've changed your mind about—"

She answered by pulling him into a kiss. Soon he was under the blanket with her, just kissing, and Moria decided that while kissing standing up was all very well and fine, kissing horizontally was an entirely different thing. It was body against body, hands in hair, legs entwined, deep and hungry kisses that seemed to go on forever. Even the position changed, and with each new configuration, there was some new sensation to delight in. Tyrus on top, the weight of his body on hers.

Moria on top, straddling him and discovering . . . Well, discovering something to rub against, something that sent waves of pleasure through her and made him gasp and push against her until he stopped abruptly and lifted her off to lay beside him.

"We ought to slow down," he said.

"Why?"

"Because otherwise, this will be finished very quickly. Or my part will, and though that won't affect my willingness to complete yours, it will change the tenor of things."

"Why?"

He chuckled and seemed ready to brush off the question with a joke or some opaque explanation. Then he saw her expression, sobered, and explained in detail and seriousness. While Moria understood the basic act of sexual congress, it appeared that significant and important details had been left out.

"Yes," she said. "We'll slow down then. And thank you for explaining."

He kissed her. "I will explain anything you want, Moria. If I dodge a question, make me answer. I am simply not accustomed to discussing such things."

"You make a very good teacher."

"It helps to have an eager student."

"I *am* eager."

He pulled her back to him. "So am I. Yet if I do anything you decide you do not want, stop me."

"I will."

The kissing started again, slower this time. They were pacing themselves, embracing but no longer entwined. His hands slid under her tunic, carefully, growing more confident when she sighed in pleasure as his fingers touched her bare skin. His hands slid over her stomach and sides, gradually making their way up to her chest, and when they found their goal, the difference between Levi's groping and Tyrus's touch . . . ? It was like the difference between fouled water and honey wine.

It was . . . incredible. There was no other word for it. His hands on her, exploring and touching and finding every spot that made her sigh and gasp and moan. That a simple touch could make her feel that way seemed beyond imagining. The heat she'd felt in her own exploration mounted to a fever pitch and then . . . And then . . . There were no words for the rest.

Afterward, kissing and embracing and whispering, and then feeling him against her, and whispering, "I don't know how . . ." and letting him show her. And that was almost as wonderful as her own pleasure, watching his face, hearing his sighs and moans and gasps, and bringing him to the same place she'd been and taking him over the edge, leaving him shuddering and holding her, face buried in her hair, telling her how wonderful she was, how she was everything he wanted.

And then, remarkably, there was still more for her. It seemed that her "end" was not as final as his and he took her back there, and when he was done, they fell into exhausted sleep, curled up together.

Moria woke to a sound from outside the tent. Or so it seemed, but all was silent and she could see Daigo's dark form at the door, meaning nothing was amiss. Tyrus still had his arms around her, seeming too tired even to shift in sleep. She kissed his lips and nuzzled against him, but lightly, trying not to wake him. While there was some temptation to do exactly that, it was more curiosity than physical need. Her body was satiated and content. Her mind was still open to more exploration. Was it all right to touch and explore when one's lover was asleep and unable to give permission? Likely not. She'd have to broach the subject with him.

Daigo scratched at the tent flap. She opened the tent to see him gazing into the predawn night. She could make out a figure and she tensed, ready to grab her dagger and warn Gavril. Then she looked to see no sign of his sleeping pallet and realized the figure was him. His back was to them. She squinted into the sky. While she could make out streaks of light at the horizon, and they'd walked half the night, he ought not to be up and about yet. Especially with his sleeping gear.

She took her daggers and donned her cloak. After one glance at Tyrus, who'd fallen back into deep sleep, she hurried off after Gavril, Daigo following.

She caught up with him in only a few running strides. He seemed in no hurry, trudging even. When he heard her coming, he turned. He said nothing, but waited for her to catch up.

"Where are you going?" she asked.

"I . . ." He hefted his pack and glanced away.

"You're leaving? Without a word?"

"I left a note."

"All right then. Let's return to the first part. You're leaving?"

"I . . . thought it might be best. Tyrus is here and you do not need a guard."

"I don't ever need a guard, Kitsune."

"I misspoke. You now have a companion for your journey, someone to fight at your side. And so does he. You are both in good hands. The best possible hands."

"Forgive me, but I was under the impression that we were pursuing a shared goal."

"I thought it might be wise for us to part. Each time we are seen together, it only lends credence to the rumors."

"I do not care about the rumors."

"It is not only about you, Keeper. If Tyrus and I were found together, it would damage his claims to innocence. It would appear he was not merely duped by us but complicit in our betrayal of the empire."

"We have no say in that decision? Despite the fact that it is about us?"

"How does that help, Keeper?" His quiet voice gave way to his usual impatient snap. "If I ask your opinion, you will be bound to tell me I'm welcome to stay."

"I am not bound by any such thing."

"Tyrus then. He will feel honor bound by our past friendship to stand by me."

"Then let me answer for him, having spoken to him before he fell asleep in my tent. If he woke up to find you gone, he would feel as if you have turned your back on him, as if you are saying in the clearest possible way that you are no longer friends, that such a thing is no longer possible, and that you do not even wish to be his ally or his companion."

"That is not—"

"I would feel the same. There's no reason for you to leave, and doing so only complicates matters. He would need to decide whether we should leave you be, as you seem to wish, or go after you to watch your back, only to risk being rebuffed again. If you wish to make amends with Tyrus, you do not do it by slinking off in the night."

"I was not slinking."

"You were and it doesn't suit you."

He seemed inclined to argue, but after a moment, said only, "In my defense, I was still considering, and probably would not have gotten far before I returned."

"Good, but the fact that you considered it at all tells me you're unsettled by more than Tyrus's arrival. Obviously, what happened the other day—"

"I'm fine."

"If you wished to talk about it . . ."

"I'm fine."

"All right then. I'll leave you alone."

She started back for camp. After she'd gone about five steps, he called, "Keeper?"

When she turned, he strode over. "Perhaps I would like to speak of it. Briefly. If you aren't tired."

"I'm not. Let's walk."

THIRTY

The next day, Moria said nothing about Gavril's attempt to leave. By the time they'd finished talking last night, he'd been quite embarrassed about the whole thing and agreed that, yes, lingering grief over his mother had caused him to react foolishly to the new travel configuration.

They spent most of the day walking companionably, as quiet conversation turned to lighthearted storytelling and heated debates. Of course, they did not forget they weren't merely strolling through the steppes. They were still hunting for Alvar's camp. They'd decided that, having not seen a shadow stalker since the previous afternoon, they'd either encountered all who had escaped or they were headed in the wrong direction. Since the latter seemed more likely, they changed course. After a half-day's walk they found an empty shadow stalker corpse. The man was not one of the bandits. Nor was he dressed as if he'd come from Edgewood or Fairview. He was perhaps in his fifth decade. His coloring suggested he was native to the steppes, and his bag contained items that had clearly come from the bandit's wagon, meaning he'd happened upon it and helped himself to the abandoned goods. They found another corpse—a woman around the same age—also carrying a satchel of stolen items. She had not been turned into a shadow stalker, but rather set upon by the man, likely her husband.

Moria said a few words for the dead, primarily to ease Gavril's grief. If she'd spoken the words of passing for his mother, but did so for no one else, then it would suggest she did not honestly believe them useful. Tyrus didn't question it, only lowered his head and spoke a few pious words to the ancestors himself, bidding the spirits safe passage to the second world.

As they set out again, Daigo found blood on the ground. A trail of it. They followed it for quite a distance. Daigo could not track well, but his nose was still better than theirs and he did a decent job of it. They walked some ways before they heard moaning. They fanned out, trying to find an angle to see from. With the long grass and flat land, it wasn't easy, and they all ended up within a few paces of the sound before Moria lifted a finger, motioning that she could see the source.

It was a young man, similar to the couple in both dress and appearance. Their son, she supposed. He lay in the grass, clutching his stomach and groaning. Daigo left Moria's side and slunk forward, crouching to stay hidden in the long grass, but his black fur was still visible, and the young man let out a cry on seeing him. He did not, however, leap up, and that was what they needed to know. All three converged on the spot.

"I . . . I have nothing," the young man said, his words coming with difficulty. "You may check. I have nothing of value."

"Are your local bandits often dressed and armed as imperial warriors?" Tyrus asked.

The young man lifted his head and took in Tyrus's face and blades. Then he glanced at Gavril. Moria slipped her daggers under her cloak and waved for Daigo to stay hidden.

"I—I'm sorry, my lords. I did not realize."

"You've been injured," Tyrus said. "Fortunately, my companion is skilled in battle medicine."

"I wouldn't say skilled," Moria murmured as she walked up beside him.

Tyrus gave her a look that said it was best if the young man didn't realize that. Hope was as important as medicine in recovering from injury.

Moria moved toward the young man. Gavril tensed and gripped his sword, his gaze on the injured man as if expecting him to leap up like the young bounty hunter. Moria knelt beside him and stripped off her cloak.

"Show me where you are hurt," she said. "I can see blood . . ."

It was his stomach. She winced at that. A wound to the gut was beyond her skill. Yet he had traveled far before collapsing, and that was a good sign. When he peeled back his blood-sodden tunic, there appeared to be five deep cuts, the edges ragged. Shadow stalker claws.

"I can clean and cauterize the wounds," she said. She glanced at Gavril, and he nodded to say that he would add

229

his healing magics. Moria said, "Tell us what happened while I work," giving Gavril the chance to kneel behind the young man and begin casting unnoticed.

The young man's story began as they expected. He'd been with his parents, on horseback it seemed, returning from market in a distant town and heading to their farm. They'd happened upon the bodies and then the wagon. His mother had been frightened by the deformities they'd seen on the dead wagon driver, but his father insisted it was simply caused by the trampling.

They had helped themselves to the goods left in the wagon storage.

"For safekeeping, my lords," the young man said. "We do have bandits out here, and we would not wish them to strip the goods from those poor travelers."

"We do not require an explanation," Tyrus said. "We trust your intentions were honorable. Continue."

They had finished removing the goods when a "smoke" came over his father.

"A spirit, it must have been," the young man said. "The lost and enraged spirit of one of those poor travelers. It possessed him and . . ."

And the thing that had been his father had turned on his mother, and her son had been powerless to pull the creature off. Then it had sunk one clawed hand into his gut, and it could have finished him off, but the "spirit" left his father in a whirl of black smoke. The young man fell, unconscious from the pain and shock. When he woke, he was alone with his parents' bodies.

"My father's true spirit had remained in that creature," he said. "He cast it out and saved me."

Moria did not disillusion him, but she suspected the shadow stalker had realized the young man made a far better vessel. Either it could not make the leap into him or it had discovered the injury it had inflicted had ruined that vessel. Either way, the young man had awoken alone, the horses long gone. He'd started for home, but became weak and disoriented, and ultimately fell.

"Is your home near?" Tyrus asked.

"It is, my lord, and if there is any way of your accompanying me there, I would gladly offer you all of our meagre hospitality. Your horses are nearby, I presume."

Tyrus gave a grunt that the young man could interpret as a yes if he wished.

"We'll need to cauterize the wound," Moria said. She looked over at Gavril. He'd finished his healing magics and moved off to use sorcery to start a fire a short distance away. He put his dagger into the flame, to heat it.

"You will likely pass out from the pain," Tyrus said. "But we will carry you home. Can you provide directions?"

When he did, they realized it was not "near" at all, and there was no way they could carry him so far.

"What other settlements are close by? Any that might have a healer?"

"There is a . . ." He glanced between the two warriors. "My family is well aware of imperial law and would do nothing to break it."

Gavril tapped his leg with impatience, but Tyrus spoke, his

voice low and soothing. "I know that the steppes are home to many unusual communities. Religious groups, bandits, smugglers . . . The emperor understands that reporting suspicions of criminal activity can be a dangerous undertaking and so he does not expect it."

"It is . . . none of those. I mean to say that we do not know exactly what it is, of course, but there are rumors, and my parents had every intention of reporting the matter as soon as we saw an imperial warrior, which is a rare occurrence in these parts . . ."

He blathered for a few moments longer. Gavril and Moria shared eye rolls, but Tyrus heard him out and then said, "Slavers."

The young man stiffened. Moria and Gavril did, too. Bandits and smugglers were one thing. But slavers? It was indeed the duty of every citizen to report those engaged in human trafficking.

The young man babbled more about how he and his parents had no proof, and how they'd been awaiting proof—along with a convenient, passing imperial representative.

"How recent is this camp?" Tyrus asked.

"Very recent," the young man said. "Less than a moon. I truly know very little of it, but I did hear word from someone who traded with them that they had healers. Several of them."

Sorcerers more likely, as it certainly sounded like the shadow stalker camp. Tyrus asked the young man for directions and got them. Then Gavril returned to the fire to reheat his blade.

"We cannot take you to a slaver encampment," Tyrus said.

"It would be unsafe. Rather, we will bring aid to you. From there or elsewhere. We will ensure you're safely hidden with food and water and, if you are correct about the distance, we'll be back by sunrise."

The young man nodded. His gaze was fixed on Gavril, who was returning with the red-hot blade, and he seemed to pay little mind to Tyrus's words. As Gavril approached, the young man dug his fingers into the dirt, pulling himself backward.

"Is this necess—?"

"It is," Gavril said, and put the blade against the young man's stomach wounds as Moria and Tyrus each grabbed an arm to hold him still. The young man screamed. Moria was ready with a scrap of cloth to shove in his mouth. Then his screams took on a note that had her hackles rising and Daigo charging back from his prowling, letting out a yowl himself, and as he did, Moria felt a familiar dread, one she now recognized. She shouted, "Begone!"

Tyrus looked over in shock, but Gavril was already reacting, his blade at the young man's throat. Too late he seemed to realize it was his heated dagger rather than his sword. The red-hot steel hit the young man's throat, and he let out the most horrible, inhuman scream. A familiar scream, though—or it was to Moria and Gavril.

Tyrus had recovered, and even if he had no idea what was going on, he leaped up, bringing his foot to the young man's chest, pinning him and pulling his blade. But before he could get it clear, the young man grabbed Tyrus's boot and, with a heave of superhuman strength, sent him flying backward.

That's when the young man's face began to change, to contort into the twisted visage of a shadow stalker.

"Begone!" Moria shouted.

Gavril swung at the creature with his sword. The thing reached out to stop the blade and it cut right through its clawed hand. Blood spurted, yet the shadow stalker seemed not even to notice. It was lunging for Tyrus, who was on his feet. Tyrus's blade cleaved halfway through the creature's torso, but the thing only pulled itself free.

It leaped at Tyrus, as if unharmed, and Moria saw Tyrus's blade in flight and saw Gavril's, too, and Daigo leaping, and she knew it would do no good, that they could hack and claw and rip and the thing would keep coming. She repeated her command, pouring all her rage and fear into it, and finally the black smoke surged from the young man's body, and she started to heave a sigh of relief. Then the smoke shot toward Tyrus.

"No!" she screamed. "Begone!" She rushed at it, and she shouted for it to begone, and the smoke turned on her and everything seemed to stop. Dimly, she could hear Daigo's snarling yowl and Tyrus's shout of "Moria!" and Gavril's "No!" But their voices seemed to come from so far, as she stood, transfixed by the black smoke. By what she saw in the smoke. Faces. Human faces, contorted in agony and blind animal terror. Then she heard voices, coming clearer than Tyrus's or Gavril's. Whispers and whimpers and cries.

Keeper.

Help us.

Goddess, please.

Keeper, please.

234

Stop it.

Please stop it.

Keeper, please.

"I set you free," she said. "By the ancestors and the goddess, I set you free of this curse and I bid you peace and safe passage."

The smoke hovered there. It made no move to come closer, just writhed and twisted, the faces writhing and twisting within it. She kept saying the words, feeling them, opening herself up to the spirits' pain, and sincerely and fervently wishing the spirits peace and safe passage. The black smoke gathered on itself, as if the magics were resisting her, but she kept repeating the words of peace and freedom and, finally, of forgiveness. For whatever these spirits had done. She poured all of her power and all of her strength into that, granting them forgiveness and beseeching the goddess to do the same.

That's when the smoke exploded. Burst apart into a thousand particles of black dust that scattered in every direction.

A voice whispered past her ear, *Thank you, Keeper.* And then they were gone . . . and Moria collapsed to the ground.

THIRTY-ONE

Moria woke to Tyrus desperately trying to rouse her, his voice sharp with panic, his face above hers, Daigo pushed in right beside it.

"Tired," she said. "So . . ." She couldn't even get the rest out. Exhaustion threatened to pull her back under, and her eyelids flagged. "Sleep."

"Does anything hurt? Do you feel anything?"

"Just tired."

"She doesn't show any outward signs of trauma." Gavril's voice came from somewhere behind Tyrus. "Her heartbeat is strong and her breathing seems—"

"How do you *feel*, Moria?" Tyrus said, cutting Gavril short with an uncharacteristically sharp look his way.

"Just tired. Give me a moment. I'll be . . ."

She drifted off before she could finish. When she woke again, she was curled up with Daigo, Tyrus right there, anxiously crouched beside them. She barely had time to open her eyes before he was pushing a waterskin to her lips.

"How do you feel now?"

"Better."

"Drink. There's dried fish here. Whatever happened, it drained your energy. You need to get it back."

"Yes, your highness." She favored him with a smile and pushed to sit up, then drank and ate as he hovered and Daigo paced. The other member of their party was nowhere to be seen.

"Is Gavril . . . ?" She looked around.

Tyrus waved impatiently. "Somewhere. He did his healing magics and then wandered off. He's not much of a nursemaid."

"Eager for me to snap out of it so we can get back on the trail."

"No, just . . ." Another wave, and he said, "Gavril," as if that explained all. Which it did. "Can you tell me what happened?"

She did, finishing with, "The stories of shadow stalkers aren't like those of fiend dogs or other twisted spirits. They don't say *what* those spirits are—the vengeful dead, the angry dead, the lost dead, the traitorous dead. They are simply described as spirits, turned into shadow stalkers by sorcerer magics. I think that's because it's exactly what they are. Not twisted spirits. Simply spirits."

"Many spirits," Tyrus said. "Bound together with terrible magics."

She nodded. "They may think they've done something to deserve their fate, but I don't believe they have. Not truly. It's like when something terrible befalls an innocent person and they search for some way they have offended the ancestors or the goddess."

"When they haven't. No more than anyone does, in everyday life." He looked over her head. "Is she right? Her theory?"

"I have no idea," Gavril said, and Moria turned to see him approaching. "As I've told Moria, my father doesn't discuss the sorcery for shadow stalkers with me. The point is simply that we may finally have a way to expel them—permanently. Which will be useful if we ever get to that camp."

She looked at Tyrus. "I told you he was getting impatient."

"No," Gavril said. "I'm merely suggesting that if you are feeling up to it . . ."

"Yes, yes," she said. "You wish to get moving. And so we will."

They found the three horses that the dead family had ridden, and Tyrus declared that if the horses balked, then the goddess did not favor their endeavor. When the horses came easily, he took it as a divine sign. Or at least a reasonable excuse.

The horses were excellent steeds, and Moria decided that when she got one of her own, she would like a steppes horse. They were neither as large nor as sleek as imperial horses, but the shaggy beasts were sturdy and sure-footed. They had a mind of their own, and Gavril grumbled when his mount exercised it, but Moria rather admired this trait in a beast. Yes, she would have a steppes horse for riding and exploring the world. Once she had time to ride and explore the world. If she lived long enough to ride and explore the world.

They followed the landmarks the young man had given, and before dusk, they spotted the encampment. The steppes seemed an odd place to hide, given the open land, yet the barrenness and lack of road meant only locals would come this way, and Tyrus doubted they'd turn in the supposed slavers. He said he wouldn't be surprised to learn the locals had been trading with them.

They found a place for the horses to drink and graze and left them there. Then, as the sun dropped, they surveyed the situation.

The camp was quite literally in the middle of nowhere. Meaning sneaking up was nearly impossible. No rises to hide behind. No trees to climb. The occupants had even cut down the long grass in a wide swatch surrounding the camp. There weren't, however, any obvious guards posted beyond the low fence.

"The sun has dropped low enough that I can slip through the grass," Gavril said. "I cannot get close enough to see past the fence, but I'll be able to hear inside, and ascertain the likelihood it contains shadow stalkers."

"Can your sorcery detect them?" she asked.

"I mean I can listen for them."

"They don't make any sound unless they're screaming."

"Yes, Keeper, that is the point. If I hear nothing, then I will know it is shadow stalkers."

"Why? If it was slaves instead, would they be allowed to roam freely? Talk among themselves? Plan their mutiny?"

He gave her a hard look.

"As much as I'd prefer to stay out of your bickering," Tyrus said, "Moria has a point. Slaves are kept bound and gagged until they reach their destination beyond our borders."

"Thank you. Now, Kitsune, if you have no magics for detecting shadow stalkers, might I remind you that I *can* detect them."

"You didn't notice the one hiding in that boy."

It was her turn to give him a hard look. "Because it was *hiding*. As soon as it manifested, I sensed it."

"Yes, and as soon as it manifested, I *saw* it. And you cannot get close enough to detect them because you glow in the dark like a lantern, Keeper."

She pulled up her hood. He reached out and tugged a lock of her pale hair. She scowled and stuffed it in.

"I am still better suited for sneaking up at night," he said.

"Through this grass?" She shook a handful of the golden stalks. "That boy spotted Daigo coming before he spotted us."

"Again, Moria has a point," Tyrus said. "You are too dark for this task, Gavril." Gavril opened his mouth to protest as Moria shot him a satisfied look. "And Moria is too pale."

"What?" she said.

"The mission, then, goes to the one who can best blend with the grass. Which would be me." He shucked his cloak. "Thank you both for pointing that out. Now, if you insist on following me part of the way to watch my back, I will not argue. However, I'll ask that you refrain from bickering. I know that will be difficult, but it does get rather loud."

They both glowered at him. He kissed Moria on the nose and headed out.

THIRTY-TWO

Moria, Gavril, and Daigo followed Tyrus until he lifted his hand, telling them they'd gone far enough. Daigo continued after him, slunk down on his belly to hide himself as much as possible. Moria reached out to touch his tail and he turned. He gave a chirp, which she interpreted to mean he would go as close as he could to watch over Tyrus while not attracting any undue attention. She murmured a thank-you under her breath and he set out.

As they watched Daigo go, Gavril whispered, "He is still bonded to you."

"Hmm?"

Gavril cleared his throat. "I have noticed Daigo seems quite attached to Tyrus, and I thought that might bother you."

"He watches over Tyrus when I cannot. I'm glad of it."

"Oh. I had not interpreted it that way, but yes, your

affection for Tyrus is obvious to anyone, even a beast. Or, I suppose, *particularly* a bond-beast."

When they reached the longer grass, they discovered *why* it was longer—the ground was moist, almost bog-like. Once Moria had gotten as close as she dared, she settled in. Daigo appeared, slinking through the grass. She scratched him behind the ears and said, "I'm fine. Go back to Tyrus," and he chuffed and left.

"I'm fine, too," Gavril called after him.

Daigo snorted as he crept away through the grass. Once he was gone, Moria discovered an advantage to their spot—they were downwind of the encampment, which meant they could likely hear better than Tyrus. When she caught faint voices, she glanced over to ask Gavril if he heard them, and found him watching her with a look she knew well.

"What have I done now?" she whispered.

"Nothing."

"You have something to say."

"This is not the time."

A few more moments, then she sighed. "Say it. I cannot concentrate with you giving me a look that says you wish to speak."

"I can speak anytime I wish."

She growled under her breath and turned away, saying, "You are in a mood."

"I am not in a mood. Perhaps you are."

"Enough, Kitsune. We aren't going to argue about who is in an argumentative mood. If you wish to say something to me, do it so we may get back to listening."

More silence. Just as she caught a voice from the camp, Gavril said, "We still need to speak."

She tried not to growl again. "On what?"

"Me. What I did. The rest of it. I know it will not . . ." He shifted position. "It will change nothing, but Tyrus has heard it all, and I would prefer you heard it from me."

"He would never tell me your story. That is yours."

"But he might allude to it, thinking you already know. I am not saying we need to speak now, Keeper. I'm simply asking that you allow me to finish, when there is time."

"All right."

He paused. Then said, "You agreed too readily. You are trying to silence me."

"Yes, blast it, I'm trying to silence you so I can *listen*."

She could hear voices now. One raised, telling someone to stop something.

"I realize you are—" he began.

A cry cut him off. A sudden and high-pitched cry, and her first thought was of the shadow stalkers, but it was a far more ordinary sound. The cry of a child. Moria went still, straining to hear, and Gavril did the same.

She caught a man's voice. Telling the child to stop her howling or he'd give her a reason to howl. Then another child—a boy—said that the girl was only frightened and yelling at her didn't help.

"I . . . I know that voice," Moria whispered.

"Niles," Gavril said.

She looked over, surprised that he would actually recognize the voice of a child from Edgewood, let alone know his name.

"He used to come around the barracks," Gavril said. "He said he was looking for chores, but I suspect he was watching our lessons, hoping to learn how to use a sword, which I told him was pointless for his caste."

"But it *is* Niles." She looked toward the camp, which had gone quiet now. She turned quickly back to Gavril.

"We've not found the shadow stalkers. We've found—"

She scrambled to her feet without finishing. When he grabbed her arm, she tried to wrench away, but his grip tightened.

"Yes," he said as he fought to hold her still. "It is the children."

"How can you be so—?" She broke off with a sharp shake of her head. "Of course you can. You didn't care about anyone in that—"

"I care about you, Keeper," he said, his voice chilling. "I'll not let you run blindly into danger. Yes, I do not feel for the children of Edgewood as you do. They grew up with you, and you with them. They adored you, and you them, however much you pretended otherwise. That does not mean I fail to feel compassion for their situation. I want them free as soon as the safe opportunity presents itself. Safe to them and, moreover, safe to you."

He released her. "You have accused me of paying no attention to those in Edgewood. That is correct. I did not because I knew I must betray my post, and could not afford to form attachments. Which is why I rebuffed all attempts at friendship. Even yours." He adjusted his sword as he knelt to look out and then mumbled, "Especially yours. It was difficult to be

244

cold toward people who were kind to me. If you condemn me for that, then I'd ask you do so once, thoroughly, and be done with the constant reminders."

"I do not mean—"

"You do not mean to be cruel. I know. But now we have another task. Rescuing your village's children."

"It *is* them."

An annoyed look. "Have we not ascertained that?"

"It's just . . ." Tears prickled. "I wanted to search for them. I always wanted to be searching, but then other things would arise, and I would feel so guilty, Gavril. So blasted guilty."

"Don't cry."

"I'm not—"

He moved closer and put an awkward arm around her. "You've found them, Moria. They will not wonder why you didn't come sooner—they will only be happy that you've come."

She leaned against his shoulder, letting the silent tears fall onto his tunic. He stiffened, and she was about to back away, but he tightened his arm around her, still awkward, mumbled equally awkward words of comfort until a voice said, "What happened?" and Gavril pulled back so fast that Moria would have tumbled face-first onto the ground if Tyrus hadn't caught her.

"Moria?" Tyrus said, his eyes widening as he saw her tears. She started to speak, but he pulled her against him, and she buried her face in his shoulder as he said, "Gavril? What happened?"

"She's upset. And happy, I think. But also upset. She . . . was . . . crying."

"I can see that. Again, what happened?"

Moria pulled back and wiped her eyes. "It isn't the shadow stalker camp. It's the children."

"Wh-what?"

She stepped away. "The children. Of Edgewood and perhaps Fairview and Northpond. I heard a boy I recognized and Gavril did, too. It's them. It's truly them."

Tyrus looked toward the camp, rising, his hand going to his sword pommel. Gavril grabbed and yanked him down.

"Apparently this is why you two need me here," Gavril said. "So you don't run headlong to your deaths. Yes, the children are there. Yes, we are obviously going to rescue them . . . if such a thing is possible. And if it is not, then we will return with aid."

Tyrus looked at Moria and broke into a broad grin. "It's the children. You found them."

"Yes," Gavril said impatiently. "I believe that has been acknowledged—"

Tyrus threw his arms around her neck and hugged her, whispering, "I'm so glad. For them and for you, Moria." He grinned down at her, and it was a breathtaking grin, as if the children were from his own village, as if it did not matter that he knew them not at all. What mattered was what they meant to her. And she loved him for that. She truly did, and she wrapped her arms around his neck and hugged him as tightly as she could.

Behind them, Gavril sighed. "I thought you were in a hurry."

"Yes, yes," Tyrus said. "Stop grumbling and give us a

heartbeat to enjoy the moment, Gavril." One last hug, then, "There. We're done. Now . . ."

"What did you see, Tyrus? From your position?"

"I couldn't get close enough to see or hear, but I did spot a wagon leaving. I was coming to suggest we waylay it to determine the exact nature of the camp, but now that we know it, clearly we must—"

Gavril grabbed Tyrus's arm when he started rising again.

Tyrus glared at him. "I was merely looking."

"Don't. You'll call attention to us, and there's nothing to see. Now may I suggest that since I view this situation most dispassionately, I should plan our next move?"

"What do you have in mind?" Moria asked.

He told them.

THIRTY-THREE

The farther they followed the wagon, the more anxious Moria grew, seeing the camp disappearing behind her and feeling as if it truly was disappearing, like a mirage in the desert.

They had to follow on foot, leaving the horses behind. They continued at a distance, until the camp vanished into the darkness and Gavril proclaimed they'd gone far enough.

Moria hurried on with Daigo, getting far enough ahead of the wagon and its two guards that she could slip into their path and collapse there. Well, fake a collapse. She sprawled on the trodden path they used as a road, her cloak abandoned in the long grass with Daigo. She'd left her boots there, too, so she was barefoot. Gavril claimed her skin glowed in the moonlight. She rather thought he exaggerated, but it was pale enough to be spotted in the darkness. She fanned her long hair out, too, in hopes that would help keep her from being trampled.

Eyes closed, she listened to the pound of hooves and the squeak of the wagon wheels, and with each passing moment, her heart beat faster and the urge to peek was almost overwhelming.

Daigo will protect me.

So she trusted, yet those hooves and that squeak grew closer and closer until she could hear the heavy breathing of the horses and she swore she could smell them and—

"Hold up!" someone called.

The horses whinnied to a halt, and Moria exhaled a soft sigh of relief.

"A pretty girl lying on the road?" One of the men snorted. "Clearly the local bandits have heard too many bard songs. You two head out. Find where they hide and take care of them."

This was exactly as Moria expected. The ploy was so hackneyed that no one would fall for it. She did peek then, since they did not truly think her unconscious. The man giving the orders was the wagon driver. He sent the warrior guards to find the bandits. Then he climbed down, approached Moria, and bent beside her.

"So, girl," he said. "You thought you'd take a wagon full of riches, did you?" He laughed. "You'd have been mightily disappointed. We've nothing in our wagon but a prisoner. You waylaid a supply wagon on the wrong leg of its journey."

Moria said nothing, just kept her eyes open enough to watch him.

"This might be an inconvenience," the wagon driver said. "But you'll repay us for that." He reached out and toyed with a lock of her hair. "Amuse us enough, and we'll bring you home.

If you do not . . . well, there are brothels that will pay richly for a pretty Northern girl."

Moria leaped up then, not with her daggers, but simply jumping to her feet to run. The man grabbed her. She struggled about as hard as he'd likely expect from a girl, which was not much at all. He easily hefted her over his shoulder, with her weakly kicking and pounding at his back. Then he carried her to the wagon. As he opened the back flap, he froze.

"Release your hold on her," Gavril said. "Or I shove this sword through your neck."

Moria kicked the wagon driver's stomach as the first note of his call for help escaped. He fell back with an *oomph* and dropped her. By the time she got to her feet, Gavril had him on the ground, his sword at the man's throat. Daigo crouched beside him. At a motion from Moria, the wildcat took off for Tyrus, who was stalking the two warrior guards.

Moria searched for weapons on the wagon driver. While he did not appear to be a warrior, he had a blade, plus a dagger in his boot. She disarmed him and climbed into the wagon to search for something to bind him.

When she caught sight of a figure in the wagon, she readied for attack. Then she saw that he was slouched against the side, facing away, his hands bound behind his back and she remembered the driver saying they were transporting a prisoner. He seemed to be unconscious, and she was about to ignore him, but . . .

There was something about the prisoner. Something familiar.

Moria opened the flap and thrust out a torch she'd carried in her belt.

"Light this," she said to Gavril. And then added, "Please."

He cast a quick spell and lit it with his fingers. Moria pulled back into the wagon and took hold of the young man's shoulder. As she was about to give him a shake, something happened outside. Gavril snarled at the driver not to move or—

The wagon jolted as if one of them had fallen against it. Moria stumbled. The prisoner fell and jerked awake, his limbs flailing, one catching her in the leg before she pinned him with a bare foot.

"Ash?" Ronan stared up at her, blinking hard. Then he looked at the foot planted on his chest. "Moria?"

The wagon flap opened and Gavril pushed through, the driver hanging from one hand, the other brandishing his sword.

"Gavril?" Ronan said.

Running footsteps sounded outside, and Tyrus appeared, breathing hard and flecked in blood. Daigo was at his side, breathing just as hard and looking just as blood-speckled.

"Thank the goddess the driver lives," he muttered as he walked toward them. "Daigo and I had less luck with our targets. Neither was very interested in being captured and—"

"Tyrus?" Ronan said, scrambling up.

"Where's Ashyn?" Moria said.

"I . . ." Ronan blinked hard, as if his sleep had not come naturally.

Moria grabbed him by the shirtfront and gave him a shake. "Wake up, blast it. Where is my sister? Is she with you?"

"I . . ." Ronan's eyes snapped open and he pulled from her grip. "We need to go to her. *Now.*"

"We will," Gavril said. "As soon as you explain."

"No, *now.* I'll explain on the way."

THIRTY-FOUR

As much as Ashyn missed Ronan, she was, in one way, glad that he was not there, or she'd have been enduring his grumbling all day. It seemed time did not progress the same in the North as it did in the rest of the empire, because apparently "day" extended to cover the following dawn. That's when the ritual would take place.

Still, she missed him. There was no denying that. As kind and friendly as Edwyn's people were to her, she was keenly aware that she and Tova were among strangers. Edwyn had tried to make her day pass quickly with preparations. Ashyn didn't know the purpose of any, and all were conducted in a foreign tongue. None required much more of her than her presence, which meant a very boring day. Between rituals, Edwyn had entertained her with histories of the North, but as keen as Ashyn normally was to learn, it all became a bit, well, tedious.

Later, when she reunited with Moria, she would be far

happier about having Edwyn in their lives. Right now, though, her thoughts were consumed with worry about everyone she'd left behind, most of all Moria.

Night came but sleep did not. She'd gone to her tent too early, partially from boredom and partially from excitement for the day to come. But excitement certainly did not calm the nerves for sleep, particularly when night dragged doubt in its wake. What if she failed the ritual? What if she failed her grandfather—was not the girl he expected?

She kept thinking about the Seeking rituals. That was how all this started. Her first venture into the Forest of the Dead to soothe the souls of the convicts who'd died in exile there. She had gone in with the Seeking party from Edgewood . . . and emerged with Ronan, one of those exiled convicts. Everyone else in her party had perished horribly, killed by shadow stalkers, and all she'd been able to think at the time was "I did this." That somehow she'd conducted the rituals wrong and raised these creatures, and it was all her fault. She knew better now, but that didn't stop her from remembering how it felt. That crushing guilt and horror. What if this time she truly did fail? Or if she woke the dragons . . . and they massacred everyone around them and then flew into the empire and—

So she did not sleep. Not for a very, very long time, and only then after one of the women came to check on her, discovered she was awake, and withdrew in alarm, returning with a cup of wine.

"You must rest, child. You truly must."

Telling her she had to rest only added to the anxiety over *not* resting, particularly when Ashyn began to worry that a lack of rest could *cause* her to fail the ritual.

Surprisingly, though, despite her knotted stomach, sleep did come. Perhaps there was more than wine in that cup. The next thing she knew, she was waking to a commotion outside her tent.

She heard a shout in the common language, the words drowned out by the scream of another. Then the clang of steel and an oath, and she grabbed her dagger and cloak, Tova already at the door, growling. She pushed open the flap to see three unfamiliar warriors, blades raised, encircling a fourth, prostrate on the ground. The downed man seemed dead, unmoving, and Ashyn let out a gasp. She heard another oath, this one from a woman, and turned as one of Edwyn's people ran toward her, saying, "Back inside, my lady! Quickly!"

Ashyn ran *along* the tent instead, with Tova at her side, the woman calling after her. Strong arms grabbed her. Tova snarled and leaped, and her captor let out a strangled cry as the hound's fangs dug into his arm. He dropped Ashyn. She twisted to see another unfamiliar warrior and lifted her dagger to plunge it into his arm, when the woman who'd chased her shouted, "No, my lady! He is one of us!"

Ashyn stopped short. She stared up at the man. He was brown-skinned and dark-eyed, like Ronan. Not Northern-born and very clearly no one Ashyn had met in camp.

"He is with us," the woman said, gripping Ashyn's arm.

Tova backed off, still growling.

"But we are under attack," Ashyn said. "Those men—the warriors—"

"They are ours."

"I am sorry I frightened you, my lady," the warrior said, dipping in a slight bow. "I thought you were panicked and running blind."

"No, I was escaping the apparent attack."

She returned back to the front of the tent. The three warriors had lifted the corpse, a man with wildly curling dark locks and bronze skin. A lantern light fell over the dead man, and she saw his face and his tattooed arms. Swirling wolf tattoos.

Ashyn gasped. "That is—you've killed—it's Dalain Okami."

"He is not dead, my lady," the warrior said. "Merely knocked unconscious. My fellow warriors and I were coming to join you for the ritual, to control the dragons if needed. We found the young Okami skulking about the perimeter of camp, and we captured him. He seemed to come along willingly. Then he pulled his blade as we reached camp so we were forced to disable him."

"That is correct," said a voice beside them. Edwyn walked over. "I'm sorry this startled you, child. We had no warning ourselves. It seems the young Okami had followed us here to finish what he began in the woods outside his father's compound. We will not harm him, of course. His father is a staunch ally of the empire. His pursuit of you is merely misguided. I will attempt to speak to him, and if all goes well, he will join us tomorrow for the ritual and witness what you are doing for our empire so he may set the story straight with his father and others."

"Might I speak to him? That may help."

"Of course, child. Once he regains consciousness. I fear my

men had to give him quite a blow to avoid using their blades. I suspect it will be dawn before he recovers, but you will get a moment with him if there is time. Now, come along back to your tent . . ."

Shortly after Ashyn returned to her tent, one of the women brought her wine again. She tried to refuse, saying she was quite tired enough, but the woman insisted. So Ashyn took a long drink from the skin, sank into her blankets, waited for the woman to leave, and then spat the wine onto the hard ground. The slight fuzzy feeling in her limbs told her that the earlier wine had indeed had more than fermented honey and rice in it. She had consumed enough of the sedative already to quickly fall back into slumber without needing more.

When Ashyn woke again, it was to another noise—the sound of ripping fabric. She rose, blinking against the darkness. Tova didn't even twitch and she wondered if she'd dreamed the noise. Then she saw a knife blade cutting through the rear base of her tent. She grabbed her dagger and shook Tova. The big hound only grumbled in his sleep. She was about to shake him harder when the knife withdrew and a slender hand pulled up the cut flap. A girl poked her face in the hole. She had bronze skin, like Dalain, and dark, wild hair like his, though nothing in her features suggested the resemblance was more than regional.

"Oh, goddess be praised," the girl said. "It *is* you, Ashyn. I thought I heard the hound snoring, but I could not be sure. It would be my luck to slice into the tent of those blasted warriors."

"Who are you?"

The girl gave a slight smile. "My apologies, little Seeker. You look so like your sister that I forget we have not met. I am Sabre. My father is a subject of Lord Okami. I came with Dalain to find you."

"You say you have met Moria?"

"Yes, I told her I'd join the hunt for you." The girl peered at her. "Ah, I see. You do not believe me. Clever girl. All right, then. Hmm. How is this? She said Tyrus was a fine swords-man, and I teased her about his . . . other sword skills, and she said she did not know about that but hoped to find out. Does that sound like your sister?"

Ashyn's cheeks burned. "Yes."

"Excellent. Now we need to clear up this mess. It does not appear you are being held captive."

"No, I'm with my grandfather. He . . . It's a long story."

"But the short of it is that we mistook the situation for a kidnapping, and the people here mistook Dalain for a kidnap-per himself. We must straighten this out and get him free."

Ashyn sat up, shaking her head to clear the sedative from it. "You said Moria sent you after me?"

"Well, Tyrus asked Dalain to find you, given that he lost you the first time. Of course he was already looking. Warriors. So blasted honorable. Anyway, I told Moria I was going along to help Dalain."

"My sister is well?"

Sabre shifted, adjusting her position, which must have been uncomfortable, peering into the tent like that. "She was well when I left her."

"And with Tyrus?"

Another shift. "I saw her with Tyrus, yes. Now—"

"I am to trust Dalain then? I'm sorry, but I find that difficult to do when he shot my companion in the throat."

"What? Dalain would not—"

"He did."

"No, little Seeker. Neither Dalain nor his men would do such a thing. Tyrus asked Dalain to watch for you and your warrior boy while he searched for your sister. Dalain handled it poorly—not surprisingly—but he certainly did not shoot your companion. That would be dishonorable."

Sabre withdrew as if looking about, and when she poked her face in again, her whisper was softer still. "I must go and find Dalain's men. We were separated. I simply came here to explain and to ask that you insist on speaking to Dalain and straightening out this misunderstanding."

"I will do it now."

"Thank you."

THIRTY-FIVE

The hardest part of making her request came right at the start. Tova did not appreciate being roused again and moved sluggishly enough that Ashyn would almost think he'd taken the sleeping draught meant for her. But she managed to get him moving and then went out and spoke to one of the warriors. He fetched Edwyn, and she told him what Sabre had said.

When she finished, he led her away to sit on a mat by the still-smoldering campfire.

"You say you had never met this girl?" he began.

"No, but she knows Moria and proved it to my satisfaction."

"The fact that she's met your sister does not mean it was under good circumstances, child. Is it not possible Moria and Tyrus were captured as traitors?"

Ashyn shook her head. "The proof she gave would only

have come from someone my sister felt comfortable enough to joke with. I do not doubt the girl. Her story makes sense. Tyrus entrusted Dalain with escorting us to Lord Okami. Dalain simply handled it poorly, and we fled before he could clear up the misunderstanding."

"But that does not change the fact that he nearly killed Ronan."

Ashyn paused. Sabre had been emphatic on the matter, but if it had not been one of Dalain's men, then who?

She answered slowly, "It may have been one of Okami's men, but I accept that Dalain himself played no role in that. If I can speak to him, perhaps we can clear this up further."

Her grandfather nodded slowly, his blue eyes troubled, and she braced for him to deny the request, but after a moment, he said, "His father is known as a man of great honor. I trust his son is the same. We will speak to him."

Edwyn took her to the tent where Dalain Okami was being held. The young man lay on his back, his tunic removed, his left arm bandaged, more healing plasters on his chest. When Ashyn gave a small cry of alarm, Edwyn said, "It was a sword fight, child. He is lucky to have gotten off so easily." Then his voice went grim as he said, "Two of our men did not. One is badly wounded. As for the other, I will be asking you to say a few words for his spirit in the morning."

"I'm sorry," she said.

"It was not you who attacked them."

"I'm still sorry that it happened."

He squeezed her shoulder. "You have a good heart, child."

Then, to the healer, he said, "We need to wake him. Has he stirred?"

"No, my lord. He is deeply unconscious, and I very much doubt you can rouse him, but you may certainly try."

They did, to no avail. Dalain was alive, but indeed deeply asleep.

It is exactly like Ronan, Ashyn thought. And then, *Is that not odd?*

When she expressed concern, she said merely that she found Dalain's condition troubling, and the healer assured her that rest was simply the body's way of healing. While Ashyn knew that to be true, he did not appear to be badly injured, and when she asked about that, the healer seemed offended, as if Ashyn was questioning her diagnosis.

"Speaking of rest," Edwyn cut in, "Ashyn needs hers. It has been a very tumultuous night, and that raises concerns about the ritual. It must be done at dawn. If we postpone it, then all the earlier rites must be repeated, which I know you do not want, Ashyn."

She absolutely did not want that. And she could see she would get no further answers here. So she agreed to return to her tent and asked her grandfather to wake her early, so she could try to speak to Dalain again.

When she was given yet another draught of wine in her tent, she repeated the process—feign drinking it and then spit it out. Once the camp seemed to have fallen silent again, she shifted over to Tova, who was already deeply asleep.

That's not mere exhaustion. You know it is not.

Tova had been drugged. Her stomach clenched at the

word. No, not drugged. Merely given a draught to help him—

No, he had been drugged.

Could someone be trying to thwart the ritual? This was a group dedicated to caring for, and ultimately waking, dragons. Glorious in its potential. Also terrifying in its potential.

What better way to stop the ritual than to ensure Ashyn was in no shape to perform it? True, killing her would be more effective, but that only meant whoever was interfering wasn't a monster, but simply a person who thought he was doing the right thing for his empire.

Or *her* empire.

Who would have access to the sleeping draughts? Who had tended to Ronan when he'd been so deeply asleep? Who now tended to Dalain, in an equally unnatural sleep?

The healer.

Ashyn did not understand the purpose of keeping Dalain unconscious, but it was easy to see with Ronan. He had been her companion. For all the healer knew, he was her lover, too. The healer had only to suggest it might be unsafe to move him, and Ashyn would balk and the ritual would be postponed until the woman figured out a more permanent way to stop it.

Ronan had complained of his water tasting off. He'd done what she had with the wine: dumped it. And he'd woken when they'd been dealing with the fiend dogs and the healer's assistant had been killed, the healer herself with Ashyn. Leaving no one to give Ronan drugged water when he stirred.

What if the woman had done something to Ronan last night? If he had not truly left—

No, there was the note. Undeniably Ronan had left of his own volition. The healer's only tool seemed to be her sleeping draughts.

But why drug Dalain?

He must know something. Perhaps when the healer had been treating his wounds, he'd woken and . . .

Ashyn had no idea what Dalain might know or have said, but it wasn't important. Her hound was deep in a drugged sleep and could not help her. The young man who'd mistakenly come to "rescue" her was also unable to help. Two potential allies rendered useless. That had to mean something. To solve this mystery, Ashyn needed to wake Dalain.

Ashyn left Tova behind. There was nothing else she could do. By the time she decided it was safe to take a closer look at the situation with Dalain, her hound was impossible to wake. She reassured herself that his heart beat strong, and then positioned the blankets so, to anyone glancing in, she would seem to be asleep beside Tova.

She seemed to have waited exactly the right amount of time. The camp had gone silent, only a lone warrior prowling on guard duty, and the horizon showed no sign of dawn yet. With her cloak pulled tight, she darted from tent to tent, circling around while keeping out of the guard's way.

The tent where they were keeping Dalain was guarded, so she followed Sabre's example and cut a peephole in the back wall. Inside, the young warrior was alone and asleep.

Ashyn sliced a larger cut with her dagger and managed to wriggle through. There were things Ronan had taught her, not so much intentionally, but in spite of himself. By example. How to move quietly. How to use subterfuge. And how, sometimes, to harden your heart, just a little, and do something you'd otherwise consider cruel. Like digging her dagger tip into a bruise on the side of an injured young warrior when she was unable to rouse him.

She hoped applying pressure to the spot would be enough, but he never even stirred, so she kept pressing until the sharp tip pierced the skin and Dalain woke, struggling and gnashing against the cloth she quickly shoved in his mouth. Then she leaned over, so he could see her as she whispered, "It's Ashyn." Then, "Shhh! Please! They'll hear."

His eyes were glazed from the sedative, and he continued to fight as she reassured him, but after a few moments, her words seemed to penetrate. He went still and looked at her. Then he lifted his head to see his hands bound on his stomach.

"Are you calm?" she whispered.

He nodded.

"Do you understand that I'm here to help you?"

He nodded.

"Do you understand that there's a guard outside who is *not* here to help you?"

With his final nod, she tugged the cloth from his mouth.

"Where's Sabre?" Those were his first words, and she reassured him that Sabre was fine and had gone to find his men.

"Blast that girl," he muttered.

Ashyn arched her brows. "For fetching your men? Being free? Or being fine?"

He muttered something under his breath. Then his gaze moved down to her hands.

"You are not a captive?" he asked.

"No," she said. "There has been a misunderstanding. Several, it seems."

She explained as quickly and succinctly as she could.

"Did you say . . . dragons?"

"I know it sounds mad, but they're here. A mother and her two whelps. Sleeping. I've seen them, and I've felt them breathing. Now, apparently, I'm going to wake them."

"Wake the dragons . . ." He whispered the words, his gaze going distant, as if he was falling back into his thoughts. "Why would the Seeker be the one who can do such a thing?"

"The Seeker or the Keeper. Either of us can. While those are our titles in the empire, Seekers and Keepers can come from any region, any bloodline. They are simply twin girls with powers. In the culture of the North, one of their powers is—"

"Twins," he breathed the word. "Yes, twins. There is a very old story. We had a bard from the North who used to say that the way to wake dragons was—"

He looked to her, his eyes wide with dawning horror. "No." He began to struggle. "Cut my bonds, Seeker. Quickly. Please. We must get you out—"

The tent door opened. The healer came in with the guard at her shoulder. Ashyn backed up quickly, her dagger raised. The woman looked at her, no shock on her face. Just anger.

"Take her," she said to the warrior.

"No!" Dalain said. "Ashyn, run!"

The approaching warrior blocked the door. She twisted, diving to wriggle through the hole she'd cut. The warrior grabbed her. The healer pressed a stinking cloth over her mouth. Dalain shouted, trying to tell her something, but his words were lost as she fell into darkness.

THIRTY-SIX

Ashyn woke staring at dragons. She flew up, expecting to find herself bound, and nearly fell onto her face when she wasn't. Hands caught her by the shoulders.

"Careful, child."

She turned to see Edwyn. He smiled down at her, his hand resting on her shoulder.

"Thank the goddess you've woken," he said. "I'm only glad we had enough strong warriors to carry you in here."

She was in the dragon's den. A half dozen of Edwyn's people watched her with mixtures of relief, anticipation, and concern. Three were warriors. The other three wore cowled hoods, their faces hidden, but from their shapes, two seemed to be women, the third a tall man. The flames of their torches caught the gold and jewels, and the whole room seemed to dance and glitter. Ashyn had to blink more, getting her bearings.

"Tova . . ." she whispered.

"I fear your hound is in no state to join us," Edwyn said. "He must rest until the effects of that sleeping draught have passed."

"Sleeping draught . . ." She struggled to remember what had happened the night before. Something about a girl. And a young warrior. A blade cutting through a tent. She rubbed her eyes hard. When she looked at Edwyn again, his face had gone solemn, his blue eyes alight with anger.

"It seems we had a traitor in our midst," he said. "The healer sought to prevent—or delay—the ritual. I do not know her reason, but she confessed it when we could not rouse you or your hound this morning."

Yes. The healer. She'd drugged Ronan and Tova, and she'd tried to drug Ashyn. And there was someone else. A young warrior with dark hair and gray eyes and wolves—

She looked up sharply. "Dalain Okami. Where is—?"

Edwyn's gaze shifted and she followed it to see Dalain bound and gagged on the other side of the dragons. When he saw her, he strained at his bounds, eyes wild.

He'd been trying to tell her something about raising the dragons . . .

"I must speak to him," she said. "He does not need to be bound. It is a misunderstanding—"

"Perhaps," Edwyn cut in. "But we believe he may have been working with our healer. There are many who oppose the very thought of dragons. It's safer to keep him bound while he bears witness."

Ashyn stifled her protests and lowered her gaze. "As you

wish, Grandfather. I trust your judgment. After all, he did nearly kill Ronan."

Edwyn seemed to exhale softly, as if he'd expected her to argue.

"May I do something before I begin?" Ashyn asked.

"We truly must—"

"I would feel better returning this," she said, tugging the dove bracelet from her forearm. "I would not wish Isobo to wake and discover I have stolen it."

"All right. Give it to—"

"I must return it from where it was taken."

Ashyn was already walking toward the pile of treasure behind Dalain. She circled around him, turning away when he tried to motion frantically. She bent at the pile directly behind him, fussed at getting the armband off, and then set it on the pile before returning to Edwyn's side.

"You are wise," he said. "I am proud to call you my granddaughter."

She smiled weakly up at him. "Hopefully, you will be even prouder soon. If I can conduct my duty as you hope."

He embraced her and whispered, "You will, child. You will."

He led her to the dragons, had her kneel in front of Isobo, and positioned her just right.

"We don't want you to be the first thing she sees when she wakes," he explained. "She may be hungry."

When she looked up, startled, he chuckled and pointed at the carcass of a goat partially covered by a blanket.

"*That* will be the first thing she sees," he said. "I should not have jested, child. We are prepared for trouble." He waved at the warriors. One was holding a braided rope. "But there should be little need of food or restraints. She will wake as sleepy as you were. We'll bind her respectfully and then feed her and all will be well."

He adjusted Ashyn's position again. She was right beside the dragon, wedged in at Isobo's chest, rather like the two whelps to her right. He had Ashyn bow her head and shut her eyes, and then he chanted in the old language of the North as the others joined in.

Ashyn had words to say as well, words he'd taught her, something about entreating the goddess and asking her blessing and so on.

Instead Ashyn whispered prayers to the goddess, prayers for protection and for guidance. And if she reminded the goddess of all she had done and all she had been through and how her faith had never wavered, well, she meant no disrespect, but right now, she needed all the help she could get.

When Edwyn laid his hand on her shoulder, she began the words he'd taught her.

"Are your eyes closed, child?" he asked.

She nodded as she continued speaking.

He squeezed her shoulder. "You are trembling. With excitement I hope."

She nodded and continued speaking, but kept her eyes the slightest bit open. In her mind, she continued her entreaties to the goddess. Protect her loyal servant. Show her the way. Show her truth from lie. But above all, protect her. Please please please—

Look, Ashyn of Edgewood. Quickly.

She heard the words whispered at her ear. A spirit's whisper. Ashyn glanced down and saw a dagger sliding around to her throat. She swallowed.

Wait, Seeker. Wait.

The dagger paused. And then . . .

Now!

She fell backward, away from the blade as it slashed toward her throat. She grabbed for it, and it felt as if her arm was pulled, guided like a puppet's, somehow managing to avoid the slashing blade and grip the hand that held it. Then she squeezed with everything she had as she heard the others cry out, heard a voice shout, "Maintain your positions!"

It was the voice of the person wielding the dagger, and even though she knew who it had to be, she'd somehow, in that moment, convinced herself she was wrong, that someone else had stepped up behind her with the dagger.

But the voice was Edwyn's. The hand she clutched was Edwyn's. The hand wielding the dagger that had nearly slit her throat was Edwyn's.

She wrenched his hand, and perhaps it was the goddess's strength that filled her or perhaps it was the simple rage of deep betrayal. She wrenched it and bone snapped and Edwyn gasped and she grabbed his dagger and spun, backing against the sleeping dragon to stare at her grandfather.

My grandfather? What proof did I have of that? None but his word and stories that could come from anyone because I know nothing of my mother's family.

She looked down at the dagger. "Blood. That's what you

needed. Not my power. My blood."

"Your blood *is* power, child. Think of what you do for the empire. You will save it, child. Your life will save it."

He put his hand out, as if he honestly expected her to dutifully hand over the dagger and offer her throat.

"I think the empire can save itself," she said.

Edwyn lunged, and she stabbed him. Again, she could say the goddess guided her hand, but no. Ashyn stabbed him. Of her own volition. She felt the blade sink in, and he let out a gasp of shock and pain and then—

A cry. But not from Edwyn. Then a shout and a clatter of swords, and Ashyn looked over to see Dalain grabbing a sword from a warrior who lay on the cave floor with a dagger between his shoulder blades. Her dagger. She'd hidden it in the pile of treasure behind Dalain, as he'd looked back to watch her. She'd prayed to the goddess that he'd seen what she did and would be able to free himself without anyone noticing. That if she failed, he'd be able to get free before he became the dragon's first waking meal.

Dalain had the fallen warrior's blade and was striking a second warrior, who'd not yet recovered enough to counter the blow. The blade went in. The warrior went down. A third one attacked, and as their swords clashed, Ashyn saw Edwyn dive for her again. She darted away from the dragons, getting to open ground. That's when she saw the tall, cowled man pulling a blade from under his cloak as he moved behind Dalain, who was immersed in his fight.

"Behind you!" Ashyn shouted.

Dalain turned, and as he saw the other threat, his original

target took advantage, swinging hard. Dalain barely avoided the blow, dodging so fast he stumbled. Both men started for him and—

"Stop!" The voice rang through the cavern. A familiar voice. Wonderfully familiar.

"The next man who moves catches my dagger in his heart," Moria's voice called from the shadows.

"Or my stone in his head," Sabre said.

One of the warriors moved. Daigo's black shape leaped from the darkness and took the man down as Tyrus lunged.

They came out into the light then, having come through the cave passage while Dalain had been fighting. A fourth figure was still entering, and when Ashyn strained, she could hear the distant sounds of battle coming from outside.

"Step away from him," Tyrus said to the cowled man, who still stood behind Dalain. Then, to Edwyn: "And you step farther away from her. Ashyn, are you hurt?"

"No."

"Neither am I," Dalain said.

"No one asked you," Sabre said.

The fourth figure hurried through the doorway and jogged for Ashyn, and when she saw who it was, she swore her heart stopped.

"Ronan?"

"Get away from her," Ronan said to Edwyn.

"I am far enough—"

"No, you are not, and if you give me any excuse, I swear I will kill you, old man."

As Ronan approached Edwyn, Moria hurried over to

Ashyn. Ashyn went to embrace her twin, but Moria gripped her arms, holding them up instead so she could inspect her for hidden knife wounds.

"I'm fine, Rya," Ashyn said. "Truly I am."

"You were about to get your throat slit to wake dragons. That is not fine."

Ashyn smiled. "Only if they'd succeeded." She pulled her sister into a hug and felt Moria melt against her, trembling slightly, the only sign of how terrified she must have been.

Ashyn kissed her cheek and whispered, "I wouldn't abandon my little sister."

"A heart-warming sentiment," said the man in the cowl. "And I agree. You ought to leave this world as you came into it: together."

Moria paled as she turned to the man.

"No," she whispered.

Ashyn frowned. Yes, it was a threat, but an idle one, given that they'd vanquished Edwyn's warriors. Yet the look on Moria's face . . . Then on Tyrus's, a slow widening of his eyes, dawning recognition. And then, from across the cave, a fifth figure, running through the doorway, breathing hard as if he'd been finishing a fight outside. Ashyn saw the newcomer's familiar face and dark braids.

"Gavril?"

It was, and the look on his face as he stared at the cowled man was the worst of all. He lunged for them, shouting, "Moria!" and the cave went dark.

THIRTY-SEVEN

Moria heard Gavril shout her name, and then the cavern went dark, every torch extinguishing at once. She yanked out her daggers and pushed her sister against the wall, guarding her as Ashyn whispered, "Moria?"

"Sorcery," Moria said. That was all she said. All she dared say. She would not speak his name, as if to do so would—were she wrong—somehow bring him, manifested like a spirit. Yet she had no doubt who the cowled man was. That voice was branded on her brain.

Alvar Kitsune.

She had asked Gavril what his father had planned next. Gavril had said he didn't know, but feared it was sorcery. Now they had their answer. More than sorcery. Alvar had planned to murder Ashyn to raise dragons.

Ronan knew the plan to raise dragons meant sacrificing Ashyn, which is why they'd raced here as quickly as they could. The fact that his captors had stopped at Alvar's camp suggested Gavril's father was involved in the scheme, but it was only now, seeing him here, that they knew those fears had been well-founded.

When darkness fell, chaos exploded. Shouts erupted from Tyrus and Dalain. Daigo growled. Metal clanked. Moria stayed poised, not daring to take a step, lest she leave Ashyn exposed. She had to trust the young warriors.

Trust them to do what? Fight in the dark? Somehow not butcher one another?

"Gavril!" she shouted, but even as she did, she saw light, Gavril raising his glowing left hand. He brandished his sword in his right, but the long blade could not be wielded single-handedly. He pulled out his short sword instead and swung it awkwardly when a dagger-armed woman lunged at him.

Daigo and Dalain advanced on the still-cowled warrior. Ronan had Edwyn against the wall, his sword at the old man's throat. Sabre guarded a second woman, her slingshot in hand, ready to send a stone flying where needed.

From beyond the cave, Moria heard more sounds of fighting. They'd had to battle their way through, the Okami warriors at their side. They'd left them out there, fighting Edwyn's men, who were apparently Alvar's men. When she glanced toward the entranceway, drawn by the sounds of that distant fighting, a figure appeared. Another warrior—and not dressed in the Okami colors. A second followed him.

"Gavril!" Moria shouted.

He was still trying to use the short sword, but when she shouted, he pulled his long sword instead, gripping it in both hands . . . and his light went out. Blades clanged. Someone gasped. An *oomph*. A thud. Then Tyrus's voice: "Gavril!"

"Busy!"

Another thud. This one followed by the wet sound of a blade slicing through flesh. A howl of pain and Moria froze. Then Tyrus again: "Gavril!"

A grunt. A clang. "What?"

Tyrus didn't answer for a moment. When he did, it sounded like he'd moved closer to Gavril. "Light! Now!"

Another *oomph*. Another thud. Then light, and Moria could see Tyrus fighting the two newcomers. Gavril stood at his shoulder, his blade in one hand, light in the other, his gaze fixed on the fighters, his body tense.

"I need the light more than I need help," Tyrus grunted between blows.

The warrior Tyrus had been fighting earlier lay dead a few paces away. Ashyn darted from behind Moria. Moria let out a grunt and grabbed for her sister, but Ashyn snatched the warrior's blade, ran back to Moria, and said, "Trade?" then took one of Moria's daggers and handed her the sword.

"I know you're better with the daggers, but you can use that," Ashyn said. "And I don't need to be shielded in a corner, Rya."

Moria murmured an apology, and they surveyed the battlefield together, hunting for the best target. Seeing how they could help without getting in the way, given the poor lighting.

Ronan still had Edwyn pinned. Dalain and Daigo had backed the cowled man into a corner. Their opponent had sheathed his weapon, his hands raised in surrender.

Surrender? Does that mean it is not Alvar?

No, that voice . . . She'd known it and so had Tyrus and Gavril, but both boys seemed to have forgotten him in the heat of the battle. Or perhaps they'd realized they were mistaken, and—

She yanked her gaze away as another warrior barreled through the entrance. With Ashyn at her side, she began rushing toward him. Then Gavril's light went out. The last image Moria saw was Gavril looking up at his hand in surprise, meaning he had not extinguished—

Hands grabbed her. It happened so fast that she didn't have time to respond. Hands wrenched her away from Ashyn. Ashyn screamed. Moria slashed with her dagger but blindly, feeling it slice through air and then—

Her feet slid out, her face crushed against something bitter cold. Then light returned and she was staring at dragon scales, someone pinning her against the beast.

Moria fought wildly. She heard Ashyn call out, trying to find her, then Tyrus's roar of rage, Gavril's shout of "No!" and then there was a flash of light, blindingly bright, and the hold on her neck eased just enough for her to twist as the dagger plunged toward her.

THIRTY-EIGHT

The blade sliced into her side. She slammed down her own dagger, hitting a bare arm, seeing blood arc, seeing dark skin and the nine-tailed fox splitting as her blade cut through it. She looked up to see Alvar Kitsune's face. She stabbed again and so did he. His blade into her side, hers into his shoulder. Ashyn leaped at Alvar, dagger raised, but Alvar snarled something, some sorcery, and she flew back into the wall.

Ronan twisted toward Ashyn, letting out a curse, and Edwyn tried to fling himself free, but Ronan spun on him, blade flashing, blood spraying. Tyrus grabbed Alvar hard enough to throw him off balance. He went to catch Moria before she toppled, but Gavril pulled her away, and Tyrus wheeled on him, shock in his eyes, his face then contorting into a snarl, his blade rising.

"I can help her," Gavril said. "Heal her. I can't . . ."

He glanced toward his father, and they knew what he meant. *I cannot fight him.* Gavril's gaze dropped, as if in shame, but Tyrus was already bearing down on Alvar as the older man got to his feet. Edwyn lay on the floor, dead, Ronan's blade bloodied. Ronan was helping Ashyn up, but she pushed him off, then grabbed a torch from one of the fallen women and ran to Gavril, letting him light it as he held Moria. She glanced at her sister, her face dark with panic.

Moria mouthed a weak, *I'm fine,* and motioned for Ashyn to stand where she could light the cave for the others.

"Tyrus," Alvar said. "I would barely have recognized you without that ink on your arms. No longer a skinny boy tagging after my son like a lost puppy."

"Unsheathe your sword," Tyrus said. "You are not raising dragons this day."

"I have no intention of raising them."

"Do not lie. You collaborated with this Northern sorcerer to trick Ashyn and raise dragons against my father. Dragons to fight a Tatsu, proving even the goddess favored you. Which she clearly does not, as you see."

"I deny none of that, except the part about the goddess. She does favor me, as you will see. I meant only that I will not raise these dragons. That is what these girls are for."

"Unsheathe your sword!" Tyrus snarled. "Now!"

"And there it is: proof that you are both the boy I remember and the true son of Jiro Tatsu. An honor-bound fool. You could have killed me. Cut off my head while I attacked the young Keeper. Even now, you could try. Swing before I can pull my sword."

"Gavril?" Tyrus said, still advancing.

That was all he said, but it snapped Gavril out of his trance, and he lowered Moria onto the sleeping dragon.

"I have her," Gavril called back. "She'll be fine."

"Oh my," Alvar said. "You take orders from Jiro's bastard now, Gavril? You are even weaker than I feared. And what do you take orders to do? See to the girl, because young Tyrus cannot fully devote himself to this fight if he thinks she is dying. That is not mere piety, is it, Tyrus? You do not simply worry about her because she is a Keeper."

"Unsheathe your sword," Tyrus said.

"She's his lover, Gavril," Alvar said. "Are you too naive to have figured that out? Or is this what it's come to? I offer you an empire, and you choose to serve the emperor's bastard and his whore."

Gavril just kept lowering her to rest against the dragon. When she touched the cold scales and jumped, he murmured, "I have you," and she looked up at him and said, "I know."

Sabre and Dalain held the remaining two women and surviving warrior at bay. Ronan guarded Ashyn. Tyrus had Daigo, prowling back and forth at his heels.

"My father will not fight," Gavril whispered to Moria.

"Like you outside Lord Okami's compound."

Gavril shook his head. "I would not risk hurting Tyrus. My father will not risk *being* hurt. He has seen Tyrus's skill." He shifted her to rest more comfortably. "Now look at me."

When she didn't, he said, "Keeper? Look at me. I need you to relax so I may examine your wounds, and you cannot relax if you are tensed to leap to his rescue. If I hear any sign of trouble, I am at his side." He paused, then said, "Tyrus's, I mean."

She looked up at him and said again, "I know."

He nodded and peeled back her blood-soaked tunic. The sodden cloth seemed to have been holding the wound closed, and blood gushed. Gavril cursed. Ashyn gasped. Tyrus started to turn, pulled by Ashyn's gasp, and Alvar reached under his cloak—

"Tyrus!" Moria shouted.

The young warrior spun, his blade spinning with him, swinging for Alvar. Ashyn's torch flashed out. The sound of a blade hitting flesh. A hiss of pain. Moria yelled, "Tyrus!" pushing herself up to standing, and then light appeared again from Gavril's fingers as he ran, sword raised.

But Tyrus stood there alone, his bloodied blade held aloft. There was no sign of Alvar. They caught the sound of feet echoing through the passage. Dalain's blade struck the remaining warrior, putting him down fast. Dalain ran for the doorway, through which someone was already leaving. He said, "Sabre!" before following the girl. Tyrus lunged after them, telling Dalain to come back, telling them both not to follow—

"Blast it!" Tyrus said. He swung his sword in frustration, blood flicking from the blade.

"Go," Moria said. Then she stumbled, her knees giving way as blood flowed between her fingers, and she fell back onto the dragon.

Ronan took off, saying, "You stay here. I've got this, and I'll find Tova," as he ran for the exit. Ashyn let out a gasp and a "No!" but he was already disappearing through the doorway.

"Daigo, please," Moria said as Gavril dropped beside her.

The wildcat didn't hesitate. He tore off after Ronan.

"Ashyn," Moria whispered, the pain in her side making her struggle for breath. "Stay. Please."

Ashyn didn't hesitate either. She ran over, discarding her cloak and dropping beside Gavril, and the two worked to staunch the bleeding while Tyrus hovered, blade in hand. Edwyn's two women had left, scrambling out when they got the chance.

Moria lay wedged between the mother dragon and one of the whelps. *A dragon throne*, she thought, and chuckled, and the sound had all three of the others looking over in alarm. She felt oddly disengaged from her body, as if she was already half spirit, fluttering there by a tether.

"I'll stay tethered," she murmured, and they all froze, eyes wide with encroaching panic.

"Sorry," she mumbled, her words coming thick. "I only mean I'll not go."

Which was not, she reflected, the right thing to say, as panic grew in three pairs of eyes and Ashyn and Gavril worked harder, Gavril whispering magical words, healing words, his voice trembling as much as Ashyn's fingers.

I ought not to speak. I ought to simply focus on staying. That is the important thing. Staying.

She thought the words with a truly unnerving calm, as if she was deciding simply to remain for breakfast. Perhaps the fact that it was a question at all ought to worry her, that floating sensation saying she was, indeed, treading the boundary of the second world.

No matter. I'll not cross it. I'll stay on my throne of dragons. A trio of—

Scales moved under her outstretched hand. She pressed her fingers against the dragon whelp's flank as it seemed to twitch.

That would be odd, wouldn't it? If I woke a dragon in spite of everything.

She tried not to giggle at the thought. That's what she wanted to do—giggle as she'd not done since she'd last drunk too much honey wine. That was how she felt, floating there.

Of course, she was simply hallucinating the movement. The dragon was still cold.

Cold . . .

Dragons . . . snakes . . . lizards. What did they have in common? Beasts whose blood ran cool. Lizards lay in the sun to warm themselves because they were not naturally warm-blooded.

Interesting . . .

She rolled her head to the side. Her eyes closed, as if the effort of keeping them open took too much strength. Ashyn cried out. Hands flew to Moria's throat—not Ashyn's soft fingers, but rough ones, pressing hard. Then other hands, on her shoulders, trying to rouse her even as Gavril growled to stop shaking her.

She opened her eyes to see the face of a dragon. And Tyrus's above it, watching her anxiously, exhaling in relief when her eyes opened.

"The dragon . . ." she whispered. "It moves."

"She's in shock," Gavril said. "Tyrus, I know you're worried, but get *back*."

284

"No." Moria fumbled for Tyrus's hand and pressed it to the dragon's side. "Do you feel that?"

When she looked into his eyes, she swore his warm brown irises turned to amber, the round pupils to slits.

"Your dragon," she whispered.

"She's hallucinating," Gavril said. "Tyrus, get back."

"I'm not in your way," Tyrus snapped. Then he turned to her. "Tell me about the dragon, Moria. Keep talking. Focus on me."

"She does not have the strength—" Gavril began.

"He's keeping her calm." The snap in Ashyn's voice startled Moria. It also shut Gavril up.

"Tell me about the dragon, Moria," Tyrus said.

She smiled up at him and watched his eyes shift from human to dragon and back again. She saw images, like memories, real and solid, and when she spoke, it was as if she heard words not her own.

"I see dragons and I see empires," she said. "I see you and I see your dragon and I see your empire. I see blood and I see fire and I see peace. I see you on the imperial throne and I see a dragon at your gate, a huge and beautiful snow dragon."

"And you?"

When she didn't answer, he bent forward, blocking her view of the dragon, his eyes right above hers, still flickering from human to dragon, both forms dark with worry.

"Moria, tell me that you see yourself. That you are there. With me."

She smiled. "Of course. I'll always be there for you. You will have an empire, and you will have dragons."

"And I will have you."

Before she could reply, she went still, pressing Tyrus's hand against the dragon whelp. His eyes widened, and she smiled. "I'm not hallucinating, am I?"

"The dragon," Tyrus breathed. "Moria's blood."

Hands together, they pressed the dragon whelp's side as it heaved with slow heartbeats and slower breaths. One foreleg twitched. Then the clawed foot clenched and unclenched.

"It wakes!" Gavril said. "Tyrus, get back now!"

The whelp opened one eye. Tyrus turned, and that was the first thing the dragon saw: his face.

As it should be.

Moria smiled, that floating feeling washing through her now, liquid warmth that made her head swim. She saw Tyrus, and she saw the dragon, and she saw them reflected in each other's gaze.

"Tyrus, move away *now*." Gavril's voice was low with warning. Tension and fear clouded his face, and he held his sword raised. Seeing that made a little of the euphoria fall away as the world became brighter, clearer.

Moria blinked.. The dragon caught the movement and looked at her, and she met its gaze and looked into its eyes. For a moment, she fell back into those strange visions, those images. Blood and fire and then victory and peace.

Not now, a voice seemed to whisper in her ear. *That is not now.*

Of course it was not, because the Tyrus she saw in the images was no boy, nor the dragon a whelp.

And where was she in that vision? That's what Tyrus had

asked, and the truth was that she did not see her place. She knew only that she was there. For him. Always.

"Tyrus," Gavril said. "I'm going to ask you again. Back up. Moria? Move slowly toward me. If that beast so much as opens its jaws, I will—"

"No, you will not," she said. "It will not, and so you will not."

Gavril's mouth worked, but something in her eyes made him lower his gaze. His sword stayed up, though.

"I'm going to ask you, Keeper, please . . ."

"He's right," Ashyn said. "The dragon is small, but the dragon is not tiny. Let's all just back up and watch. No sudden moves." She glanced at Gavril. "That goes for you, too. Lower the sword, please."

"If they back away, I will lower it."

They did. The dragon only watched them, looking from Tyrus to Moria, seeming sleepy and confused. The beast made an odd little noise, almost like a mewl. Then it moved. A sudden move that had Gavril jumping, but it was only the dragon trying to get to its feet and instead falling forward. Moria dove to catch it. Tyrus let out a cry, but the whelp had stumbled into Moria's arms and come to rest there, shaking against her, still mewling.

The whelp was as big as Tova. Its scales seemed white at first, but when Moria looked closer, she could see they were iridescent. It had a thick, serpentine body, tapering to a long tail that ended in what would someday be spikes, but were for now, only bone nubs. Likewise, the nubs on its head would grow to curving horns, with more spikes radiating out around its face and down its spine. Its wings ended in single claws, like a bat, but it had both forelegs and hind legs, each pair already thickly clawed.

Moria rubbed its cold sides, feeling them warm under her touch. The dragon nuzzled against her.

"It needs heat," Moria said. "And food. Is there—?"

"There's a goat," Tyrus said. "I'll cut off some if Gavril can start a fire."

THIRTY-NINE

When Tyrus walked away, the dragon whelp let out another little mewl, its head rising to watch him go.

"He'll be back," Moria whispered. The dragon leaned against her, keeping warm as Ashyn gingerly approached and reached out a hand to pet the beast.

"You have a dragon now," Ashyn said, smiling.

Moria chuckled. "It's not mine."

"Did you truly see a vision of—?" Ashyn broke off and leaned in to hug her sister. "It does not matter. How do you feel?"

"As if I've drunk an entire skin of honey wine."

Ashyn laughed softly. "You look as if you have, too." She kissed Moria's forehead. "My sister, curled up with a baby dragon. If I wasn't seeing it, I'd not believe it."

"The dragon? Or me as a nursemaid?"

"Both seem equally unlikely."

Moria rubbed her eyes and looked around. "Where are my—?"

Ashyn handed Moria her daggers.

Moria stuck the blades in her belt and shook herself a little, throwing off that oddly intoxicated feeling. The dragon mewled, but only repositioned itself once she stopped moving.

"Zuri," Ashyn said as she stroked the beast's neck.

"Hmm?"

"Her name is Zuri. The female is the smaller, and Edwyn told me her name is Zuri. He said . . ." Ashyn trailed off, and Moria was about to pursue it, to ask her more about what had happened here, but as soon as Ashyn said the name and looked at the old man's corpse, everything rushed back.

"Alvar . . ." she said. "Tyrus! Gavril! We need to—" Pain ripped through her as she tried to move. The bleeding had stopped, but Gavril's magics could not completely heal her so quickly. "Alvar," she said again.

"We were just discussing that," Tyrus said. "All seems quiet beyond the cave, and I would like to think that is a good sign, but if we have not seen Ronan or Dalain . . ."

"Neither Ronan nor Dalain nor any warriors of Alvar and Edwyn," Ashyn said. "Which means a battle still wages. It has simply moved where we cannot hear it."

"I'm going out to look around," Tyrus said, handing a chunk of meat to Gavril.

He started for the exit, but when Zuri saw him leaving, she began to mewl and weakly flap her wings, and tumbled off Moria. She scrambled after the dragon and hissed in fresh pain. Moria had to stop, and Ashyn went after the dragon, who was trundling along on unsteady legs, trying to get to Tyrus. Zuri snapped at Ashyn, who drew back quickly.

"I'll go," Gavril said. "There's nothing more I can do for Moria, and that beast is going to give us all trouble if you leave."

"No," Tyrus said. "I must lead—"

He stopped short, and in his eyes, Moria saw a thoughtful look, as if perhaps he was reflecting back on what Alvar had said, mocking Gavril for following Tyrus's orders.

They are not their fathers. Yet there are similarities, and they must be careful not to fall into the same traps.

Tyrus took the meat from Gavril. "Yes, you go. Please. Tell them—" He clapped Gavril on the shoulder. "Just be careful."

Gavril nodded and headed for the doorway.

"Kitsune?" Moria called. When he turned, she said, "Be *very* careful. And stay away from . . ."

"I know," he said. "I suspect he is long gone. Running from battle is a talent of his. Stay here and rest."

He left, and Tyrus lifted the small dragon, grunting as he did and saying he did not plan to play dragon-nursemaid himself. Yet he moved her to the fire and took pains settling Zuri and then began cutting meat off the chunk. He tried laying it in front of her. She ignored it, until he was putting down another piece . . . and she snatched it from his hand.

Ashyn laughed. "Apparently, she expects you to feed her, too."

He sighed, and between bites, Zuri's adoring gaze followed his every move.

"She's imprinted on you," Ashyn said. "Like a bird."

He sighed again.

Moria snorted. "It's a *dragon*, Tyrus, not an inconvenient stray kitten. When is the last time that a Tatsu even *saw* an actual dragon?"

He leaned over and mock-whispered, "I know, it's amazing, but I don't want her getting too full of herself." He looked at the dragon. "You'll need to behave and pull your own weight. Or I'll have the girls put you back to sleep."

Tyrus shifted to sit against Moria, his arm going around her and pulling her close as he leaned to kiss her cheek. She turned and kissed him back.

"So . . ." Ashyn said. "I've been gone a while, it seems."

Moria smiled at her. "Just a little."

"Missed a few things, did I?"

"Just a few."

Moria could feel her sister's gaze on her, evaluating, assessing, then nodding and smiling. "I'm happy for both of you."

"Thank you," Moria said. Then she turned to lean against Tyrus and face her sister. "Tell me what happened."

"I'm not even sure where to begin."

"With him," Moria said, pointing at the dead old man. "Ronan says he told you he was our grandfather?"

"He is not."

If Moria had already decided she hated the old man for deceiving her sister, hearing the bitterness in Ashyn's voice hardened that to loathing. With the death of their father, they'd lost their connection to their family, to their ancestors and their past. Moria had been able to forget that—there was no time to dwell on it—but she knew how much it had bothered Ashyn.

To not have any family was almost as great a tragedy as the actual loss of their father.

"We do have family, Ash," she said. "Somewhere. We will find them."

Her sister managed a smile. "Of course we have family. We have each other."

"And we'll not be separated again. Now tell me—"

"Later," said a voice from the entrance as Ronan ran in, breathing hard, Tova and Daigo at his heels. "We need to get out of here."

Gavril followed him in. "All had gone quiet because Dalain and Ronan were pursuing my father and Edwyn's men. Pursuing them into a trap. I had Sabre climb the tallest tree, and she confirmed it—a small army waits on the horizon. When they realize we've stopped following, they'll march back for us."

Dalain and Sabre came in. Zuri clearly decided this was far too many strangers, and she rose, her wings extending as she hissed. Tova stopped short, snorting in alarm. Daigo growled.

"That . . . that is a dragon," Dalain said.

"Brilliant deduction," Sabre said. "Well, since both you girls are alive, I suppose it didn't need that much blood. My suggestion, though? Let's leave the big one sleeping. Now, if we can please get aboveground before that army arrives?"

"But . . ." Dalain looked at her. "It's a dragon."

"Yes, dragon." She jabbed an emphatic finger at the cave exit. "Army. May we go, your lordship?"

"Moria's injured," Tyrus said. "She cannot—"

"No, I think I can . . ." She pushed to her feet and staggered, Ashyn and Tyrus leaping up to catch her before she fell.

"You cannot, Keeper," Gavril said as he strode over. "But Sabre is right. We need to move."

"I can wait here," Moria said. "I have my daggers and my wildcat. And a dragon."

Gavril gave her a look. "All of which only means they will be captured *with* you. Then my father can drain the rest of your blood to wake her." He pointed at the mother dragon.

"Gavril, you should take her," Ashyn said. "I know you would rather fight, but she'll need someone to help her move to safety. Someone skilled with a blade and with healing magics in case her wound reopens."

Gavril said he would, and tried not to look relieved. Moria and Ashyn both knew he would rather *not* fight, given who led the opposing army. Her sister was giving him an honorable way out, even if it did mean separating moments after saying they would not. Sadly, no such promises could be given anymore.

They made plans for reuniting. Gavril would get Moria to an abandoned farmhouse they'd passed on the way in, and she would rest there until Ronan came to fetch them. Tyrus would lead the others, fighting or fleeing, depending on the situation.

With both Gavril and Tyrus supporting Moria, they headed out of the cavern, Tyrus giving orders to the others as they walked. As for the dragon . . . when they started to leave, she seemed to have eaten enough to regain her walking strength. Moria had grabbed the hunk of meat and was cutting strips for her as they moved. She hand-fed the dragon—whose head reached her waist—but by the time they got out of the cave, Zuri was using her wings to propel jumps and snatch the strips as soon as Moria cut them.

"Here then," Moria said, giving her half the rest. "Serve yourself."

A flurry of teeth and claws and chomps and growls . . . and the chicken-sized hunk of meat was gone.

"Everyone?" Sabre said. "Keep your hands away from the dragon baby."

When they prepared to separate, Zuri hesitated, looking from Moria to Tyrus. Daigo moved alongside Moria with a grunt that stated his intention to stay with his wounded bondmate, and Zuri flew to Tyrus.

Partings were quick. Ashyn gingerly embraced Moria and told her to stay safe. Tyrus did the same, adding a kiss. The kiss seemed brief enough, until Sabre told them to hurry it up. Then Gavril put his arm under Moria's and helped her away, Daigo prowling ahead of them, watching for trouble.

FORTY

The camp looked like a battlefield.

Because it was.

A half-dozen bodies lay strewn across the blood-spattered ground. As Gavril led Moria past them, one stirred, his clothes so bloodied she couldn't tell which side he'd fought on, but Gavril lowered Moria to the ground, went over, and ended his suffering without a word. Then he gathered her up and continued on.

Riding in, the farmhouse had seemed so close. Now, as Moria realized exactly how badly she'd been hurt, their destination felt an impossible distance away.

Her side split open again. She felt the blood drip and told herself it was not enough to warrant stopping. Then it began to stream down her side, and she knew she ought to tell Gavril, but that's when they spotted the farmhouse in the distance—and riders on the horizon—and Moria knew if they paused, those riders would draw close enough to spot them. So she gritted her teeth against the pain and said nothing.

Daigo had been scouting ahead. When he circled back to them, he lifted his black head above the long grass, his nostrils flaring. Then he bounded to Moria and growled.

"I'm fine," she said.

He growled at Gavril.

"Yes," Gavril said. "I'm doing something wrong. I have no idea what it is, but I'm sure I am doing something you disapprove of."

His voice was weary, laced with frustration, and he stared straight ahead, supporting her as he walked. Perhaps wishing he *was* in battle instead of playing nursemaid to a wounded girl?

"Go scout," Gavril said. "Leave me to get your Keeper to safety. You may disapprove of my methods later."

Daigo stopped in front of him, so close that Gavril—his gaze on the horizon—nearly tripped over him.

"Blast it, Daigo! Can't you see I'm supporting your Keeper? Trip me and you trip her. Let me get her where we're going."

Daigo let out a plaintive yowl.

"Keeper?" Gavril said. "Can you please tell your wildcat that blocking my path does not help either of us?"

Moria knew Daigo was trying to tell Gavril that she was wounded, and they needed to stop.

"Daigo, please," she said. "We're almost there."

Daigo stalked back into the grass but stayed close, anxiously monitoring their progress.

When they finally reached the farmhouse grounds, Moria's

legs gave out, and she collapsed, dead weight, startling Gavril enough that he dropped her.

"Blast it," he said, helping her to her feet. "We're almost there. I need you to just take a few more—"

He stopped and slowly withdrew his hand. It was covered in blood.

"No," he whispered.

He lowered her to the ground, cursing more. He fumbled to open her cloak. It stuck to her side, plastered by blood she could feel soaking her tunic and dripping down her leg.

"No, no, no. Blast it, Keeper! When did this happen? Why didn't you tell me?"

"We could not afford to stop."

"So we can better afford to have you die from loss of blood?"

He let out a string of curses, the likes of which she'd never have imagined him knowing. When Daigo growled, Gavril spun on him with a snarl of his own.

"Do not blame me, cat. If this is what you were trying to tell me, then you need to have been clearer. If I'd had any idea her wound had reopened, I'd have stopped."

"We need to get inside," Moria said, and she meant to speak the words with full authority, but they came out a papery whisper. She blinked hard. "Help me up, and I can walk."

"You cannot. You should not." He turned his glower on her. "You are as bad as your wildcat, Keeper. You expect me to know something is wrong, and when I do not—"

"I expected nothing. Now, if we don't get inside, then all this has been for naught."

"All what?" he said as he scooped her up. "All your bravery?

Is that to be your epitaph, Keeper? She perished because she was too blasted stubborn to . . ."

He continued, but her mind went fuzzy, less euphoria this time and simply a feeling of floating, barely tethered. She blacked out, coming to inside a dark, cool room, his fingers gripping her chin hard enough to make her wince.

"Good," he said when her eyelids fluttered. "Now keep your eyes open. I don't care how tired you are, I swear if you close your eyes and give me any cause for alarm . . ."

Again, he continued talking. Again, she seemed to float away from his words, thinking, *He's frightened*, and mumbling, "I'm sorry, Kitsune."

"I don't want apologies. I want you to stay alive. Tyrus entrusted me with your care, and I am not going back to tell him I failed. I will not. Do you understand that?"

"He would not blame you."

Gavril stopped, his mouth open as if to retort something, and he froze there, not moving, poised over her, his panic palpable.

"I have no intention of passing into the second world, Gavril," she said, her words oddly calm and measured. "But if I do, Tyrus will not blame you. You needn't worry."

He blinked hard and swallowed. "I did not mean . . . That is not why . . ." He shot back onto his haunches, the rage finding a fresh target as he said, "If you pass, I will kill my father. I swear by the ancestors and the goddess that I will put a blade through his heart, and I know that should be for everything else he's done, everyone else he's killed, but it won't be. It'll be . . ."

He stopped and rocked, rubbing his face. She looked at him, that oddly distant feeling growing, as if she was divorced from the scene and merely observing it. Observing him. Yet she did feel something, and she could not put a name to it, only looked at him and at his fear and his panic and felt an overwhelming sense of some nameless thing. She reached for his hand and squeezed it weakly and said, "I forgive you." Then, "For everything."

From the look on his face, she might as well have spat curses. His eyes went wide and he scrambled to his feet, dropping her hand.

"No," he said. "No, no, no. Not that, Keeper. You cannot forgive me until I've told you everything, and even then you probably will not, so don't speak the words. I do not wish them, and they are not true. You only say that in case . . ." His voice hitched and he shook his head. "*No.* In case of nothing. You haven't lost that much blood. You will be fine. So there is no need to say anything. I will get you water, and I will heal your wounds, and you will be . . ."

She passed out.

FORTY-ONE

Moria was not dead. She'd only lost consciousness, and Gavril hadn't let her lose it for long. She woke to Gavril's anger and Daigo's rough tongue, and the two of them snapping and snarling at each other. But she did wake, and after that, she tried harder to stay that way, because Gavril seemed to think that merely shutting her eyes was a sign of her imminent departure from this world. So she drank water, and let him clean her wounds and cast magics on them, and she endured his misdirected anger and curses—at her and at himself and even at Daigo. That was how he dealt with panic and fear and uncertainty, and she let him.

When the wound closed again, he ordered Daigo to stay put while he went in search of water. He found a stream nearby and brought back a skinful. She drank as he washed her wounds and bound them using the only cloth available—his tunic. She did rouse herself enough to argue about that, but he only snapped at her and she fell silent again. When he finished, he realized she was shivering. Shock, he said, and piled his cloak and hers on her. Daigo curled up beside her, but still she shivered, and finally, Gavril lay on her other side.

He did not exactly curl up against her like the wildcat. It was rather like leaning against a wooden board, Gavril as tense as if he expected her to sink her dagger between his ribs. But when she kept shivering, he pulled her against him and she rested her head back against his chest, listening to the beat of his heart, and he told her she could sleep then but only for a while. She closed her eyes and drifted off, and the last thing she heard, after he must have thought her asleep, was his whisper.

"Don't ever scare me like that again, Keeper."

Having reached a horizontal position, Gavril and Daigo must have fallen asleep, thoroughly exhausted. The next thing Moria knew, a cry from Gavril penetrated her dreams, and she caught a knee in her back and a claw in her leg, as both Gavril and Daigo clambered to their feet, Gavril with his blade out.

Moria rose on her elbows, blinking hard in the dim light. There was one window in the room, but enough light shone in for her to see they were alone.

"Kitsune?" she said as she reached for her dagger. "Did you hear something?"

He surveyed the room in silence. Then he blinked hard and shook his head. "It was but a nightmare. I apologize for disturbing your rest, Keeper."

She watched him as he walked to the window. He'd sheathed his blade, but his hand remained on the hilt and trembled slightly.

"Gavril?" she said, her voice softer.

He didn't turn. "I am going to walk the grounds."

Before he reached the door, she said, "The nightmare . . . Was it of your mother?"

He stopped, his back still to her, sword hand trembling enough that his blade clinked against his short sword, and he pulled his hand away from the hilt.

"I'm sorry," she said. "I ought to leave you to your grief. I only wished—"

"He killed her," he blurted, still facing the door. "My father did that." He paused. "No, he had it *done*, and not because he couldn't bring himself to do it, but because he was too busy with his other schemes. Burying my mother in the dirt and leaving her to die was, in the larger context of his plan, a minor ploy."

The agony and bitterness in his voice pushed Moria to her feet. She ignored the stab of pain as she stepped toward him. She stopped a pace behind and said, "You had a nightmare. He would not—"

He turned then. "Would not? Truly, Moria? He tried to whore you to me as if you were a mere vessel for his imperial lineage. He tried to have your sister's throat slit to raise dragons. When those two plans failed, he tried to kill you instead. And I know, in the greater scheme of what he has done— slaughtering entire villages—killing you is but a small thing, but it was, for me, the true proof that he is responsible for my mother's murder."

"I don't under—"

"My father would not allow me to form other attachments as a child. That is why he took me from my mother to be raised by an endless parade of caretakers. An attachment to him was filial piety. To anyone else? A sign of weakness. When I was young, Tyrus gave me a puppy from a palace litter. My father killed it in front of me."

Moria inhaled sharply.

"It was but one of many lessons in the danger of attachments. I cried for the puppy, and my tears proved me weak and made his point. That is why I fought so hard to pretend I did not care about you."

"For my own safety."

He nodded. "But he knew. I could not . . . I could not properly hide it. I allowed you to be kept in a dungeon, but after the guard attacked you, it became clear to him that I cared. I believed the betrothal was a political ploy, as he claimed, but you are correct. He intended to see it through and force me to . . ." He swallowed. "Use sorcery or charms to . . ." He turned away. "That would be a lesson to me. Take someone I cared for and make her loathe the sight of me. And when that plan went awry? He substituted you for your sister to raise dragons. A punishment both for forming an attachment to you and renewing one with Tyrus."

"I still do not think he would—"

"I tried to keep my fears for my mother concealed. To show only the proper concern of a son for his mother. But I did show that concern to him. I said that I wanted to see her, to reassure myself she was safe and well."

"Which is, as you say, only proper."

"We were not abducted by imperial bandits, Keeper," he said. "Toman was my father's man."

"What?"

"Does that not make more sense? That they were lying in wait for us, knowing the road we'd take back to my father? Wouldn't that explain why he tried so hard to convince us of the evil plans the emperor would have in store for us? To frighten us? Why he would not attack a small band of my father's recruits? Why he knew exactly where my mother was being held? Why he played the game of having me search the house, of having my hopes raised that she'd escaped or my fears raised that she'd been taken . . . only to discover she'd suffered a far worse fate? *That* is my father, Moria. It is exactly how he would do it."

She said nothing. Could say nothing. Daigo rubbed against her, sensing her mood.

Gavril continued. "As with all his schemes, it accomplished multiple purposes, because it is not enough simply to teach me a lesson or to stop my asking about my mother. Killing her in the traditional way of the Tatsu clan pins the blame on the emperor. Toman would have found some way to return me—perhaps my father's men would have faked an attack and rescued us—and I would tell the tale of my mother's death and my father could work up righteous rage and grief and the story would spread."

"But it won't now. Your father is losing control of his

shadow stalkers. They escaped and killed Toman and foiled that plan, and now we have foiled the greater one. He did not raise dragons. The goddess is punishing him."

"I wish I believed that, Keeper," he said.

She walked over and leaned against his shoulder. "I do, Kitsune. I truly do."

FORTY-TWO

"Alone again," Ashyn murmured as Tova bumped her hand. She smiled and scratched behind his ears.

"You don't count."

He rolled his eyes. Then he looked at everyone surrounding them and rolled them again.

"Yes," Ashyn whispered. "But you know what I mean."

True, she was surrounded by people, and few of them were strangers. She could see Ronan scouting ahead. Tyrus had been at her side, but had gone ahead to speak to Ronan. Dalain and Sabre were behind her, watching for trouble. A half dozen Okami warriors and several of Sabre's father's men could be spotted in the sweep of an eye. There was even a dragon, intermittently flying over Tyrus's head and then taking off for parts unknown, stretching her wings and exploring her world after nearly an age of sleep.

Yet someone was missing, and right now, that was the only person Ashyn truly wanted: her sister.

Tyrus circled back to her side. "Gavril will take care of her," he said, as if reading her thoughts. "I'd not have let her go with him if I doubted that for a moment."

"Nor would I have suggested it if I had doubts."

However confused Ashyn felt about Gavril—seeing him fighting at Tyrus's side, tending to her sister's wounds—she did not question his loyalty to Moria. That felt naive, after all he'd done, but she'd seen his face when her sister was hurt, seen his terror when they'd been trying to staunch Moria's wound, and when Ashyn had suggested he go with her, it was as if everything between them had vanished, and he was once again the young man who'd traveled with them through the Wastes.

Ashyn looked over at the young prince, now more than a friend to her sister. That, perhaps, in its odd way, had her most unsettled of all. So much had happened during their separation, and while most was larger and far more significant, this was what stuck in her mind. Her sister had fallen in love, and Ashyn had not been there to witness it. She'd missed Moria telling her of their first kiss. Missed Moria confessing her feelings. Missed the joy and excitement of sharing her sister's first love. They'd shared every landmark in their lives, and now . . . Life was changing. For both of them.

How did Ashyn feel otherwise about what had transpired? Pleased. She'd said she was happy for her sister, and she truly meant it. Tyrus was a worthy partner for Moria, and Ashyn would not have said that of anyone else. Except perhaps . . .

That only complicated matters, didn't it? Best to put it aside and leave it uncomplicated. Tyrus loved Moria, and Moria loved Tyrus, and their feelings were clear to anyone who saw them together.

"We'll be reunited with her soon," Tyrus said.

"I know."

"When we get her back, I'll not . . ." He glanced over. "I know you have been parted nearly a fortnight, and I know how painful that was for her, so I am certain it was the same for you. Things may have changed between Moria and me, but when she comes back? She's all yours."

Ashyn smiled and leaned her head briefly against his shoulder as they walked. "Thank you. I'm sure I'll want to steal her away and let her regale me with tales of her grand adventure, but I'll not keep her to myself for long. I did mean what I said. That I'm happy for you. Thrilled, in fact."

They both looked up to see Ronan jogging toward them. Tyrus strode forward, Ashyn hurrying to keep up. Ronan cast her a quick glance. They'd had little time to do more than exchange a few words. Ashyn desperately wanted to speak to him, to hear what had happened, if he'd returned to his brother and sister and then somehow found the others. But it had not been the time. Tyrus needed Ronan scouting, with his full attention on that. She'd resisted the urge to ask Tyrus how he'd found Ronan. She wished to hear the story from Ronan himself. Which meant it had to wait.

"I've spotted riders," Ronan said. "Three, possibly four. Scouting, I presume. They've broken from the main group and they're headed in this direction."

"How far?" Tyrus asked, straining to see against the bright midday sun.

"Perhaps a thousand paces. And riding fast."

Tyrus cursed. "And the rest of the troop?"

"Still distant enough that I cannot see them."

"Which means they cannot see us if we raise extra dust. All right then. Stay back here. Alvar is about to lose his scouts."

Ashyn would play no role in planning the attack, nor in executing it. Her sole task was to survive it. And, preferably, not to be taken hostage.

Tyrus had found her a place to hide with Tova. Which made her feel completely and utterly useless, and only strengthened her resolve to improve her battle skills. From her spot, she watched as the others found places of their own to hide, one of the warriors taking the horses and riding off to the other side of a distant outcropping of rock.

Then they waited. The scouts were riding hard, presuming that on the open ground they'd see trouble. There were four of them. An easy battle. Still, Ashyn gripped her dagger. She would not blindly run in at any provocation, but if there was a situation where she could safely help, she would not stay hidden behind a rock.

The riders closed in. From her place, she could see Tyrus and Ronan together. There was a rock in front of them, but not large enough to do more than throw them into shade and shadow, and they had hunkered down in the long steppe grass. Dalain and Sabre each had half of the Okami men hiding in other patches of grass. They were all far less hidden than

Ashyn, and as soon as the riders drew near enough, they'd need to leap up and charge before they were—

A shadow passed overhead. Ashyn craned her neck and at first saw nothing but the brilliant blue midday sky. Then the sky itself seemed to ripple, and she smiled and whispered, "Zuri." On the ground, the dragon whelp's camouflage was imperfect. If the light hit her at the proper angle, she'd blend with her surroundings. Otherwise, well, an iridescent white dragon was rather easy to spot. In the sky, though, with the sun blazing, she was all but invisible, and Ashyn watched in wonder as the dragon soared and swooped, visible only by that telltale ripple.

Zuri let out a cry, not so much a roar as a yowl. The riders looked up, and Ashyn's heart stopped as she frantically searched them for signs of bows and quivers. There were none, and as the warriors continued peering into the sky, she looked toward Tyrus, hoping he could take advantage of their distraction. Then Zuri let out another of those yowls, and Ashyn realized what she was doing: searching for Tyrus.

"No!" Ashyn whispered, and she motioned for Tyrus and Ronan to hide themselves better. They weren't looking her way, though, and a moment later, Zuri spotted her quarry. She let out a victory cry and swooped down to perch on the rock partially hiding Tyrus. She squawked and danced in place, wings fluttering, head bobbing, clearly very pleased and relieved to have found her master and eager for him to recognize her triumphant return.

The scouts, not surprisingly, stopped in their tracks to stare, unable to believe what they were seeing. The shock wouldn't last long, though, before they realized the young dragon was very intent on something in the long grass.

Tyrus whipped a chunk of meat. Zuri let out a joyful squawk and dove after it. She caught it in midair and gulped it down, and before she could zip back for more, Tyrus threw another piece that landed in the grass, meaning she had to hunt for it. This would have been an excellent idea, except apparently the dragon whelp had eaten quite enough and wasn't interested in food that required work. She gave a cursory look and then flapped her wings, taking to the air and heading back for Tyrus.

Ashyn saw the prince flatten himself face-first on the ground, doing his best to hide, but the dragon spotted him with a chirp, dove, and grabbed his ponytail. She didn't get far with it, yet it was enough for the scouts to spot him. They lifted their heels to spur their horses . . . and twin shouts rang out from either side, as Dalain, Sabre, and their men burst from the long grass, having crept up behind the scouts while the dragon provided a distraction. Ashyn breathed a sigh of relief as they charged.

Three scouts wheeled their horses to face their attackers. The fourth, though, spurred his forward, blade out, battle cry on his lips as he ran straight at Tyrus. The prince leaped up, as did Ronan. Zuri heard the scout's cry, turned in midair, and saw him charging Tyrus. She let out a shriek—pure rage—and shot down at him, jaws opening. One day, if the legends were true, her breath would freeze a man in his tracks, but while Ashyn saw the whelp's throat expand and contract, all that came out was a puff of white air, and the scout was running at her, his sword out, pulling it back, the dragon low enough for him to strike.

Ashyn tore from her hiding place, dagger raised, but Tova was already leaping past her. He launched himself at the horse, his fangs sinking into its rump. The horse screamed and reared and the scout flew off its back, Tyrus on him the moment he hit the ground.

The fight was quickly won. Then it was Ashyn's turn to do her bit, tending to the dead and the wounded. Fortunately, their side had incurred only minor injuries. Tyrus came over while she was checking on the lead scout, ensuring he was dead. From the extent of his injuries, it seemed certain, but she still checked. As Tyrus saw those injuries, he stopped short and turned away. When he turned back, he seemed himself, but she'd not missed the look in his eyes.

"Chewing ginger or mint leaves will settle your stomach," she murmured as she rose.

"Moria told you then."

"Moria told me nothing. She would not, if it was said in confidence, though back on the road from Fairview, she did ask what settles stomachs. Having seen your expression, I now know why. Your secret is as safe with me as it was with her."

"Thank you. I came to say that the rest of Alvar's men will head this way once they realize their scouts are missing. By then, I plan to be long gone. We'll split up, making us more difficult to track. Ronan? I'd like you to go meet up with Gavril and Moria. If they're safe at the farmhouse, keep them there and I'll join up after nightfall. Take one of the horses. Ashyn? Would you like to ride with Ronan?"

She hesitated. "I ought to tend more to—"

"My apologies," Tyrus said with a smile. "I forgot I'm not speaking to Moria. Ashyn, I insist you go with Ronan. You and Tova can watch his back, and your sister may need your healing skills more than Dalain's men do."

"Yes, your highness." A quick kiss on his cheek. "Thank you, Tyrus."

FORTY-THREE

"I did not leave you." Those were Ronan's first words when they were away from the others.

"What?"

"I mean that I did not leave you by choice." He glanced at her. "And I can see that comes as a shock. I had hoped . . ." He looked forward, tugging the reins to turn the horse a little to the north. "I had hoped you would know better. But given how many times I have left or said I wanted to leave or that I should leave . . . I do not blame you for not believing me when I said I'd never leave you, Ashyn. You considered my history, and you decided I'd changed my mind."

"Um, no. I read the letter. In your hand. Saying things that only we could know. Are you telling me you did not write it?"

"Under duress. They threatened Tova—"

"Tova?" She looked down at the hound, who glanced up.

"At that point, I thought Edwyn was truly your grandfather,

315

so I'd not have believed a threat against you. But they said that if I did not write the letter convincingly, they'd kill your hound. Moreover, I feared that if you did not believe I'd left willingly, you might stir up trouble, and that would be more dangerous for you."

"So you wanted me to believe you'd gone. You wrote a letter designed to convince me of it, saying things no one else could know. And now you're disappointed that I believed it?"

"I would not say I am disappointed . . ."

"You are mortally disappointed."

He turned to her then, saying hotly, "I am not—"

"Yes, you are." She leaned over and kissed his cheek, much as she had Tyrus's, a sisterly kiss that could not be mistaken for anything else. "You wanted me to logically accept you'd gone, but deep down, to wonder and to pine and to hope—"

"I did not expect you to pine."

She grinned at him. "Yes, you did. You may say you're only a thief, but you wish to be the hero. My hero. Saving the poor and helpless girl, who will ache for you every moment you are gone."

"Now you mock me."

Her grin grew. "I've been mocking you for a while. Did you only just notice?" She rode closer and reached to squeeze his hand. "I'm teasing you because you are being very foolish, disappointed because I believed a letter that you wrote in a way that ensured I *would* believe it. But if you want the truth, Ronan, if not for that letter, I'd have suspected a trick. Even with the letter, I did not wish to believe you'd gone. However, given that you'd also just told me a story about being distracted by a girl and blamed that for your brother's death . . ."

316

He nodded. "All right. I concede your point."

They rode in silence until she said, "I did miss you. Terribly. You can ask Tova."

He smiled over. "Thank you. I'm sure I *would* have missed you, too, if I hadn't been going mad with worry, knowing you were about to be sacrificed to raise dragons."

"I thought you believed I was safe?"

"I did when they made me write that letter. Then I was supposed to return to the city. I had no plans of doing that, of course." He glanced at her. "I said I'd never leave you, Ash, and I meant it. I planned to walk far enough so they'd think I'd left and then circle back to watch over you."

"Which didn't happen, because they didn't trust you to simply walk away."

He made a face. "Of course, *you* see that. I didn't. Once I was far enough that I couldn't shout and alert you, they jumped me. That's when I learned the truth—I overheard my captors speaking about the ritual. I realized they needed your blood, enough of it that you would not survive. I also discovered that Edwyn wasn't your grandfather. Apparently, he knew your family in the North, but only because he tracked them down, knowing you and Moria could wake his dragons. He knew enough about them to fake it. You'd had no contact with your mother's family, so he could make up stories about them."

"Which I believed."

"Because you were desperate for family, as he would also understand. But this means that you do have family in the North, which I hope comforts you."

She nodded. "It does."

317

"And I have bigger news, unless Moria told you. Which I doubt, because you had little time together and perhaps I should allow her to—"

"What is it?"

When he hesitated, she bumped her leg against his. "You cannot set that up and then leave me dangling, Ronan. What is it?"

"When they took me, we stopped briefly for supplies in a camp of Alvar Kitsune's, a half-day's ride from here. It is where he keeps the children of Edgewood and Fairview and Northpond."

They found Gavril and Moria at the abandoned farmhouse. Moria was eager to start the journey back to the children, but Ashyn pointed out that they had no idea where to find Tyrus and therefore had to wait for him to come to them.

"Moria cannot travel anyway," Gavril said as Moria returned to her sleeping spot. "She lost more blood. Her wound opened, and she was too stubborn to tell me."

After they got a fire going, Gavril glanced over and said, "Are you asleep yet, Keeper?"

She didn't answer, but although her eyes were shut, they knew she was not.

"I'm going to tell your sister my story," he said. "If you wish not to hear it . . ."

"I said I would," Moria replied. "Go on."

Gavril looked over at Ashyn. "Do *you* wish to hear it? I am not trying to excuse my actions. I was not held captive nor tricked nor manipulated by magics. I made choices. Poor ones."

"I'd like to hear it."

"You have probably deduced that I did not end up in Edge-wood by accident. That was part of my father's plan. Though he was not in the forest—nor had he been since his exile—he wished to make a symbolic first strike from there. I was to be nearby when he did. I'd requested the post. Initially, Emperor Tatsu refused. He thought I was punishing myself, but eventually I convinced him that this was my way of facing my father's crime. He relented, albeit grudgingly."

He pulled his legs in, one arm going around them. "As for what happened in Edgewood, I was told my father would take the village captive. The massacre . . . The shadow stalkers . . . I knew nothing of them, and I say that not as an excuse but as an admittance that I was foolish and naive and trusted my father, despite a childhood that should have taught me otherwise. Even after what happened, I was convinced that the magics had gone wrong or my father had been betrayed and these horrors done in his name. That is what I expected to hear when I joined him."

"And you did not."

"He made no attempt to deny what he had done, and if I was appalled, then he was disappointed in my lack of spine. It was then that I realized what he truly is."

"Yet you stayed."

"Because that seemed the best way to thwart him. Stay and be the son he wanted, which would allow me to be a full party to his plans, and take them to the emperor." He looked back toward Moria, who was sitting up now, watching him. "And there is my greatest and most shameful confession, Keeper. I wanted to march to court and throw myself at the emperor's feet and not only win his pardon but his thanks. I would be both martyr and hero. Betray my own father and save my empire. You may laugh now."

Moria's voice was uncharacteristically soft. "I never would, Kitsune."

He nodded, his gaze down, and Ashyn looked away, feeling as if she'd intruded on something private between them. She looked at Ronan. He was listening but remaining silent.

After a moment, Gavril continued. "Needless to say, it has not exactly worked out as I planned."

"Because I got captured by Lord Jorojumo," Moria said.

"Which I proceeded to make a mess of, as I did the rest of it."

"You did not—"

"I did, Keeper. Perhaps there was no good way to handle it, but there must have been a better one. I failed to find it." He raised a hand against her protest. "I'll stop there. Wallowing in self-pity is neither productive nor flattering. I am . . . out of sorts."

"With reason," Moria said, her voice softening again.

"Thus ends my story. The only thing I hope you will take from it, Ashyn, is that I know what my father is, and I will no longer feel any filial duty toward him. If that damns my spirit, then so be it. I turn my back on him, completely and unequivocally, and I hope that you will believe me when I say that I can be trusted not to betray my empire. If you are concerned about my resolve . . ." He looked toward Moria again. "Speak to your sister. She can detail what he has done and you will realize any duty I still felt toward him is gone now."

"I understand."

He looked over, as if sensing that Ashyn meant more than simply that she understood his words.

"I'm sorry for what you've gone through," she said. "For what your father put you through. For what you've suffered."

His face hardened then, and she knew she'd said the wrong thing. But he kept his voice low and steady as he said, "I appreciate the sentiment, Ashyn, and I know you mean well, but I have inflicted more on others than I've suffered."

"I don't believe that."

She said the words gently, but at a noise from Moria, she saw her sister shake her head. Others might take comfort in her words. For Gavril, if anything, they made him uncomfortable. He wanted to accept the blame, and she should let him.

FORTY-FOUR

A little later, as they sat around a fire inside the farmhouse, Ashyn recalled another moment, seemingly a lifetime ago. The four of them, traveling from Fairview to the imperial city. Ashyn twisted the silver and garnet ring on her finger and remembered the night Moria had given it to her, along with their father's note, and they'd cried and grieved together.

Before that, though, the four of them had sat around a fire not unlike this, Ronan and Moria deep in conversation about . . . What had it been? Oh, yes, quills. Moria and Gavril had killed some twisted beast in the Forest of the Dead and she'd been showing Ashyn the quills, and Moria and Ronan had gotten into a deep discussion of how they could be used for nefarious means.

Ashyn had been content to sit and listen to them. Gavril had, too, offering a comment here and there, but mostly just listening and looking happier and more at peace than Ashyn had ever seen him. There had been something perfect about that night. Their journey had been terrible—the massacre, their father's death, the trip across the Wastes, and then, sent with a missive to the emperor, a missive that would decide the fate of Edgewood's children. There should have been no place for laughter and conversation and, yes, peace on such a journey. But around that fire, they'd found all of it. A camaraderie and a comfort Ashyn had never felt with anyone outside her family. And now, remarkably, they had it again. One magical night when it felt as if everything that had come since the last one did not exist, or if it did, it did not matter.

Moria and Ronan were talking about dragons this time. The uses for a young dragon and whether Zuri could be trained for them. As one might expect, Moria imagined martial applications while Ronan envisioned her as a spy. Gavril pointed out that Zuri was a very small dragon and would take many summers to be more than a pet—if indeed, she even decided to stay with Tyrus. They told him to save his logic—they had no use for it, and he'd laughed then, and he'd joined the debate, and Ashyn had rested, seeing them happy and feeling that wash over her.

It should be like this always, she thought as she watched them.

Of course, it could not be, and even to think that felt uncomfortable. A war simmered beyond those walls, and while they could not see it, nor could they escape it—it was their war, as much as anyone else's. Perhaps even more theirs, because they were the ones on the front line, facing Alvar, who seemed more interested in engaging *them* than facing Emperor Tatsu's armies.

And it was not simply the four of them anymore. They had allies, the most important being Tyrus, who was as much a part of this now, and as much a friend to Ashyn and Moria as Ronan or Gavril were. A new configuration. Different yet even stronger than before.

Conversation twisted and turned, and sometimes Ashyn took part, but mostly she was content to listen, and eventually she caught Gavril giving her pointed looks, and she realized he was saying it was time for the evening to end. Tyrus would arrive soon and they needed to leave at dawn. Moria had to get some sleep, and Ashyn was the only one who could make her get it. So, with no small reluctance, Ashyn brought the night to a close.

After Ashyn convinced Moria to go to sleep, she headed off to perform her nightly ablutions. Ronan went with her, possibly because when Ashyn wandered off in the night, trouble seemed to follow.

The stream was a good distance from the house. When Ashyn had finished, Ronan said, "If you're not tired, I'd like to walk a little."

"Certainly. Is something wrong?"

He shook his head, but she could tell it was—after chattering nonstop at the fire, he'd barely said a word since they set out. It was a silent walk for at least fifty paces, before he pulled something from his pocket. When he held it out, her breath caught.

It was the dove bracelet.

"I took this." He wrapped his hand around it, as if hiding it from view. "I know you might not wish it back. In fact, I'm quite certain you don't. I took it as a reminder of . . ." He shrugged, still looking away. "Of that night. In the dragon's den. But for you, I suppose it would be a reminder of the rest. Of Edwyn and . . ." He looked at her then. "How are you doing? You never complain, but I know you must be upset."

"I've been too busy to be upset," she said with a wan smile. "If anything, I feel foolish, but I won't whine about that."

"You never whine, Ash. You can talk to me about anything, at any time. But I understand if you don't want this back."

"Can we trade?" she asked.

He looked over, frowning.

"A trade," she said. "I have something for you, in return for that. But if I take it, then you must take what I offer. Unconditionally."

"I will take whatever you offer, Ash. Unconditionally."

She reached into her deepest pocket and took out her fist, bulging. Then she opened it. Jewels and coins tumbled from her overflowing hand. Ronan saw that, threw back his head, and laughed.

"You took—"

"*Stole* is the proper term," she said. "Yes, I stole it, and I do not feel a flicker of guilt. Edwyn and his people owe us, and therefore, by extension, their dragon does. Do not argue with the poor logic of that."

He grinned. "I see perfect logic in that. I simply cannot believe that you took it." He bent to pick up the pieces that had fallen. Then he stopped and looked up at her, his expression unreadable. "You did not take them for yourself."

Before she could answer, he went on, "No, that is a foolish question. You have no need of gold and jewels. You are the Seeker—the empire will provide whatever you require. And you would never fill your pockets with pretty baubles. You took them for me."

She took a deep breath. "It is not charity, Ronan. I know perhaps it feels like that, and I hadn't considered it that way. I simply wanted you to have—"

He cut her off with a kiss, making her jump, and when she pulled back, he was smiling. "I know you did not intend charity, Ash, no more than I intended this"—he lifted the dove cuff—"as a reminder of troubles. Our intentions were both good. I was simply surprised. And . . ." He seemed to struggle for more, and then settled for kissing her cheek. "Thank you. If you will take the bracelet, I will take these."

They exchanged their thievings. She put on the cuff, and when she looked up, he was right there, his face over hers.

"There is more I wished to say," he said. "When I was taken captive, I realized how much you meant—no, that's not right." He met her gaze. "I've long known how much you meant to me, Ash, and I tried to tell myself it was simply friendship, but it has not been friendship for a very long time, and when I was captured, I made a vow that if I ever saw you again, I would not waste another moment—"

"No."

The word was soft, but he flinched nonetheless. "You are saying . . . ?"

"I am saying no. I can see where this is heading, and I will not allow it to head there."

When he pulled back, the look on his face was almost enough to melt her resolve. "All right," he said slowly. "I cannot pretend I don't understand. I hurt you and abused your affections and I do not blame you for refusing me now, but the reason I retreated—"

"I know why."

"Then you know it was certainly not a change of heart. Can we then—"

"No."

His gaze dropped, and he nodded slowly. "All right. That is your choice—"

"It is."

"Because of what I did."

"No, because of what you *think* you did."

He looked up.

"You think that you got your brother killed because you were smitten with a girl. Because you were paying attention to her and not him. In truth, your brother died because a cart lost control and because he was simpleminded and because your father did not know better than to entrust his care to another child. You *were* a child, Ronan. Leaving Eder outside while you visited a girl is something any boy of thirteen summers could have done, and what happened was a tragic accident. But you were not driving the horse."

"I was responsible for Eder."

"Yes, you were. And now you are responsible for Jorn and Aidra, and if anything should happen to them while you are on the road with a lover, you would truly never forgive yourself. So you are not on the road with a lover. You are on the road protecting a Seeker and an imperial prince while fighting for your empire."

He went quiet, processing her words. "And when I am home again? Do I dare to hope that anything will change then, Ash?"

"You can hope." She smiled and lifted up to kiss his cheek. "I'd not want to make it too easy."

When she moved back, he caught her face in his hands and pulled her into a kiss, and it was nothing like the kiss at the gate, the one that haunted her dreams. That had been a sweet and pleasant surprise. This was . . . Well, not to be too blunt about it, but this kiss was not sweet. It was fire and passion, starting as a spark, hungry but contained. Yet the moment she reciprocated, it turned into a blaze that consumed all thoughts except "Oh, *this* is a kiss" and "I want more of this." She wrapped her arms around his neck and kissed him back, and when they finally parted, they were both short of breath, and Ashyn had to disentangle herself quickly before she completely forgot her intentions.

"I do not believe that is what I had in mind when I said we would wait," she said.

He grinned. "So now it is not merely hope? We are only waiting?"

She flushed. "I didn't mean—"

"Too late." He caught her hand. "We are waiting. Which means one kiss like that per day. So that we do not forget what we are waiting for."

"I don't think—"

"I do. One kiss. Each night. No more and no less, until we are home in the city."

She smiled. "And then less?"

"It depends on how I like the rest of the kisses." He winked at her. "I wouldn't want to make it too easy. Now come on. You've had your kiss, and Tova is telling us we need to get back to the farmhouse."

FORTY-FIVE

Tyrus arrived almost as soon as Ashyn and Ronan returned. Moria awoke long enough for a brief exchange of words and a kiss, and then he settled in next to her, and everyone went to sleep.

Moria's wounds did not heal overnight, but between Gavril's magics and Ashyn's healing, she was in good enough shape to ride. And they all *could* ride, Tyrus having brought two more horses. They were on the road not long after dawn and eventually rejoined Dalain and the others at their camp.

Tyrus, Gavril, and Moria had come up with a plan on the journey. Ashyn and Ronan had listened in, but it was mostly those three who determined their course of action. They would free the children first. No one even suggested they ought to ride straight for the imperial city. The children were close enough that it made no sense to rush straight to the emperor and risk losing them.

Did it concern Ashyn that her sister had stumbled on the children so easily? At first, yes, but once they explained the situation with the shadow stalkers, she understood it was no unlikely coincidence. The so-called bandits had been working for Alvar. They'd brought Gavril intentionally to show him his poor mother's corpse. Alvar had been keeping her in this wasteland on the edge of the steppes. And he'd been using the same general area to hide his shadow stalkers and the kidnapped children. It was a simple matter of efficiency.

They did keep their eyes open for the shadow stalker camp. It was likely within a half-day's walk of the children. Understandably, though, Alvar wouldn't keep it *too* close. They'd notify the emperor and he could send men to find it when they did not.

They did worry that Alvar might have stopped at the children's camp as he headed back to his military base. But if he had, it was only temporary and he'd moved on before they arrived. The children had only five guards and a small staff to tend to them. Tyrus spent a quarter of a day ensuring that— scouting to be certain there were no hidden troops waiting to spring a trap. There wasn't. At sundown, they launched their strike.

This time, they used Zuri to their advantage—Tyrus and Moria got the dragon whelp flying above the camp, as she traveled between her two favorite people, both armed with fresh meat. The sight of a dragon sent the camp into a tizzy, and from there, the guards were easily routed. The servants seemed ill-inclined to fight, particularly on seeing an imperial prince and their own lord's son leading the charge with a Keeper at their backs. The older children rose up, too, the girls as well as the boys, grabbing whatever they could find as weapons, in case the servants attacked. They did not. The warriors were easily beaten and the caretakers easily cowed.

And that was it. The camp was taken.

That's when Moria and Ashyn got their truest reward. Their reunion with the children of Edgewood. The others stayed back for that. Even Ashyn had been inclined to linger on the fringes. She'd been friendly with the children of their village, but it had always been her sister whom they loved. Or so she thought. Now, they embraced her and they clung to her and they climbed on Tova. And she realized that, perhaps, she had never been overshadowed by Moria quite as much as she'd *felt* overshadowed. The sisters were different. But that only meant they had their own strengths. And while the older children clamored about Moria and chattered to her and told her all that had happened, the little ones curled up with Ashyn, on her knee and in her arms and leaning against her, and they cried and she comforted them.

Then the children wanted to see Tyrus. After all, he was an imperial prince and certainly no word of his alleged betrayal had reached their ears. For them, it was like meeting the emperor himself. Even better, because Tyrus was young and friendly and handsome and had stormed in to their rescue, blade flashing. Along with Moria, he was the hero of their childhood dreams. Someone else was, too. A young warrior they remembered from Edgewood, now fighting at Tyrus and Moria's side: Gavril.

The children did not seem to realize his father was

responsible for their captivity, or if they did, they did not blame him. He was Gavril Kitsune. From Edgewood. He may not have been friendly or even well-liked, but that was forgotten now, because he was familiar and as much a hero as Moria and Tyrus. Gavril took one look at those glowing faces, heard one joyous shout of "Gavril!," mumbled some excuse about the horses, and bolted from the compound.

Moria and Tyrus exchanged a look. Tyrus whispered something to Moria, and she nodded and left the children in Tyrus's care, promising them something truly magical if they behaved.

While Moria went to speak to Gavril, Ronan came in from securing the camp with Dalain and Sabre. Some of the children recognized Ronan, and, like Gavril, it didn't matter *what* he'd been before. They saw not an exiled thief, but the young rogue who'd escaped the inescapable forest, who'd joined their heroes and come to their rescue. Then there was Dalain, and when Tyrus said who his father was, the older children stared in awe, having heard tales of the Gray Wolf. And a bandit king's daughter? A girl who'd charged into the camp, alongside the warriors, armed with her sling? For once, Sabre didn't insist her father was no bandit. Clearly the children were entranced, and she let them be, showing the older girls her sling as she chattered away.

Moria returned shortly after that. Gavril followed, staying at her back. It helped that she brought with her something guaranteed to turn their attention from the reluctant hero. The children promptly forgot the warriors and the thief and the bandit girl and the prince and even their own Keeper and Seeker. There was a dragon in the camp. Nothing else mattered.

Zuri seemed a little uncertain, with so many children, but Tyrus was there and Moria was there, and Daigo, too, sticking by Zuri's side like her appointed protector. She accepted some petting and such, and by the time Tyrus declared it was time to leave, they had a camp filled with very happy and very tired children, all ready to collapse, asleep, in the Okami wagons.

In short, the rescue and the reunion were everything Ashyn could have imagined.

FORTY-SIX

Moria lay beside Tyrus in the wagon. They were fully dressed, which was a shame, but she was still recovering from her injuries, and this was hardly the time for more exploration. They also both had too much on their minds to devote their full attention to that, as it deserved. For now, what they needed most was quiet time together, away from those other thoughts and responsibilities. So they'd retreated to the wagon to "talk and rest," and while they were in a recumbent position, they'd been too busy kissing to talk. Lots of wonderful and delicious kisses, which made Moria decide that while the exploration was very fun and satisfying indeed, there was something to be said for simply lying in each other's arms.

"Does this hurt your side?" Tyrus whispered as he tugged her on top of him.

"I do not care if it does," she said.

He chuckled, startling Daigo and Zuri, who were curled up at the other end of the wagon. Being careful with her bandaged side, he wrapped his hands in her hair, and their lips had barely touched when a rap came at the wagon door.

"Tyrus?" Dalain said. "May I enter?" He lowered his voice. "I will keep my gaze averted."

"Come in," Tyrus said.

Dalain stepped inside—backward.

Tyrus chuckled again and said, "We are fully dressed."

"But not lying with a handbreadth between you, I'll wager."

"I find it more restful without space between us," Moria said.

Dalain turned, smiling, and shook his head. "I know I'm the oldest one in the party when the others accepted your excuse of 'resting and talking' without comment. I am sorry to interrupt, Tyrus, but I need to speak to you. I'll keep it brief."

They talked, mostly Tyrus and Dalain, though Moria listened in, and Tyrus would glance over, taking in her thoughts with a look, amending his plans if she displayed any sign of doubt. Tyrus would never be a bold, blustering leader, certain that every word that came from his lips was divinely inspired. He consulted those around him when their skills were better suited to a task. And he consulted her as a sounding board, a trusted confidante who would always tell him exactly what she thought.

This was their second night on the road. They were still traveling—continuing through the night, taking turns resting in the wagons. They would arrive at the imperial city in another day. And Tyrus was terrified.

Dalain had sent two of his men to his father's territory, to convince Lord Okami to join them as they neared the city. Yet what they asked was dangerous. It placed Lord Okami firmly at the side of several supposed traitors. What they planned to do might force Emperor Tatsu's hand more than he could afford to have it forced in a time of war. They'd agreed, though, that it was the only way. No more skulking about, caught between the two sides, accused of betraying both. They were marching on the city, possibly to end up in its dungeons. And if they did, then it did not matter that all had agreed—Tyrus would blame himself.

When Dalain left, Tyrus fell back onto the sleeping pallet, sighing. Moria moved against him again and he smiled for her, pulling her into a kiss. They lost themselves in that distraction for a few moments longer.

They were breaking for a brief meal, when the messenger they'd sent to speak to Lord Okami came riding hard.

"He comes," the young man panted. "With an army at his rear."

Tyrus exhaled in relief. "He joins us then."

The messenger only swallowed, his gaze downcast.

"Does he *not* come to join us?" Dalain said.

"I—I know only that he comes, my lord. He said to tell you that . . . and then sent me off at the tip of his sword."

Moria glanced at Tyrus.

"We hold our ground," he said. "And we pray."

* * *

It seemed to take forever for the dust of the approaching army to appear. They did spot riders before that, presumably sent to follow the messenger onto Tyrus's path. First they saw the dust clouds. Then riders—at least thirty of them. And behind the riders, rows of marching warriors. While Lord Okami would have left men behind to guard his lands, he had brought the bulk of his army, quickly gathered from nearby posts.

The army halted far enough that Moria was just barely able to make out the wolf head helmets of the warlord and his elder sons. The Gray Wolf then broke from his ranks and approached alone. He rode up to Tyrus, who stood in his path, Dalain at one side, Gavril and Moria at the other, all slightly behind him.

"So," Lord Okami called as he approached. "By what right do you order me to raise an army for you, Prince Tyrus?"

"It was not a demand but a request."

"From a member of the imperial family, it is always a demand."

Tyrus dipped his chin. "It was not intended as such."

"You requested my help. My men. After you escaped my custody. Turned me into an imperial traitor."

"What? No. I—"

"You escaped my custody when the entire empire knows you apprenticed under my family. Either I betrayed my emperor by releasing you or I am such a weak and sentimental old fool that I let you play on my affections and escape."

Dalain cut in. "But Tyrus has proven he is no traitor, as I'm sure the messenger told you. He will return to the city in triumph, and everyone will see that he was aligned with both

338

the Keeper and Gavril Kitsune *for* the empire, not against it. You alone saw through the lies and allowed him to prove himself. By marching at his side, you take control of the story, Father."

"Now you advise me in matters of state?" Lord Okami turned his steely gaze on his son. "Tyrus escaped my custody. You found him. And you failed to return him. You had the opportunity to save your family's good name . . . and instead you joined the alleged traitor."

"Because of the dragon, Father. The dragon proves—"

"Ah, yes. The dragon. Let's see this beast that someone has convinced you children is a dragon."

Tyrus turned and Ronan opened the wagon, luring Zuri out with food. When Tyrus whistled, she flew over with a happy squawk and swooped to tease Daigo before landing at Tyrus's side. Moria glanced at the Gray Wolf, expecting to see shock in his face, but he only crouched and gave the whelp a critical once-over.

"Snow dragon," he said. "Not the most useful variety. And it's very small."

Zuri hissed, blowing cold air in his face.

"Ah," he said. "Now I see her use. She'll chill honey wine for the warriors." He stood. "I heard there was a full-grown one. Why did you not wake her?"

"Because it would have cost the Keeper's or Seeker's life," Tyrus said.

The Gray Wolf looked at Moria, and then over her shoulder at Ashyn as she approached. "Neither of you was willing to sacrifice your life for your empire?"

"No," Moria said simply.

Ashyn walked up behind her. "Particularly not when the result would almost certainly be a very unhappy, newly woken, full-grown dragon who would have killed us all. These things never end nearly as well as they do in bards' tales. Which people always fail to realize until it's too late."

Lord Okami looked as if he was biting his cheek to keep from laughing. "All right, then. So you have a dragon. A very small dragon. I'll take a wolf."

"What?" Tyrus said.

"Did you catch an arrow in your ear, boy? I want a wolf. Preferably gray. That will be the price of my fealty."

Tyrus stared, but Dalain shook his head. "He's teasing you, Tyrus. As he has been since he first rode up here. Or not so much teasing as performing. He is the Gray Wolf—he cannot come gamboling to your side like an eager pup. He must be fierce and proud and fearsome, and you must tremble and stammer and then woo him to your side."

"With a wolf," Lord Okami said. "There's one in the mountains. A legendary she-wolf. You'll bring me one of her next litter as a living representative of my totem. Like that." He pointed at Zuri.

"All right," Tyrus said slowly. "I owe you a wolf."

"Good." He slapped Tyrus on the back. "You have explained yourself to me, convinced me of your innocence, and bought my forgiveness with a wolf cub, to be delivered at some future time." He glanced at Gavril. "If you ever wanted your own nine-tailed fox, this is the time to ask."

"That one would be slightly more difficult to deliver," Gavril said.

Lord Okami winked at him. "Which is the point of making the demand. Come then, children. Let us march on the imperial city while you tell me your plan, so I may fix it for you."

FORTY-SEVEN

"I can do this," Tyrus said, sitting atop his steed, his cloak hood pulled up. Moria had just rejoined him, after riding with Ashyn. They'd been snatching what time they could together, talking about everything they'd been unable to speak of until now. Over a fortnight had passed and they had been separated. There had been much to discuss. Now, though, it was time for Tyrus, because the city gates drew near.

They waited on the same side road that Moria, Gavril, and Ashyn had used to approach the city the first time. They were almost in the exact spot where Ronan had left them to sneak in a back way. From the look on Tyrus's face, he was seriously contemplating asking Ronan to point that route out.

"What's the worst thing that can happen?" Tyrus said. "The dungeons. That's not so bad. I hear they're relatively nice in the springtime. Not too cold. Not too damp. They'd be quiet and peaceful." Tyrus looked at Gavril. "Tell me I can do this."

"Why? There's no doubt you can. The question is simply whether you'll survive it."

"Thank you. Thank you so much."

"We have not heard that your father has reinstituted capital punishment. Of course, we haven't heard news from the city in many days."

"You are not helping."

Gavril shot him a quirk of a smile. Tyrus laughed, which was as good to see as Gavril's smile. As tense as Tyrus was, Moria knew his show of anxiety was partly for the benefit of Gavril, who seemed almost to hope that the goddess herself would smite him before he reached the gate. Of course, Gavril would say no such thing. Or even show it. So Tyrus did the fretting for him.

"Are you ready?" Moria murmured as she moved her horse closer to Gavril's.

He nodded.

"Then turn." She motioned, and he twisted in his saddle. She reached over and undid his cloak. He let her push it off his head and shoulders. Then he removed it. She took it and laid it over the back of his horse.

"You want this," she whispered. "As hard as it is. You want to face the emperor. To face the city. To say that you made a mistake. I would gladly sneak you in the back and spare you that. But this is what you want. What you need."

He dipped his chin. "It is." He hesitated, then looked toward the back of the caravan. "Perhaps, though, I ought to ride farther away from—"

"No, you are Tyrus's friend, not his captive. If it makes you uncomfortable having me here, given the rumors, I'll ride back with Ash and—"

"No, stay." He lowered his voice. "Tyrus needs you." Another hesitation. "And I . . ." He trailed off and straightened. "You'll ride with us. Anything else would be hiding."

"And none of us need to hide." Tyrus passed Moria a strained smile. "I'll just keep telling myself that."

She moved her horse to him and leaned in to remove his cloak.

"I think I'm going to vomit," he whispered.

"Which is why you had no breakfast."

"Hmm. I still might."

"If you're serious, then we'd best step aside."

"I think I'll be all right. But I would not mind a moment to check on the children, perhaps settle my stomach."

"We'll do that then." She raised her voice. "Gavril? We're saying a few words to the children, in case they are anxious."

He nodded. "I'll wait here."

Speaking to the children settled Tyrus's stomach and his nerves. They thought him a hero, so he would be one for them. As Moria watched him tease and joke with the children, knowing each by name, and she saw them beam under the attention, she thought of the wild visions she'd had on waking the dragon whelp. Visions of Tyrus on a throne. She watched him with the children of Edgewood, and then with the warriors, more words for them, and she realized they were not such wild visions after all. He did have what it took to be emperor, and she might have no idea how he'd get to that throne, but he would. She'd no doubt of that.

Then it began. A test more daunting than any battlefield. Tyrus marched on the city that had declared him a traitor. He marched at the side of the enemy's son and the young woman who'd supposedly betrayed him. He marched with the Seeker of Edgewood and with an exiled thief who bore a warrior's blades. He marched with Goro Okami, who followed with his son directly at Tyrus's back. Wagons followed him, too. Two wagons filled with the children of Edgewood and Fairview and Northpond.

And Tyrus brought something else. A dragon.

They'd argued about that. Tyrus had wanted to find a way to contain Zuri, possibly in one of the wagons.

"You bring a *dragon*," Moria had said. "And you wish to hide her?"

"I fear . . ."

"You fear what?"

He'd shifted, uncomfortable, casting a glance at Zuri, who was ripping apart a leg of deer with Daigo.

"You fear insulting your father," Gavril had said, quietly listening in.

"How?" Moria had asked. "The dragon is your totem. You return to the city bearing your actual, living totem, who chooses to stay at your side. If that is not a sign of the goddess's favor . . ."

"That is the problem," Gavril had said.

She'd understood it then. If anyone should have a living dragon, it was the emperor. So Moria devised a solution, one that allowed Tyrus the awe and majesty of returning with a dragon, while not claiming the goddess's favor over his father. Now Zuri flew far overhead, circling the wagons and the troops, but always returning to her master, making sure he did not leave her.

They attracted quite enough attention on the secondary road, but when it joined the Imperial Way, Moria truly realized what they were doing. One might say that an empire is never so unsettled as when it is at war. That was, Moria reflected, not true. Being on the edge of war was worse. Tensions ran high and everyone was looking for a scapegoat. And now they brought three of them into the city. Three traitors, leading a small army.

Last time they'd been met with catcalls and mockery. Now it was hatred and fear. Lord Okami's men had to surround them to keep them from being attacked. Even then, they could not stop the rage-fueled words. Or the stones and fruit and whatever else could be hurled. Moria deflected a few of the missiles before they struck Tyrus, and she hurled snarls back, Daigo echoing them, but Tyrus stopped her.

"Ignore them," he said, without looking her way. "To acknowledge their anger only feeds it."

Gavril grunted in agreement. Moria glanced back to be sure Ashyn was fine, riding behind Lord Okami. Her sister caught her gaze and looked anxious, but the mobs growing along the road were leaving her alone. Their targets rode at the front. The three traitors.

Moria seethed and fumed and fidgeted in her seat. When someone shouted an insult about Gavril's mother, she could not help herself. She wheeled toward the offender, daggers raised. Gavril leaned over swiftly and caught her arm, and then whispered, "Be calm. You are the Keeper."

"I cannot stand to hear—"

"Do you remember when we first walked into the city? And you defended me? I never forgot that. Whenever I would try to tell myself I had not betrayed you, I would remember you leaping to my defense."

"I—"

"What I mean, Keeper, is that it was more than I expected then and it is far more than I expected to ever have again. So . . ." He fussed with his reins. "I simply mean thank you."

Tyrus leaned over then. "Believe me, I would have liked to draw my sword on that idiot myself, but this is one time when we cannot—"

"Are you bewitched, bastard?" someone shouted.

"At least bastard is an epithet I can own," Tyrus said quietly to Moria. "And I will also accept bewitched."

He grinned at her, and she smiled back.

"The Kitsune traitor has used his sorcery on you," the man shouted. "He whispers treachery to the Keeper bitch and you still smile for his whore—"

Tyrus had his blade out before the man could finish. Gavril lunged, nearly falling off his horse as he leaned across Moria to grab at Tyrus's arm. He couldn't reach, but Tyrus looked over, their eyes meeting.

"He cannot call her—" Tyrus said.

"It is but a word," Moria murmured.

Tyrus's eyes still flashed, and Gavril lifted in his seat,

straining to see the gates, cursing at how far off they still seemed, their party slowly making its way through the growing crowd.

"Do you not like that, you traitorous bastard?" someone else yelled. "Perhaps you aren't ensorcelled after all. Perhaps you simply tell yourself that your whore did not spread her legs for Alvar's brat. Or perhaps you don't care. Whores have their attractions—"

"Enough!" Gavril said, then shook his head sharply, as if angry at himself for reacting.

And with that, the crowd realized how to break their stolid facade. The trio would not react to insults against themselves. But to one another? Oh yes, that worked. They fought to hide it, all of them gripping their reins and looking straight forward, but when the crowds insulted Tyrus's honor and Gavril's mother, Moria knew there was a limit to what she could endure. Lord Okami rode closer and counseled them to stopper their ears, but there was a growl in his voice that belied his words, one that said he was on the verge of drawing his own sword, and Dalain already had his out, carried at his side, spoiling for a fight. Which was not what Tyrus or Gavril wanted. Not at all.

There was, then, only one thing to be done. Moria squinted into the sky. Zuri had been flying in ever wider circles and ever higher, confident now that Tyrus would not escape her, boxed in as he was by the crowd. The bright sun meant she was but a shimmering patch of light, visible only to those who knew what to look for.

Now Moria lifted her hand over her head, with a piece

of squashed plum between her fingers. Then she whistled. Zuri heard her above the crowd and circled sharp. The whelp saw what appeared to be food and began her descent. Before she could realize she'd been tricked, Moria dropped the plum and merely waggled her fingers. It was enough. Zuri swooped down and nipped at them. Nipped playfully, thank the goddess, though her teeth still dented the skin. She landed beside Tyrus's horse, walking alongside him and chirping. He reached into his pocket and threw her a piece of dried meat and she dove after it.

The moment Zuri had appeared, the crowd had gone silent. Now they stared, dumbfounded, as the whelp leaped and walked alongside Tyrus, snatching meat from his fingers.

"What?" Moria shouted into the crowd. "You act as if you've never seen a dragon before."

Tyrus snorted a laugh. Even Gavril cracked the barest smile. Behind them, the laughter carried through their party.

"You thought dragons did not exist?" Moria called out. "Then you are wrong. Perhaps you are wrong about many things. Tyrus Tatsu returns to the city—to his *father*—and he brings a dragon, his totem beast. If that is not a sign that the goddess favors our emperor, then I do not know what is."

Murmurs ran through the crowd.

"Perhaps you ought to give him way," Moria shouted. "Considering that he brings a *dragon*."

There were a few laughs and chuckles then, from the crowd itself. Not everyone moved. But enough backed away, heads bowed, that they were able to pick up speed, and no one challenged or insulted them until they were near enough to the gates for the guards to step out, swords at the ready.

Tyrus stopped his horse. "I will not enter the city gates without my father's permission. Please tell him I am here."

The captain of the guard gave a curt nod, one that could not be mistaken for a proper bow in any way. Then he turned on his heel and walked into the city, and they were left to wait.

FORTY-EIGHT

They waited in silence. Tyrus kept glancing at Moria, and she wanted to move closer, to whisper with him and reassure him, but she knew that would only get the crowd grumbling again. The Keeper who had seduced him and continued to bewitch him.

It might seem a pretty fantasy to one who imagined her some beautiful and delicate maiden, but it seemed impossible to fathom that they could see her—with her dusty breeches and plain tunic, face dirty from the long ride, her hair messily braided—and imagine a girl who seduced both an imperial prince and the enemy's son. It was a feat worthy of an artful enchantress, not a village girl barely past her sixteenth summer.

Worse, they believed it with absolutely no evidence beyond the fact that she'd been seen in the company of both young men. It seemed that was all the proof anyone required, that now they were engaged in a deeply torrid love affair, ready to betray their empire and their families and their ancestors to be together.

"We ought to speak to the others while we wait," Moria said. "Reassure them that all will be well."

"Of course," Tyrus said, nodding, and he waved for her to go ahead. Gavril stayed where he was at first, sitting as still as a statue, a trickle of sweat the only sign of his terror.

"Gavril!" Tyrus called, waving to him. "Ashyn has a question for you."

Her sister had said no such thing, but Ashyn caught on and formulated one. As Gavril was talking to Ashyn, Tyrus moved up beside Moria and whispered, "You are well?"

"I am." She looked over at him. "Whatever happens next, remember this: it is not your fault."

"I—"

"Your father believes in you. He loves you. He is proud of you. He knows you have done absolutely nothing wrong. Well, except for escaping from Lord Okami's compound, but I'm sure he expected no less. If anything, he will be secretly pleased you managed it." She moved closer. "He will do what he must for the empire, but if we are to go to the dungeons, it will be only temporary, while he works this out, because there is no doubt in the mind of anyone here that you have done your best, and there will be no doubt in the mind of your father either. He is proud of you, and I am proud to ride at your side. Truly proud."

He dropped his gaze. "Thank you, Moria. I only hope that I will earn that momentarily."

"You already have. You have earned my regard and my

loyalty and my love." She met his gaze. "Always. No matter what."

"And you have mine. Always. No matter what."

Dalain cleared his throat, and they looked to see the gates opening.

Tyrus started forward, moving his horse close enough to discreetly squeeze her leg. Then they returned to their places as the gates swung open and Emperor Tatsu walked out.

Everyone dismounted as the emperor approached. Most of the retinue bowed deeply. Tyrus, Moria, and Gavril got to their knees and bent until their heads touched the ground, in what had once been the customary greeting for an emperor but had fallen out of favor, except in circumstances where mere bowing seemed insufficient. This qualified.

They stayed like that, heads touching the road, eyes on the cobblestones, waiting for permission to rise. Moria could hear the click of the emperor's shoes until they came to rest just before them. Then he stood there, saying nothing. Moria cast a glance Tyrus's way at the same time he looked hers, and he truly did seem about to vomit, his face shiny with sweat, his eyes bright with fear.

"Rise," Emperor Tatsu said.

They did, as gracefully as they could manage. The emperor looked from one to the other, his expression unreadable. Moria recalled her words to Tyrus, reassuring him that if his father acted harshly, it was as emperor, not as father. But in that moment, seeing him so stone-faced, panic darted through Moria.

What if I was wrong? What if I misjudged? What if . . . ?
What if.

She glanced at Tyrus. He had his speech planned, but now he seemed frozen with his lips slightly parted, her own panic reflected in his eyes. As soon as she looked at him, though, it was as if she'd kicked him instead, and the words came, strong and true, ringing out over the silent crowd.

"Father, I return to you. I return to my empire and to my city to offer my sword and my body and my spirit, in any way you see fit to use them. I failed you at Riverside. My men were massacred. I survived. That is unacceptable, and I will accept any punishment for that with no words in my defense except these: you trusted me and I failed."

"Why did you fail?" The emperor's words came soft but rang as clearly as Tyrus's.

"It does not matter. I failed."

Emperor Tatsu turned to Moria. "Keeper. Tell me why he failed."

The panic in her gut crystalized into terror. *Do not put this on me*, she wanted to say. But what did that mean? That Tyrus ought to bear the brunt of the blame? No. She would answer truthfully, no matter how much trouble this might cause.

"He was too young for the charge you gave him, your imperial majesty. You misjudged the situation, and he was forced into a position a seasoned general could not have handled."

Anger and outrage rippled through the crowd. Tyrus looked over sharply, but she refused to glance his way.

"Continue, Keeper," the emperor said. "Tell me everything that happened."

"The people of Fairview were dead. Tyrus and the counselors knew Alvar's men would march on another town, and there was no time to return to the city for reinforcements. Tyrus chose Riverside as the most likely target. The counselors supported him. We came upon a man who claimed to have seen shadow stalkers marching on Riverside, which appeared to seal the matter. When we drew near, we found a camp of Alvar's men—a force twice the size of ours. Tyrus sent for the local warlord. Lord Jorojumo came and seemed to fight with us. Then he turned on us. Our forces were overwhelmed. I was taken, and Tyrus was poisoned and left for dead, rescued and returned to life by my sister and her guard."

"I take responsibility—" Tyrus began.

"Keeper? Your assessment?"

"I am not an impartial judge. Nor am I a martial expert. Tyrus did the best with the information he had. His biggest mistake was trusting Lord Jorojumo, but he had no reason not to, and your imperial majesty knows that if his son has a flaw, it is trust. He will not make that mistake again. On the battlefield, he fought better than any man there, which is how he survived. He left the field, not by choice, but because he was taken from it, poisoned and unconscious. Neither the counselors nor warriors questioned his choices at any point. His failure comes down to one thing: his youth."

"And an emperor who misjudged the situation."

"I said that once. It seems unwise to repeat it."

Emperor Tatsu's laugh rang out, startling everyone. He walked to Moria and embraced her, saying loud enough for all to hear, "I cannot count on you for manners, child, but I can count on you for the truth."

He stepped back, sobering. "Now, tell me what I asked of you."

When she hesitated, he said, "I met up with you after you escaped from Alvar Kitsune with my son's help. And then I asked you to do what?"

"Return to Alvar Kitsune's camp," she said, her voice low, in case he expected her to lie.

"Louder, child."

"Return to Alvar Kitsune's camp."

"With whom?"

She looked at Gavril. "Gavril Kitsune."

"Who was acting as a spy for me in his father's camp. Because the atrocities his father committed were too great even for filial piety. The empire came first. Is that correct, Gavril?"

The emperor's words suggested Gavril had been a spy from the start, which he had not. Wisely, the emperor was not asking Moria to confirm this.

"Yes, your imperial highness, I did turn against my family," Gavril said. "I understand the crime I committed in that, and my ancestors will judge me for it."

"But your conscience would not allow you to act in any other way. My charge to you then, Keeper, was to return with Gavril and do what?"

"Spy on Alvar Kitsune."

"And?"

"Kill him if I could."

Tyrus stiffened at that, his eyes filling with outrage. "You asked—" He clipped his words and shut his mouth, but his eyes still blazed.

"I presume you did not?" the emperor said.

Moria lowered her gaze. "No. Like Tyrus, I failed my mission."

"Because, like Tyrus, you were tasked with one you lacked the experience to carry out."

"It does not matter. I failed."

Tyrus looked over, and the outrage in his gaze turned to pride. He straightened and said, "Yes, Father. She lacked the experience to carry it out. She is a Keeper, not an assassin. In asking her to do so, you misjudged. I apologize for saying so, but I must."

"Yes, you must." The emperor stepped forward and squeezed Tyrus's arm. "I gave both of you tasks you were too inexperienced to carry out. Yours, because I did not foresee what happened. Hers, not because I expected her to carry it through, but because I hoped if she had the opportunity she would take it. It was a seed planted with little hope of sprouting."

"We may have failed our missions," Moria said, "but we did find the children of Fairview, Northpond, and Edgewood, and we have brought them home, safely."

Emperor Tatsu's brows shot up. "You . . . ?"

"We have the children, your imperial majesty. In the wagons." Moria waved toward them and the crowd and the emperor looked and saw several of the older children, grown restless and standing alongside the wagons.

The emperor hid his surprise, and quickly turned to the

warrior behind him, ordering the man to take the children inside the city walls.

"The guard said you brought something else," Emperor Tatsu said. "Something more exotic." He looked up, over their heads. "But it did seem rather unlikely." He tried to hide his disappointment, but he looked like a boy who has been told he can have a pony for his Fire Festival gift, and then finds no pony with his presents.

Tyrus lifted his fingers and whistled, and Zuri swooped in, landing beside him.

Emperor Tatsu stared at the dragon and then said, "Or not."

Tyrus fought a smile. "The one Alvar hoped to raise was much larger."

"I should hope so."

"This is her whelp. And while I had hoped to do this with a little more ceremony . . ." Tyrus cleared his throat and bowed. "I would like to present you, Emperor Tatsu, of the dragon clan, with the living embodiment of your totem, brought to life by the blood of the Keeper of Edgewood and given to me by the goddess herself, to bring to you and present to you. A dragon." He looked at Zuri. "She'll grow."

The emperor laughed and stepped forward to embrace his son. When he moved back, he looked at Zuri again, staring for a moment, as dumbfounded as any commoner. Then he shook his head sharply and turned to the crowd.

"My son has returned. He has brought with him the honored Keeper and the equally honored son of my former marshal. I gave them tasks that set the entire empire against them, that brought them into grave danger, and branded them as traitors. Yet while they were not entirely successful, they accomplished feats greater still. They returned our lost children to us. And they woke a dragon. For the empire. Taking her from the clutches of Alvar Kitsune. If there is a surer sign that the goddess smiles on us, I do not know what it is."

A cheer rose from the crowd. Emperor Tatsu embraced the three of them again, more formally now, then moving to do the same with the Okamis and Ashyn and Ronan and even Sabre.

"You are welcome into the city," he said, his voice echoing. "As our most honored guests."

FORTY-NINE

They were going to war. Come dawn, Moria would set out with the emperor and Tyrus and Gavril. While they'd been off on their adventures, the emperor had been mobilizing his troops and sending spies to assess the situation. A target had been located—a camp a day's walk from the imperial city. The emperor knew better than to hurl his entire army at one camp, but he was no longer sitting and waiting for Alvar to make the first move.

Alvar knew his son had switched sides. The emperor would strike, at the head of a contingent of his men, with his sons at his side.

War. Moria would actually see war. Yes, she was going primarily as a figurehead. But while Emperor Tatsu refused to put her into battle until she was better trained, she would do as she had done outside Riverside—watch from the front lines and offer support in any way possible.

She'd left Tyrus speaking to his father and wandered into the gardens. Now she and Daigo sat beside the pond, watching the huge golden fish mouth the surface for the grass seeds she stripped and threw in.

"If you do not wish companionship, I will stay back here," a familiar voice said. "But I do not think, even in the court grounds, that you ought to be alone, Keeper."

She turned to find Gavril and managed a smile. "I was not, but I seem to have misplaced my guard."

He shook his head, and she patted the ground next to her. He came over and sat at her side.

"So . . ." she said. "War."

He nodded.

"I know a warrior is not supposed to admit fear . . ." she said.

"But I will. To you. I am not, however, as afraid as I was the last time I was in this garden with you. That is something."

She looked around and realized this was indeed the garden where he'd begged her to run away with him, before she discovered who'd sent the letter to the emperor.

"Do you wish we'd done it?" she asked.

"Do I wish you'd been spared everything that came after? Yes. But do I wish I'd tricked you into life in exile? Never. You lost and you gained."

"More gained than lost."

"As did I. While I would wipe my mother's death from my mind if I could, she would still not have lived had I run. Whatever I've been through, I needed to endure it. To defy my father. To pledge myself to my empire. Even reconciling with

Tyrus, though that may seem a small thing . . ."

"Friendship is never a small thing."

He dipped his chin. "I have begun to regain something I lost and mourned more than I realized. And I have begun to find myself, where I belong. I see a future. I never did that before."

She leaned against his shoulder, carefully, half expecting him to pull away, but he only put his arm lightly around her waist.

"Now we just need to survive a war," she said.

"Apparently."

"In light of everything else we've survived, how hard can it be?"

"How hard indeed."

She smiled and rested against him as they watched the fish in the pond and said nothing more.

It was night, and Moria was alone with Tyrus. Unfortunately, it wouldn't be for long. There would be no nights together for a while. Moria did long to spend private time with her sister, but she'd still hoped perhaps she could begin her evenings with one and end with the other. She quickly realized that would be neither seemly nor wise. On the road, they were adults, in charge of their days . . . and their nights. Here in court, they were little more than children again, surely not nearly responsible or mature enough to be trusted in such matters. If they shared a sleeping pallet, babies and scandal would be the inevitable result.

"We'll work something out," Tyrus had said when they'd

shared their mutual disappointment. "I neither plan to forgo our nights nor to sneak about as if we are doing something wrong. We will not be in the city past tonight anyway."

Gavril had retired for the evening. He was struggling, and Moria was learning when to go after him so he could talk and when he truly did just want to be alone with his thoughts. Tonight was the latter, so she stayed with Tyrus, walking through the darkened gardens, talking and finding shadows for embraces and kisses and lovers' whispers.

Daigo was with them, of course. Zuri was . . . somewhere. She was more like a pet falcon than a dog or a cat. She amused herself, exploring and such, returning now and then to reassure herself that her master had not left. And despite Tyrus's "gifting" her to his father, there was no doubt who her master was. Even Emperor Tatsu had already decreed that Zuri should stay with Tyrus . . . for training and such.

They were heading to see the children before bed. There'd been talk of commandeering a few city inns, but some of the older children had asked to stay in the palace grounds for a night or two.

"It is so beautiful here," they'd said. "And so safe."

It was the last part that had swayed the emperor. So the children were there, under the care of nursemaids.

"My mother wishes you to dine with her," Tyrus said as they headed through the gate into the palace grounds. "For tea before we leave."

Moria said nothing. Daigo bumped against her, sensing her anxiety. When Tyrus looked over, she said, "Of course. If that is what she wishes, I will be . . . delighted?"

The last word rose as if in question, and Tyrus squeezed her hand.

"You will survive the encounter," he said. "My mother is not Dalain's. She won't devour you."

"I know. I . . ." Moria took a deep breath. "If she feels some obligation to host me, please assure her that I do not expect—"

"She wants to." He tugged her hand, steering her toward the children's quarters. "She is very anxious to meet the young woman her son has fallen madly in love with."

That was exactly what Moria feared.

"I—I will be honored to take tea with . . ." She trailed off, losing the words.

Tyrus turned her back against the guesthouse and put his hands on her hips. "What is the matter, Moria?"

"Nothing. I'm simply unsettled tonight and—" She paused and then blurted the words. "I fear I will not be what she expects. What she wants for her son. I fear I am not a proper consort for an imperial prince."

"Ah. Let's see. Could she find you not intelligent enough?" He met her gaze. "Impossible. Not strong enough? Impossible. Not pretty enough? That won't be one of her concerns, but again, I assure you, impossible. There are exactly two things my mother cares about: whether you make me happy and whether you are good to me. There is no question of either. You make me ecstatically happy, Moria. More than that, you make me a better person, a stronger person, a more decisive leader. I watch you with others, and I wish to emulate that."

"I, umm, don't think everyone would agree with my particular course of action . . ."

He grinned. "Too bad. My father did earlier today. I stood up to him, against all convention, because it was the honorable thing to do. Because I was following your lead. You make me a better person, Moria. And as for being good to me?" He leaned in, kissing her. "No one could be better. You know when I need comfort and when I need a kick in the arse. You care for me and you respect me, and I could ask for nothing more."

"And I love you."

His grin broadened, eyes sparkling in the moonlight. "Except perhaps that." He leaned down to kiss her. As he did, something thumped against the wall behind her, and he stopped short. Another thump from inside. Then a yelp and a hiss of pain. The sound of hand striking flesh and a child's voice saying, "Stop that!"

Tyrus sighed. "Seems the children may be safe from others here, but they are not safe from one another."

"They're restless and anxious," Moria said. "We'd best get in there before the fighting spreads."

FIFTY

The children were being kept in several guesthouses, each with a guard and two servants. As Moria and Tyrus approached the front door of the nearest one, Tyrus was nearly knocked flying by the exiting guard. The man barreled past without pause and headed into the darkness of the palace grounds.

As Moria watched the guard, her gut twisted with anxiety. She'd been on edge ever since they'd been escorted through the imperial gate, as if unable to believe it had gone so well, expecting dagger-wielding assassins behind every post. It would pass, and she'd accept their good fortune, but it did not take much for her to feel that worry again.

"Perhaps he did not recognize you," Moria said.

"No," Tyrus said grimly. "Not everyone will accept my father's word on my situation. They will still wonder if I am a traitor. I will expect that but not tolerate it. I'll speak to the man tomorrow."

They entered the guesthouse. All was silent and dark. The hair on Moria's neck rose. Daigo growled. Tyrus frowned as he looked about.

"Hello?" he said.

A head popped from around the doorway. An Edgewood girl named Chera. She rubbed her eyes, sleepily, then saw who it was and ran out, saying, "Moria!" and threw herself—not at Moria, but at Daigo, who huffed in alarm. Tyrus laughed as the girl buried her face in Daigo's fur. Moria reached over and patted her head.

"Everything is well, Chera?"

The girl looked up. "No, it is not."

Moria bent beside the girl. "What's wrong?"

"They made us go to bed early."

Behind Moria, Tyrus laughed, and Moria relaxed.

"Ah," she said. "That is a tragedy."

"Yes," the girl said. "We told them you had promised to come. Ashyn visited earlier, with Sabre, who said some of us could try her sling, and he made them leave."

Tyrus frowned. "The guard made them leave?"

"No, Hogan did." It took Moria a moment to place the name. It was one of the oldest boys from Fairview.

"And by what right did Hogan do such a thing?" Moria asked.

"No right at all," the girl said, lifting her chin. "He's awful. He bosses everyone about. He told the nursemaids that we ought to go to bed early, and then when Ashyn and Sabre came, he told them we were sleeping, which we were not. He's mean, and I hate him."

"Ah," Moria said. "It sounds as if someone takes his

responsibility a little too seriously. We will speak to him."

"Is he awake?" Tyrus asked.

"No," Chera said. "He fell fast asleep. That's why he made us go to bed early. He was tired. It's not fair."

"No, indeed it is not," Tyrus said. "But as a prince, I overrule him, so you may stay up." He leaned down and whispered, "And he will miss all the fun, because he is asleep. Now, where are your nursemaids and guard? I ought to speak to them before I steal you away to help me feed Zuri."

At the mention of the dragon, the little girl squealed. A few more faces popped from doorways, and Tyrus motioned for them to come out quietly. Moria told him to take the children outside, so they would not wake the others. She'd speak to the guard and nursemaids.

Tyrus bustled the children out. Moria stood there, looking about the dark guesthouse. Daigo slunk around her legs, whipping them with his tail, the fur along his spine raised. Which could mean that she had reason for feeling as unsettled as Gavril. Or it could simply mean that her anxiety had spread to her wildcat, as her emotions often did.

"Let's do this and get back outside, where we may watch over Tyrus," she whispered.

Her nerves settled a little as she began to search. There were only five rooms. The first held sleeping children, as did the second. The third, a washbasin and toilet pit. The fourth a small kitchen. The fifth . . .

"More children?" she whispered to Daigo as she opened the door. "Blast it, where are the servants?"

And the guard. Yes, they'd seen one walking out, but that

only meant he'd been relieved of his duty. Speaking of guards, what was the point of having one if he was so otherwise pre-occupied that they could spirit off the children on his watch? Was he playing a game of capture-my-lord? Or another sort of game, with the young women assigned as nursemaids?

"He'd best not be," Moria grumbled. But as she searched again, she knew she would not stumble over the guard with a servant. There *was* no guard here.

She imagined Gavril's voice at her ear, *You feel unsettled, Keeper.*

I am simply worried—

You know that is not it.

I know nothing—

Yes, you do. You know exactly what is wrong. You fear saying so and being proven wrong. Being shown a fool. Will you feel better if you are right . . . and you told no one?

Moria raced outside. Tyrus was there, with Zuri, showing Chera how to feed the whelp without losing fingers.

As soon as he saw her expression, his grin fell away.

She motioned him aside and said, "That *was* the guard we saw leaving. The *only* guard. The servants are also gone."

"What? They left the children—"

"I feel . . ." She took a deep breath. "I sensed something, when the guard passed. I may be wrong . . . I'm sure I am because there's no way . . ."

Tyrus laid his hands on her shoulders. "Tell me, Moria. Whatever it is."

"I sensed shadow stalkers."

FIFTY-ONE

A shyn felt guilty about the children. She'd gone to see them with Sabre, and one of the oldest of the Fairview boys said they'd gone to bed early, and Ashyn had felt not disappointed but relieved. Hence the guilt.

While she did want to see the children, she'd wanted to see Ronan more. Not for a romantic interlude, but to hear what the emperor said about his situation. Ashyn herself had already met with the emperor, summoned to give her story. She ought not to have been surprised at that—who better to explain about Edwyn and the dragons? Yet earlier, when riding to the city gates, Ashyn had taken her place *behind* Moria, Tyrus, and Gavril. Taken it gladly, to her surprise.

Moria would be quick to say that she'd ridden with Tyrus and Gavril because she was their co-accused. Ashyn and the others had been charged with no wrongdoing, so they did not need to face the emperor.

That was true. Yet there was more to it. Moria, Gavril, and Tyrus were the heroes of this story. That did not belittle Ashyn's own contribution. Nor Ronan's. But they were not warriors. They were not fodder for legends.

Moria had confessed her vision of Tyrus as emperor. Ashyn did not doubt it for a moment. No more than she doubted that this was simply the beginning for all three of them.

Bards would sing of the girl whose blood woke a dragon. They would not sing of the one who'd *nearly* done so. Perhaps the tale would twist and the bards would sing that Moria had saved her fair sister from the blade. Moria would set them straight—at the point of her dagger if needed. Ashyn did not care. She had escaped on her own, and everyone who mattered knew that, and that was what would be important in her life— that those she loved truly valued the role she played. And she would continue playing it, working with them, whatever they needed of her. She was a hero . . . to those who mattered.

In speaking to the emperor, she'd also learned the fate of Simeon, the young scholar who'd tried to woo her and then later betrayed them all, accusing Tyrus of cowardice on the battlefield. Simeon had been taken from the city "for his own safety," and then interrogated at a hidden location. Interrogated under torture, she presumed, though she tried not to think of that. He had, in the end, confessed to his lies. Now he was being held prisoner, while the emperor waited to see if he'd need him to provide a public statement.

She'd also asked after the court Keeper and Seeker, Thea and Ellyn. They'd been out in the empire, sent by Emperor

Tatsu to investigate reports of increased spirit activity, and had returned two nights ago, now resting their aged bones. That was all well and fine, but Ashyn had a hard time forgetting that they'd not lifted a finger earlier to help the girls who were supposed to be under their tutelage.

While she'd been in conference with the emperor, Ronan had been home with his siblings. He'd returned as soon as he knew Jorn and Aidra were well. Or he'd attempted to. There'd been some confusion at the palace gates, over the boy in the mended breeches and filthy shoes and dusty hair, demanding to speak to Prince Tyrus. It seemed Ashyn wasn't the only one overlooked. At least people noticed her. Ronan had entered the city without even that, all eyes on the prince and the Keeper and the Seeker and the Kitsune boy and the Okamis.

The guards at the gate had mocked him at first and then threatened him with the dungeons if he persisted in his charade. So Ronan had left. Then, when their interview with Emperor Tatsu ended, the four of them had gone to the gates, to see if anyone had spotted Ronan. That had been rather awkward.

Ronan had been recovered, and they'd all dined together. Then Ronan had been summoned to speak to the emperor. Now, with the children asleep, Ashyn was in her quarters with Tova, pretending to read a book while anxiously awaiting news of Ronan's meeting.

She'd finished the slim book—without processing a single word of it—when there came a rap at the door. A tentative rap, almost as if whoever was there hoped she'd not answer. It wasn't Ronan then.

She considered *not* answering. Several of the court ladies had stopped by earlier, leaving notes that said they hoped to take tea with the Keeper and Seeker. Moria had snorted that their true hope had been that they'd find Tyrus and Gavril there, and could take tea with all of them and regale the other court ladies with gossip.

Ashyn had no desire to entertain court ladies. And certainly no desire to suffer through a late-night visit with those who secretly hoped someone more interesting would stop by. So she ignored the knock. But when it came again, Tova moved to paw at her feet, whining and looking at her questioningly.

"Yes, it is my duty to answer," she said. "But I have decided there is more to life than obedience. I avoided death at the hands of a mad dragon-cult leader. I will not perish of dishonor if I fail to answer a door."

Tova growled.

Ashyn sighed. "All right. I will look. But if it is a social call, I will pretend I didn't hear the knock and trust the goddess will not smite me for my impudence."

As she approached, another knock came, equally light, then a voice, whispering "Ash?"

Ashyn hurried over and opened the door to see Ronan standing there, wearing no cloak. No weapons either. He hadn't brought them into the palace grounds, of course—that was a crime. But she had hoped when he left his meeting with the emperor, he would be wearing the twin blades, rightfully, his caste returned to him.

He had his arms crossed, as if against the chill night air, and the first words that came to her lips were, somewhat ridiculously, "Where's your cloak?"

He shrugged, and when he turned to her, all her hopes for him plummeted like stones in her stomach.

"Wh-what happened?" she said. "Surely the emperor—"

"Walk with me, Ash."

She shook her head and stepped back. "Come inside."

"It isn't proper."

"I don't care. You're cold and—"

"I'm fine. Fetch your cloak and walk with me, Ash. Please."

FIFTY-TWO

"Have I done something wrong?" Ashyn asked as they circled the fish ponds for the second time.

"Of course not."

"I must have. I've somehow displeased you and now you're punishing me."

"Why would you think—?"

"You just came from a meeting that will change your life, for better or for worse, and from the look on your face, it is clearly not for better. I am obviously beside myself with worry, and I've asked you twice what happened and you haven't even given me the courtesy of a reply. I must conclude that you are angry with me, though I've no idea what I could have done wrong."

"Nothing, Ash. You know that. I . . ." He looked at the pond. "Can we walk a little more?"

"Why? Because you must see the fish a third time? The forest a second? The teahouse a fourth? If you wished to walk and clear your thoughts, then you ought not to have brought me along. I do not appreciate being tortured with silence."

When he smiled, the sparks of anger ignited. "I'm glad you find my discomfort amusing."

"No." He took her hands, ignoring her when she tried to shake him off. "I am simply thinking how the girl I met in Edgewood would not have said that to me. She'd have *felt* it, but she'd have held her tongue and done what she thought was right."

"If you wish for that girl again—"

"No." He tugged her closer. "I thought that girl was pretty and clever and sweet, but the girl you have become?" He bent until his lips were over hers. "I would never want you to be anything else." He kissed her, lightly, murmuring, "Ash, my Ash. My wonderful, perfect Ashyn."

She let him kiss her. Then she stepped back, still holding his hands. "I'll not be distracted."

An almost sad smile. "I know, as much as I wish you could be. I want to walk with you and talk with you and find secret corners and kiss you and tell you . . ." He looked away.

She dropped his hands. "What happened with the emperor?"

Silence passed long enough that she was about to grow angry again when he said, "I have been pardoned."

She threw her arms around his neck, though in truth, neither had doubted that particular outcome. The law was clear—if an exiled convict survived a winter in the Forest of the Dead, he would be pardoned. Ronan's initial fear had been that he might be thought a party to the massacre. After all that had happened, there was no longer any such possibility. He had not only survived the winter but had been a loyal subject and aide since then.

"I have been paid as well," he said. "Handsomely. I'll be given a house and enough money to set myself up in any business."

"That . . ." She tried to say that, too, was wonderful. But the last part stopped the words in her throat. The last part suggested that, while he'd gotten what they'd expected, he had not gotten what he truly wanted.

"Your family's caste will not be returned to you," she said.

"A caste will. I am no longer without one, nor will my brother and sister have to grow up casteless, and that is what I truly wanted."

No, what he'd dreamed of wasn't simply a caste, but the one that would allow him to carry two blades.

"He will not allow you to be a warrior." She took a deep breath. "All right. We feared that. Giving caste to the casteless is difficult enough."

Ronan said nothing, just took her hand and started walking.

"So it was not enough that your family had once been warriors," she said. "Revoking that is permanent. No matter how long ago it was."

"It was longer ago than I believed. When Tyrus told the emperor, he had his clerks look into their files. That could not have been easy. I did not even know my former clan. My father would claim it was Mujina, Tanuki, Okami, Bakenko, depending on what served his purpose. The clerks knew, though. The stripping of warrior caste is significant enough that it was easy to find, particularly since I am not empire-born."

"So what was it?"

"Tsuchigumo. Which my father never included in that list of possibilities, for obvious reasons."

Tsuchigumo meant spider, like Jorojumo, the warlord who had betrayed Tyrus. Jorojumo, though, referred to web spinners. Tsuchigumo were ground spiders. Also known as "dirt spiders." And it was the name sometimes attributed to a group of disgraced warriors who had established themselves as a renegade clan.

"So that truly is their clan name?" she said. "I thought it was merely a derogatory term. I'm sorry, that sounds rude."

Ronan gave her a twist of a smile and leaned over. "To be honest, I expected as much. My family denied it, but I had a feeling it would be a little coincidental to be from a disgraced family that was not connected to a disgraced clan. It was also longer ago than I was told. At least seven generations."

"And that did not help? That you are so far removed from the renegades? The blood so diluted? Or did that make it worse—the dilution of warrior blood?"

He shrugged, and they walked a little farther.

"All right," she said. "So is it merchant? Is that what you'll be?"

He nodded.

"I know you hoped for better, but I'm merchant caste."

"You're a Seeker. You are above caste."

"I still consider myself—"

He kissed her nose. "I know. Thank you. I would be honored to be merchant caste. And I will be." He nodded sharply, leaning to kiss her lips now and take her hand. "I'll be a merchant and I'll be proud of it and I'll never regret . . ." He straightened. "I'll never wish for more."

"What would you regret?" She caught a glimpse of his expression. "There's more, isn't there?"

Ronan started to walk again, tugging her along, but she yanked him back, her hand wrapping tight around his.

"What else was there?" she asked.

When he didn't answer, she said, "Ronan? I will find out. I have only to ask Tyrus—"

"I can be warrior caste."

"What? No, there's more, isn't there? Some test?"

He shook his head. "It's mine if I want it. I just . . ." He took a deep breath. "If I am to be raised to warrior caste, I must devote myself to the service of the emperor."

"You must join the army," she said. "Perform your term of service there, as a lower-born warrior."

He didn't answer.

"Not a term of service," she said. "Permanently."

"The emperor recognizes my past service, and he has decreed that I have earned my caste . . . if I continue that service. Specifically to Prince Tyrus. As part of his personal guard. In whatever capacity Tyrus sees fit."

"All right," Ashyn said slowly. "I'm sure you'd like more autonomy in your future, but warriors *do* serve. And to serve Tyrus . . . ? Would that be such a bad thing?"

"Not at all. He would naturally be my choice. I've been doing it already. Voluntarily and gladly. As for service in general?" He shrugged. "I understand the limitations that come with warrior caste for the lower-born, and I certainly did not expect to be excused from them."

"Then why would you ever consider rejecting his offer and becoming a merchant?"

"I'm seventeen summers of age, Ash. If I am to serve Tyrus, I cannot be a half-trained boy. I am expected to do as other young warriors would, when they came of age. I'm to serve a warlord for one round of seasons. Then I am to serve at an outpost for another. Possibly two if I require additional training." He looked over at her. "I need to leave for as many as three summers, Ash."

"Leave your siblings? Surely the emperor understands that you did all of this for them, and he cannot expect—"

"They would come with me. My first term would be with Goro Okami, who has agreed to take us all, to begin training my brother and to offer Jorn an apprenticeship when he is old enough."

"You are being offered apprenticeship under Lord Okami, who apprenticed Tyrus himself. Goro Okami, whom you know and respect. He'll take you and your siblings, and he'll train your brother, too. And you plan to refuse? Are you mad, Ronan?"

"So you see no problem with the arrangement?"

"No, Ronan. Truly I do not."

He let go of her hand and his voice changed, gruffer, harsher. "Then I suppose I have my answer, don't I? No need to stay."

"What?"

"If you do not care if I leave, then I have no reason to stay, do I?"

"You—? Are you—? You're considering staying for *me*?"

"And that, I believe, answers every question I had. I'm sorry if I misinterpreted your regard, my lady. I'll take my leave now and apologize."

He turned stiffly and began to walk away. Ashyn ran after him and grabbed his arm.

"You are telling me that you considered giving up warrior caste to stay with me?"

"No, of course—" He stopped and gave his head an angry shake. "Yes, Ash. One word from you, and I would have stayed. I thought—I misinterpreted obviously. You enjoy my company. You are quite happy to dally with me, kiss me, but that hardly means there is any depth to your regard."

"Depth—? You honestly doubt—?"

He shook his head again, his tone softening. "I didn't mean it like that, Ash. We're friends. We're having fun being more than friends. It is a dalliance, and I ought not to have expected more."

She stared at him. "You expected . . . ?"

He opened his mouth. Then he studied her expression, and hope glimmered in his eyes. "You did not realize that. Of course. How could you? We couldn't speak of the future, under the circumstances. You wished me to get home to Jorn and Aidra first. Yes, Ash, I want more. I want you. For as long as I can have you, and I cannot imagine being without you. At a word from you, I will happily be a merchant. So long as I have you."

Ashyn continued to stare at him, and as she did, he seemed increasingly pleased with himself. He'd professed his love and now she would profess hers back, and all would be well. It was simply a matter of letting her know how he felt. Which proved he did not understand the situation at all.

"At a word from me . . ." she said slowly.

"Yes."

"If I tell you that I wish you to stay, you will."

"Yes. That's all I need, Ash." He took her by the arms and held her there, his face above hers. "Just speak the word."

"You wish me to tell you that I am committed to you. That I love you, and I will stay with you always, and that you do not need to fear turning down this opportunity, only to have me wander off after the first handsome young man who smiles my way."

His own smile flickered, and he shifted his weight. "Not like that. I just want you to tell me that you feel the same, and that I have reason to stay."

"Reason to give up your dream. To rob your family of a chance at warrior caste. Rob your brother of a chance to be a warrior. And it will be my fault."

"It isn't like that."

"It's exactly like that," she said, looking up at him. "You are asking me to promise that I will be worth the sacrifice. That *we* will be worth it. And how exactly do you think that would work out, Ronan? Every time I am angry with you, I'll remember what you did for me and feel ashamed of myself. Every time you are angry with me, you will remember what you gave up for me, and hate me for it. And if your siblings ever found out?

382

That you'd sacrificed their futures for a girl you cannot even marry? You are asking if I love you. And you are asking me to prove it by forcing you to do something that, if I loved you, I would never want you to do. Blast you, Ronan! Blast you to—"

She couldn't finish the oath. She wrenched from his grip and ran. She'd barely made it around the next building when she stopped. Tova whined and she laid her hand on his head.

No, I won't do this. I won't run. Not this time. We're going to talk it out.

As she marched back, she saw a figure approaching through the shadows.

"Ronan, we—"

The figure took another step and Ashyn made out the uniform of an imperial guard. She straightened quickly. "I'm fine," she said. "We're playing a game and—"

The guard moved into the moonlight and she saw his face, his horribly twisted face. Then he sprang.

FIFTY-THREE

The shadow stalker attacked with claws and fangs, ripping through Ashyn's cloak as if it was the thinnest silk. She yanked apart the fastening and dodged clear of her cloak, leaving the creature still ripping into it, snarling like a rabid beast.

The distraction lasted barely long enough for Ashyn to unsheath her dagger. Then the shadow stalker lunged at her. She stabbed it—in the throat, in the chest, in the head, wildly stabbing, all her frustration over Ronan fueling her rage. She heard a snarl and Tova vaulted over her to grab the thing by the neck. Both went down. The shadow stalker clawed and screeched, but Tova flipped it onto its stomach and pinned it there, letting it claw and bite the ground instead.

I have to banish it.

But that wasn't her power.

It didn't matter. She recalled Moria's words.

They are tormented spirits. Not innately angry or vengeful but forced to be so by sorcery. Many spirits, bound together in false anger.

Meaning the trick was to calm them. Which Moria had done, despite the fact that calming was Ashyn's power.

Beyond Edwyn's lies, he'd spoken truth, too. Their powers were not merely spiritual—the empire simply utilized them for that. Which meant that while Ashyn might be stronger at soothing, perhaps she could banish as well.

She set about calming the spirits. Setting them free. Wishing them peace. She wove a little banishing power in there, as well, perhaps being firmer in her requests, not so much begging them to leave as telling them, in the most respectful manner. Combining the powers of the Seeker and the Keeper, soothing while sending the spirits on their way.

It was like untangling a knot of spirits. She would hear one whisper its thanks or apologies and slip away. Then another. And another. Some needed less soothing and more banishing. But with each that left, the shadow stalker's struggles weakened until finally it lay still.

Ashyn stared at the creature as Tova nudged it, making sure it was dead.

There was a shadow stalker in the imperial court.

How could that happen? While they took the form of smoke as spirits, they seemed limited in how far they could travel in that shape. Otherwise, they could have slipped into the emperor's chambers and killed him in his sleep and ended the war before it began.

When they'd struck in the forest, they'd attacked men there. At Fairview, Alvar had captured the town, making it easy to unleash the creatures on the site. In human form, they could travel, as anyone could, but this warrior wore the uniform of an imperial guard. He'd been possessed *here*, in the palace grounds.

And while you are considering how such a thing could happen, Ashyn, perhaps you ought to consider the unlikelihood that Alvar unleashed only one shadow stalker?

Ashyn ran, leaving her cloak behind and Tova to catch up, which he did in a few short bounds.

Ronan was only a few paces from where she'd left him, tackling another shadow stalker. Or, not so much tackling it as trying to avoid getting sliced open by its claws and fangs. And perhaps it was not truly until that moment, seeing him struggling without his blade—punching and kicking and wrestling—that she realized the full horror of what Alvar had done, unleashing those creatures onto a world where the common folk had no such defense.

Like her father.

As she ran—trying not to think of the court and palace filled with defenseless women and servants and, yes, children—she began her entreaties to the spirits in the thing attacking Ronan. Then she leaped on its back and plunged her dagger into its neck. It howled, but did not release Ronan, gripped in its clawed hands.

"Begone!" she snarled. "Begone spirits or the wrath of the goddess herself will consume you and snuff you out and your descendants will be cursed for all time!"

It was, perhaps, overkill. Blasphemy even, to presume to know the goddess's will, but Ashyn reasoned the goddess certainly wouldn't be *happy* seeing her subjects murdered by vengeful spirits.

The shadow stalker hesitated in its frenzied attack, and when she struck again, it released Ronan. She stabbed the thing in the back now, knowing it would not kill the creature, but it certainly seemed to slow it down, perhaps even weaken it. When she yanked the blade out, she shoved the creature hard enough to make it stumble. Ronan leaped, as if starting from his shock. He went to push the shadow stalker down, but Tova beat him to it, knocking the creature to the ground on its stomach.

Ashyn slapped her bloodied dagger into Ronan's hand. "Use that if it breaks free. I must dispel it without distractions."

He took the dagger. "I was trying to get to you. When I saw the creature—"

"Yes, yes. Now, please, watch it while I—"

"You came back for me. Despite what I did."

She gave him a hard look. "No, I would let you perish at the hands of a shadow stalker because I am angry with you."

She expected him to look chagrined. To her surprise, he laughed softly under his breath. "I truly do not deserve you, Ash."

"No, you do not, which is why you don't have me. If you wish to discuss that, you'll need to survive tonight. Starting by—" She pointed at the shadow stalker.

He grinned and dipped his chin. "Yes, my lady. I will watch the creature while you dispel it. I will also stop talking."

"Good."

He walked to the shadow stalker and stood there, dagger

ready while Tova pinned the creature and Ashyn dispelled it with a combination of soothing words and harsh ones, a little more soothing now than harsh, with the creature disabled and Ronan safe. The spirits slid away, one after the other, the knot freeing more quickly now as she gained confidence. When the body lay still, Ashyn turned to Ronan.

"We need—"

"To find Moria," he said, handing back her dagger. "I know. Let's go."

They were passing the tea gardens when the scent of roses made Ashyn slow. She looked at the building beyond the gardens. When Ronan glanced over, she turned away from the building so he would not determine her thoughts, but he looked there anyway.

"The Chamber of the Divine," he said. "You are thinking of notifying Thea and Ellyn, the court Keeper and Seeker. If you can dispel the spirits, they can, too."

"I . . ." She looked longingly toward the palace grounds.

"If you wish, I'll go and warn Moria while you speak to the old women. But I would rather not leave your side."

He meant that he wanted to protect her. Which was very sweet. Under the circumstances, though, given that he was unarmed, *he* was the one who needed protecting, so she shook her head and veered toward the Chambers of the Divine.

"We'll do this quickly," she said.

FIFTY-FOUR

There was a guard posted at the door to the chamber. One who seemed under direct orders not to let Ashyn pass.

"As long as you are in the city, our Keeper and Seeker must remain in their quarters," he said. "The combined force of your powers—"

"That is a load of horse dung," Ashyn said.

Ronan choked on a laugh behind her as the guard stared, incredulous.

"My lady," the guard began.

"I'm not a lady. I'm the blasted Seeker of Edgewood, and as such, I outrank you, which means you will step aside, and if you babble on about the combined force of our powers, I shall scream. Moria and I have been in and out of the city, sleeping within a hundred paces of Thea and Ellyn, and the palace has not exploded yet. Now, there are shadow stalkers in the court—"

"Shadow stalkers?"

"Is that not what I said when I first demanded you step aside?"

"I—I misheard. B-but my orders—"

"Tova?"

The hound sprang in front of Ashyn, and Ronan moved up beside her. The guard's hand fell to the hilt of his sword.

"Pull that on him if you must," Ashyn said. "But bear in mind that the last warrior who drew on my Hound of the Immortals is now in the second world."

Which was true, though one thing had nothing to do with the other.

The warrior removed his hand from his sword.

"Good. Now step aside."

He didn't, but when Ashyn took hold of the door, he made no attempt to stop her from going in. Tova and Ronan followed.

The Chambers of the Divine was one of the largest buildings in the court. It served spiritual functions as well as housing the Seeker and Keeper. Moria and Ashyn had never been in it. One could say that was because Emperor Tatsu believed the old stories that their "combined power" could be disastrous, but Ashyn suspected he'd done it merely to keep the old women from complaining. Just as Ashyn suspected that Thea and Ellyn avoided the young Keeper and Seeker because they viewed the girls as rivals. Which, Ashyn supposed, they were now.

With Ronan leading the way, Ashyn headed through the darkened ritual rooms, deeper into the building, where she found the Seeker and Keeper's quarters. She found the Seeker and Keeper, too. As she watched the old women, snoring on their pallets, she wanted to stride over and shake them as hard as she could.

Their beasts were not with them. Ashyn had heard they kenneled them in the night, like common pets, but she'd not dared believe it. Bad enough they'd never named their beasts. To voluntarily be parted from them all night? The thought horrified Ashyn. Even Tova looked about the bedchamber, as if confused, expecting to see the old beasts in a nest of blankets nearby.

Ashyn strode in past Ronan, who respectfully remained outside the bedchamber door. "Thea? Ellyn? I need your help."

She had to say it again, louder, before Ellyn leaped up, dagger at the ready. Thea only lifted her head, blinking sleepily. One would think, then, that Ellyn must be the Keeper. She was not. Which only supported Ashyn's theory that perhaps the difference in their powers arose more from training than innate ability. In her case, she'd gotten the position better suited to her temperament. Ellyn had not.

"Ashyn?" Thea said, still lying there, blinking.

Ellyn advanced on her. "How dare you come into our chambers, at night no less—"

"There are shadow stalkers," Ashyn said quickly. "In the court. I've come to get your help."

"You brought shadow stalkers?"

"I don't know how they infiltrated the court, and it's not important. They're out there. I came to warn you so you can dispel them here while I warn Moria and the others."

"The others? Like Prince Tyrus?"

391

"Of course. I presume he's with my sister—"

"I'm sure he is. Seducing an imperial prince. I always told Thea that Moria wasn't nearly as honorable—or as dull-witted—as she pretended."

"My sister is—" Ashyn clipped her defense short. "I need you and Thea to dispel the shadow stalkers with us."

"You give me orders, girl?"

Ashyn held herself still to keep from stamping her foot in frustration. "There are shadow *stalkers*. In the *court. We* have dealt with them before. *You* have not. We've figured out the best way to dispel them."

"You? You're little more than children."

"The shadow stalkers are like a knot of spirits. Normal spirits, I think. The magics bind them and make them angry, make them wish for revenge, and that rage consumes them."

"What are you talking about? Everyone knows shadow stalkers—"

"No one knows anything about shadow stalkers," Ashyn said. "Because no one alive has had to deal with them. We have. Now, I don't have time to—"

"Ash!" Ronan said.

Ashyn turned to see the guard advancing down the hall. Only it wasn't the guard anymore. Not truly. His twisted face and hands gave that away.

Tova leaped, but the shadow stalker was already in flight. Both Ronan and Ashyn backed away fast. Ashyn shouted a warning to Ellyn, standing in the doorway, but the old woman charged.

"No!" Ashyn shouted. "Don't—"

Too late. Ellyn's charge met the shadow stalker. She stabbed the creature in the gut.

"Begone!" Ashyn said, dispelling madly, yelling at Thea to use her Keeper skills, but the old woman just lay on her pallet, staring bug-eyed as her sister was knocked down by the shadow stalker.

Ronan and Tova jumped in. Ronan stabbed it in the neck, Tova leaping on it, but the shadow stalker had Ellyn on the floor, and before Ronan could even stab it again, the thing ripped out Ellyn's throat. Bit in and tore at it like a frenzied beast, blood spraying, Ellyn's scream dying at the first gurgle.

Ashyn closed her eyes. It was all she could do. Close them and focus on her powers, on soothing and dispelling the spirits, on telling them that they'd murdered a Seeker but that it was not their fault, that it was the fault of the sorcerer who'd done this to them, and if they left now, the goddess would forgive their madness.

"You must go," Ashyn whispered, stoppering her ears to Thea's screams and Tova's growls and Ronan's curses and the creature's shrieks. "Please, please, please. It is not too late. Go now and the goddess will understand."

She kept saying the words, squeezing her eyes tighter and tighter, struggling not to look, trusting that Tova and Ronan were fine and that this was still the best thing she could be doing.

It didn't take long. Perhaps, despite the frenzied attack, enough of the spirits within were still aware of the horror and the blasphemy of what they'd done, slaying one of the goddess's chosen, and they seized on Ashyn's words as their last hope for redemption. They left and the shadow stalker weakened, and the rest either realized what they'd done or gave up. Soon the creature lay still, and Ashyn opened her eyes to see Ellyn's ruined body, her neck nearly bit through, the room sprayed with her blood.

Ashyn looked at Ellyn, and she didn't think of all the times the old woman made her feel like she'd never be a proper Seeker. She recalled the rare moments of kindness during their training, the moments of shared success, when Ashyn would perform a ritual exactly right, and she'd see a glow of pride in the old woman's eyes. Only a momentary glow, as if with every one of Ashyn's successes, Ellyn had seen her own power weakening.

It didn't need to be like that. It *shouldn't* have been like that. Any threat Ashyn posed to the old woman had not been Ashyn's fault. Only now did she realize that and felt, not anger but pity and grief for what they'd missed out on—a true bonding of mentor and student and, ultimately, of equals.

Ashyn turned to Thea, frozen on her pallet, staring at her twin.

"We need to—" Ashyn began.

A scream cut her short. A scream from deep in the courtyard—in the direction of the palace.

"Quickly!" Ashyn said. "I will tell you how to dispel them on the way."

"My sister . . ."

". . . is gone. Mourn her later. Honor her now. We'll find Moria and with the three of us, we can fix this."

The old woman looked up at Ashyn, her gaze blank.

"Please," Ashyn said. "We cannot wait."

"No," Thea said, her voice monotone. "You are right, Seeker. I cannot wait. My sister is gone."

She started to rise. Then her hand moved and Ronan shouted, "No!" and Ashyn saw the flash of the blade as Thea drove her dagger into her own gut.

FIFTY-FIVE

Moria and Tyrus were working their way toward the court, Tyrus shouting for others to take cover while Moria dispelled the shadow stalkers. She had to get to Ashyn. Yes, her sister could help, but more than that, Moria needed to know she was safe.

Moria had told Tyrus to go to his father and his mother, but he would not leave her side. He'd sent the children to warn his father—trusting that the shadow stalkers would still be under orders not to slay the young. His father would watch out for his mother, and there was little he could do that others could not. It was Moria's skill they needed. Hers and her sister's.

They were almost at the gate when a figure came running through it, braids swinging. Moria heard Gavril's exhalation of relief from ten paces away.

"You are both safe," he said as he ran to them. Daigo

growled, and he said, "Yes, you, too. If you're running for Ashyn, she's not in her quarters. I was in the court when I saw one of the stalkers. I went straight for your chambers. No one is there."

"She was waiting there for Ronan," Moria said. "He must have come. Good. He'll watch over her, and she knows what to do. But we must find them."

"Your highness!" a voice called.

They turned to see a guard running toward them. All three stiffened and reached for their blades. So far, all the afflicted had been guards, and while this man had clearly not been turned, that did not mean the creature was not inside him, waiting to come forth as it had with the farm boy in the steppes.

"Keep your distance, Nao," Tyrus said.

The guard stopped short and nodded. "Yes, your highness. I understand. I will not come close, but I bring an urgent message. Your father has ordered everyone into the palace. He has secured it. Your mother is there, as well as your brothers."

"Go," Moria said. "I'll find Ashyn."

"I'll stay with Moria," Gavril said.

The guard shook his head. "The Seeker is already there. I'm to bring all of you. Quickly, please. The creatures are everywhere."

Moria nodded, and they broke into a run, following the guard.

"Where is Ashyn?" Moria said, striding through the main palace chamber. It was a vast room, seeming big enough to hold a hundred. Yet there were fewer than twenty people there, and clearly no girl with red-gold hair nor a giant yellow hound.

"She's not here," Moria said, as Gavril and Tyrus walked on either side of her, scanning the knots of people. "Blast it, she's not—"

Moria nearly collided with a court lady who stepped into her path. She was about to circle past when she stopped short. The woman was imperial-born, perhaps barely into her fourth decade, and more well-rounded than was the current fashion. What stopped Moria, though, was her face. She saw it, and she knew exactly who this was and bowed as deeply as she could manage, stammering, "L-lady Maiko. My apologies. I was—"

"Searching for your sister. Not the best time to make your acquaintance, I know. *My* apologies."

Tyrus embraced his mother with one arm, the other still clutching his sword. "I am glad to see you are safe. I was going to look for you. I just—"

"You're busy trying to solve the current crisis. As you should be." She lifted up to kiss his cheek. "I'll not interfere with that. I saw Moria searching for her sister and wanted to say that she is not here."

"What?" Moria said. "The guard told me—"

"I suspect the guard told you whatever he needed to get you in here." Maiko cast a look behind Moria. "Which would not be the young man's fault."

Emperor Tatsu approached. "I did not tell him to lie about Ashyn. But yes, he could have extrapolated that when I said bring you all here by force if necessary. I have men searching for your sister, Moria."

Moria turned toward the door. "I need to find her."

The emperor stepped into her path. "I know you're worried about your sister—"

"It's not just that. Um, and excuse my interruption, your imperial highness."

Maiko's lips twitched in a smile as Moria hurried on.

"While I am of course worried about her, I *need* her. We can dispel the shadow stalkers. That's the only way to stop them. Well, short of hacking them into tiny pieces and . . ." A glance at Maiko. "Apologies, my lady. I did not mean to be so blunt."

The concubine smiled. "Continue, child. Please."

"I need Ashyn. If we can get the court Seeker and Keeper, we can do even better. Together, we can end this quickly."

"She's right," Tyrus said.

The emperor nodded. "All right. But you will be guarded—"

"That . . . Again, um, apologies. But the stalkers have possessed guards. Sometimes they do not manifest immediately."

"Again, Moria is correct," Tyrus said. "Which is why I was trying to find you to tell—I mean *ask* you to put the guards outside. Do not tell them why. Simply order them to stand guard *outside* the doors."

"Is that *your* order?" the emperor said.

Tyrus flushed. "Deepest apologies. Like Moria, I am rattled, and in my attempt to be efficient—"

"No, I believe her forthrightness is rubbing off on you. I would say I was glad to see it, if that would not imply I'm encouraging insubordination from my son. I will admit only that I'm not displeased to see it. Your point is taken, Moria. If the guards are infected, they should not go with you."

"I can," Gavril said. "They'll not bother me when I'm with the Keeper."

"I will as well, naturally," Tyrus said.

"*Naturally* you will not," the emperor said. "I need you here."

"No," Tyrus said carefully. "You wish me here so that I will be safe. You *need* me with Moria, to add my blade to Gavril's and bring Ashyn and the court Keeper and Seeker back."

"When I said I was not displeased to see you being more forthright . . ."

"He is correct, though," Maiko said. "As much as I would love to keep him safely here, he serves better out there. His companions will watch out for him."

"We will, my lady," Moria said, and Gavril seconded it. After a quick embrace between mother and son, the three of them were off.

"We'll focus on Ashyn first," Tyrus said as they strode toward the exit. "Daigo? You can help with that, correct?"

The wildcat gave no reaction.

"Don't pretend you don't understand me. I need you to track Ashyn and Tova, and I know you're already doing that, and I know you won't admit to it because you aren't a hunting cat and you don't want to be seen failing."

"Do you truly think he understands you?" Moria asked.

"Every word? No. More than he lets on. Yes. Mostly, I can just predict his behavior because I know his Keeper. He will do whatever you would."

"I don't think that's exactly—"

"Completely true."

Gavril grunted in agreement. She looked at him.

Gavril shrugged. "The cat is your bond-beast. He's as difficult as you are. It's his nature."

Tyrus smiled as Moria glared at Gavril. Ahead of them, the main doors were opening to let someone in. They paused to let the newcomer pass, their attention still on one another.

"Back to the plan," Tyrus said. "Daigo will attempt to track Ashyn and Tova. We will follow him while not relying on his nose. The point is—"

"The point is," said a voice in front of them. "That you have given your last order to my son, Tyrus."

The figure stepped forward, pulling back his hood. Even before he did, Moria knew who it was. She would never again mistake that voice.

Alvar Kitsune.

FIFTY-SIX

Tyrus, Moria, and Daigo all lunged at Alvar . . . and he extinguished the lights, as he had before. Gavril got his sorcerer's fire lit, but by then his father was gone and the hall had erupted into madness. There was no other word for it. Simple madness.

Alvar had not come alone. He'd brought a troop of warriors, who'd apparently been living in the imperial city and who'd easily marched through the palace gates while everyone dealt with the shadow stalkers. Then they were in the palace itself—the warriors plus the palace guards turned shadow stalkers. Tatsu's men fought hard and fierce, and soon a dozen bodies littered the floor—half of them Alvar's men—but between the sorcery and the shadow stalkers, they did not stand a chance. One moment Moria was dispelling the last of the shadows stalkers while Tyrus and Gavril fought off those who would stop her. And then every lantern burned bright again and Alvar

Kitsune stood on the throne dais, Emperor Tatsu pinned with a sword at his throat.

"No!" Tyrus was the first to shout it. The only one to shout it. The only one to rush forward, his blade out.

"Stop," Alvar said. "Or I *will* kill him."

Gavril grabbed Tyrus's arm. The prince went to throw him off, but Moria gripped his other arm, and Tyrus stopped.

"Good," Alvar said. "You play at being leader, but you bend easily to the will of stronger friends. Sound familiar, Jiro?"

The emperor stood motionless, blood soaking his tunic. Not his blood. He'd fought as hard as any warrior and had been captured not by skill but by sorcery. Moria was certain of that.

"Do you think I plan to kill you, Jiro? No. That would be too simple. You will survive tonight. Then your suffering will begin in earnest, as you look back on this day and realize that everything that happened here was your own fault."

A long moment of silence.

"Not even going to defend yourself?" Alvar asked.

"To whom? To you, old friend? You know what happened. You know what you did, and what I was forced to do in return. Put whatever slant on it you like, but there's no sense defending myself to the person who knows the truth as well as I do."

"Brave words. Do you believe them, Jiro?"

"I believe the truth."

"So do I. Let's talk about the truth. The truth is that you stole my life to protect your throne. Then, to continue protecting it, you attempted to steal my son. To leave me no heir, in hopes that would kill my spirit. Shall I tell you a secret, Jiro?" Alvar leaned down to the emperor, a handspan shorter than he.

In a loud, mock-whisper, he said, "My son never truly returned to yours. He betrayed you. Again."

Gavril stiffened, his green eyes widening, and in those eyes, Moria didn't see guilt. She knew she wouldn't. Tyrus didn't even glance over to gauge Gavril's reaction. What Moria saw was what she would have expected: shock. It was not until that moment, realizing she did not believe Alvar for a heartbeat, that she knew she'd forgiven Gavril. That she trusted him as much as she had that first night in the garden. He'd made mistakes. He'd suffered—horribly—for them. But he had, in his own way, never truly betrayed her or Tyrus. Nor would he now.

Alvar's lips pursed. "Perhaps betrayed is not the right word. My son . . . struggles. He is a young man caught in a storm, uncertain where to find shelter. He turned to you, but his heart was not truly in it, because his heart—his loyalty—remains with me. He is young, though, and more naive than I would have hoped. That is his mother's influence."

"Which you put an end to," the emperor said.

"Is that what he said? That I'm the one who killed her? As I said, he's confused. I would never do such a thing."

Emperor Tatsu snorted. Alvar's eyes narrowed, and he pressed his blade tip into the emperor's throat.

"Go on," the emperor said. "Please."

"There is no more to say. My son is confused. He ran from me, but I am his father. I understand, and I forgive him." He turned to those assembled below. "Gavril? Join me."

Gavril hesitated. Moria murmured, "Go. We know," which meant that she did not doubt his loyalty, and that he was safer going along with his father's delusion. *They* were also safer if

404

he did, putting him in a position where he might be able to do something. Tyrus gave the smallest nod, seconding Moria's words, and Gavril stiffly made his way to the dais.

It wasn't until Gavril started up the steps that Moria had another, horrible, thought. What if Alvar was tricking Gavril? Was that not exactly what he dealt in—tricks and misdirection? Get Gavril on that dais so he could punish him for his betrayal?

Moria rocked forward, ready to run and grab Gavril back, knowing even as she did that it was too late, that if she'd been mistaken . . .

She was not. While Alvar did not let his gaze linger affectionately on Gavril, as the emperor did with Tyrus, he glanced over, satisfaction glowing in his eyes. Satisfaction with a flash of arrogance and self-pride. *Is he not a fine young warrior? Of course—he is my son.*

It was not truly unlike Emperor Tatsu with Tyrus. Except with Tyrus, the emperor had no doubt of his son's loyalty. Alvar did . . . and refused to believe it. He had deluded himself, perhaps as much as he had about the crimes that had gotten him exiled. An ego that did not allow for the possibility he'd been wrong—about his friend, his exile, or his son.

"There," Alvar said as Gavril approached him. "His loyalty to you, Jiro, and to your fool of a son? Temporary and convenient. My son spends too much time in his head. I would not wish otherwise, or I'd have one like that." He waved a dismissive hand at Tyrus. "But a young man who thinks too much also questions too much. Doubts too much. He will outgrow that and be a brilliant emperor. Sadly, your son will not outgrow his

405

foolishness. No more than you did."

"You seem quite fixated on insulting Tyrus," the emperor said. "Careful, Alvar, or we might think you see him as a threat. I hear he faced you in single combat, and you ran from it. Fled a fight you could not win? Tell me again how you did not run from the battlefield."

Alvar pushed his blade tip into the emperor's throat, blood trickling down. When Emperor Tatsu didn't even flinch, Alvar closed his eyes briefly, as if getting his temper under control. Behind him, Gavril shifted, his gaze fixed on Alvar, his blade still in hand.

Could Gavril kill his father? Risk eternal damnation for it? Even if he had the will, his father made him stand too far away, where Alvar could still see him. Wanting to trust his son . . . but knowing not to press the matter.

"I speak of Tyrus because I am reminding you of his faults," Alvar said. "I'm helping you to make a decision, Jiro."

Now he got his reaction, the emperor tensing, his gaze swinging to Tyrus.

Alvar chuckled. "You don't even make an effort to hide your affections, do you? As big a fool as he is. As soft, too. You love him best because he reminds you of yourself. That is a breathtaking act of ego, my old friend."

"No," the emperor said carefully. "I love all my sons for the young men they are, for all the ways they are *not* like me."

"Oh, such pretty words. Let's test that love."

Alvar waved and Moria looked over to see the three imperial princes standing together. The fourth . . . ? She looked around quickly, only to see him on the floor. Dead. She sucked in a breath. In the chaos, she hadn't even realized one of Tyrus's brothers had perished.

She was still staring at the prince's body when Tyrus lunged, and she thought he'd only just realized his half brother had died, and it didn't matter if they'd never shown him a moment's kindness, he would still care. She looked over, though, to see his gaze elsewhere—and before she could see what he was running toward, he stopped short, swinging back to her, his blade rising.

That's when she felt cold steel against the back of her neck.

"Don't prove yourself to be the fool you seem, boy," Alvar said. "Lower your weapons to the floor. That goes for every armed man—and woman—here. Blades on the ground or I put mine through your emperor's throat."

When Tyrus hesitated, the blade dug deeper into Moria's neck. She did not flinch, but Tyrus still put his blades down.

"Good, now retreat to her side and stay there. My man will remain where he is. If you move from that spot, Tyrus, the girl dies."

Rage whipped through Moria, and she wanted to say it didn't matter, that Tyrus should pay her predicament no mind. She would say it if he could kill Alvar. But there was no chance of that.

When Daigo growled, Alvar laughed. "Same goes for you, wildcat, and let's hope you truly are imbued with a human soul and can understand me. Otherwise, your dear Keeper may die for nothing."

Daigo pressed against her, as if to say, *I'm here*, but he stopped growling. That's when Moria looked up at the dais and realized why Tyrus had leaped forward. Guards had brought one of his brothers up. The other two—the crown prince and his next younger brother—stood where they'd been, not needing anyone to restrain them, their expressions saying they were simply glad they hadn't been chosen.

"Kneel," Alvar said to the prince beside him.

The young man did.

Alvar turned to the emperor. "Would you like your son to live?"

Emperor Tatsu glared at him. "That is obvious and—"

"Is it obvious? Let's see. You may let him live. Simply order Tyrus to take his place."

"What?"

"You heard me. Give the word. Your bastard dies. Your legitimate son lives."

The emperor's glower only hardened.

"Is that a no? Not surprising, I'll admit."

Alvar nodded and one of the guards restraining the prince lifted his blade over the young man's neck. A woman in the crowd screamed. Tyrus shouted "No!" but he did not move, could not move, and even if he had, it would have been too late. The blade came down and the prince's head fell to the floor. Two women shrieked and rushed for the dais, and Moria looked to see what had to be the young man's mother and his wife. Guards restrained them.

Alvar had the next son brought up. That's when the crown prince did react—he tried to pull his sword, not to save his brother, but knowing what was coming next. More of Alvar's warriors had arrived during the commotion. They restrained the crown prince and Tyrus, just to be sure, and they held the women at sword point.

The emperor tried to get free then, even if getting free meant a blade through his throat. But before he could do more than grab for Alvar, warriors were there to restrain him.

Alvar gave the emperor the option again: have Tyrus change places with his other son. Emperor Tatsu spat curses and raged. But he did not agree. And the guards executed the second prince.

When they hauled the crown prince to the dais, Emperor Tatsu could barely form curses, snarling that the ancestors and the goddess herself would make Alvar answer for this.

"No," Alvar said. "The goddess will understand. This is my revenge. She smiles on me in my victory. The question is what will *you* allow, Jiro. You have one legitimate son left. One heir to your throne. True, you will not have a throne much longer, but I don't expect you to believe that. Now comes the true test, when you have the chance to prove yourself a worthy leader . . . or a sentimental old fool. Make your choice."

"There is no choice!" Emperor Tatsu spat. "You seek only to hurt me. You will not allow any of them to live. You wish only to hear the words, to hear me grovel and beg for my sons, to make the terrible choice of sacrificing one for another, but I will not, because there is no choice."

"Oh, but there is. You have my absolute word on that. One of your sons will survive tonight. It is up to you to choose who. Your heir or your bastard."

"I will not—"

"Of course you will not, because you cannot. You choose Tyrus. You may say you don't believe me, but you know me to be a man of my word. You only pretend otherwise so that you are not judged for your choice. Say the word and Tyrus takes your heir's place."

The hall went silent. And Jiro Tatsu said nothing.

The guard lifted the blade.

"I'll do it!" Tyrus shouted.

Moria turned to him, words stoppered in her throat, telling herself he was not saying what he seemed to be—

"I will give my life in my brother's place. For the empire."

Moria looked at Alvar, her heart beating so hard she could barely draw breath. *Tell him no. I don't care if it's wrong. Just tell him—*

"Approach and take his place then."

"No!" Moria screamed and threw herself forward, not caring that there was a blade at her neck, thinking only that she had to stop this, in any way she could, and whatever happened next, all that mattered was that she could not live knowing she hadn't tried.

Daigo sprang, too, but more guards grabbed Moria and one kicked Daigo in the head, hard enough for the wildcat to fall. Moria screamed again, and Tyrus fell beside Daigo, his hands going to the beast's heart.

"He's fine," he said. Then he rose, slowly, his gaze on Moria. "I need to do this."

"No, you do *not*," she said, struggling against the men who held her. "They wouldn't do it for you. They'd wield the blade themselves if they could."

410

"That doesn't matter. It isn't about them. It's about the empire. Leaving an heir."

"What heir? Him?" She jabbed her finger at the crown prince. "He's one-tenth the man you are, and your father knows it."

"But I cannot be heir."

"My vision. I saw—"

"No, Moria." He walked over and put his hands on her face. "It's not about me or about my brother. It's about keeping the empire whole." He leaned in and kissed her. "I love you."

"If you—" She bit off the words. She could not say that. Would not. It wasn't fair, no matter how much she longed to say whatever would work. It wouldn't work, and he'd go to his death with that: *you'd not do this if you truly loved me.* He was right. It wasn't about them, not any of them. It was honor and it was duty, and that came first, however much she railed against it.

She kissed him. She tried to throw her arms around his neck, but the guards held her back. So she kissed him and told him she loved him.

"You still have my amulet band?" he whispered.

"Of course."

"Good. Then I'll see you on the other side. I don't expect you to wait for me—"

"I will."

He pressed his lips to hers. "Don't. Just know that I'll see you and, perhaps, we can start again. Perhaps that is what you saw. That's when we'll be together."

One last kiss, and he turned, and she tried not to scream,

she bit her lip so hard it bled, blood mingling with her tears. She still fought. She couldn't *not* fight. She fought, and she told herself this would not happen. That her sister would rush through the door with an army at her rear. That Zuri would find a way to swoop in. That Daigo was only feigning unconsciousness and would save Tyrus. That if all that failed, the goddess herself would intervene.

Tyrus walked onto the dais and bent. He moved his hair aside for the blade. Three warriors restrained the emperor. Another two flanked Gavril. That's when she saw Gavril's expression. The horror and that look she knew so well, the one that said his mind was whirring as fast as it could to come up with a solution.

He glanced at her then. She mouthed, *Please, please, please,* straining against the guards, tears streaming down her face.

Please do something. Please help him. Use your sorcery. Use your blade. Use whatever you can, Gavril. Please, please, please.

Gavril saw her pleading, and he nodded. That's all he did. Nodded. And she knew it would be all right. That he had a plan. She held her breath, waiting, but Alvar gave the signal and the blade began to drop and—

And there was a flash of light, as there'd been in the dragon's den. Moria fell back, blinded. Then she saw Gavril lunging at Tyrus, pushing him out of the way, but the blade was still falling and—

"No!" Moria screamed with everything she had as she saw that blade falling. On Gavril. Gavril not only pushing Tyrus to safety but taking his place under that terrible blade. Moria threw herself forward and in the shock of it, her guards released her and she ran for the dais, still screaming.

The blade fell. It cleaved into Gavril's back and his body jerked with the force of it, the blade sinking in, blood spraying. Tyrus was already on his feet, Gavril's own blade in his hand, swinging it on the executioner, striking so hard he cut the man in two. He dropped the blade and fell beside Gavril, and Moria was there, seeing . . .

She refused to understand what she was seeing. Refused to comprehend it. The wound could not be so great. She could not be seeing bone and viscera and blood, great gouts of blood pumping. She could not. Tyrus had his shirt off, and they wrapped it around Gavril, turning him onto his back as they did.

Gavril's eyes were closed.

"No," Moria said between gritted teeth. She took his chin in one bloodied hand and shook it as hard as she could. "Wake up, Kitsune. Blast you, open—"

His eyes fluttered open. He saw her and he smiled. "Keeper."

"Stay with me. You said that to me. Now I say it to you."

"I cannot."

"You will."

A slight shake of his head. "I cannot. I'm sorry, Keeper. I'm sorry for everything."

"You have nothing—"

"I do."

"No." She met his eyes. "You have nothing to be sorry for, and if you think you do, then yes, you are forgiven. But you—"

His eyes began to close.

413

"Stay with me, Kitsune. Please, please, please." Tears streamed down her face onto his, and his eyes opened barely a crack. He fumbled for her hand, and she took it, squeezing it hard. "Please, just—"

"I was never good at obeying your orders, Keeper. But for once, I wish I could. Just stay here." His hand gripped hers. "Stay here, and tell me a story, one of your silly stories . . ."

His eyes closed. She wanted to shake him again, to shout at him to wake up, but she knew he wouldn't. She had seen the wound. She knew what it portended. Now she crouched there, crying and clutching his limp hand. Then she leaned and kissed his lips.

"I'll see you on the other side, Kitsune," she said. "Do not forget me."

I never could, Keeper, his spirit whispered as it slipped past, and she fell onto his bloodied body, sobbing like she would break in two.

FIFTY-SEVEN

When Moria finally rose, she saw Tyrus there, kneeling beside Gavril, tears rolling down his cheeks. She reached for his hand and he took it but said nothing, just rose. He stood with her as their gazes went to one figure standing on that dais.

Alvar Kitsune stood as if frozen in one of his own spells. His gaze was locked on his son, and his expression . . . Moria didn't care about his expression. Didn't care if he looked like he was going to fall on his own blade. She'd not let him. She'd wield that blade herself. And so she rose, and in her hand she held a dagger—Gavril's own dagger.

Tyrus walked at her side, his own blade raised. She met Alvar's gaze, and he did not flinch. Gave no expression at all, just looked at her with eyes as dead and empty as his son's.

"He hated you," Moria said. "That's the last thing I want you to hear, Alvar Kitsune. The last thought I want impressed in your mind. That your son despised you. That he was ready to give up his afterlife if that's what his betrayal cost him. What happened here? You have no one to blame but yourself. You killed him as surely as if you wielded the blade."

One of the guards moved forward, but Alvar lifted a hand to stop him. Then his lips began to move.

"Casting magics?" Moria said. "That is your only true power, isn't it? The only reason you stood a chance of winning. You raised the dead and you twisted innocent spirits and you slaughtered innocent citizens with them. You snuck spirits into the city in the bodies of *children*."

She expected him to deny it, or at least to sneer and gloat at how easily they'd been trapped by their sentimentality, bringing the children into the very palace grounds. But he said nothing. Just continued to whisper.

Moria raised her dagger and Tyrus his sword. No one moved to stop them. Alvar's own guards stood stock-still. Emperor Tatsu met Moria's gaze and then Tyrus's, as if to say that he would do this if they could not. They both shook their heads. Moria stopped in front of Alvar Kitsune and lifted her dagger.

"Wait," he said, and his voice was oddly soft. "Let me finish."

"Finish casting your spell?" She gave an ugly laugh. "Of course, my lord. I'll let you finish so you may turn out the lights and escape."

"If I wanted that, I'd have done it. Plunge that dagger into my gut, Keeper. Start me on my way to the second world. But let me complete my magics before you finish me off."

416

Of course she would. He was the nine-tailed fox. He'd trick her with his dying breath. Yet as she lifted the dagger again, a passing spirit whispered *Wait*, and she hesitated, thinking it was Gavril, and the pain of that, of hearing him as a spirit, of remembering his broken body behind her—it stopped her hand. Then the spirit said, *Wait, child*, and she realized it was not him. Yet she paused, just a moment, unwittingly long enough for Alvar to finish.

"There," he said. "It is done. And so am I."

He reached as if to pull open his tunic for the fatal blow. Instead, he grabbed his sword. Before he even had it out, Moria was on him, stabbing him in the chest, thoughts of Gavril fueling her rage as she stabbed him again and again, expecting to feel his blade at any moment. Instead, he said, "Best not to attack an unarmed man. It is dishonorable." Then he smiled. An odd little smile. And there was a *thwack*, and the smile was gone, his head gone, blood spraying. Tyrus pulled her back out of the way, his bloodied blade still in hand. She stumbled and he caught her and they both stared at Alvar Kitsune's body.

"There's a trick," Moria whispered. "I know there's a trick."

But there wasn't. Alvar Kitsune lay on the dais, his head against the wall, his life's blood flowing into his son's. Moria couldn't look at Gavril. It was as if, by not looking, it would not have happened like this. That instead of throwing himself under that blade, Gavril would have killed his father. But Moria knew why he'd made this choice. Because killing Alvar wouldn't have stopped the blade. Even dragging Tyrus aside would have changed nothing. Alvar would only have restrained Gavril and killed Tyrus and perhaps the crown prince, too, reneging on the deal in his rage. No, the only thing that would truly stop Alvar? The death of his son. Of his only heir.

It had been about Gavril. All about Gavril.

No, she imagined Gavril's voice. *It was about him. His legacy.*

Which was true, but Gavril *was* that legacy. Alvar hadn't been securing the throne for himself. He was older than Emperor Tatsu. He'd not have ruled for long. He would win the empire, rule briefly, then hand it to his son and watch his legacy unfold.

Gavril had given his life. To stop his father. To save his friend. Moria had begged him to do something, anything . . . and he had done everything. Given everything.

And she would never forgive herself for that.

She felt Tyrus's arms around her then. They were shaking, and she reminded herself that she was not the only one who'd suffered this loss. As much as she cared for Gavril—no, as much as she *loved* him—Tyrus had loved him first. Loved him. Lost him. Gotten him back. Lost him again.

Moria turned in Tyrus's arms and hugged him, letting her dagger clank to the floor, as his sword did the same. They stood there until they both realized the room was no longer silent, that people were milling about, freed from their shock.

They both looked to see the emperor standing there. They parted, and he embraced them, first his son and then Moria, whispering "I'm so, so sorry, child."

She nodded and pulled back. Maiko was there, on the dais, and she hugged them both as well, gripping Moria with a fiercer embrace than Moria would have expected of the concubine. When Tyrus and Moria finally pulled away from both his parents, Moria looked . . . and saw an empty blood pool where Gavril had lain.

"Where—?" she began.

"They've taken him," Maiko murmured. "He'll be tended to."

"I want to see him."

"I know. Someone will lead you there. Both of you."

Moria stepped back. Then she saw Daigo, and she broke from Tyrus, leaping off the dais and running to her wildcat. As soon as she touched him, his eyes opened.

"Ashyn," she whispered to Daigo. "We must find Ashyn and Tova."

Tyrus was already there, helping her up, his sword back in place. "We'll go now. Daigo? Are you well enough—?"

The wildcat was on his feet before Tyrus could finish. They all started for the door, everyone falling out of their way.

"Moria!"

She stopped short and turned to see her sister racing in a side exit, Tova and Ronan at her heels. Moria ran to her and caught her up in a hug.

"We were locked outside with Sabre and the Okamis," Ashyn said. "We only just got in. You're . . ." She pulled back, staring down at Moria's blood-soaked clothing. "What happened? Are you hurt? Where are you—?"

"It's not mine. Gavril . . ." She swallowed, the pain surging again. "He . . . he . . ."

"Moria is fine," Tyrus said softly. "Alvar Kitsune is dead."

"And Gavril?"

Moria met her sister's gaze and shook her head. That was all she could manage. A head shake. It was enough. Ashyn pulled Moria into her arms and they both began to weep.

FIFTY-EIGHT

Gavril had been taken away for his body to be prepared. It took time to find him, and Moria grew angry, even Tyrus's patience fraying until finally he snapped at the woman in charge of preparations, when she admitted she wasn't sure where the young warrior lay.

"He's . . . still in the palace," she said. "In one of the rooms there. His body . . . it was not in good . . . they did not wish to move him far."

Moria saw the sword falling on Gavril again, slicing into his back, and she teetered, shaking her head when Ashyn and Tyrus both reached for her and leaning on Daigo instead for support.

When they turned to head back to the palace, the woman hurried into their path. "You ought to wait—"

"No," Tyrus said, and brushed her aside.

They found the room easily then, in the rear of the palace. Easily because two guards raced past them on the way, and there were two young healers outside the room babbling to a older man so fast Moria couldn't catch more than a word or two of what they said.

Tyrus broke into a run, Moria behind him.

"What's going on here?" he said. He looked at the closed door. "Is that where Gavril Kitsune lies?"

The older man stepped in front of the door. It was one of the senior household stewards, looking as shaken and frightened as a newly appointed clerk.

"Y-yes, your highness," the steward said. "But you ought not to go in there. The body . . . it is not in any condition . . ."

"We were at his side when he died," Tyrus said. "We bound him. We know exactly what condition he was in. Now step aside."

"T-there is a problem," the steward said. He bowed awkwardly, sweat dripping from his brow. "I beg deepest forgiveness, your highness, but I must ask you to wait. Your imperial father has been summoned—"

"My father is dealing with the death of three of his sons. And the death of many more of his people. As much as he cares for Gavril, this is not the time to bother him with funeral arrangements."

"I-it is not that . . ."

"Sorcery," one of the girls whispered. "It is sorcery."

The steward spun, hand raised as if to strike her. Tyrus caught the man's arm and then turned to the girl.

"What is happening?" he said. "And remember who you address."

422

The girl bowed her head. "Yes, your highness. I—I cannot say exactly what happened. I know only that it is sorcery. When we saw . . ." She swallowed. "We fled the room and summoned the steward and the guards."

Sorcery. The spell Alvar had cast. The girl said something about the body. Had he done something to Gavril's body? Some final indignity? Revenge on his son for his betrayal?

"We have to—" she began.

She didn't need to finish. Tyrus's hand was already on the door, his glare silencing the steward.

"Ashyn? Ronan? I'll ask you to wait here. Moria and I will see what this is."

"And you'll bring us in then, correct?" Ashyn said, meeting his gaze. "If it is sorcery, Moria and I may be able to do something."

Tyrus nodded. "I will summon you as soon as we've determined it's safe."

"Or as soon as you've determined it *isn't*," Ronan said.

Another nod, and Tyrus opened the door. Moria and Daigo walked in, and he closed it behind them. Gavril lay on a raised platform. He was naked, a sheet pulled over him for propriety. He lay on his back, his wound partially bound. There had been some initial attempts to clean the flecked blood on his face and shoulders, as if the girls had started there while awaiting a surgeon to sew up the terrible wound on his back. The bindings had been pulled away, preparing for that, and Moria stopped short, not wanting to see that horrible wound. Except . . .

Moria stopped. She stared. Then she jogged past Tyrus to Gavril's side and pulled the binding back farther. She kept tugging, certain she was mistaken about the wound, the size

of it, the horror of it, and that at any moment, she'd reveal the bloody slice that had ended his life.

There was no wound. Moria grabbed a cloth from the bowl and hastily wiped at Gavril's side. There, under the blood, was the mark. Not the gaping tear that had nearly ripped him in two. Just a mark, like a long-healed scar.

"It must be farther up his back," Tyrus said.

She nodded and pushed Gavril up, Tyrus helping. But there was no gaping wound, only that scar. She stood there, Gavril's body cold against her fingers.

Why would Alvar do this? Spend his last moments closing his son's wound? Was this a custom from the mountains, from before the Kitsunes *became* the Kitsunes, before they became an imperial clan? Ashyn had once mentioned a tribe that would stitch its dead back together fully, in the belief that they would not be able to enter the afterlife otherwise.

"I don't understand," Moria whispered.

Tyrus shook his head. "Nor do I. But if it's sorcery, it isn't with evil intent. I don't see how it could be." They lowered Gavril's body to the platform. "I'll tell the girls to resume their work, and we'll stand guard, in case they're concerned about evil magics."

He headed for the door. Moria stood there, looking down at Gavril, thinking of Gavril, seeing him again, his glower, his scowl, hearing his snapped words. And the rest, too, that slight smile, that low laugh. Rare moments. Too rare. She reached for his hand and took it, feeling the skin warm as if from her touch, and she thought of those last moments, Gavril on the dais, meeting her gaze as she'd silently pleaded with him to do something.

"I'm sorry," she whispered. "I'm so, so—"

His hand twitched, and her heart stopped. She stared down at him. He lay as still as ever. His lips as still as ever. His chest as still as ever. It was her imagination. Her treacherous—

Gavril's lips parted and his chest moved and she shouted for Tyrus, her hands flying to Gavril's neck, feeling the barest pulse of life. Then his eyes fluttered and opened, looking into hers as his lips curved in the faintest smile, and his lips parted to whisper, "Keeper." And she threw her arms around him and wept.

FIFTY-NINE

"C"ome," Moria whispered in Ashyn's ear. "Let's leave them alone."

Gavril was sitting now, talking to Tyrus as one of the young healers ran to find her mistress and the guard ran to inform the emperor.

"If you wish to stay . . ." Ashyn whispered, but Moria shook her head and said, "Gavril died for him. They should have a moment alone. And they'll not get it once everyone hears what has happened."

What *had* happened? Ashyn still didn't know, to be quite honest. Gavril was alive. Alive and healed, and she'd checked him herself, as Moria had tentatively put questions to him, ensuring it was no sorcery. He'd passed her sister's tests. It was Gavril. Alive. And as Moria walked from that death chamber, she glowed as if lit by the fire of the goddess herself.

"Do you know what happened?" Ashyn asked.

"Perhaps. We can speak of that later. For now . . ." Her sister turned and caught her in a hug so fierce it took Ashyn's breath away. "For now, *you* are alive. That is the most important thing, and I want to talk about you. Not Gavril. Not Tyrus. Not you either," she said as she turned to Ronan, who'd been following, and waved him off with, "Begone, boy. I wish time with my sister."

He only smiled, bowed, and said, "As you will, my lady," and headed back toward the chamber.

Moria looked at Daigo and Tova. "I suppose you may both stay. But see that you do not interrupt my time with Ashyn."

Tova harrumphed and Daigo rolled his eyes, but they fell back, trailing them as Ronan had been.

"Thea and Ellyn are dead," Ashyn said, which was not, she suspected, what Moria wished to hear, but she could not go further without telling her.

Moria's smile faded and she bowed her head. "I am sorry to hear it. I suppose we ought to go there, to say blessings for their departure."

"I did so quickly, as I left. But yes, we ought to." She looped her arm through her sister's. "We'll take the long way, to avoid others. You can tell me what happened in the palace."

"You first," Moria said. "You're the older one. You can start."

Ashyn managed a smile at that. She was a half day older, and Moria had always hated the reminder. She tugged her sister closer, and she began.

Four days had passed since the horror of that night. Ashyn was where she'd been every afternoon since, in the tiny apartment

that Ronan had once called home. He'd paid his last rent and was preparing to move his siblings to the court, at the emperor's insistence. It was temporary, of course, but with everything that had happened, it wasn't the time for long-term plans.

Ronan had offered his services as the emperor struggled with the loss of over half his imperial guard. That's what Ronan was doing now while Ashyn watched his siblings.

Though it had been four days, there had been little time for personal conversations. Ronan's time was split between court and home, and Ashyn's was, too, on the opposite schedule, as she prepared to take over as court Seeker while Ronan was home with Aidra and Jorn. He'd tried to speak to her several times, but she'd brushed him off, not unkindly, simply making it clear that this was not the time.

She was reading to Aidra while Jorn feigned disinterest in the story, yet never moved far enough away that he couldn't hear it. When Ronan arrived, he had to duck to enter the dark, dingy apartment. Even the dim lighting couldn't hide his exhaustion. But he walked straight to her, as he always did, bending to brush his lips across her cheek and whisper, "Thank you."

"Are things getting any better?" she asked.

He made a face. "Better, yes. There's still much to be done."

The court was in turmoil, and they were all dealing with it. Alvar might be gone, but the emperor still had to deal with the warlords and warriors who'd betrayed him. Politics rather than war, which was some relief, though it meant little rest for anyone as they handled the aftermath and stitched the empire back together.

"Will you finish the story tomorrow?" Aidra asked,

climbing off her lap and giving Tova a farewell hug.

"I will," Ashyn said. "But I'm not leaving just yet. Ronan has some very exciting news, and I want to be here when he shares it."

Ronan mouthed: *I do?*

"Shall I tell them?" Ashyn asked.

He frowned in confusion.

"I will then." She turned to the children. "Your brother has done something incredible, and he's been too modest to share it with you. Your family has been raised to warrior caste again."

Ronan's eyes widened, and he madly shook his head, but she ignored him. "Yes," she said. "In return for his service to Prince Tyrus, you are all elevated to warrior caste."

Aidra shrieked and threw herself at Ronan. Jorn rose from where he'd been sitting and stared at Ashyn.

"You mean . . ." Jorn said. "I am to be . . ."

"Trained as a warrior," she said. "And there's more. Ronan will personally serve Prince Tyrus. First, though, he must train. He'll do that with Lord Okami."

"The Gray Wolf?" Aidra said, her eyes rounding.

Ashyn chuckled. "He isn't nearly as scary as his reputation suggests. But he is a great warrior, and he will train both your brothers."

"When?" Jorn blurted.

"You'll start as soon as you arrive at Lord Okami's compound. The emperor needs Ronan and the Okamis here a while longer, but when they leave, you will travel with them."

Aidra stopped shrieking. She turned, very slowly, her huge brown eyes fixed on Ashyn. "And you'll come with us?"

When Ashyn didn't answer, Jorn said, gruffly, "She can't, silly. She's court Seeker now."

"But . . ." Aidra looked at Ronan, who had his face turned away as if struggling to find the right expression. When he glanced back finally, he hadn't managed it, and Ashyn could see the devastation in his eyes.

"That's it, then," he said. "Your choice."

"Yes," she said. "That is my choice. You will take the offer, because you could not live with yourself if you did otherwise."

"And if I cannot live without . . ." He trailed off, looking aside again.

"You'll train under Lord Okami. You will return when you are able. And I will go to Lord Okami's compound when I can. The lord himself has assured me I may visit as often and as long as I wish. Apparently, his wife greatly appreciates female companionship."

"Does that mean . . ." He turned, looking at her.

"Can we walk?" she said. "Jorn will watch Aidra while you escort me back to the palace."

SIXTY

They were out of the casteless district before Ronan spoke.

"When you say . . ." he trailed off. Then he cleared his throat. "Does this mean . . . ? That is, when you speak of visiting, do you mean . . . as friends?"

"Yes. I am going to travel three days' ride as often as I can because we are friends." She gave him a look. "I certainly hope if I make that ride, I can hope for more than pleasant conversation."

He studied her expression. Then, slowly, he began to grin. Before she could say a word, he caught her up in an embrace, Tova barking in surprise as Ronan swung her off her feet.

He swung her clear into an alleyway, into the shadows there, before setting her back on her feet.

"I have you, then," he said. "I truly have you."

"For now," she said. "And if you go changing your mind a

fortnight from now, I swear I'll—"

"Never," he said, pulling her into a kiss. "I will never change my mind."

Ashyn was back in court later than she expected. Ronan had not been content with a quick kiss. Nor, admittedly, had she.

She and Tova walked through the first door into their quarters. Ellyn's hound rose from his pillow and walked over, stiff-legged with age. Thea's wildcat lifted her head and stretched, favoring them with a look of greeting. Everyone had expected the beasts to perish after their Keeper and Seeker died. That was the legend. When they had not, there'd even been talk of "laying them to rest with their bond-people." Moria had sworn to use her daggers on anyone who tried. The old beasts deserved a quiet retirement, which for now, they could get with the girls.

There were pictures on the walls. Drawings from the children. Their extended families were coming for them, as news trickled across the empire. If no family could be found, there were homes—so many had volunteered to adopt the children that the emperor had put Ashyn in charge of a committee to find the best applicants. It was a weighty responsibility, but she took it gladly. The only sadness there was knowing that they'd lost a handful of the children—the ones who'd been possessed, like Wenda, their own spirits gone. At peace, Ashyn hoped.

When she returned to her quarters, she opened the door to hear voices arguing, and she stopped to smile and lean against the doorpost. Four days ago, she'd thought she'd never hear such a familiar sound again. Moria and Gavril bickering. They

were playing a game of capture-my-lord. Moria had made one of her mad, bold moves, and Gavril was chastising her on the foolishness of it, telling her she ought to think before she plunged in. Which, if she ever truly did, she would not be Moria.

What had happened that night in the palace? Alvar Kitsune had ended his life with perhaps the only good and selfless act he'd done in his life. He hadn't let Moria and Tyrus kill him because he'd been crushed and beaten. He'd accepted death to resurrect his son. The darkest form of sorcery: death magics. That was the spell he'd been casting. The one that offered his life in return for his son's.

Perhaps it wasn't purely selfless. As Moria had said, Alvar's goal had not been a throne but a dynasty. He'd given his life to keep his blood alive.

Gavril was still mending, and the girls had insisted he recuperate here, where Moria could watch over him and Ashyn could tend to him. Physically he was whole and well. Yet he was weak, as if his spirit had not fully recovered from the shock of leaving his body. Each day he gained a little more strength. Now, when Ashyn walked in, he had left his pallet and was sitting cross-legged on a cushion as he played with Moria.

Her sister looked over quickly. Seeing Ashyn, she said, "Ah, it's you."

"Sorry."

Gavril shook his head. "Tyrus is late for their sword practice, and she's hoping he comes soon so she will be spared the indignity of saying 'You were right,' when I defeat her."

"But you are not right," Moria said. "Whether I win or

lose, I stand by my move. It was my only chance of winning. Therefore I took it. That was all I could do."

Silence. Moria had her head bowed, studying the game board. Gavril watched her, the expression on his face making Ashyn look away, before he said, softer now, "Yes, I understand that."

Which he did, of course. That was how he thought, as much as Moria, in his own, quieter way. Moria, bold and brash. Gavril, thoughtful and subdued. Tyrus, honorable and resolute. All of them willing to make the hardest gamble for what they believed in. Tyrus taking his brother's place under the sword. Gavril taking Tyrus's. Moria risking her life to avenge Gavril.

Could Ashyn do the same in the same situation? Likely not. Heroes made the bold moves. Heroes risked their lives. Others kept the troops at ease, tended the wounded, fed the hungry, and soldiered on, and the world could not survive without them any more than it could without heroes.

Before Ashyn could sit to watch the game, Tyrus burst in as if he'd been running, saying, "I know, I'm late, but we still have time before the—" He stepped into the room and exhaled. "Good. You're keeping her occupied. I was afraid I'd run through that door and find myself dodging daggers."

Moria didn't favor that with a reply. Tyrus was busy, as they all were, and it was just as often that Moria missed their scheduled engagements.

A new life. One that promised many challenges. But this was what they wanted, all of them. To play their role, whatever it might be.

"Finish your game," Tyrus said as he snatched up a sitting cushion.

"No, take her," Gavril said. "Please. She's restless, and it makes her a very poor player."

"I'm not the only one, Kitsune," she said. "On both counts. You ought to come watch us. Get some air and exercise."

Tyrus seconded the invitation, but Gavril demurred, saying, "I'll enjoy the silence."

"Ashyn's not leaving," Moria said.

"As I said, I'll enjoy the silence. Comparatively speaking."

Moria made a face and got to her feet.

"If you change your mind . . ." Tyrus said.

"It'll be a long council meeting tonight," Moria added. "Take the exercise where you can."

"I'm fine. Go on."

They left, with Daigo following along. The door had not yet closed before Tyrus said, "Zuri!" and Ashyn smiled, knowing the dragon whelp must have soared out of nowhere again, having developed the habit of swooping on Tyrus and grabbing his ponytail, which was apparently her idea of an affectionate greeting.

"Uh-uh," Moria said. "Not this time, girl. I—"

Moria cursed, and Ashyn laughed to herself. Zuri's greeting for Moria was to walk behind her and goose her in the rear until she produced treats.

"One of these days I won't have treats for you," Moria said, but Ashyn knew she would, she always would. The dragon might be Tyrus's "beast," but she was as devoted to Moria as Daigo was to Tyrus.

Their voices faded, and they could not have gotten past the next building before Gavril tentatively rose, his gaze on the door.

"Go," Ashyn said. "It's a swordplay lesson. Nothing more. They'd like you there, and you would like to get out. Moria's right. You're as restless as Daigo."

He nodded and started for the door. He'd barely made it there before Ashyn blurted, "Are you happy, Gavril?"

She regretted the words as soon as she said them, and braced for him to stiffen, that good mood to evaporate as he pretended to have no idea what she meant.

He turned slowly. "Yes, I'm happy. For the first time in . . . Perhaps in my life." He rubbed his face, as if embarrassed by the sentiment, then said, "It's like . . . like I'm finally able to breathe. I know that doesn't make sense."

She reached and squeezed his arm. "It does. It completely does. You have a future again. A normal life. And friends. People who care about you."

He nodded, definitely looking embarrassed now.

"And Moria?" Ashyn said softly.

"Yes, she is a friend, as much as Tyrus."

"And that's what matters."

He nodded. "It is," he said, and walked out the door, his strides lengthening as he hurried to catch up.